"A dreamy tale that unravels with hypnotic precision. A story of love and secrets, all played out against a backdrop of meticulous, flowing writing. The best stories are the ones that leave readers with decisions to make: about themselves, about life, about the world. *Twinless Twin* leaves readers with all of those difficult choices and more. It's a novel that relies heavily on the established traditions of rural storytelling—with its tropes of magic, danger, and folklore—while grappling with contemporary themes with no loss of momentum or impact. In short: a wonderful story."

—JASON MOTT, author of *Hell of a Book*, winner of the National Book Award

"Reader beware: This amazing first novel is haunted, not just by mysterious creatures in the Appalachian deep woods, but by enduring humans facing mortality all around them—births, deaths, horrible accidents, and even more horrible cruelty from within their own kith and kin. It's like a surreal Southern fever dream from which no one can awake, yet in the end the characters find hope in the fractured hearts of others, and in items that can fit in the palm of your hand: coins, teeth, a pocket watch, a railroad spike, a rock. I loved *Twinless Twin*."

—MARK RICHARD, author of *Fishboy* and *House of Prayer No. 2*

"In *Twinless Twin*, Dean Marshall Tuck takes us by the hand and leads us into a twilight world that exists just outside our everyday perceptions. The mood is uncanny and the prose haunting. His language is lyrical, engaging, and emotionally precise. And the voices of his characters sing with heartbreak, joy, and deep love. This is a book about a family unlike any you have ever encountered. But by the end, it's also about your own."

—RICHARD HATEM, writer and producer of film and television, scriptwriter of *The Mothman Prophecies*

TWINLESS TWIN

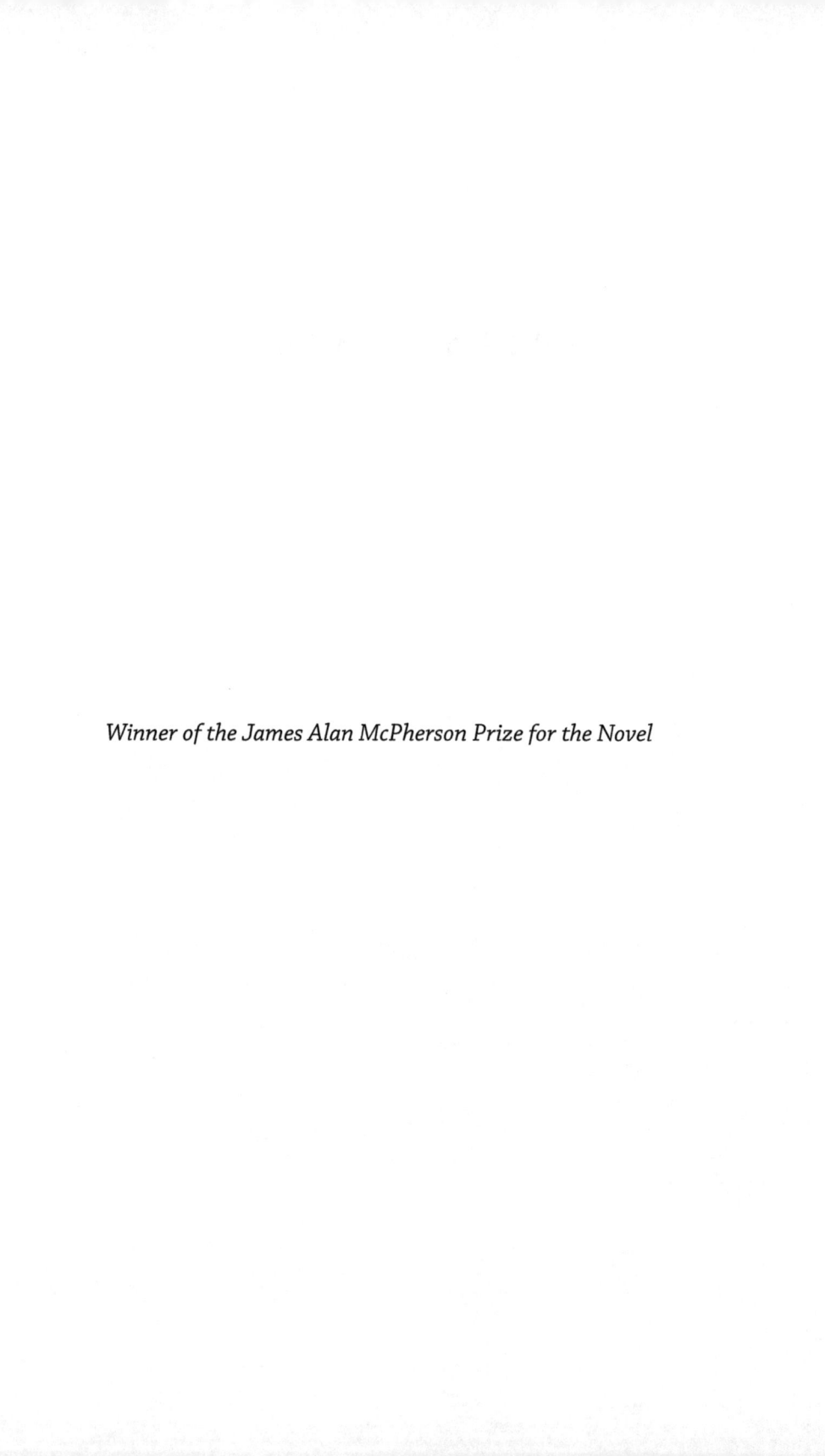

Winner of the James Alan McPherson Prize for the Novel

TWINLESS TWIN

A Novel

Dean Marshall Tuck

University of Nebraska Press
LINCOLN

Acknowledgments for the use of previously
published material appear on page 295, which
constitutes an extension of the copyright page.

The University of Nebraska Press is part of a land-
grant institution with campuses and programs on the
past, present, and future homelands of the Pawnee,
Ponca, Otoe-Missouria, Omaha, Dakota, Lakota, Kaw,
Cheyenne, and Arapaho Peoples, as well as those of the
relocated Ho-Chunk, Sac and Fox, and Iowa Peoples.

For customers in the EU with safety/GPSR
concerns, contact:
gpsr@mare-nostrum.co.uk
Mare Nostrum Group BV
Mauritskade 21D
1091 GC Amsterdam
The Netherlands

Library of Congress Cataloging-in-Publication Data
Names: Tuck, Dean Marshall, author
Title: Twinless twin : a novel / Dean Marshall Tuck.
Description: Lincoln : University
of Nebraska Press, 2025. |
Identifiers: LCCN 2025008183
ISBN 9781496244215 (paperback)
ISBN 9781496244673 (epub)
ISBN 9781496244680 (pdf)
Subjects: BISAC: FICTION / Literary | LCGFT: Novels
Classification: LCC PS3620.U2848 T95 2025 |
DDC 813/.6—dc23/eng/20250602
LC record available at https://lccn.loc.gov/2025008183

Designed and set in Chaparral Pro by K. Andresen.

For Deniz, Mia, and Tessa

O lost, and by the wind grieved, ghost, come back again.

THOMAS WOLFE

CONTENTS

TWINLESS TWIN

TWINLESS TWIN

Maybe it was because he always played alone by the railroad tracks. He must've picked up every loose railroad spike between here and Saluda County. I didn't think much of it until one day I noticed there were enough around the house to fill a five-gallon bucket. We couldn't afford many toys, so whatever he found was fair game, and with these spikes, he had discovered his building blocks. He'd line them up, side by side like crossties on the floor, heads of the spikes alternating so they fit perfectly until he'd laid out his own railroad track indoors. At first he preferred circle and oval designs. Later he'd lay these winding paths, beautiful curving shapes. He made sure they always met back at the start. He'd walk barefooted along his track, around and around, always quiet and with such concentration—walk himself into a kind of trance. You'd look in his eyes and never know where he was at. I imagine it was his way of bringing the railroad feeling home. I didn't care for all the rusted metal dirtying up the house, but since we had so little, I let him do as he pleased. Maybe if our carpet had been a little newer, I might've objected, but something about the calm it put on him—I couldn't take that from him.

At first I wouldn't let him play out there. Too dangerous, and you never know who or what you'll find. But his sister was too young to play, he rarely had a school friend, and that's all he wanted to do—walk up and down the rails all day searching for things to fill his pockets.

He was a sweet child, mostly, and happy, I think. I remember when he would still put his arms around my neck and kiss my cheek before bedtime. He never liked to be touched. Even as a baby, he wouldn't let me rock him to sleep. He'd cry until we set him down.

It was a difficult birth. A painful blur. I don't know what my mind did with the memory, but the body knows best—what you can handle, what you can't. He was a long time coming, and when he finally arrived, no crying. The nurses feared the worst. Then, when his brother came along and everyone knew, it was like his little lungs awoke. He cried.

His brother was lost. The doctor couldn't make sense of it. One of those things you act like you get over but you never really do. It bothered Dr. Thorne. All the checkups and the visits every year since, all the shots, tongue depressing, ear gazing, and heart listening, was the doctor trying to figure it out. When he got older, the doctor started asking all sorts of questions—what he liked, what he didn't, what made him happy, what made him sad, was he upset, did he dream, what about . . . . I didn't know what to make of all the questions, but Dr. Thorne said it was standard cognitive something or another. I watched his face while my son calmly answered his questions.

That's when I knew this child was special.

I tried to be more cheerful when I was carrying him. Maybe all the fear corrupted him. They say what you do—what you eat, what you listen to, what you say, what you think—your attitude, all that stuff matters for the baby, will determine the kind of person he'll be.

I was full of fear.

Not the kind of fear that keeps you in bed all day but the kind that keeps you awake too long, makes you forget what you were thinking of, makes you lose your place in a conversation.

"Perk up," Mother said to me over so many cups of coffee. But I needed a sign, something out there to show me everything would be okay. In the morning I watched from our kitchen window: mockingbirds worrying the crows, robins back and forth to their nests, buzzards' shadows moving across the yard, scurrying squirrels about their mysterious business, big black lizards lounging in the sun. During the day: dust devils, sudden showers, unexpected visitors, drowsy visions, strangers' words, items found in peculiar places, sounds in the wind. On the porch at night, I listened for a message: mourning doves, whippoorwills, hoot owls, cicadas, locusts, crickets, bullfrogs, a bobcat crying. Nothing.

I started going back to church. I spoke with the old folks, smiled at the women who acted like we were friends, paid attention to the pastor's words the best I could, and prayed to God: Quiet my soul; let me know everything will be all right; release me from this dread I feel; help me be the happy expecting mother I ought to be.

When he was little, no more than four, he asked once: "Where's my brother, Mama? Where's my brother?"

"You don't have a brother," I told him.

He wouldn't understand. He must've known about his twin. Though I made Ray promise to never tell him, I know he did anyhow, maybe not sober but one of those nights he would come home shuffling after a few drinks with the men after their shift at the sawmill. Sometimes I'd find him sitting at the corner of the boy's bed whimpering, not enough to wake him, whispering his whiskey words, muttering little prayers, Mother said, teaching him to talk to his lost brother. Who knows what he told him? These midnight sittings, spun out like a record, always repeating, Ray speaking and him sleeping.

I know he listened because years after his daddy had left, I would hear him in the night, half-awoke from a dream, mumbling words I couldn't make out. Another language. Mother called it "squabbling." There'd be sounds coming from his room, not quite words, but you knew he was talking to someone. The words would come in low and grow into sounding the way children talk with no adults near, when they're learning and explaining the things they don't yet know. He'd be chewing on those words, like he was trying to lock them in, to swallow them up, but on he'd talk, half an hour or so. I'd hear his soft murmuring through my wall, and I'd know he was speaking to his brother:

Aaron.

I wish to God we'd never given him a name.

But we gave him a happy childhood. He was almost three before he said his first word. Ray and I worried. He'd grunt and make motions and faces. Mother said: "Don't worry. Children won't speak until they're ready to be heard, and the smartest ones don't speak until they know we'll listen."

She was right. When he spoke, he didn't start with words but sentences. Before a year had passed, it was questions. A few years more, and he had answers to our questions: What did you learn in school today? What's your teacher like? Who's in your class? Why do you favor this color? Don't you want to sleep with more covers? What did you find today? What's your favorite animal? What's your favorite book? What's your favorite subject? When's your favorite time of day? Suddenly, we were his students. We wanted to learn our son. We wondered at his words, his ideas, how it all seemed to spring from nothing.

"What did you expect?" Mother said. "He could climb before he could walk. He could run before he could crawl."

He loved to roam and play outdoors. Ray was proud. When he was old enough to play on his own, he'd walked over and learned every inch of our yard and the woods and nearby fields. He'd come home, pockets filled with buttons, coins, smooth stones, pieces of glass of all colors—anything he found that cried out to him.

One day he brought home one of those beetles, the ones with the long, jagged tusks. Of course, he'd already placed it in my hands before I realized. I hollered and dropped the monster. He laughed to see me startled and picked it up to show me it wasn't moving. He poked its horns, moved its legs, turned its head, and sure enough, it never moved. He hopped on his bed and placed the beetle on the windowsill.

Each day afterward, that's all I could see when I went to straighten his room—that black monster and its terrible jowls. How could he sleep with it watching over him in the night? For two days it sat above his head, and for two nights I dreamed of hellbeasts the size of tanks, crawling out from cracks in the ground, lurching forward in their smooth black armor, destruction all around.

On the third day, I had to do something. I walked into his room, and there on the windowsill where the dead creature once sat was a jar lid filled with water. I called him in from the yard and asked him what happened to the bug. He ran to his room to find the beetle gone. Gone where? I'd like to know. He didn't seem surprised to find the bug missing. Said he'd probably just walked home. Honey, the bug was dead, I reminded him, but that didn't seem to matter to him. "He wasn't ready," he said, and took the jar lid to the backyard and sprinkled the water in the grass.

Bug nightmares the rest of my life is what I thought, but Ray thought otherwise. He said life is never a bad omen—more like a second chance. He hugged me close, his arm around my side, his hand resting on my middle. We just knew everything would be okay.

Maybe it was because Ray took him hunting too young. He told me not to worry, that he was half his age when his father took him coon hunting the first time. I could tell when they returned something had happened; they both seemed changed. The boy drifted off to bed. Ray wouldn't talk. The next morning this is what he told me:

Everything started fine. He seemed to like walking in the woods at night, liked carrying that heavy old flashlight buckled to his waist. Trapper was trailing as soon as I let down the tailgate. He ran off full-cry howling, and the boy would've chased after him, but I kept him back, told him to wait, let the dog wear him out, bring him back to us. We listened to him hunt. Once or twice he'd go silent, and again full cry. Then it sounded like they were getting farther away. I got a sick feeling the coon had led Trapper down to the beaver pond.

We started for the pond as fast as the boy could walk. Every hundred yards we'd stop and listen and make sure we were headed in the right direction. When we finally neared the pond, something had changed. Trapper sounded funny. His barking was muffled. I knew the worst was so, that the dog was swimming after the coon.

We ran down to the edge of the water and shined our lights toward the sounds: splashing, growling, and screeching. It was hard to make out. At times you could see just the coon, and sometimes you could only see Trapper, hear him snorting out water. I turned my light on the boy's face. He never even blinked. His eyes were dark and wide, his mouth caught open, and for a second I forgot the dog was out there fighting for his life. Something went haywire. He went wild. Crying. Thrashing. He darted for the water. I said, "What in God's name are you doing?" and caught him by the scruff of his jacket just before he could wade out past his rubber boots. I shook him, tried to get him to act sensibly, but there wasn't any reasoning with him. He fought to get away, out there in the water. I didn't know what to do, so I took the leash and tied him to a pine tree. I just panicked. I couldn't both hold him and somehow save the dog. All the while the boy was shuffling and scrambling, clawing and biting. He'd stopped crying, but he sounded like something wild. Struggling there, grunting, yelling like fear, rage, and hate all rolled into one, squirming and pushing away from the tree—I was afraid he'd hurt himself trying to get loose from the leash. I left his flashlight on the ground pointed toward the tree and went running along the bank until I could better see the animals. When I got close, I raised the gun to my shoulder, spotlight against the gun with my steadying hand, and lined the sights on the animals.

Luckiest shot of my life. Trapper emerged from the water half-drowned but clutching that ratty coon in his mouth. I caught my breath, relieved, until I remembered him back at the tree. I held to Trapper's collar the walk back. Then my light died. I stopped in the complete black and listened, but I couldn't hear much aside from Trapper panting and the leaves under our feet. We followed the edge of the pond until I could see a faint shine on the trees where I left him. Again, I stopped and listened. Nothing. And the same sick feeling came over me, like when I knew Trapper was in trouble. I ran to the tree, worried to my soul I'd find him somehow gone, and if he was, how on Earth would I ever find him, but there he was, not quite standing, still held up by the leash chains, a pile of scrubbed-off pine bark all around the tree. His knees were locked, and he was leaning forward, his head hung down like he was ashamed, staring at his boots. I picked up the light and looked into his eyes. They were open but not alert. He was out.

I loosened the leash and laid him down. Shook him. Shone the light in his eyes and called his name over and over. Finally, he came to and looked around. I stood him up and brushed him off. That's when I noticed his pants were soaked through. I tried talking to him, tried to get him to say if he was *okay, but he wouldn't talk. I clipped the leash to the dog, picked the boy up, and toted him to the truck—who knows how many miles—carrying him like a stack of chopped wood. He never spoke the whole way back, never put his arm around my shoulders. Just deadweight.*

Ray looked empty telling the tale. Just stared into his coffee. "I broke him," Ray said. "I think I broke him."

We didn't know how he'd take the news about a new baby sister. He seemed to understand, but what could prepare him or anyone for the changes to come?

And he was always very stubborn about even the smallest of changes: always wanted his chair in the exact same space at the table; resisted changing to shorts in the summer or back to pants in the winter; hated haircuts and clipping fingernails; wanted everything always in its natural place—food in the refrigerator and the pantry, toys in their boxes, books on their shelves. One day he came home from school, and I had shampooed the carpet. The carpet was still damp, and I'd rearranged the living room furniture. He went on a tear. I'd never seen him so agitated. I grabbed his little shoulders and tried to tell him how unreasonable he was being. At the same time that Ray walked across the kitchen to check on us, he'd thrown his arms around me hard and landed his head into my belly.

I was maybe four months along then, and it looked worse than it hurt, but Ray was on him in a flash. Ray grabbed his arms and, pinching them to his sides, lifted the boy into the air and shouted in his face. I begged him to put him down, but Ray was in a state. I thought he might throw him across the room. He kept shouting, the boy squirming, kicking, making a strange sound almost like crying. I put my hand on the back of Ray's neck and spoke calmly, telling him everything was okay, it didn't hurt, he didn't mean it, he's just worked up because of the house, and who knows what I said before he finally lowered him. The boy ran off to his room. Ray lifted my shirt and moved his hands across my stomach, gently in slow, wide circles. He kissed my side and then my cheek, wet with tears, and whispered to me, "Never again," and I held him to me firm like I might not let go. I think he never loved me more than he did then.

Cindy was born on a hot July afternoon. Nine months, very little sickness, no panics or dreams, quick labor, and everything fine.

My first time I went into early labor with two months left. The whole time I carried them I had so many dreams—me giving birth to all manner of horrors: babies with their spines poking out through their skin; babies joined together at the hip; sometimes two heads or four arms or no eyes or mouths with full sets of teeth or hair all over their bodies or bodies no bigger than your hand.

Mother said it was the same with her. She said Grandmother cured her from these dreams when she carried me: said you have to stew a chicken; you eat the pulley and get the pulley bone; break the bone in two with the father; take both pieces and bury them in an open jar; dig up the jar on the next full moon. If the bone has disappeared, the dreams will end.

So I cooked us a chicken that night and told Ray about my latest dream. As I cleaned the meat off the pulley, I thought to tell him about what Mother said, but instead, I just ate the chicken and kept my mouth shut.

I handed him one end of the bone. He paused, looked at that spindly little bone and then into my eyes, and we snapped it in two. I gave him the long end with the wish. I always do. That's the secret to that little game. You can look at the bone and tell who'll get the wish. I always give the wish away. He asked me did I have a wish in mind, and I nodded no—wishing's for children. A woman makes things happen.

"What'd you wish for?" I asked him.

"Twins," he said.

He was nearly five years old when his sister was born. He never had a close friend his age that we knew of. We thought a new brother or sister might help heal him in the particular way we never could, but he never seemed too interested in his sister.

Soon it was summer, and the baby needed most of our attention. I couldn't bear the thought of him playing alone for three months, but Ray said he'd been a loner as a child too and to leave him be, but I wanted him to have a friend. I got Lois to bring her Calvin over. They were in the same grade. They got along okay, though Calvin seemed more of a tag-along really, following him everywhere. Still, I worried less when they were together.

When summer was over, I pulled a few strings with the principal to have them in the same class. I explained to Mrs. Pittman how having the two together might help him come out of his shell. She agreed.

They kept on after school like this. We'd watch the two disappear into the woods with their walking sticks—persimmons Ray had cut, carved, and stained. "See," Ray said, "he can make friends like anybody."

One Saturday morning, Calvin comes running in through the back door, crying. He gathers his things, wipes his cheeks, and I try to get in a word or two, but he says he wants to go home, and he doesn't want to ever come back. About the time I reach for the receiver to call Lois, Ray walks in and wants to know what's the matter. They talk as I try to explain to Lois that Calvin's ready to be picked up. I overhear a few words: *train tracks, bones, dog.*

When Lois arrives, we apologize, but she won't hear it, just leads her son to the car. She spins gravel behind her, and then it's dust and quiet. Across the yard, we see him coming from the woods. I hear Cindy crying in our room, so I go back inside, but Ray tells me the rest, late that night in bed.

I look him in the eyes, tell him, "Calvin told me. I want to see." He leads me to the tracks. We walk maybe a mile or more. Along the way, he looks like he's counting. Railroad ties, I guess. Then he crosses the tracks and makes his way into the woods. We walk until we reach an open area, and there it is. A pile. Stinking like hell, rotten, awful. I grab his stick and poke around the carcasses—possums, raccoons, rabbits, even a small deer—some nothing but bones, some dried-up leathery messes, and others covered with worms and filth breaking it all down to nothing. Then I find what Calvin said. There's the dog, only a few days dead, I guess. I pry open his mouth, and it's true. I grab his shirt and yank him to me, yell at him to show me. He reaches into his pockets and pulls out a handful of teeth, yellow, white, and pearl. I slap the boy's hand and teeth scatter over the ground. I look back in the pile, in the empty mouths of all the animals, and then I look in his eyes. He didn't look sad or sorry or even confused. Just nothing, and that's when I knew there was no fixing him.

Ray says to me, "There's a kind of sickness you don't get over as long as you live. All it does is fester and worsen, until your whole life becomes one long heartache." I can barely make his face out in the moonlight, only a cheek and the tip of his nose. "It'll end you before it ever ends, Martha," he says, and then he rolls over and goes to sleep, never stirring or waking. I know because I laid there awake, running the whole mess over and over in my mind. What to do.

I thought I would talk to Lois and Calvin, ask them at least to keep it secret. What if they told the school or a counselor and they shunned him or studied him or took him away? Would he ever make another friend? Wouldn't he be poison to everyone from then on?

I thought about Ray's words "no fixing him," like he was a windup toy with a spring popped out. What if he was right and this was the sign of more to come? But then, he didn't *hurt* anyone. It was certainly peculiar, but something about it must've made sense to his child's mind.

The next day I run to town for a few groceries. When I come back, the kids are alone. I call for Ray, but nobody comes. Like a fool, I look in the backyard. The truck is still there. I walk around the house calling, but I know he's gone. I knew it when I stepped through the door.

I search our room. Nothing much is gone. Maybe some clothes. Then I see on the kitchen table the strongbox he kept all the deeds in, title to the truck, few savings bonds, warranties, receipts, old letters, and pictures. Sitting on top of these is a birth certificate: Aaron's. I pick up the paper and find underneath a small pile of folding money and pocket change, and I see he gave everything he had.

I kept him in school. I raised Cindy on my own. We made do with my one paycheck. Of course, Mother helped. Cindy grew healthy and was walking before long. I believe he loved his sister, though he didn't know how to show it. He wouldn't let her touch him, but occasionally, he'd let her play in the same room, at least until she started crying. Still, I was encouraged.

He never did make any more friends at school. Mother said, "Something so sad about watching a child play alone." We'd see him outside at the edge of the yard with a couple bricks. He'd gather small stones, place one on a brick, then lift the other high before bringing it crashing down on the stone, like cracking a walnut. Afterward he'd sit and study the rock like it had changed into a diamond. He'd blow away the dust and run his finger along the new edge. Sometimes he'd bash a stone until it turned to bits and dust. "You going to let him play like that? Don't look right," Mother said, but he wasn't hurting anyone. I think he liked the colors, how bright and new the insides of these stones looked. Even an old piece of gravel looked pretty on the inside. He'd come show me all kinds—the white insides of smooth cream-colored stones, the speckled look of crushed granite, the cracked beauty of broken quartz. His favorites ended up on windowsills and in boxes and drawers. Once or twice, I saw him displaying them to his sister. I almost cried. The way he collected and cared for all the things he found—I thought, he knows beauty, he knows pride, he knows love.

We'll be fine.

Then he fell from the sycamore tree.

I was at the sink washing dishes. I looked out the window just in time to see him hit the ground. It takes your eyes a second to make sense of a thing like that. I ran outside to check on him. He was completely still. I lifted him, even though I know I probably shouldn't have, and held him to me. He was bleeding from the back of his head. I ran my fingers through his hair and saw he'd gashed it open. The second my fingers passed the cut, he gasped awake in one deep breath like he'd just swam up from a river bottom. Blood was all over my hands. He was relearning how to breathe when he saw his blood on my dress, and he whipped himself free from my arms like an angry cat. He scrambled away holding the back of his head, and I tried to tell him what happened. I'm not even sure he could hear for his panicky breathing, me saying over and over, "You fell, you hurt your head. You fell, you hurt your head." When he finally settled down, I took him to Dr. Thorne.

He needed stitches, of course. The doctor said to keep him awake until midnight and talk to him every so often. Ask him questions, and if I feel like something isn't right, bring him back.

At midnight, though he was quieter than normal, he didn't seem all that different. But as the days wore on, I knew the whole thing had shaken him because he rarely played outside anymore. One night he complained about a bad headache, so I took him back to the doctor. He had a look and said everything seemed normal, that a few head-aches were to be expected but if they persist, we might arrange to have a special doctor look at him. Anyway, I gave him some headache pills the doctor prescribed, told him to take a nap, had him drinking more water, and kept the lights low until he felt better.

In a week or two, the headaches let up, but I felt we weren't out of the woods yet. He was different in little ways. He slept later, spent more time indoors, ate less. Truthfully, he began to talk more, and to all of us. At the same time, he seemed more temperamental. He'd suddenly get frustrated trying to talk, and we'd hardly ever know why. Still, I could manage him; I could calm him down. One day after a fit, I talked him down, and we spoke like never before. I asked him why was he so irri-table these days, why can't he control himself. He said he didn't know, that he felt like he couldn't focus anymore and he often felt confused or frustrated when he'd lose his place. I tried to tell him it would pass; he needed more rest.

"Why don't you play outside like you used to?" I asked him.

"I'm scared," he said. "I'm scared I won't come back. I'm scared I might start walking along the tracks, forget how to come home, and never come back."

In time he played outside again. He seemed more like himself. I knew he would. Then the weather changed.

Almost the whole month of June, rain every day: storming, light-ning, thundering, flooding. And every day he spent penned up in the house, he grew more agitated.

One evening I said: "What about your railroad spikes? Why don't you try lining those up again. Show your sister how you used to do it." He dragged an old crate from the closet half-filled with railroad spikes. One, then another, and another. After he'd taken them from the crates, which took some time, he arranged them carefully while his sister watched. He spent the better part of an hour, and when he finished, he had a beautiful curvy design similar to the "and" symbol you see on signs between lawyers' names.

I told him what a good job he'd done, but he didn't seem to notice.

He was walking along his track like always, but the calm wouldn't come. When he stepped to the end of the design, finding the track broken bothered him. He kicked around the spikes, bickering with himself. He stopped, took a deep breath, and went back to work. Again, he laid down a looping, curving line that crossed over itself once and twice, and when it seemed he'd solved this strange puzzle, he'd run out of spikes again. He grew worse. I pulled Cindy away, said: "Give him time. Let him sort it out."

An hour later we walk in the room, and he's got it—the shape he wants, a simple figure eight, but it's a complete design that ends where it begins, and this seems to please him.

One foot after the other, he walks along his track like a tightrope walker, like I'd seen him walk the rails of the train tracks behind our house plenty of times. And I'm proud and relieved to see him with the railroad feeling clearly on his face, severe yet serene.

Cindy's proud too. She moves to her brother, sits with her knees touching his track, and stares as he follows the path so careful and silent. He traces the route over and over with Cindy watching, passing a dozen times before the calm settles on us all.

Without a word, without a sound, Cindy stands and falls in line behind him; he doesn't even notice his sister following, matching him step for step. He makes the pass, the turn, and sees his sister has left a void by the track. He halts, his face scrunching up, and he buries the backs of his fists into his clenched-shut eyes. He's confused, startled, and angry, all in a flash. Cindy, eyes still on the track, bumps into him, and in an unthinking motion, he spins and lunges like a jungle tiger with claws landing on her shoulders, and he's on top of her, and Cindy's falling backward, tottering on her heels, flailing, crashing against the dresser, banging her forehead before hitting the floor, awkwardly pinning her arm with the full weight of her body. I rush to them both, pulling him off and shoving him away. Cindy has broken her little arm, and her face is red with crying. Blood is starting on her temple. I lift her and jolt to the kitchen, snatching my car keys from their hook, leaving him alone in his bedroom, standing there staring at the floor, spikes strewn everywhere, pointing in all directions.

Several years passed before the accident. I can't think of it. Strangers call me sometimes. It's all anyone wants to know, but I tell them I won't think of it. I've forgiven him. I pray they all do. They took him from me then, I realized, for good, but I knew there was no other way. I knew it had to be, just as I'd learned the day he was born, anything can be taken from you. Nothing is yours.

Mother said to me: "Rest, Martha. Now you can rest. You've done all you can. He doesn't need your protection now." For three days I slept without dreaming. When I awoke, Mother and Cindy were by my bed waiting, and I felt a tremendous peace come over me like the quiet way the earth begins to mend itself after a storm, like the way a tree heals a lightning scar, slowly closing, growing through the years.

Maybe his great uncle Sammy resurrected in his blood, like Mother said. Mother said bad blood doesn't ever run its course, on it flows, often unseen through generations like blue eyes, illness, or twins. I had only seen Uncle Sammy once when I was a girl. Daddy needed a part welded to an old tobacco trailer, so he took me with him to my uncle's shop one winter day. We walked in, and an old tomcat scooted in behind us. Some men, no more than seven, stood or sat around an old barrel stove, talking, smoking, drinking. My head was spinning with the smells of woodsmoke, tobacco, whiskey, grease, and sweat. I grabbed Daddy's hand. There he was, sitting closest to the stove, smoking a cigarette, whittling a piece of wood down to a sharp point. The cat moved across my shin. Daddy addressed the men and Uncle Sammy. Everyone stopped. All you could hear was the wood fire crackling. Finally, Uncle Sammy nodded, started back whittling, and everyone went on talking. Daddy began talking to a few of the men farthest from Uncle Sammy. After a few exchanges, he moved down the line to the men next closest to him. All the while he was talking, I couldn't stop watching Uncle Sammy whittling away at the piece of wood. Occasionally, he'd stop and test its smoothness against his cheek. I could almost hear it scrape the stubble. Then he'd run his finger across the sharpened edge of the blade.

Daddy talked. Uncle Sammy smoked. All of a sudden, the cat jumped up on Uncle Sammy's lap and settled like he wanted petting and to fall asleep by the stove. Uncle Sammy stopped, the knife in one hand, a wooden stake in the other; the cat looked up at him, and Uncle Sammy pushed him off his lap with the back of his whittling hand. The cat lazied away, inspecting the woodpiles and around the tools and benches for mice. My heart was jumping.

When Daddy finally worked his way to Uncle Sammy, I felt dizzy. The heat from the stove was unbearable. I could feel the sweat starting under my flannel and upon my face. They spoke, but I couldn't hear a word. I stared at his face, his mouth in particular, that thin line of a clamped jaw, only opening now and then to mumble out a few words to my father. Just as Daddy was about to mention the trailer, the cat hopped back on his lap.

"One thing I can't stand's a damn cat," he said. He looked at me for the first time. I tried to smile. He put the knife and the wood in his overall pocket; he grabbed the cat by the back of his neck and rose from his seat like he hadn't stood in hours. Then, in one quick movement, he lifted the lever on the stove door, creaked it open, flung the cat in the flames, and slammed it shut.

The sound that cat made I will never forget. I took a deep breath, the kind that comes before a scream or a cry, and before I could make a sound, Daddy picked me up and headed for the door. Over his shoulder I could see Uncle Sammy sitting again, resuming his whittling. Some of the men shook their heads, some laughed, and some kept talking.

Meanness is the only word I know to describe it. You could see it in his eyes and in the way he set his jaw. God marks His creations so you know where you stand. Like a streak of white down a skunk's back or the rattle on a snake, you get a flash, and it moves under your skin telling you to keep your distance, turn right around, and don't look back.

But I have never seen anything of the sort in my child—no streak, no rattle, no flash. Not that kind of meanness. Not like Sammy. Not my child. The accident, what they say he did, was awful, unforgivable maybe, but I will not believe it's the meanness of my uncle Sammy's blood.

Maybe we never knew him. I remember one day he'd suggested all three of us walk with him along the tracks. This is one of the handful of times I recall his inviting us, but I remember this trip distinctly because once we began on the trail, he took both of us by the hand, and we three walked this way for quite some time. I felt an easiness in him as we made our way through the woods.

The trees thinned, and I could see the hard black line of the rails. We climbed up to the track and walked along, crunching on the gravel. Cindy skipped from tie to tie. In the clearing the sun shone down, and everywhere around us was deep summer green. Cindy laughed. We were all happy.

We walked a good way, and then I felt a change in the way he held my hand. He told us to stop.

He went ahead, maybe twenty yards, and kneeled, studying something on the ground. He picked it up, held it away from him. Something dead. A possum maybe. I couldn't say except for that rat tail it dangled by. He walked the animal to the other side of the tracks and swung it into the woods.

He returned without a word, a faraway look in his eyes. As we continued, he made sure to keep between us and the possum side of the woods. Later he took our hands like before, and we walked quite a while.

After supper we were all so tired that we fell asleep on my bed, safe and sound under one roof, together. This is the way I like to think of him: a small, lonely boy, tenderhearted, protective, curious about his world, in love with his home.

Sometimes I walk up and down these train tracks, wondering like this. All I ever come up with is "maybes." A maybe's about as worthless as yesterday to a dying man. All of these reasons, all of these maybes, searching our past, trying to make it all add up, but I'm never any closer to understanding what happened before they took him from me for good. Even now, after so many years, newspaper and TV people still want to talk to me, record everything I say, but what more is there to say? I've made it over in my mind hundreds of times and still don't understand.

No one wants to think their child is capable of anything like what he did to hurt so many people.

Before Mother passed, her last words to me were: "Don't take it to your grave, Martha. You couldn't stop it from happening, and you can't change what's done. All you can do—all you could ever do—is love him. When love isn't enough, it's in God's hands."

My days now are happy enough. Just me and Cindy. She's a good girl. She takes after Mother. Knows her sayings and all of her stories like an encyclopedia somehow. We do everything together: cook, clean, sew—whatever needs our attention. And if we don't know how to fix it, we figure it out.

I send my son letters—not so many as I used to. He never writes, but they tell me he reads them and that he's making improvement, though they never explain how.

In my prayers I whisper each of my children's names. I wish for them a happiness perhaps this world cannot abide.

Some nights, before I fall asleep, I wonder about Ray. I imagine him hurrying through the house with what little he took, walking up the road with his thumb out. I picture him catching rides all over the countryside, rambling wherever the spirit leads him.

I no longer begrudge him for leaving. For some, staying home comes naturally—others, it's not in their blood. Like the two sons in the Bible. One stays home and grows bitter, and the other leaves and finds out for himself what this world's all about. And neither one is bad—they just have different paths.

Some nights I imagine he's taken up in a new town, working odd jobs, meeting new people; then he's catching new rides, making new friends—off again.

When I dream, I dream of a strange young man, dark yet familiar, tall and skinny with Ray's eyes and my chin. I call his name. He approaches me with the ease and liveliness of youth. His perfect face knows no cares. Though we have never met, he receives me with the smile of a child awaiting one's arrival—a smile that says, "You're here."

RECESS

In my memory of him during those school days, I can see him, now, always at least fifty yards away, a slender white figure in the woodland shade of the playground's periphery, watching the other children play or weaving in and out of the little copse of cedars at the corner of the lawn, marveling at the caterpillars and cocoons he'd find there.

Mother charged me with looking out for him—she has spent her lifetime fretting over my brother—but I was his little sister by nearly four years, and with him a teenager, that gap couldn't be wider. What could a meager nine-year-old do to protect her teenaged brother from big boys who would harm him or older girls who would speak ill of him? I asked Grandmother as much. "He'll need to learn for himself how to meet the trouble that finds him," she said. "But if he can't see it coming, Cindy, you point him in the right direction. Sometimes a protector only needs to keep her eyes and ears open."

A protector. I often thought on this during lulls in the school day when we quietly scribbled through our lessons. A sword and shield for my older brother. By this time I already knew he needed it. He had no friends. Most younger children avoided him. Those his age, having grown with him in the fringes of their classrooms, had long been accustomed to never thinking of him. His presence was as unnoticeable as a crack in the plaster wall or the dusty, sun-bleached globe on its shelf by the window. But protect him how?

Maybe if my brother hadn't liberated the classroom pet, a rabbit named Charles, a few weeks prior, then the ill wind would have never stirred and two weeks of murmuring schoolmates wouldn't have caught up with him; he could've remained the little white glint beyond the schoolyard, an evanescent blur one might easily blink into oblivion.

Charles wasn't one of the garden-variety rabbits your headlight beams catch alongside the road or in the yard. He was gray with a large head and a big, flat face. Though he had a sizable cage, there wasn't much he could do aside from chewing pellets and flaring his nostrils all day, so he grew twice the size of any rabbit I'd ever seen. One couldn't help but feel a little sad for him.

The playground was a long, wide yard adjacent to the cafeteria building, nestled in woodland at the farthest points. The boys played out in the yard or on the equipment placed at the far end near the bordering woods while most of the girls would watch the boys and talk in the shade of the old utility building. We stood out of hearing distance from the two teacher assistants present, who sat in weathered wooden chairs that never came inside, only casting a rare begrudging glance to the children during conversation lapses or after sips of coffee or cigarette puffs. It was a short morning recess, but a third of the school's children were there—the middle grades my brother and I belonged to. These were the last years before the junior and senior high schools were built across the county, and the school still held kindergarten through high school.

"I'll bet a wolf ate him," one of the older girls said.

"We don't have wolves around here," another said.

"That's not true. My daddy says people see red wolves every once in a while."

"Dogs and coyotes probably."

"Dog, coyote, *wolf*, whatever. Something likely got him," the older girl said, and the rest agreed. "I don't know why your stupid brother had to do that." She looked at me, and they all looked at me.

"He felt sorry for him. He looked fat and sad in there with nothing to do all day," I said.

They couldn't deny it.

"And kids had let him out of his cage before. He's not the first," I said.

"But no one had shoved him from the window," the older girl said. "Letting him roam around the classroom isn't like setting him loose in the yard."

Everyone agreed.

"He wanted Charles to have some grass to munch on instead of that moldy hay," I said.

"Well, it was stupid," the older girl said. "Your brother's so weird. Look at him."

Far across the schoolyard, the trees made an L-shaped border that blocked one corner of the school grounds. Near a patch of cedars where he spent every recess, completely self-possessed as always, my brother was nimbly stepping from one exposed root to the next, around the trunk of an enormous willow oak. Like a centaur or satyr, unguarded, I thought, but none of these girls would even know what I was talking about.

Two girls my age, Mira and Samantha, stood silent by my side. They were my best friends in the school. Mira was a small, mousy girl with sad, blue eyes. Samantha was taller than the two of us, with straight, long hair. She was skinny and precise. Mira wouldn't speak if more than two people were around, but I'd hoped Samantha could at least divert the conversation. I looked to her, and she merely waited for my reply.

"Maybe he's in the woods looking for Charles," I said.

A boy from my brother's class named Calvin had joined the group. It is my understanding he was once my brother's friend. He had been making a habit regaling the girls with stories at the end of recess. "Probably looking for railroad spikes," he said.

The girls laughed.

". . . or dead possums," the older girl said, winking at Calvin.

"What's that supposed to mean?" Samantha asked.

Before he could answer, the teachers finally rose from their chairs and waved their arms in wide, swooping motions like lifeguards bringing beachgoers in from the ocean. Makeshift playground equipment assembled by local handy fathers and welders stood not far from the edge of the woods—a row of swings, a trapeze, a rope ladder, and a few gymnast rings. I saw my brother linger in the woods, then race to these while everyone else headed to the schoolhouse. I saw him shuffling his feet in the dirt below the playground equipment, and after kicking up dust, he scrambled on the ground on his hands and knees. I called for him. Like a deer, he perked up at my voice, and in a flash, he bounded across the yard to meet me. He shoved his hands in his pockets. "Dust your pants off. You're filthy," I said.

My memory of those school days seems to consist largely of the time we spent on and around the playground. What happens to all those dreary classroom hours of our childhood spent in forced silence while a world outside spins its sunshine and songbirds by those blurry windowpanes? Were we ever children then? Only during recess, I suppose.

Though recess had its share of chaos, it also brought its own order, with children falling into their regular places: Samantha, Mira, and I jump roping; my brother off to himself at the edge of the woods; Calvin and the others sitting in the grass gossiping.

Mira and I had to swing a looser, slower turn for Samantha to jump; she was so much taller than we were. When she jumped, a gold pendant rose and fell against her chest. Her mother had found a pendant set shaped like a heart, fractured into three pieces, and she'd bought three tiny chains for each of us to wear our section. I had the middle, which to me, seemed like the most important part—the part to bond the other two together. With its jagged edges, it looked like a key, and I suppose that's how our little friendship trinity felt to me then.

Above our jump rope chants, I overheard Calvin's nasal pitch nearby followed by girlish giggles. Again, he'd rejoined the group for story time. In their laughter I could sense not a meanness necessarily but a casual brand of self-satisfaction that I felt was collectively achieved by dumping dirt on the head of my brother.

I wasn't wrong.

"... *Probably*," Calvin said with finality.

"Probably what?" I asked.

"We think we've gotten to the bottom of the mystery of Charles's disappearance," the older girl said.

Calvin snickered.

"We think your brother ate him," she said, much to the rest of the party's delight.

"Don't be stupid," I said.

"Stupid?" Calvin said. "I've seen what he does. I've seen where his animals end up."

Everyone was silent at this.

Of course, he was referring to an apocryphal moment from my brother's past that I need not further substantiate with retelling. Suffice it to say, a few animal carcasses near forested train tracks doesn't make my brother a blood-thirsty, primeval wildman of the woods.

"Does that look like a dog killer or a live rabbit eater or whatever foolishness you've said about him this week?" I pointed to my faraway brother under the cedars. He was baring the pale underside of his forearm in all its gleaming whiteness, watching a caterpillar inching up and down his arm.

"Watch to see if he eats it," the older girl said.

The teachers waved in the children. I attempted the most nonchalant dawdling I could muster, watching and waiting for my brother, and sure enough, like yesterday, he kicked and scrambled under the playground equipment until the last possible second, and just before I was about to call after him, he raced across the yard to find me.

We caught up with the rest under the breezeway that led back to the schoolhouse. Our building, the larger of the four, held most of the older grades' classrooms, and an older building that used to be a one-room school long ago had been converted to the youngest grades' building. As we waited to file into the schoolhouse, Mr. Perry, a maintenance man, stood watch. The older boys liked to talk and cut up with Mr. Perry, who, aside from Vice Principal Vance, was the only man on campus. The boys were slapping his hand as they walked by. An older boy named Doug slapped his hand, spun around, and grabbed the set of keys that dangled from Mr. Perry's side. The keys extended on a kind of chain that, when Doug let go, retracted back to his belt with a zip. The boys laughed.

Mr. Perry smiled and said, "Best watch yourself, boy."

"What you gonna do, Mr. Perry?"

The boys waited to hear what he would say. They envied the way Doug spoke with him.

"Don't you know what they did to thieves back in the old days? Back in Arabia?"

The boys shook their heads.

"What they teaching you in there anyway? Give me your hand."

Doug stuck his hand out. It wasn't much smaller than Mr. Perry's, though his fingers weren't as wide. He held the boy's wrist with one hand, pulled an imaginary scimitar from his side, and swiped his fingertips close to the boy's arm with a "Hah!" The boys laughed. "You'd lose that hand, boy."

"I'm going to get me one of them keychains," Doug said as the last of us reached the entrance.

"Best get you some doors, first!" Mr. Perry yelled back at him.

And recess proceeded and ended in this fashion for several days—Calvin's stories, my attempts at quelling them, and after everyone had begun the walk back to class, my brother's peculiar, dusty ritual. It seemed we'd put enough distance from Charles's disappearance, and so the children grew less concerned with my brother. Of course, such lulls only serve to leave you all the more vulnerable.

This day's recess conversation wasn't about anything until Calvin arrived, out of breath from having been "it" too long. He sat down beside the older girl, and soon they began laughing. Samantha stopped turning the jump rope to hear, with me caught mid-cadence, my legs trying to figure the fun was over. Before I could hear the day's story, the teachers began waving in the children. I waited to see if my brother would come, but this time I wasn't alone. Calvin, the older girl, Samantha, and Mira lingered with me. If I'd thought leaving would make them follow, I would have gone, but I knew better, so we all waited and watched as he darted to the playground, kicking and scrambling in the dirt. "What's he doing?" Calvin asked. I called to him like so many days. This time, however, his loping stride was made awkward by having shoved his fists in his pockets along the way.

"Beat the dust off," I said when he arrived.

My brother didn't smile very often, and when he did, I doubt others would even recognize his peculiar version of the expression, but I could tell he was pleased with something. He removed his fists from his pockets and opened them to show me. Among a few scattered coins was a cat's-eye marble, clear glass with bands of yellow, like two criss-crossing ribbons forever caught in motion. He plucked the marble from his palm and, bringing it closer to my face, trapped the late-morning sunlight in this perfect little crystal. I can see him now, standing before me: the slight frame, unkempt hair and placid smile, the open arms by his side, a few dusty coins in one hand, the other bearing this tiny star, suspended between the closed circle his finger and thumb made.

"Where'd you get all that money?" Calvin's voice shrill and impertinent.

They waited for him to speak. He seemed confused. "The playground," he said. "The swings, the trapeze, the jungle gym . . ."

"You mean it's kids' money," the older girl said, "and you're taking it." Her voice sounded indignant, self-assured, a prosecutor's closing speech. Samantha and Mira seemed to study her eyes as she spoke.

"He didn't steal anything," I said. "He only found it."

"He sits there in the woods," Calvin said, "waiting for money to fall out of kids' pockets."

"He's a vulture, Cindy, a spider. Your brother's a spider. You're a spider," the older girl said to him.

He put his hands back in his pockets. I could see his eyes cloud over. We were entering a storm now, and we weren't likely to see its end for a long time.

"He can't help what he finds," I said. "I guess you all would just pick it up and give it to the teacher. Except for you." I looked to the older girl. "Maybe you wouldn't even bother to pick it up. What's a few coins when your dad makes more money than—"

"Kids!" one of the teachers shouted at us, and we all scrambled up to the breezeway and to the door.

We dispersed to our separate classes except for Samantha and Mira, who were in my class. Back at my desk, I didn't hear a word the teacher spoke the rest of the day. My thoughts were consumed with my brother's situation, how to explain his behavior this time. I tried to imagine him in the classroom, dutifully doing what he's told, never speaking except to whisper a question to the teacher, and window gazing whenever possible at squirrels scampering up one of the oak trees outside. On a typical school day, I would only see him at recess and lunch. There wasn't much I could do to watch over him the rest of the time. Still, I made a habit of working the details of his day out of him on the bus ride home. Being his protector, I had to be informed.

By the end of the day, word had traveled from student to assistants to teachers to the vice principal. This was clear from the note each of us was made to take home to our parents. I waited until my brother and I were in our seat on the bus to take mine out to read.

> Parents,
>
> It has come to my attention that students who do not bring exact change for school lunches are prone to losing the extra nickel or dime they receive in change, often on the playground, and this has created some unfortunate behavior from the students. Please, whenever possible, provide exact change for your child. Furthermore, we will be piloting a new practice in which students give their money to the teacher at the beginning of the school day. Students who have overpaid will receive the difference at the end of Friday's class day.
>
> Thanks for understanding,
>
> Vice Principal Vance

Though I was perplexed by his usage of *piloting*, I felt the mounting dread of the day begin to subside. The note didn't mention his name, nor was there any clear indication of wrongdoing on my brother's part. *Unfortunate behavior.* That could refer to my brother or the tattletales who would accuse him.

"I got a note too," my brother said, and reaching into his bag, he produced a stapled, folded sheet of paper.

I carefully removed the staple and unfolded the note, holding it so we could both read.

Dear Martha,

Several students today observed that your son had his pockets full of coins, presumably some money he'd found on the playground after having watched children lose their lunch money and loose change. I wish not to judge his actions or true motivation (only he and his conscience know for certain), but to the parties concerned, he is believed guilty of stealing innocent children's money. In the future, I would like you to discourage your son from exhibiting this behavior to avoid any further trouble or ill will between him and his classmates. Please send me a brief note stating that you understand and will comply with the school's wishes.

Sincerely,

Ms. Gladys Baker

After reading, I held the note loosely in my hands. My brother's eyes had trailed to the brown patent leather of the seat in front of us. He seemed to be staring through the fabric. He sighed and took the letter from me. He folded it in half—I thought so I could replace the staple—but then he folded it again and again. He took out a pair of safety scissors from his bag and began cutting little squares into the note.

I gasped and swallowed hard. "What are you doing?" I whispered.

He went on cutting like he didn't hear me.

"Where'd you get those scissors?" I asked.

"They think I'm a thief," he said, posed almost like a question though devoid of any note of surprise.

"Why'd you do it?" I asked

"I was hoping to save up enough, maybe buy the class a new rabbit or at least a guinea pig."

"I mean the *letter*. Why'd you cut up the letter?"

He unfolded the note to reveal a kind of grid of rectangles. It looked like a window with twelve windowpanes. He held the paper up to his face and looked me in the eyes through the paper window. "This is how they'll always see me," he said.

I didn't understand.

But the truth of my grandmother's words struck me then, like a church bell clapper hammering around my ribcage, reverberating throughout my entire body. *Now. Now. Now. Now.*

"Give me that," I said and took the note. I swept up the cut pieces from the floor, picked them up, and folded them into what remained of the note. I grabbed his scissors and jabbed a one-inch slit into the upholstery of the seat facing us, and I fed the tattered note into the slot. I handed him the scissors. "Put these back where you found them."

I had the rest of the day to figure out how to handle this trouble.

From the moment we arrived home to late in the evening, I kept to myself. I pretended to do my homework in between pacing my room and standing by my bedroom window, gazing into the darkening woods outside.

"Cindy?" My grandmother peeped her head in the doorway. She had joined us for dinner that evening.

I turned and smiled, expecting her to say goodbye before leaving for home, but she asked if she could come in, which was unlike her.

She walked over to the window and looked with me upon our small yard and into the woods. The shady green blotted the view from every vantage point, but in the fading light, with the sky grown lavender, there were short, craggy fissures of yellow sunlight like frozen lightning carving out the edges of the clouds. "Pretty sunset," she said. I agreed. "You seem like you're carrying a little extra weight with you tonight— worrying like your mama. What's going on?"

I wasn't so old yet that parental inquiries were met with eye rolls or quarter-turns in the opposite direction. Even then, my grandmother had more access to my thoughts and troubles than my mother. When Mother worried, her mind fell into familiar ruts that rarely led to anyplace helpful.

"Remember what you said to me about my brother?"

"You'll have to give me more than that, darling."

"You said he would need me at school or anywhere outside of our home. You said once in a while he'll need a protector," I said.

"Oh. Yes. Sure. That's true. You should each be protecting each other, even if he is your big brother. I recall saying that."

"You said he'll need to learn to take care of himself, but he might need me to see when he's in danger."

"That's true." She seemed to be studying my face. "Has something come up?" she asked.

"He's been in a lot of trouble lately. Both times I haven't seen it coming. The children at school like making things up about him. I try to explain why he acts the way he does, but no one ever believes me, if they're listening in the first place."

"I see."

"How do I protect him? I only see him at recess and on the bus. What about the rest of the day? I'm littler than everyone who would hurt him. Right now, it's all talk, but what if it comes to real fighting?"

She sighed, touched my cheek, and ran her thumb upward, smoothing my brow. "You'll wrinkle, like me." She seemed to be choosing her words, then said: "Your brother is a special case. Only God knows what he'll do next or why he'll do it." She laughed at this. "Well, a protector need not be the biggest person in the room or the smoothest talker, but it helps to be quick. Quick in every way you can be, like a rabbit. But not just fast on your feet, you need to be sharp as a needle—smarter sooner. That's the best kind of quick."

"How do I get smarter sooner?"

"That's the great trial of this life, Cindy, getting smarter sooner. First you have to consider what you already know: you can't predict your brother, and you can't explain what he does, so fretting on either is a waste of time." She thought on this a moment. "So nobody listens anymore?"

"Right."

"Maybe you're not telling the right kind of story." She leaned against the frame of the window. The golden streaks were gone, and the clouds were now a deep lavender. "And maybe you're telling the story too late."

A click behind us turned the nightstand lamp on.

"What are you two plotting in here?" my mother said.

"Women stuff," Grandmother said.

"I'm women," Mother said.

Grandmother wished us good night, and Mother walked her out. I kept looking out the window. The lamplight behind me glared in the double panes at such an angle that a pair of two yellow lights reflected before me. I swayed my head from side to side, and the twin lights seemed to follow me, almost like a pair of glowing eyes peering into my room.

I still had *my* note. I would give Mother mine for the both of us. But what did the end of *his* note say? I was beginning to regret having hidden it in the seat. Something about a reply?

Before we all went to bed, I presented my note to Mama with an additional two pieces of notebook paper and a pencil. I told her that though the note neglected to mention as much, we were verbally instructed to bring to school a signed note from a parent to say that she had received the note and understood the new policy. Mother wrote two notes stating as much, signed them, said, "Guess I'll need to get my paycheck in rolled coins from now on," and handed me the notes.

The next day I gave one note to my brother just as he departed for his classroom. "Put this on her desk as soon as you walk in the room," I said. He pinched it between his fingers, but I didn't let go. "Stop looking for coins on the playground," I said, looking into his eyes more sternly than a little sister has any right to. He took the note and ambled down the hallway. Later I pulled out the other note from my bag, erased every word that was not my mother's signature, folded it neatly into the back of my math book, and prayed the whole mess was finished. I knew, of course, it wasn't.

At recess the usual forum loitering near the school building had grown its numbers, one particularly troubling addition being Doug, who was roughly my brother's age, though much larger. He reminded everyone of Mr. Perry's words, how thievery was punished long ago.

"Maybe we should corner him and break a finger or two," Doug said.

"He wouldn't be so quick to steal kids' lunch money then," Calvin said.

Calvin spoke with a little extra zeal behind Doug. Calvin found a mentor in him, and as Doug's protégé, he didn't mind probing any angle of yesterday's happenings to win a little favor in his eyes. Calvin had already instigated a discussion about the total sum of pocket change my brother must've amassed over the last week. Based on yesterday's small sample, they extrapolated over the full week, multiplied by weeks in the school year and so forth, until he had our family practically sitting on a gold mine like the older girl and her father.

Through all of this, I listened.

Next item on the agenda was what my brother would do with the money. What was he saving for? Hot sauce for all the sunbaked roadkill . . . I listened . . . bus fare so he could ride across the country and track down our father . . . I listened . . . a friend since he didn't have any . . . I listened . . . a wooden chest to hold all the notes he'd made from watching other children . . . I listened . . . a .22 rifle he could come shoot the school up with . . . I listened . . . a shovel to bury his victims . . .

"Poison," I spoke.

This time *they* listened.

"Of course, it doesn't have to be anything fancy. Rat poison, antifreeze, any old household cleaner corrosive enough . . . ," and I rambled about how nearly anything within my brother's reach could be used to give a child all sorts of maladies, from a sore throat, head or stomachache, to a heavy sleep they might never wake from, and the longer I spoke, the more their faces changed, starting with the girls, moving to Calvin, the one older girl, and finally resting on Doug, and the more their faces turned, the more I felt bubbling inside of me a kind of caustic elation having at last verged on the discovery of what Grandmother must have meant in charging me with the care of my older brother, how words uttered after the matter were a waste of breath, how the truth can be a fangless snake. I was building up to something, I knew not what. "You think he just *found* all those animals dead in the woods? I'd think longer on that one. I don't know what he wanted with them or why he thought to collect them, but nothing changes the fact of where they ended up, but you keep running your mouths, well, I think that would be a real shame." I looked Calvin dead in the eyes. "Well, maybe not you so much."

The joyful sounds of children playing could be heard in the distance but here only silence as I looked each child in the eyes, pendant-wearing Mira and Samantha included.

"Where is he?" Mira asked.

"What?" I said.

We all looked over to his usual spot. He wasn't there. I winced at the feeling in my stomach. Any moment my icicle dagger words would shatter on the ground. The children would begin discussing his whereabouts, each guess another insult, but then: "Oh. There." One of the younger girls pointed back toward the school.

He was walking along the breezeway unattended, returning to the playground. Anyone else, this would seem like the least remarkable sight in the world, but with him there was something so lonesome about it, so perplexing, yet given everything I'd just finished saying, electric, dangerous. Everyone, myself included, wondered why he had no adult supervision, where he'd been, what he'd been doing, yet no one dared ask. We watched as he made his way back to the trees, but before he could return, recess ended.

The rest of the school day was a meditative blur of pondering, relentless questions, each with numerous conjectures. How long had he absented himself from recess? Where had he gone? What was he doing? I wondered what would become of the seeds I'd sowed. I imagined—I hoped—in every classroom, whispers and scribbled notes on tattered paper secreted away into books, desks, and pockets and, with them, a disquieting fear sweeping through the school like a plague, up and down the rows of desks and cafeteria tables, telegraphed from one grade or one group of friends to the next on the playground and in the buses. I wondered how long would it take for everyone to simply leave my brother alone.

On the bus ride home, I felt my curiosity welling up within me again, ready to burst. My brother looked out the window, shadows passing over his face from sunlight through the trees. A blunt "Where were you?" nearly escaped my lips, but I pressed them tight and held it all in. For as far back as I can remember, my brother has always had very little to say, yet everyone in his life has always leaned into him with a barrage of questions, and the harder they leaned, the stonier he grew. They only wanted to know him better at first, to understand him, but these one-way conversations could quickly assume the tenor of an interrogation. I didn't want to bully information out of him like so many have, but I had to know.

Instead, to my surprise, he spoke first. He unzipped his bag and revealed a tall, slender canvas-bound book. It was a faded blue canvas, threadbare at the edges. I couldn't make out any print on the spine or the cover, only the subtle imprint where ink must've once been.

"I found this in the library today." He handed me the book.

Inside were glossy pages with pictures of paintings, scribblings, and sketches, some in black and white and some in color.

"Leonardo da Vinci," he said. "I'm doing a report on him for history."

We flipped through the book together. There were colorful pictures of beautiful, pale-skinned women and bearded men with long, curly hair, but he was mostly enamored with the backward script and unusual sketches. "Look here," he said, "a flying machine." He turned a few pages. "A kind of tank . . . a sort of carriage with knives that spun around . . . a huge crossbow. Here, look!" There were skeletons and exposed muscles, frighteningly old faces, bird wings. He turned to a page with a baby curled into a ball, tucked into itself so you couldn't see his face. On this he paused for quite a while.

"Won't it be hard to do a report with mostly pictures?" I asked.

"There's writing." He flipped through the book again and pointed at a few of the lengthier captions. There was an infrequent page or two of biography or context interspersed within the pictures. "I mostly picked this one because it was skinny, and the teacher didn't like any of my other ideas."

"She didn't?"

"'Nothing mysterious!' she kept telling me."

"What did you want to write about?"

"The Bermuda Triangle. There was one book about it. Planes and ships and boats just kind of disappear out in the ocean. They get turned around or the planes can't tell which way is up or down, and then they crash or sink, and nobody ever hears from them again."

"What else did she turn down?"

He proceeded to tell me about old monster movies, Bigfoot, the Loch Ness Monster, UFOs, mythical beasts like unicorns and dragons, the massive stone carvings of Easter Island, Stonehenge. I kept imagining each excited discovery ending with a dejected walk back to the shelves to return these books.

"She pretty much dragged me to a different section of the library, said, 'Pick one,' and then we left. I don't know what she's got against mysteries."

The next day at recess, everyone was much quieter, in my presence at least. The children watched me instead of my brother. They didn't talk about him, nor did they talk to me. I decided to meander about the playground, maybe eavesdrop. I wanted to overhear children speaking about my brother. I wanted to hint at more portentous possibilities should they even think of further maligning him, but most children simply grew silent as I approached. I took this for a sign that it was working. I made my way to the far corner of the yard, then walked along the outer stretch with the playground equipment and back to the cedars to find my brother gone.

In the shade there, I scanned the entire property and playground, woods and all, every group of children, and at last I noticed him passing along the old school building adjacent to the new one and turning the corner. Yet again, it seemed he was unaccompanied by a teacher or assistant. Of course, being a teenager at the time he didn't need anyone to watch over him, but it still seemed odd to me that he was given free rein. Maybe the lax supervision was simply the laziness of a few women tired of leaving their chairs and their cigarettes—it was their break too—but this confirmed my suspicion that the teachers and assistants didn't want to be around him either.

It was cool and pleasant under the cover of the trees, so I sat on one of the exposed tree roots. This ancient oak among the cedars had sprawling roots that spun a kind of wild, serpentine web in the ground, creating spiral stairsteps here and undulating like massive tentacles there. Children of all grades were discouraged from playing under them, but I don't recall my brother ever being reprimanded. He'd have felt like a prisoner exiled from the woods.

I watched, waiting for him to return, when at last I saw his form appear from between the two buildings; almost instantly, the teachers began waving the children in. I walked briskly to join the rest. Calvin and the others were in the back. Were they watching me like we'd watched for my brother? I ran up behind Samantha and Mira, but they didn't see me. They were walking nearly shoulder to shoulder, elbow to elbow, so I fell in step silently behind them. At one point I could see they held something in their hands. Their pendants. They had taken them off and were piecing the two outer ends of the heart together. They fit surprisingly well.

After another day of this behavior from my brother, it was time for an intervention. Once he made his usual escape to his woods, I joined him there.

"Welcome to the kraken," he said when I arrived. He chuckled and began stepping from root to root. "Don't you think the bark looks like crocodile hide?" he asked.

Unlike the trunk, the bark on the roots was less flaky, more like scales. I agreed.

"They're like great monsters, don't you think? There's some old trees this size in the woods around our home, but you have to walk a long way," he said. "Maybe I'll take you to see them sometime."

It was a humid day. I squinted to see if the group was watching. My brother kept circling the tree, stepping upon its tentacle roots.

"You know, Leonardo da Vinci wasn't just a painter and inventor—"

"I need to ask you something," I said. "Where have you been going these last few days?"

"Here," he said.

"You *start* here," I said, "but then you leave."

"I have to go to the bathroom sometimes."

". . . and you don't just go behind a tree out here?" I asked.

He made a sheepish look. "Don't you think I shouldn't?" he asked.

"I never see you talk to Mrs. Tedder. Don't you ask before you go?"

"I asked a time or two. She said, 'Stop asking and just go.'" He seemed to be bristling at my questions. We'd settled nothing, in my mind. "Speaking of—I need to go." He balance-walked up a root to the trunk and picked up his bag from behind the tree.

He nearly vanished in the haze. In the wavy heat, I saw his blur turn the corner. I thought I might rejoin the old group and wait out recess, but instead I sat and watched them. Something seemed different, particularly in the posture of the boys. Then I noticed Calvin, having left Mrs. Tedder, headed in my brother's direction. A short time later, my brother returned, though much sooner than usual. He seemed lost with the extra time. He began walking toward the cedars, but then Calvin caught up, tapped my brother's shoulder, and spoke to him. I couldn't tell if he answered back. I hoped he didn't.

My brother spoke very little the rest of the day. He ate practically nothing for dinner. Mother asked was everything okay. I butted in and answered that it was, though I knew better. I wouldn't learn until tomorrow. I didn't pray a lot back then—nor do I now, I suppose—but each time I awoke in the night, I prayed for guidance, not to be a worthless, dim-witted kid sister, the kind who sleeps while her brother sweats blood in his midnight garden; I prayed, my brother's name on my lips, whispered in the resigned way you hear men utter the name of a coming hurricane.

The next day Calvin couldn't wait to tell everything he knew. With my brother absconded to the cedars and with everyone in place, he began: "I thought something was up with your weirdo brother, Cindy. We all did. Now I know it's true."

I made no reply, but I could tell he was enjoying himself by the way he looked at everyone while addressing me.

"He's been acting more suspicious than ever since we all found out he was a thief. You've been acting weird too. 'Where's he been going every day?' me and Doug wanted to know, so I did a little investigating . . . ." My grandmother's words came to me. "I saw how he walks along the edge of the cafeteria building and leaves the playground like he's up to something . . . ." *Sharp.* "Well, turns out he is. He's been breaking in . . . ." *Quick.* "Spending recess in the hell room," he said at last.

Gasps all around.

On this side of the new school building was a much smaller, older utility building. Together they formed a kind of claustrophobic alleyway children would dare each other to explore, and just beyond the alley was a dilapidated doorway to the hell room, spray-painted with the black letters HR, with a plastic KEEP OUT sign tacked underneath. There had been horrifying speculations about the hell room—the kinds of things that occurred there, why no one goes there today, what would happen if you did. Who knows where such stories begin? Frightened children breeding fear into younger children, who pass the tales down to younger children . . .

They waited for my reply.

"It's true," I lied. "He told me as much long ago."

"What's he doing in there? And don't try to sell us anymore of that poison crap neither," Doug said.

"How's he getting in?" the older girl asked.

"He's got a key, I think," Calvin said.

"How'd he get a key?" Doug said.

"What's in there?" Samantha asked. They all wanted to know, but I was caught silent when she chimed in. Samantha had never followed the others in all their slandering conversation. Perhaps she spoke out of a genuine curiosity about the contents of the room. I wondered as much as anyone, but something about the way she watched for the older girl's reaction after speaking—well, it felt to me like she had stepped on a passenger car and left me, and maybe Mira, at the station.

"Let's go see," I said.

They looked confused.

"We'll go take a tour," I said.

"How?" Doug asked. "You think they're just going to let us all walk down there like a mob? Beat the door down?"

I laid out the plan. First, Samantha, the older girl, and I would go. We tell the assistants we're going to the bathroom together—a common enough request. Once we pass the blind spot, the two girls wait at the alley while I see if the room's open. If it is, we take a quick look and come back. Calvin and Doug could go once when we return. I don't know what I hoped to accomplish with this, but I thought it would buy me a little more time to create something new, a new way to protect my brother. In the back of my mind, the words *Quick, quick, you have to be quick.*

It's true that in those days recess was a "wild west" affair. Teacher assistants took a rather laissez-faire approach to monitoring our play unless a child broke a bone, which happened on occasion. Except for a few of the clingier children, most wouldn't interact with the assistants unless a trip to the restroom was in order, which typically was met with aversion or a dismissive wave of the hand.

I led the two by Mrs. Tedder, who wearily assented to our request. We nearly ran to the buildings. As we reached the alleyway, the older girl watched to see if Mrs. Tedder was paying attention. Before I could ask if I was clear, she whispered, "Go!"

I ran up to the door. The knob was rusty and, when it turned, sounded like metal grinding upon metal. I had to throw my weight against the rickety door to loosen it from its frame. The girls saw and hurried to my side. The hinges gave a coffin lid creak as we slipped in.

You could hardly make anything out in the darkness. There was a row of short rectangular windows at the top of one of the walls. They were nearly opaque with decades of grime. It took a moment for my eyes to adjust, but even then, the dingy windows cast a greenish brown tint to everything in sight: dusty old fluorescent light bulbs, cardboard boxes, leather cases; teacher desks stacked to the ceiling and a mountain of student chairs and desks; a once-white trellis intertwined with fake ivy; a tarnished, dismantled sousaphone and a rail hung with old marching band uniforms; a set of lockers, shelves of forgotten baseball and basketball trophies, lots of plastic buckets, yellow, white, gray, and black . . .

We each stepped carefully through the room, Samantha following the older girl. The stagnant air smelled of mold and mildew. Among the buckets were a few jugs. A blue one had a yellow label with a skull and crossbones symbol. I took the jug by the handle and sloshed it.

"We need to get back," I said to the girls from the other side of the room.

Quick! a voice inside me spoke.

I unscrewed the cap of the blue jug—it had a safety cap like on a medicine bottle—and quietly spilled the chemical on the floor until there was a good-sized puddle. I balled up a greasy rag I'd spotted nearby and ground it into the puddle. I placed the jug next to the puddle and rag with the lid off.

I circled back to the girls, who were both enthralled with the trappings of the old room, but before I did, I noticed two huge rusty machines partly obscured by the desks and chairs. They looked like they had steering wheels, dials, faces that looked like clocks, chains, and most of all—pipes—pipes everywhere around the hulking machines, connecting to each other, to other machines, leading through the floor and through the walls. I learned years later these were boilers.

Samantha nearly screamed when I tapped her shoulder.

"Let's go," I said. "Out, out."

As we neared the door, the older girl asked, "Do you smell that?"

The liquid puddling on the floor had an overwhelming odor like ammonia mixed with urine and expired perfume, a little worse than what I'd smelled sitting next to strange old women at the church Mother sometimes dragged me to. Samantha grabbed her nose and gave a little cough. I followed suit and doubled back to the buckets and jugs. "What's this?" I said. I'd left the jug sitting just so, it's grinning skull and crossbones facing the doorway.

"It looks dangerous," Samantha said.

"Let's leave," the older girl said, coughing.

I almost forgot to close the door after we ran outside but thought better and pulled it shut. When we returned to the group Calvin and Doug were nearly running in place. "What did you see? What's he doing?" they asked.

"Poison," the older girl spoke.

"What?" Doug said.

"That's what we saw," Samantha said.

"And we all breathed it in," the older girl said. "If you go, you better not stay long."

Calvin looked to Doug for confidence.

"We'll see about that," Doug said. "Let's go."

I saw them stop by Mrs. Tedder on their way. She looked annoyed but nodded yes anyway, and they ran off. "Maybe we should just hold recess in the damn bathrooms tomorrow!" she shouted for everyone to hear. "Do we need to have a half-hour potty break before recess? That'll leave about five minutes of playtime by my math." Then she continued talking to the teacher sitting beside her.

None of us spoke as we waited for the boys. Though they were probably only gone for five minutes, it felt much longer. The longer I sat there, the sicker I felt. A new dread was settling into my stomach. If they were afraid of him, wouldn't someone simply tell a teacher or parent, and then we'd be back in the same place, only worse—he might finally get into real trouble. I had to temper this deception somehow. I had to ensure I hadn't induced a kind of panic.

They returned short of breath. Doug said: "We saw it. The blue jug. We saw the poison."

"He did it," Calvin said. "Now he's going to poison us. He'll poison everyone."

"No, he won't," I said.

"He hates me," Calvin said. "I know he does, especially after what I said yesterd—" He caught himself.

"The rabbit . . . the lunch money . . . the poison . . . I can't say where my brother gets his ideas. I only know what happens when you interfere with his routines." I lifted the hair on the side of my head and showed them a three-inch scar creeping into my hairline. I pushed up the sleeve of my shirt and told them how he once had broken my arm. "I think you should take all this as a warning." I looked at each of them. "Everybody," I said. "I don't think he ever *intends* to hurt anyone, but I also know that sometimes people get hurt anyway. My head, my arm, neither time he meant to hurt me."

This much was true, but this time the truth was working. Yet somehow this truth felt ugly and cruel. A truth to seal a book of lies.

"But I will say this: he listens very carefully to his sister. Think what you will of him, but I believe speaking about him would be a bad decision." I looked to Calvin and Doug. "I'd hate if he got the idea any of you came between him and whatever he's got going on down in the hell room."

Then recess ended.

I didn't talk with my brother that day until close to bedtime. I knocked on his door, but he was entranced by his work. On the floor he had arranged dozens of old railroad spikes in a kind of spiraling fractal on the floor. It was very precise. You'd think these old, discarded spikes would be rusty, but he'd taken steel wool to each of them. They didn't shine, but underneath their rust they had a dull antique-bronze coloring.

I sat admiring his work, watching his eyes as he studied the pattern and occasionally made slight adjustments. I wasn't sure he noticed I was there, but I waited for him to speak first anyway.

"If you turn your head quick one way, it looks like it's burrowing through the floor; from here, at this angle, it looks like it might stretch across the room," he said.

I knelt next to him. It was true. I noticed he'd placed the yellow marble at the center of the spiral. A tiny glass star for a galaxy of steel.

"Cindy, the kids seem to act differently with me lately. They never really talked to me all that much, but now they seem almost frightened."

Thinking of the look on his face as he told me this still sends a sinking feeling through me, like driving too fast through a dip in the road. Though his troubles had begun long before the past weeks, I was a part of them now—I shared that stain with the rest, though I hadn't begun to understand this in the moment. Then, I only knew the pity I felt for him and the resentment of a little sister burdened with guarding her hapless older brother.

"I need to know why you've been going to the hell room at recess," I said.

"Hell room? Why would they call it that? I take my book there and read. It's cool and quiet, nobody watching. I feel like everyone's always watching me. I sit in a small space below a window, near a mirror for extra light, and I read my Leonardo book."

"Why didn't you tell me this yesterday?" A stupid question really. Keeping this secret allowed him a refuge in this otherwise unforgiving place. It was probably the one time of the day he didn't feel exposed. Nevertheless, the thought of him reading alone in that dank, dusty room, huddled over by a cloudy mirror image of himself, filled me with an irrepressible melancholy and, for some reason, a growing sense of shame. But this wasn't the time to search these feelings.

"How are you able to get in there?"

He reached in his pocket and produced a key.

"How'd you get it?"

"On the way back from the bathroom one day, I saw Mr. Perry down the alley. He was fiddling with the key in the doorknob. I guess it was jammed. He got a call on his walkie-talkie. He needed to leave, but his keys were hooked to the chain on his belt. I could see he was trying not to break it. He worked the key off the ring and left it there in the door. It only took me a few seconds to get it loose. He'd bent it a little, so I've mostly been leaving it unlocked."

"You need to return the key."

"To Mr. Perry?"

"No. Hide it nearby—somewhere he might see it—but don't let anyone find it on you." And with that I left him to his railroad spikes. No one spoke to him in this manner—direct, unwavering commands without hesitance, with the right amount of heat—not Mother, Grandmother, nor any of his teachers, for all I knew. Maybe adulthood revealed some truth about him that I couldn't see as his adolescent sister, but many years later, when pondering their indifference—or should I say inaction?—I would be filled with a growing, quiet resentment for all of them. Had they given up on him even then? I wondered. Given up finding the right pressure to raise something good in him? Did they ever try guiding him or speaking to him like there was any hope? All the same, I didn't know if he'd listen to me then or whether he intended to get rid of the key.

The next school day, a sickly third grader named Zeb had stayed home from school. This wasn't uncommon, but then I overheard someone suggest he was poisoned. At recess they asked me if this was the case; I didn't deny it. Later at lunch, one child drank two cartons of milk and vomited all over the cafeteria floor. A few children looked at me. I simply shrugged. Before the end of the day, several more children weren't feeling well. I cannot account for any of this. Looking back, it's the part that seems most miraculous to me—if you could call a few kids sick on their stomachs a miracle. It certainly helped cultivate the seeds of anxiety I'd sowed.

The following day's recess, their questions intensified: "Can your brother pick locks?" "Did he sneak into the cafeteria yesterday?" "What did he put in the milk?" "How long will he be mad at us?"

"He's not angry at anyone," I said. "He just wants everyone to leave him alone. I asked him if the kids who got sick yesterday would be okay, and he said: 'Yes. This was only intended to open everyone's eyes.'"

These were the first of the many stories I would tell over the next few years to anyone and everyone who would mention my brother in my vicinity. Speaking of him within my hearing would invite another somewhat twisted tale, painting my brother as a prescient, mystic, macabre loner, capable of puzzling acts carrying portentous significance—a walking superstition. And when the whispers had ceased and people grew silent at my passing, this served to give me more time to further contemplate his legend. I wanted every child in the school to know my brother was the kind of special you don't trifle with. And every story ended with the same familiar caveat I told the children back then: if they would simply leave him alone, no one else would have to suffer.

On the ride home that day, it became clear I was losing control. My brother said Vice Principal Vance had called him to his office. I was shaken at those words. These were still the days when the howls of children could be heard throughout the lower hall of the school building. I'd heard of everything from open hands to fists, switches to paddles, rulers to canes. Their cries only fed our terrible imaginations. Funny how this works.

This is how my brother said the meeting happened:

"You know a few children went home sick yesterday?" Mr. Vance asked.

My brother nodded.

"A few children seem to be under the impression that you had something to do with this?"

He stared.

"They're scared of you. Why?"

"I don't know," he said.

"They said something about the old storage room. I happen to know Mr. Perry has been missing a key to this very room. What do you know about any of this?"

He told him he didn't know anything.

"Empty out your pockets," the vice principal said.

I nearly passed out in our bus seat. My vision was flashing black, pink, and red. "Did you . . . ." I couldn't say it.

"I showed him—just this." He showed me the yellow cat's eye marble. "And my lunch money." He put the marble back in his pocket. "He said, 'I don't want to see you in here again.'"

I quit holding my breath.

"Why does he think I make kids sick? Is that why they're scared of me?"

I didn't know how to tell him.

"They think I poisoned the school?" he said.

The bus air brakes screamed out, and we lurched forward three times before stopping. Each time my stomach flipped. Dust flew by our window. We were home. "Get your stuff. I'll tell you everything," I said.

As we sat on an old picnic table in the backyard, he listened very patiently, stoically you might say. I waited for him to be angry or to be moved at all, but he sat quietly, letting me explain myself. In the end "I'll be fine" is all he said, and he hopped off the table and walked into the woods.

I've often wondered about the life cycles of a story. Over the years it seems people will hardly broach the topic of my brother; no one asks where he is or how he's doing or if we've heard from him; no letters come from interested strangers; no newspeople or documentarians or writers drop by requesting sit-down interviews with their recorders handy or cameras in tow . . . . And then suddenly they flood in, a few a week for several months. We get questions and visits. If you watch a person carefully, you can see how a question fills their bodies like water in a vessel, especially with the townspeople if, say, we were out on an errand: it starts in their shuffling feet, tensing their legs, churning their stomachs, lowering their shoulders, coloring their cheeks, shifting their eyes, and resting on their tongues jammed tight behind the teeth of their slackened jaws.

But children are different, naked in their sense of wonder, and at recess the next day, the forum was alive, and the cycle was in full chatter mode.

"I don't believe any of this," Doug said. "Look at him." My brother appeared to be gathering a handful of white and green flowers from the clover in the yard close to the cedars. Doug addressed me directly: "He's a dirty thief all right, and I wouldn't put it past him to poison anybody, but I don't think he's some kind of mastermind lock picker, and I ain't scared of him."

The older girl giggled and agreed. Samantha followed suit. Mira stood silently.

Almost as if he'd heard, my brother began walking back to the school, making the wide circle to avoid passing anyone too closely.

Before he made the corner, Mrs. Tedder called him over. He ran to her and spoke too softly for us to hear. She relented, and he walked toward the school, I assumed to the restroom—I prayed not to the old storage room.

"I can't believe they're letting him go anywhere alone," Calvin said.

They all agreed.

"Calvin!" Mrs. Tedder called, after my brother had been gone a few minutes. Calvin ran to her, and after a brief exchange, he nodded and followed my brother's steps back to the schoolhouse.

It has become clearer and clearer to me that the children's talk had no doubt reached the ears of many of the teachers and administration. I was a naive child then. Nevertheless, it makes me sick to think of the foolishness of it all, to think my fearmongering could be contained to the children without ascending to adult ears. I can only attribute this silly notion to the enchanting nature of our daily recesses. Entering the playground each day felt like leaving the rest of the world behind. The books, lessons, teachers, adults, home, family—everything didn't exist for the half-hour or more we were left to our own devices. I think I genuinely believed words spoken on the playground would more or less remain there.

A moment later my brother returned with Calvin not far behind him, but Calvin stopped and spoke again to Mrs. Tedder before returning to our group. "I saw him," Calvin said. "He'd been down the alley. I walked down there, but the door was locked. Could it be he'd already been in and left?"

"No," I said. "He doesn't do that anymore. He's done."

"Oh, he's done all right," Doug said. The older girl laughed. Calvin smiled.

Rabbit quick! Grandmother's voice.

I took Mira by the hand and said, "Let's swing." As we walked across the yard, I all but begged her to tell me what the boys were planning. She demurred, but I grabbed her arm above her elbow and squeezed. "I need to know. He's my brother. I have to watch out for him. He can't do it for himself. Even when he minds his own business, he gets in trouble, so I've got to take care of him." Mira had a baby brother not yet in kindergarten. I asked wouldn't she do anything to make sure no one hurt him. We made our way to the swings and sat hovering there, barely swaying.

"They want to catch him in the alley," she said. "They're going to corner him. They're going to slip around the back of the building as soon as your brother asks Mrs. Tedder. Then they're going to wait for him, make him open the hell room, force him in there, and Doug says he's going to beat him up real bad."

Though she sounded genuinely concerned, I had to wonder how long she'd known and stood silent, a feeble, tight-lipped mouse in Samantha's shadow? Why would she allow this secret to be kept from me? I gave a perfunctory "thanks," not a drop of warmth or kindness in my voice. In truth her weakness disgusted me. Mira's allegiance obeyed the slightest wind. I remember thinking, I have no need of friends like these, and I bruised it into my heart then, never to fail a friend by idling in silence when the occasion demanded words or action, that is, if I ever made another friend.

That evening he'd been out in the woods alone again. He didn't come back until close to dark. Mother, Grandmother, and I were eating dinner with an empty place setting for him. I suspect he had been walking up and down the train tracks because of his calm demeanor.

He ate very little, maybe a chicken wing, a few garden peas, and a forkful of rice. As we finished, Mother asked him when his report was due.

"Tomorrow," he said.

"Oh, you need to practice, honey. Get your papers and your book and come try it out on us," Mother said.

We sat in the living room, Mother and Grandmother in their chairs and I on the floor, and we waited several minutes for him to return. We looked at each other, each thinking he'd forgotten or decided not to, but then he walked into the room.

He began: "Leonardo da Vinci was one of history's most famous painters in his day. He lived in Italy in the 1400s." He held up his book and showed a sketch of a hanged man. "This was one of the first sketches Leonardo did. It was a criminal they hanged in the streets. Leonardo sketched everything he could see. No matter what it was, Leonardo was interested in it, and he would study it even if it bothered people. He was a kind of doctor or scientist, too, but people didn't like that side of him too much. They wanted him just to paint and draw and sculpt nice things. They didn't want him peeling back any skin to see if he could understand how muscles work or learn what people's bones look like. That's what we all look like inside, and that's what da Vinci wanted to show us, but nobody wanted to know that part of us for some reason, maybe because skeletons just mean death to some people, but skeletons are really more like . . . well, it's what makes us people. We'd be like blobby slugs without skeletons."

We were silent.

"Here's a picture of a baby." He showed us a sketch of a child in the womb. Mother made a sound, so he quickly flipped a few more pages to a portrait. "Here's a pretty lady with a pet weasel," he said. Mother and Grandmother smiled.

The next morning after breakfast, I had finished dressing and was gathering my things for school. Mother had left us both bagged lunches before leaving for work, so I went into the kitchen to collect them. Before I reached the refrigerator, I could hear a rattling behind the counter. It sounded like when a racoon or possum gets into one of the trash bins at night—jugs, cans, and bottles jostling around. I thought I heard one or two aerosol cans rattle and spray. I called my brother's name.

"Yeah?" he returned.

"What're you doing?" I walked around the counter to see him sitting on the floor beneath the kitchen sink with the cabinets open. All around him were bottles and cans of all sorts. Cleaning liquids, paint, bleach, bug killer, drain cleaner, who knows what else? "Is everything okay?" I said.

"Sure." He started placing everything back under the sink. "I'll meet you outside."

I took our bags from the refrigerator and shut the door. "You did hide the key somewhere Mr. Perry would find it, right?"

He didn't answer.

I walked out the back door of the kitchen to go wait for him at the road where the school bus picked us up. In a moment he'd joined me. My mind searched for a way to ask him what he was doing with all those chemicals under the sink, but I didn't know how to ask without sounding accusatory. How does one casually ask such a question? We stood there not talking, listening for the bus's engine. I wondered had he finally been pushed too far. I wondered at the part I'd played in bringing him to this point. Could he really make good on any of the threats I'd implied? Was he capable of doing something truly awful?

These questions burned in me the whole ride to school while he sat looking out the window, seemingly hypnotized by green forest shade blurring by. In his catatonic silence, I felt something shifting between us, and the boy I'd forever known as my older brother, an extension of my own body, seemed foreign to me now, something alien. The bus had entered a particularly long stretch of woods with an occasional pathway leading to hidden, childless homes. "You know, I've always thought if you look carefully enough through the woods or down one of these paths, you might see something unordinary in there, even if it was just a coyote or wolf or, better yet, a black bear or a panther or an enormous bird. What if it was a wild man or a bigfoot or another upright-walking thing?" he said. "Sometimes before we pass these places, I try to imagine one of them, like maybe if I see it clear enough in my mind, I can make it appear, and as the bus passes, it'd be looking dead at me; our eyes would meet. I'd be the only one to see it, a kind of secret, and as we'd zoom on by, my eyes wouldn't still be looking out the window—I'd be looking toward the road, then turning back deeper into the woods, headed wherever it is they go that nobody hardly ever sees them."

"You ever seen anything like that?" I asked.

"No, but they're out there," he said. "I've heard them. I've felt them."

The rest of the way to school, we rode in silence, looking deep into the woods for the dark silhouettes of anything mysterious, terrible, and wonderful.

I'd spent most of the day before thinking the whole thing through—the plan. Grandmother was right about never knowing what would come next from my brother, but his passions made him predictable, and this was my one advantage. It felt disloyal, even dangerous, withholding how Doug and Calvin planned to jump him in the alleyway, but I knew if I told him, it could derail the whole plan. I needed my brother to go to the storage room even if it meant confronting the boys. I wasn't sure what he'd do if he knew about the ambush.

Morning classes crawled along. I imagined everyone's actions, how to time my moves, what to say to whom, how to say it, and I tried to invent fail-safes if any part of this were to fall apart, but the more I worked to anticipate the various ways the whole scheme might unravel, the less confident I became, so instead, I rehearsed my part over and over.

My teacher let out class a little early—a bit of luck. This would allow me a chance to speak to Samantha and Mira without the boys overhearing. The teacher took us girls to the restroom down the hall before leading us to the playground. As I waited for the others to finish, I thought I could hear my brother's voice. Leaning against the wall, I scooted a little farther until I could see inside his classroom. My brother stood by the teacher's desk at the front of the class. He had nearly finished delivering his Leonardo da Vinci report. I shuffled back a step so he couldn't see me listening.

". . . Leonardo was a very clever man. He thought of everything. Not only that, but when he thought, he didn't think like everybody else. Like this: he lived to be a very old man, and when he knew he had a few days left to live, he planned out his whole funeral—all the details. Like, he wanted to make sure the service lasted for a certain number of hours, so he had a friend measure out and make the candles just the right size, and he told the church that the funeral should last until the candles burned out." He paused and looked up from his papers to see their faces, but I could tell he was speaking to a bunch of stone walls.

"Is that all?" I heard his teacher ask.

"No." He spoke to them now, without his notes. "They say Leonardo made a habit of buying caged birds when he was in the market, just to set them free. To some people, that probably looked like a waste of money. That's all."

When we were out on the playground, I took Samantha and Mira to the side.

"Guys, I overheard one of the boys saying how they were going to attack my brother today."

They both looked very solemn.

"I need you to help me. We don't have much time, but it's going to take all three of us to save him. You're my only friends. Can you help me?"

Samantha gave a slow kind of nod. Once she did, Mira followed suit.

"The boys are going to wait for him by the hell room when he goes there today. They're going to gang up on him and beat him up or something worse. We're not going to stop them ourselves, but we're going to make sure a few grown-ups do." This was a critical part of my plan. A teacher's assistant, maybe a teacher, but hopefully the vice principal needed to see these older, bigger boys attacking my brother. He was tough enough to take a few punches, and though I wasn't certain about this part, I believed he wouldn't engage in the fight—at least not until a certain instinct kicked in, which was a distinct possibility with him, but I prayed it wouldn't go that far.

After I told the girls the rest of the plan and how they were needed, the other classes joined us for recess. Everyone gathered where they typically would; Doug and Calvin hung around the shade of the building with the rest of our group, and my brother headed for the cedars.

I tried to act casually those first minutes. I jumped rope with

Samantha and Mira, but I barely took my eyes off of my brother under the cedars. I tried to read in his movements or his posture a sign that he would soon be making his way. When I couldn't wait any longer, I told them, "Now."

We walked up to Mrs. Tedder and the other assistant. I felt my chest wasn't big enough for my heart as we made this first move—the note. I'd taken Mother's second note, the blank sheet with her signature, and prepared a new note in my most careful handwriting the night before that simply read: "Please excuse Cindy from class during recess. She has a brief appointment but will return before the end of the school day," with the day's date by her name. This was a fail-safe of sorts, possibly unnecessary, but I couldn't take any chances with this part of the plan. I needed a clean exit without suspicion to ensure everyone was in place. I handed her the note. She read it without interest.

"Who's your teacher?" Mrs. Tedder asked.

"Mrs. Sykes," I said.

"Why didn't you give it to her or take it by the office this morning?"

"I forgot," I said.

"Run to the office then." She gave me back the note. "What do you girls need?"

"To go to the bathroom," Samantha said.

She scoffed and looked at the other teacher assistant, who had just lit two cigarettes. "Be quick," she said.

She muttered something as we ran to the school building.

When we reached the corner of the school by the alleyway, I stopped them. I pulled out a red marker from my pocket, and I knelt by Mira and began coloring in a heavy splotch under her knee with three or four uneven streaks streaming down from this point. Then I grabbed a handful of dirt by the sidewalk and patted it over all the red ink. It didn't look all that convincing, but it would buy us a minute or so.

"There's a small chance Doug changes his mind, or maybe my brother locks himself inside. I don't want to say there's a fight going on at the hell room and there not be." I handed Mira the marker. "That's why you're part of this. You're the reason Mr. Vance leaves his office, but when he hears a fight going on, he'll forget all about your knees. Now get this on your hands and pat a little dirt on top of that. When we see my brother turn down the alley, Samantha, you'll walk to the corner. You're the lookout. Mira, you wait here on the steps. I'll go get Mr. Vance and tell him you've fallen. Samantha—you have the most important part. You're going to scream like a horror movie actress, high as you can, to alert him to what's going on down the alley. But you have to time it right. You have to be certain the boys have begun attacking my brother, but please scream before it goes too far. He could get seriously hurt. But also, don't let Mr. Vance have long enough to see Mira's got marker instead of blood on her knees. You'll have to watch us both and make the call. If it looks like they're really hurting him, scream sooner. If the boys aren't down there, give me a sign. Understand?" I said.

She gave a look that did not inspire confidence.

"You've got two jobs: stand there and scream," I said.

Mira patted the dirt in her hands and gave me the marker, and the three of us waited inside the door. We held our breaths. I prayed no adult would happen by. If they did, I was already rehearsing my lines. Mira would cower behind Samantha. I would say something about a messy art project and washing up.

As I practiced my stories in my mind, Samantha startled and pulled us away from the doors. "There's your brother!" she said.

"Give him a second to go inside." I held her wrist. "Now!" I whispered, and she made her way to the corner. I held the door. "Mira, you go too. Just sit on the steps outside, and when you see us coming, cover your face and act like you've been crying."

I sped down the hall to Mr. Vance's office, knowing every second counted for my brother, who had no idea he was walking into their little trap. I gathered myself before stepping into his office, took a deep breath, and called him as I walked through his door: "Mr. Vance! My friend just fell on the stairs, and I—"

No one was there.

Rabbit quick.

Front of the building. Main office. Someone will listen.

I sprinted down the hall and into a little foyer that led to the main office. There were a couple ladies behind desks but, again, no Mr. Vance.

"Yes?" a lady with short, permed hair said.

"I need Mr. Vance; there's been an accident" I said.

"An accident?" The lady looked up from her work. "What kind of accident?"

"My friend's fallen on the stairs and cut her knee. Can we get Mr. Vance?" I asked.

"Is it bad?" She stood. "Nancy, page Mr. Perry," she said and began to leave the office.

The other woman walked to a little microphone. "Wasn't he leaving campus to go pick up parts? Maybe we can catch him." She pushed a button and said, "Mr. Perry, please report to the side entrance stairs."

We walked briskly down the hall. "Don't you think we should call Mr. Vance?" I said.

"If Mr. Perry needs him, we will," she said.

I was on the edge of panic. The plan was failing. Mr. Perry could break up the fight, but he knew Doug; he liked Doug. Whatever accusation Doug made would be good enough for him.

We walked through the doors and met Mira at the steps who was doing her best to cover her knees with her dirty, marker-stained hands, crying all the while. The lady automatically began trying to soothe her and to get a look at her knee, but—and I must give her credit here—Mira only clung tighter to her knees and cried harder, real tears.

"It's okay, Mira. It's okay," I said. Vice principal or no vice principal, we had to move ahead. My brother's life depended on it. I glanced over to Samantha's post, but she was gone. Where was she? Without her signal, how would I know what to do? Perhaps the boys were all talk? Maybe they were merely idle threats? Maybe Mira misheard them? What to do?

Simple.

I had to play Samantha's part.

I ran to the corner of the schoolhouse, where I had a clear view of the alleyway. A handful of children were blocking my view. They were near the hell room door. I heard a loud, wooden thump and then another, followed by the onlookers' pained reactions. I thought I could hear Calvin egging the fight on with a strand of puffed-up threats, cut short by a frantic, high-pitched shouting: "Get him off me! Get him off me!

What are you doing?" I couldn't see my brother or the other boys, but it was clearly getting out of hand.

"Help!" I didn't know what else to say.

Mr. Perry and the office lady rushed over.

"Oh, my," the lady said.

"My brother!" I said.

Mr. Perry lifted a walkie-talkie to his face. "Get down here!"

A voice crackled back.

"Storage room!" Mr. Perry shouted.

It was hard to make out what was happening. Most of the children from our group were there, including the older girl and Samantha. They both were clamoring for my brother's head. Mrs. Tedder stood behind them with a lost look on her face. The other children encircled the melee. Vice Principal Vance appeared, walkie-talkie in hand, shouting over them: "Boys! Now, boys! Listen! Boys!"

In the center Doug was grappling my brother like a wrestler, struggling to take him down. My brother was resisting with all his might, but he wasn't throwing any elbows or punches. He didn't really seem to be attempting any counter or evasive moves. It looked like he was hammering Doug's backside with the heel of his hand, almost like he was disciplining or spanking him.

Calvin, having been pushed aside by their spastic tangle, looked rumpled and dusty. He stood near the fray, yelling: "You fight like a sissy, you weirdo! Get him, Doug! Show him how a dude fights!"

"Get him away!" the vice principal said to Mr. Perry, gesturing at my brother. Mr. Vance moved in to pry Doug off of my brother, but as soon as he tried, he caught a hard elbow to the cheek, below his eye socket.

Everyone gasped. As he staggered away, Mr. Perry stepped in and forced his two brawny arms between the boys. He used his backside to push my brother to the ground, but Doug he grabbed by the throat and spoke in a commanding bass, "You best mind, little boy!" Doug clawed at the man's hand, but one look in Mr. Perry's eyes stopped him. I saw Mr. Perry's forearm flex like he was tightening on the boy's throat. The boy levitated a moment, the tips of his toes touching the ground.

Doug let loose, and his arms dangled limp by his side, like a kitten held in the air by the back of its neck. Mr. Perry dropped him in a crumpled heap.

"What—in—the—*hell* is going on here?" Mr. Vance said, still massaging his face.

"The boys were protecting us from that freak," the older girl said, pointing to my brother.

"Doug and Calvin tried to stop him," Samantha said.

"No one asked you!" I shouted at the older girl. "You neither," I said to Samantha.

Calvin looked to Doug, who was swallowing hard and teary eyed. "We were trying to save the school!" Calvin said. "He was going to poison everyone. He's got a key to the hell room. He found some chemicals in there, and he's been breaking into the cafeteria, poisoning the food."

Mr. Vance made a few exasperated grunts, but the words weren't coming.

"That's why everyone's been sick." Calvin's voice was shrill and faltering. "Look what he did to me." He pointed to a superficial scratch on his arm.

Mr. Vance stopped rubbing his cheek and straightened himself. He seemed to be contemplating the story, testing out its truth. "What do you have to say for yourself?" he said to my brother.

And this is the part I can't help returning to whenever I run through this series of days in my mind. Before he spoke, he turned to me with the most patient of looks, almost grandfatherly, with the ghost of the smile I'd seen days ago when he'd found the yellow marble, a smile only I would recognize. In this moment and in the days to come, I thought little enough of the look he gave me. But there, locked in the eyes of the vice principal, a few teacher assistants, and so many children who wished him ill and who would grow to fear him—I see now that he was trying to tell me something, perhaps that he would be all right, that these people, though he would never win the sympathy of a single one, they would never get the best of him. But that's not quite right. No, they would never *know* the best of him.

He addressed Mr. Vance: "I would never do such a thing. Every day I play by myself at the edge of the playground. If anyone wanted to join me, they could. They don't. I don't mind. But I don't know why people think I'm bad."

"He's been sneaking into this room every day or so!" Calvin shouted. "He's got a key!"

"Is that true?" Mr. Vance looked at my brother.

"I don't have a key," he said. "But I wonder if he does?" He pointed at Doug, who was massaging his neck, still reeling at having known absolute helplessness, breathing now, he knew, at the whim of this man with the strength of a python.

"How's that?" Mr. Vance's expression began to soften.

"He told me he was going to take me in there and pour poison down my throat. He must have a key to do that," my brother said.

"Check his pockets," Mr. Vance said to Mr. Perry.

Mr. Perry put a firm hand on Doug's shoulder. "Empty them, boy," he said.

Doug pulled his front pockets inside out. A few loose coins. He reached both hands in his back pockets and his eyes widened. He opened his hand and displayed the lost key.

"Give that to Mr. Perry," the vice principal said. "Take him to my office."

Mr. Perry squeezed Doug's shoulder. "This way," he said turning Doug away from the crowd, ushering him down the alley.

"*He* did that!" Calvin said. "*He* put that on him!"

"Are you okay, young man?" the vice principal asked, looking to Calvin.

"Yeah? Why?" Calvin seemed shaken.

"Your trousers are wet," he said.

"What?" Calvin looked at his jeans, everyone did, and they were stained with a milky whiteness on one leg from the front to the back. A wave of mutual embarrassment settled in among all attending. A few stifled their laughter. "What's this?" Calvin pulled a small black cylinder from his pocket.

The vice principal snatched it from him. "A film container," he said. He popped off the lid, gave a look inside, and then poured out a slow trickle. He smelled what remained in the canister, blinked hard a few times, and made a face. "What in God's name is in here?"

"They were going to hold me down and force me to drink it," my brother said.

"Jesus," the vice principal said. "Ladies, take these children back to class. I'll take care of this one." He grabbed Calvin by his collar. "I'm not finished with you either," he said to my brother. "Go with them for now. Everybody else, clear out!" His voice reverberated between the two buildings. I'd never heard a man raise his voice this way, and frankly, I didn't think Mr. Vance could command such ferocity. As he walked away, I could hear him reproaching Mrs. Tedder, something about "unaccompanied children" and "bathroom," and "what were you thinking?" was forcefully whispered a few times.

All the children fell in line, and they looked at the ground in front of them as they walked. "Hey!" I called from the back of the mob. My friends Samantha and Mira stopped. I tugged the golden pendant out from behind my shirt's neckline, yanked the clasp broken from around my neck, and threw it to the ground. I joined the rest, weaving through them to find my brother. When I did, I placed my hand on his elbow and gently pulled him to the side.

He appeared to be deep in thought, and when he turned to look at me, it was with the look one might give a sidewalk stranger. I wanted to embrace him, but this was never our way. How could he have known any of this would come to pass? How did he know what to prepare for or how to prepare? Had he kept the key all this time? He had scratches on his arms, and bruises on his face. I said, "Are you okay?" No one had bothered to ask him. His clothes were dusty, and his wild hair had loose bits of grass and weeds in it.

My inscrutable brother. Was he hurt by the part I played in all this? If he was upset with me, which part disappointed him most? That I let so many children believe he was some kind of demon, or was that too simple? Was it that I, his only sister—the *only* one he could talk to— didn't truly believe in him? I was no better than the most vapid child in our school. I was as faithless, as treacherous, as the rest. The cool, unfeeling look, maybe it wasn't so much disappointment but the final confirmation of all he'd ever suspected to be true about our nature. For all his indifferent shrugs and distant stares, it was finally clear to me now: He was the well among the sick. He was the well among the sick, and I did not see him. We wouldn't rest until we'd infected him with our own suffering or driven him into exile.

He made a wearied, bemused sound and reached into his pocket. He took my hand and placed in it the yellow marble he'd found in the playground dust. Then he left me there, alone between the two brick buildings. I stood there leaning against the schoolhouse a moment until something caught my eye, down the alley, on past the hell room and beyond the sloping hill to the surrounding woods. There in the dandelions, a flat-faced rabbit the size of a groundhog was munching on dark-green clover. His haggard gray pelt no longer had the sheen I remembered. At seeing me, he stopped and reared back on his hind feet, a move I'd never seen him make in his cage or in the classroom. We watched each other in silence a moment until, sniffing the air, he made for the woods, vanishing behind a wall of honeysuckle.

In truth I sometimes find myself dwelling on his, I mean, *our*, past more than I should. I know what Grandmother would say, the same thing she told Mother so long ago: This type of searching, this wondering, begins in daydreams and ends in obsession; fantasy soon turns to sickness. Grandmother says, we throw our bright penny wishes into the well so that we may be rid of them. The past is a luminous coin at the bottom of a pool; its only charm is that it is irretrievable.

Yet tonight my thoughts return to the evening he practiced his Leonardo da Vinci report in the kitchen, here in front of all three of us, me, Mother, and Grandmother. Every sketch and painting had its story. Though I'm not certain, I got the distinct impression that my brother was making much of it up. Part of me wondered if he hadn't simply spent all those quiet moments in the storage room gazing at the pictures, getting swept away in his imagination, dreaming up fanciful stories to go along with the paintings and sketches. He told a story about how when Leonardo was a boy, near Florence, he happened upon the mouth of a great cave. Leonardo passed by the cave for weeks, daring himself to brave the darkness, but his unrelenting fear stayed him each day. But

Leonardo could never suppress his penchant for discovery. One day he ventured into the cave, deep enough to discover a network of caverns, and torch in hand, the boy trekked deeper into the black, only to find a great empty space, a hidden room, and embedded there in the cave walls, the fossil skeleton of a titanic whale. In the opening he'd passed through, he could see the upper jaw bending down from the ceiling, a row of vertebrae above him, the great ribs a cloister archway. I picture the boy, his trembling arm, inspecting it all with a flickering torch, beating away the cave shadows until at last, shaking the cobwebs and sweat from his hair, he emerges from the ancient leviathan transfigured, exultant—a man.

BEFORE CROSSING THE DESERT

Ray leaving with nothing but the clothes on his back, walking beneath a late-spring wooded canopy. Dirt roads will lead to paved roads, paved roads to highways. A few rides, and he's a hundred miles from home. A hundred's as good as a million, but no matter where he rests nor the duration of his stay, he knows he will shut his eyes in new rooms and new towns among new people forever, gathering a thousand lives into this one lifetime—his wife, daughter, and son, merely three drops of rain in a red clay puddle, their concentric ripples echoing outward into stillness, Ray's boots stepping over, leaving, gone.

Ray listening to a woman in a diner tell how her sister-in-law was visited by pale men in dark suits after seeing the amber orbs of light rising, dancing, then zipping across the sky during those days when so much strangeness surrounded the visits of the flying gray creature with glowing red eyes. Learning how the woman lost her husband and son in the bridge collapse that marked the end of those fantastic happenings, the family car sunken deep into the murky green river bottom. Riding east with an old man who saw gruesome things during the war, who says he has a son who would be Ray's age now, who warns Ray about the dangers of hitchhiking, who trucks only to keep the lights on at home, who worries if he can afford to feed his aging hogs through the winter, who then prefers cigars to talking, leaving a trail of chewed-up stubs littered along the highways. Ray hunching against the passenger door as they cross the river, glimpsing a great sandhill crane sailing above their truck, then falling asleep.

Ray pouring scotch and soda for sweaty men who run business empires all over the country, who laugh like fraternity brothers in the dim room overlooking the tenth fairway. Ray, after nearly everyone has gone, attempting small talk with a man who owns the clubhouse, owns the dining room, owns the course, owns the mountains surrounding the lake that he owns, which his grandfather created by building a series of dams and flooding an old mining town that very few living even remember. The man sipping his drink, replying, "I don't care for football." Ray later chewing on a forkful of lobster meat—the first lobster he's ever seen—which a member has sent back to the kitchen for being overcooked. A young server from Poland laughing at his expression and later taking Ray to one of the hundreds of wooded waterfalls, this one named after a boy named Freddy who fell to his death from the top of the watery cliff. The young woman nearly slipping into the pool at the bottom, caught by Ray, his hand on the small of her back, their eyes meeting, her waiting for Ray to decide. Ray fleeing the mountains, heading east.

Ray lying in the back seat of a car, two teenagers in the front, amused at picking up a loner walking through town at night. The girl sliding across the bench seat, pressing into her boyfriend, begging him to tell Ray the story of the crazy man who lives near the mill, "But take him the right way," she's saying before he even agrees. The boy detouring into the rural suburbs. A few miles in, and it's all woods and farmland and darkness. The boy telling the story: "This fella who owns the mill and much of the land out here, his wife died when his daughter was just a girl, so all growing up, she was her daddy's whole world. He'd do anything to take care of her . . . ." Turning on a dirt road, an open field of wheat on the right, woods that meet the road on their left. "But after she turned sixteen, she went wild—boys and fast cars." Hitting the gas, spinning a cloud of dust, grinding gravel into the road. "Her daddy bought her a car so she wouldn't ride with bad dudes, but she was a wild one. Until one day she was fooling around with a guy while they were flying down this very road . . . ." The girl grabbing the boy's thigh, laughing suddenly like a woman, not a teenager. "And . . . ." The car fishtailing in the dirt before coming to a stop with the headlights pressed against the thick forest wall beside them, there the rusted-out body of an unidentifiable wreck of a car. The girl growing quiet as the boy continues down the road, taking curves too fast. The boy pumping the brakes, clicking off the headlights, saying, "Get the light, Debra." The girl reaching under the seat for the light. "This man'll shoot his .22 at us if we hang around." The car lurching along at a crawl, the girl rolling down her window and pointing a deer spotlight past the hood of the car and, with the flick of a switch, illuminating a sprawling yard with massive colored shapes and designs, turning, spinning, and swirling structures of mangled steel, creaking and moving in the midnight breeze, each with patterns of reflectors, a beaming rainbow kaleidoscope until the girl kills the light, and the complete darkness returns, confusing and unreal. The boy pulling away. "Her daddy was devastated. Went crazy. Started building this park in front of his house. A bunch of road reflectors and a whole lot of metal. He did it so folks would slow down by his house at night, so they wouldn't end up like his daughter. Some say it's a memorial. Some say he's crazy." Neither of them laughing or talking for another few miles before slamming the brakes and shouting, "What the hell is that?" Ray getting out of the car to find a bushel basket in the middle of the road filled with deer hooves, entrails, and a blanket of hide, shouting back to them what he sees before they peel out, leaving him a few miles from town, alone in the night.

Ray roaming up and down an ancient neighborhood near the waterfront, where a sign by an old oak tree says a great war began here, a fort far across the water with an illuminated flag. Passing through neighborhoods set in palmettos and live oaks hazy with moss spilling from their branches, colonial homes and their wraparound porches with white railings, their wrought iron fences around shadowy yards. Ray's thinning rubber soles molding to the mortar and cobblestone with each step down the empty streets. Resting against a building across the street from a gleaming white church with a towering steeple, sipping whiskey from a flask, humming to himself, breathing deeply, almost sleeping until a sinking feeling possesses him. Irrepressible dread. Ray watching a figure wearing something like a monk's habit, an almost brown crimson, the figure moving smoothly along the facade of the church, pausing at the door, turning in Ray's direction, underneath its hood emptiness where a face should be, a stare, then passing on, turning the corner, gone. Ray refusing to move or to tear his eyes away, an empty stillness burning within him that feels endless and sure as the grave but then, broken by the sounds of a choir, indistinct, ghostly voices, echoing through the streets, their wordless harmony freezing him all over despite the sweltering heat, the notes rising and falling like the water lapping against the monument walls out across the bay. Ray checking the time—midnight—but the voices go on singing, singing still . . .

Ray sweating, lifting full baskets from pots of boiling water, dumping the contents upon a sheet of plywood laid atop two old sawhorses: crab legs, ears of corn, potatoes, shrimp, andouille, onion, crawdad, and mussels, the steam rising up, scorching his skin, steeping his beard and clothes in spices. Ray returning the empty basket to the kitchen, swearing against the heat, sweat dripping from the tip of his nose, wishing just one of the men who sell their catches to the owners would hire him. He'd work for nothing. Some boat, any boat, so he might feel a little wind, a little lightness in this place so heavy and stifling, where the alligators, dragonflies, and snakes only move when they have to. Ray slapping his apron on the parking lot pavement, swearing, finding a train depot back in town.

Ray learning the hard way that jumping trains east of the Mississippi is a bad business, riding the rails too far north, not far enough west, the hammering of fists and clubs, fighting back and losing, tenderized but toughened, sometimes thrown from railway cars, other times thrown into jails before yet again finding a freight train to help him put the cuts and bruises, black eyes and bloody mouths, behind him . . .

Ray winding up on the streets of a city where people worse off than Ray wind up festering in their stinking rags, occupying alleys, creating their cities within the city. Ray understanding the danger of staying too long. Learning from one of the legions of homeless which sidewalk smudge belongs to the last of the real midtown gangsters. Thinking he'd like to trade places with that gangster for one of the beef sandwiches from the deli or even a couple hot dogs from the umbrellaed street corner carts. Ray growing gaunt in his travels, his clothes hanging loosely now, rarely bathing, hair flipping out from his hat, a beard long enough to tuck into his shirt against the wind. Finding rambling to be a hungry business but only at first, however many weeks it takes to learn where meals can be scrounged. Later, dreaming of when eating every day won't feel like a luxury.

Ray riding the rails with a grizzled young man who, beneath the beard and grime and the dirty brown hat and tattered corduroy jacket, is really just a boy from a wealthy family, running from becoming his father or his uncles or any occupation he might lapse into at any point on this journey—warehouse lackey, machinist's apprentice, assembler, shift captain, foreman. "Then what?" the boy saying, "another balding, pot-bellied desk sitter with an unhappily-ever-after wife and three spoiled kids and a couple mistresses and . . ." the young man's voice droning with the rhythm of the wheels on the rails, the countryside streaking past like Impressionist paintings of wheat fields, pine groves, rolling hills, and pastures dotted with barns and black cows. "That life ain't for me," the kid saying. "They can have all that. Just leave me this," the kid pointing to the endless prairie before them, its low-hanging clouds sending nebulous dark shapes passing over the horizon. "I'm gonna live it. Then I'm gonna write it. *Here*." The kid reaching into his sock, handing Ray a wad of money. "Get you an old car. This life don't suit you." Ray refusing. "I've been carrying it for nearly half a year, too scared to let it go. Now I know it's the only thing standing between me and what I'm trying to do out here—who I'm trying to be," the kid saying. Ray taking the money before leaving, telling him, "I hope you get where you're going." The kid saying, "I'm already there, man."

Ray finding a town, shaving—cleaning up—staying in a cheap motel, sleeping mostly, eating cheeseburgers, fries, and vanilla milkshakes for a few days. Buying a beat-up car he points west. Sailing through the badlands with the windows rolled down, looking like a new man. Deep in the bottom of a butte, among the feathery grasses, small yellow flowers and prairie dog cities, pale sandstone walls climbing high above him, their stripes and layers of earth stacked upon itself for millions of years, like a city made of cake and ice cream in a perpetual slow, dripping melt. A lone bobcat. Wheeling buzzards. An easy wind so gentle it cannot be heard, a silence so absolute he can hear familiar voices begin speaking inside him. Ray beating his hands in the dirt, weeping. Pausing, listening again, hearing only the wind. Ray grinding his tears in the dust with the heel of his fist, finding something harder and darker than the sandstone, a trilobite. Spitting on the fossil, brushing and breaking away the dirt and revealing its rows of legs. Ray fishing a tire iron from the trunk, chipping at the stone around the creature, taking this gift with him now wherever he goes.

Ray driving through the desert at night, talking to himself or to God or to a ghost or to no one or to everyone. Sometimes a coyote or jackrabbit flashing their eyes or crossing the road before him. At the desert's edge, finding a tiny restaurant, a family's residence conjoined with a kitchen and dining room large enough to serve a dozen people in the chance event a caravan ventures off the main highway in dire need of gasoline before beginning the empty hundred-mile stretch Ray has just traversed. Ray taking a seat, wicker chair, checkered tablecloth, and half-sheet, laminated cardstock menus. A teenage boy tying his apron on the way to the table, asking what'll it be: hamburger steak, onions with gravy, rice, and string beans. The kid ringing the service bell at the counter, calling the order into the kitchen, then leaning against the counter, asking Ray where he's from. Ray thinking on this, asking what a kid does for fun living here in the desert. "We're outta the desert here, mister. Dad farms oats and hay. I help with that." "But what about for fun?" Ray asking. "I play football. Got a game tonight actually. We play eight-man, so most of us play both sides, except the quarterback." Ray and the kid talking until a woman appears at the order window with his food. "Did you get him his drink?" the woman asking the boy, impatient, not surprised. "Dang, Ma." Rushing away. "I always forget," the kid saying to Ray as he sets a Coke down. "Drink's on the house, Ma says." The kid talking to Ray while he eats, telling him about how he drives nearly thirty miles to school one way, how they live next to the restaurant but spend most of their time in here, how they hardly serve a couple dozen people a day, how he's saving for a used car so his mom can have the pickup in the day while he's at school, how his father trucks, farms, and runs combines for other farmers and always comes home well after dark; asking Ray about his family and his home, where he's going, why. Ray not responding, thinking about lying, feeling bad about this notion, changing the subject. The woman in a floral print dress, slender yet hardy; dark, careful eyebrows with the slightest of wrinkles at her eyes when she smiles, gently reprimanding her son for bothering customers while they dine yet joining the two of them at the table anyway. Ray hearing them talk, to him, to each other, sipping his Coke, drifting a moment, forgetting to listen to their words, enjoying their voices, the earnest affection for each other in the sounds they make, ringing out like poetry—Ray, thinking of another family a half-continent away, a wife and daughter, a troubled shadow of a boy—the mother telling Ray how a person ends up running a make-shift restaurant built from a home on the edge of a desert, a cloudy haze creeping into the boy's eyes like a coming storm, a note of resignation in her voice as the mother continues, elbows propped on the table supporting her lovely face, the overcast covering her eyes too, now a fading smile. Ray panicking inside, his heart swelling with words he'd only blubbered alone to the stifling silence of the badland butte, a breath. The mother and son waiting for him to speak—another breath, a hard swallow from telling them everything. The mother sensing the tremor inside him, her eyes glazing with tears. A bell ringing above a screen door, two men walking in, seeing the three of them sitting quietly, intently, at the table of the otherwise empty restaurant, asking if they're still serving. Ray, realizing for the last half-hour he's been pretending to be the third member of this family, pitying himself, cursing himself, praying to forgive or better yet forget himself. Leaving a note on the back of his bill, "It's yours," and a twenty-dollar bill underneath the keys to his car. Studying a few family pictures framed on the wall next to the entrance, memorizing their faces, refusing to look at the father's, turning toward the kitchen to glimpse the woman's face one last time, straining to hear her voice, but she is gone. Ray walking away, catching a ride with yet another trucker, speeding through the void, headed to a green glow on the horizon, wondering if years from now they'll think of him, if they'll tell a story about him, and if, in the story, he'll be an angel, a man, or a ghost.

Ray demanding a truck driver pull over and let him out. "What the hell, fella? You crazy? Shit don't live out there," the driver pointing to the silvery white landscape. "It's like dropping a man in the middle of an ocean," the driver imploring him. Ray pulling on the door handle anyway before the truck has slowed to its stop. Ray thanking him and slamming the door, crossing the highway, the ditches, and a wire fence to step out into oblivion's fringe, black, shimmering, shapes vanishing impossibly far into the distance. Ray collecting smooth black stones the size of his fist in the blinding heat, gathering them into a pile, sweat soaking through his shirt and pants, slipping into a heat-induced delirium, stumbling, a memory of a radio preacher playing in his head . . . *God speaks, but he won't beckon but so many times, and you keep turning away, quenching the Spirit, it's a dangerous game, my friend, and it won't be long before God quits knocking on the door of your heart, leaving you with nothing but silence, forevermore, friend, isn't it time you turned from your own selfish ways* . . . Ray lifting the stones, hearing voices in them now, crying out, placing them in lines and curves next to each other, letters: the names of the family he vows never to speak of. Ray walking back to the highway, leaving them once again, never looking back.

Ray craning his neck underneath redwoods, the Pacific crashing into nearby cliffs. Emerging from the woods to find a pebbled stretch of beach. Happening upon a scarlet stone marbled with white, glazed with ocean spray—the petrified heart of an ancient merman, still to this day, swimming the deepest fathoms of the sea, sloughing his tail and growing legs once a year to wade out to shore, combing the earth in search of this most precious lost possession. So thoughtless and forlorn. How could you lose something so essential? How fortunate I should find it. *Here.* Ray heaving the stone into the ocean, dreaming of the polished ruby, sinking for days, however long it would take to tumble down to where all the deep-sea creatures look on, aghast with their empty dead eyes, scowling with their nightmare teeth.

Ray borrowing a pair of binoculars from a park ranger, a young woman with long, shiny blonde hair, stationed on a lighthouse, both of them looking at sea lions at the craggy bottom of the cliffside. Ray wondering what it might be like to stand here day after day, watching the sun set over the ocean, wishing he was still in his thirties, like this young woman, wishing he might at least stand there until sundown beside her. Later Ray ascending hundreds of stairs back to the parking lot with the first Irishman he's ever met, waiting every so often for the man to catch his breath, the Irishman, perplexed by America's youth who dream of hostel hopping through Europe, "If I lived in this country, I tell ya, I'd never leave," him saying, enamored with all of America except the Golden Gate, an ugly, rusty thing that leads to absolutely nothing. His aged mother waiting for him in their car, agreeing about the bridge before wishing Ray farewell.

Ray haunting the wharf and dive bars and bookstores and Chinatown shops and anywhere else he pleases, being catcalled by angry poets smoking and swearing behind their expensive coffees. Ray looking down from an observatory at the bridge and the prison island, recalling stories of jumpers and gangsters and men who dig tunnels in concrete walls with palmed silverware, who maybe drown, who maybe escape on crudely fabricated life rafts, who maybe live alone somewhere nobody knows, feeling hungrier and emptier by the minute, Ray grasping the handrail, hoping the next somewhere calling him will feel different somehow.

Ray accepting a free ride in a taxi, making his misgivings known. "Look, if you don't know where you're going, you might as well get part of the way there quicker." Ray not arguing with this logic, enduring the cabbie promising him all the trouble a young man could get into in a town like this, rolling up to an awning, velvet rope, limos, taxis, everyone younger than Ray—women in short, tight-fitting dresses; men in shiny, tailored suits, slicked hair. The cab driver saying, "There's more tail in that place than even a young buck like yourself could handle." Ray being ushered from the car up the carpet to the front door, two bruisers stepping aside, telling him to enjoy his evening, one of them speaking indiscernible words into his wrist. Ray walking down a dark hallway lined with strange, abstract paintings, enormous gilt frames of dingy gold. Thumping loud music shaking the chest hair beneath his shirt. Finding a lady perched on a tall barstool behind a kind of podium at the end of the hall where a large room opens, a bar on the left, a small stage on the right, tiny round tables filling the floor. The lady speaking words he can't hear, even when he leans his ear up to her lips. Ray absent-mindedly reaching for his wallet despite having warned himself about everyone in this city poised to take everything he has, until his eyes finally register the nearly nude topless dancer onstage, a smarmy emcee having just announced her, slinking backstage to a curtain, the dancer raising a black feather boa from her chest, the hostess's soft hand touching Ray's stubbled cheek, whispering now, but Ray hearing this time, at last realizing the hostess is topless as well. Ray excusing himself, pushing his way through the swarm of people in the hall and outside, holding his breath until he's safely down the street, checking his pocket for his wallet once more, not daring to look over his shoulder lest he become a pillar of salt.

Ray listening to the river rushing through the canyon, the white capping current growing less visible in the setting sun, finding a piece of ground fit for his lean-to tarp tent, setting up camp far enough from the twenty-somethings and their lanterns and campfires and guitars and beer and smoke. Ray warming a can of soup by his tiny fire, being offered a beer by a lanky young man with glasses and heavy facial hair. Ray hesitating but the kid's earnest smile and congenial manner winning him over. "You gotta join us though, mister," the young man saying, Ray already regretting but following anyway. The young man leading him to the fire with friends and strangers alike, demanding someone get Ray a beer and slide down to give him a seat. Ray learning these young people are largely unknown to one other yet they're sharing everything they have. Two clean-cut brothers with slicked-back hair, like the rock 'n' roll stars of another era standing near the fire with acoustic six-strings on matching straps. The brothers' voices melding in familial harmony— one singing higher and the other singing low, taking turns with the melody, coming together for the refrain—sung in a distinct way, the notes and the words ringing out in clear, perfect unison:

I roved and I roamed, and I traveled from home
And I left Ginny far o'er the sea
All the old men in town,
Taking turns putting down
Ol' wayfaring, wandering me.
Ol' wayfaring, wandering me.

If I saw her one day, would she ask me to stay
Could I still be in their family?
With all I am, all I lack,
Would they dare welcome back
Ol' wayfaring, wandering me?
Ol' wayfaring, wandering me.

Keep a warm firelight, hug my daughter good night,
Make sure to rock my baby to sleep,
Tell Ginny not to wait,
Not to curse, nor to hate
Ol' wayfaring, wandering me.
Ol' wayfaring, wandering me.

Ray sipping or smoking anything passing his way, laughing, singing, crying, talking, stumbling, crawling, sleeping, waking with a young woman's wavy chestnut hair in his face, smelling of sweet Betsy after rain, her warmth consuming him, the river carving through the canyon, breakfast voices, Ray lying awake with his arm pulling her close, living this way for another hour.

Ray learning trades from a man with more wealth than sense—masonry, welding, architecture, construction—building an eyesore of a castle in the wilderness, to the chagrin of neighbors and county planning and zoning, who all succumb to the almighty dollar and the best team of lawyers south of the Rockies, so declares this wild, anti-government capitalist, conspiracy theorist dreamer, zillionaire, whose tirades sound mostly like hate and rage when Ray meets him but sounding more like reason and truth after weeks living and working alongside the man. One day, assisting the man welding—applying the finishing touches high upon a steel catwalk archway, twenty feet higher than the highest treetop—Ray, looking out over the wilderness, away from the welding arc, noticing a shimmering in the woods, one tree, then an adjacent tree, then the next, like a systematic wind or an invisible brontosaurus brushing against the trunks and upper branches. Ray stopping the man, pointing, asking, "What's happening, an earthquake?" "They come around every so often," the man saying. "Good thing we're up here and not down there with them, buddy." "*Them*?" Ray asking. "Children of the sons of God and daughters of man," the man saying with a laugh more like a cough. The man squinting down at the trees, flipping his visor back on, back to his job. Ray thinking, I'm done with the woods forever, and maybe I ain't ever coming down from this scaffolding.

Ray watching the sunset, drinking beer atop a giant dune of white sand with several servers from a nearby restaurant where he's been washing dishes a few weeks. A server telling him how the military dropped all kind of bombs, missiles, and atomic weapons here. "One nuclear explosion," the girl saying, "lit the night sky for three days, swirling greens and blues and purples like the northern lights as far as you could see . . . ." Everybody thinking they were going crazy or that they'd secretly been dosed with experimental drugs or that they'd been abducted by extraterrestrials or that they'd slipped into another dimension through an unstable portal a bomb had opened or plenty of other theories. One server saying how his father had lucid dreams every night since the test. Another saying how, after the tests were finished, the bombs and the extreme heat had forged crystal stalagmites rising from the ground like great mountains of hoarfrost, how the white sand turned into jagged glass splinters, towering and protruding in all directions. Almost no civilians were allowed to witness the effects of the test, but there are rumored to be a few people in town who had broken a few crystal daggers from the mountains before they bulldozed it all back into dunes. Ray listening, wiping white sand from the lip of his bottle, drinking another beer, the sun painting the sky, changing from orange and red to pink and lavender. Before leaving, watching a slender white dust devil breezing slowly across the dunes, elegant and lonesome, disappearing.

Ray's ride pulling into a desolate rest stop one night to fill up before crossing the desert, Ray with his arm hanging out of the window. A Navajo man with long, gray hair, an old cowboy hat with a silver buckle on a black leather band, wearing ceremonial beads around his neck, approaching the passenger side to speak to him, asking if he can spare a buck or two. Ray wincing, knowing he's nearly cleaned out, unfolding his wallet outside the window where the man can see his one remaining dollar. "Yours," Ray saying to the man, giving it to him. "My last dollar." Ray smiling, the man chuckling back. "Good man, you are a good man," the Navajo telling him, giving him the two-handed shake. "Listen," the man saying. Ray hearing voices and drumming in the distance. "There's a gathering tonight, kind of like a powwow. A friend of mine's grandson is coming of age. It's a big celebration. I was going to leave, but maybe you want to see?" Ray nodding, the man smiling. Ray getting out of the truck, dismissing his ride with a wave, following the man, listening to him tell how the boy had been fasting and praying alone on the mountain for the better part of a week—all the while, the voices and drums growing louder, the smell of food and smoke growing stronger, as they approach—how soon, the friend's grandson will be emerging from a sweat lodge behind the building where all his family and loved ones have been feasting and singing and praying for him, waiting for his return, waiting to hear what the spirits have shown him, waiting to learn where his path will lead.

SILVER MAGNOLIA

In those days it was a rare occasion, going into town—in fact, this is one of my earliest memories doing so—but it was about a week before Christmas, and Mother wanted to give Daddy a present this year. I think she would've preferred to have left me with Granddaddy, but we needed him to drive us there. If I'd ever been to town prior, I don't remember. It's one of the few memories I have of my granddaddy.

Daddy worked at the sawmill in the winter, so we had no trouble sneaking away when Granddaddy rolled up to our house in that big, blue monster of a pickup. I scooted in next to him. The cracked leather seats sent cold through my clothes. Even with the three of us on the bench, I was skinny enough that a child could've sat on either side of me.

"Thanks for the ride," Mother said.

"I've got business in town myself," he said, maneuvered the gear stick, and we were off.

It was still the blue-gray time before dawn that I usually slept through, but the prospects offered by our little adventure had me wide awake. And who could sleep with so much countryside passing our windows? Though we couldn't see it at first for all the woods, the morning sun began turning the blur of forest deep shades of green. Once in a while, we'd pass the dirt path of a neighbor, but in those days most everyone kept to themselves. I assumed there were houses and farms and fields and gardens along and at the end of these paths, but I never really saw any. It seemed like we drove for many miles until a break in the woods revealed a tangerine sun hung low on the horizon over a newly harvested field of grain—everything gold and warm, with the smell of wheat straw still fresh in the air.

"Kinda young to be going to town, ain't she?" Granddaddy broke the silence. "You heard what happened to that one little girl?"

Mother made a face. "Daddy."

"Been all over the papers."

"*Daddy.*"

"Nobody's seen her in a week; another one's been gone two months down in Saluda."

"Enough," Mother said.

"I'm only saying—I was a grown man before my daddy ever let me ride to town."

"Some people are *born* in town, Daddy. Some people live their whole lives in and around town, and they fare just fine." She squeezed my hand. "You've been to town before, but you were too young to remember probably."

"It's a shame the doctors don't come around like they used to," he said.

As we rode along, the woods opened up even more. There were houses, barns and silos, pastures with livestock. Eventually, the dirt road ran up alongside a wide creek of clear water rushing over large, smooth stones. Several miles later, there was a pond and a grain and feed mill.

"Taylor's Mill Pond," Granddaddy said. "Seen it froze over once when I was a child."

"I thought you hadn't been to town before you were a grown man," I said.

"Oh, she *is* awake," he said. "Well, missy, this ain't town yet."

We passed through a little village and back into more woods as dense as the ones around home before I learned "town" was actually a city—or so the city limits sign read—once we finally got there. I'd never seen such buildings, though in truth, only a few of them were higher than two stories. Before we'd reached the center of town, Granddaddy said, "You better watch her like a hawk," in a solemn manner. "Don't let her out of your sight."

"I know," Mother said, and something about their mood dampened the excitement I'd felt at seeing all the signs, the streetlamps, the buildings, and the people passing.

"Say what you will, but folks are different out here. Just as soon steal your purse as they would smile at you. Wouldn't hold a door for you unless they thought they could get something from you."

"You act like nothing awful's ever happened to anyone out in the country. You're being unfair," Mother said.

"Am I? Young girls kidnapped, who knows what all . . ."

"Thurman—"

Here Granddaddy said a word I'd not heard before.

"Stop the truck and let us out, right now."

I'd never heard her sound so serious.

He pumped the brakes but drove on. "I only say as much so you won't forget to watch yourself and Martha. I learned long ago if you don't call a thing what it is, folks won't hear you right."

Mother sat with her arms crossed, watching the road.

As we slowly made our way, Granddaddy kept his eyes fixed on the street. "Once had a neighbor boy as a kind of carpenter's apprentice—he'd worked with me all summer. We had some roof work at this old lady's house. I said, 'You watch out for that light line, especially carrying that aluminum ladder around it.' Well, I guess we were both about delirious after laying shingles up there so long in the late-August sun. After we finally finished the job and had packed away all the tools, he was taking down that damn ladder in a hurry, walking before he could get it low, and he must've tripped on an old tree stump." We'd reached the heart of town, so Granddaddy pulled up to the curb and stopped. He turned to look at us both and continued. "He tilted the ladder high enough to touch the line, and it lit him up like a San Francisco cable car—graveyard dead—and if I had the chance again, I'd look him in the eyes," he said as he looked me in the eyes, "and that's exactly what I'd tell him: 'graveyard dead.' Maybe that would've left an impression."

Mother stepped out of the cab and helped me down. "Thanks for the warning. I think you've made an impression on *both* of us," she said, cutting her eyes at me.

"I'll tell you what leaves an impression: prying a young man's sticky hands from the rungs of an aluminum—"

Mother slammed the door good and hard. She straightened her dress and pulled her coat tight across her chest. "Better button up," she said. "We've got a bit of walking to do."

"But we're here at the grocer's," I said.

"And we've got several stops to make. Christmas presents oughtn't come from a grocery store, and we wouldn't want to carry groceries around all day anyway."

I marveled at the shop windows decked out for Christmas. Most had scenes with snow made from rolls of the white fluff Mother sewed inside her quilts, and there were trees with lights and ornaments and mannequins with sweaters, scarves, and toboggans. We walked into one store named Turner's. The apostrophe before the *s* on the sign above was made to look like a diamond. Upon first entering, I thought the store didn't seem so large. It was an open room, and in the middle of the floor were two parallel rectangles of glass display cases with a few clerks working behind them. A crystal chandelier hung over the cases.

"This is just the jewelry counter. The rest of the store's through there." Mother pointed at the back of the room, where an open doorway led to a much bigger department store. "They make customers walk by the jewelry first to make simple-minded girls think the rest of the merchandise is a real treasure."

Mother has always had an uncanny sense of the private thoughts of others, and I knew she had said this for my benefit. Still, my immediate impression was that I'd stumbled into the treasure trove of some lost civilization, and I couldn't wait to gaze upon whatever else the store had to offer—even if it was only overpriced shaving kits, stockings, and electric can openers.

"Well, hello there. Is there any way I might assist you?" One of the ladies working the floor had approached us. She wore a tight-fitting, gray plaid skirt that narrowed below the knee and a ruffled, cream-colored blouse. Her dark hair was pulled in a tight bun behind her head. She had lipstick and flawless skin. She smiled as she spoke.

"We're shopping for a Christmas gift," Mother said.

The lady gave us a quick glance-over. "Perhaps I could interest you in a pair of earrings or a bracelet?"

"I'm not shopping for myself today," she said to the lady, then to me, "We'd rather get nothing at all than to buy our own Christmas gifts, right?"

I smiled, but I was feeling too overwhelmed to reply. I looked at my mother's wrist and ears. I'd never seen her wear jewelry. Then I noticed all the women in the store wore both, pearls or diamonds. Not only this, but they were each dressed alike—a team of slender, stunning young women. I touched my own earlobes and wondered if these women had ever seen a house as deep in the woods as ours. The lady seemed put off by her answer.

"Might I ask who the gift is for?"

"Her father," Mother said. "Maybe you could find him something in the men's department," Mother said to me.

I gave another blank look.

"Go ahead. I'll be a few minutes," she said.

I thought Mother had been a little short with her at first, but before I could pass into the greater part of the department store, I heard both of them laughing at something. It occurred to me that I'd rarely heard Mother laugh this way. Daddy was always the funny one. She'd enjoy his nonsense, but I wouldn't necessarily call her reaction laughter, just a little sound through the nose to let him know she'd heard and was somewhat amused.

I could go on and on about the wonders throughout the department store—clothing, jewelry, appliances, kitchenware, bedding, home furnishing—listing the fabulous or even everyday items that caught this twelve-year-old's eye, but suffice it to say that everything between the glossy tiled floors and bright, fluorescent lights captivated me, and the best part of everything: it was all *new*. I was surrounded by, immersed in, everything new. I wanted to memorize every shelf; I would take it all home in my mind.

But in this rapture, in my mother's absence, I couldn't suppress a growing uneasiness that began with Granddaddy's peculiar warning: "graveyard dead," the ladder boy, and the missing girls. After glancing at the wares of each department, I'd return to the entryway to find

Mother still at the storefront, peering into the cases. Twice I noticed her looking closely at the display of watches. The saleslady modeled one with a silver band and a large face by laying it over the back of her hand. Even from a distance, it struck me as something Daddy would never wear.

I wandered into the ladies' department and was taken by the fabrics and styles, the lace and design—everything so dainty yet durable. On one shelf I shoved my hand among a stack of powder-blue cashmere sweaters. I felt an urgent desire to bring the soft-as-soap wool to my face, but one of the ladies had begun to watch me closely. At the fringe of the department, one rack had fur coats, brown with black accents, no doubt from some exotic creature I'd never seen or heard of. I imagined Mother in one of these, strolling around the yard on a quiet, wintry day, diamonds in her ears, pearls around her neck and wrists. It wouldn't do to see her this way in the kitchen or even the living room, but maybe outside, with a delicate snow falling . . . . Even if she'd never want these things, I could dream them for her.

Just when I thought to touch the sleeve of the coat, I noticed a man from across the aisle watching me. He had a gray three-piece suit with a deep-brown necktie that matched the leather band around the short-brimmed hat he wore pulled down over his forehead. He had a navy tweed overcoat draped over his arm. Once our eyes met, I looked away and briskly returned to the storefront, listening behind me as I walked: a high-sounding clip-clop, like a slight man walking in cowboy boots. I rushed through the store, resolving not to stray so far from Mother wherever we'd go for the rest of the day.

I found her still in the jewelry room by the watches. I stepped into her and pulled her arm around me. The saleslady was saying: "It's certainly a shame. Thankfully nothing of the sort has ever happened here."

I looked back through the corridor and thought I saw the gray man pass by.

"No, not in a place like this," Mother said, taking my hand. She leaned over to look in the case one last time and sighed. "It's getting late, Martha. We should leave."

I attempted another glance as she pulled me along. "Have a splendid day," the lady called as we reached the glass doors.

"It'll be divine," Mother said in a way fairly matching the lady's tone and style, then she mumbled something into her collar I didn't catch.

It was easy to forget the cold inside Turner's, where everything was warm, bright, and new, but now, on the street, the chill completely froze out our words. Mother took quick, furious steps to our next destination. I wondered at her reason for beginning our Christmas shopping there when it became clear to me we could afford very little of their merchandise, definitely nothing in the front. I wanted to ask why she never met me in the other departments to shop for Daddy. And I thought to tell her of the gray man in the store, but I only pulled my denim jacket tighter, flipping its collar up to cover my lips.

Our next stop was a store called O'Cleary's. Here you could see the whole store upon entering. Though smaller than Turner's, it had half a second-floor balcony, with a long glass wall that overlooked the rest of the store. I could see this story was accessible by two separate sets of stairs. As for the rest, I'd never seen a room with a ceiling so high or a floor packed with so many racks of clothing.

"We should've just started here," Mother said. "But if they ever start charging extra for looking, the men'll be the first to wear blindfolds. Then we'll just follow suit."

I rarely understood her sayings. She often said things more for herself than anyone near.

No one greeted us here. Mother didn't appear bothered. In fact, she seemed relaxed as she expertly navigated the aisles and racks to find exactly what she had in mind. A carousel wire stand by the shoes in the men's department had an array of hats with various felts, colors, and styles of brim.

She picked one from the stand. "Think Daddy would like one of these?" Mother asked.

"Are we going to start going back to church?" I asked.

"Maybe we should have just gone with Granddaddy to the hardware store—bought him a new cap." She replaced the hat. "A hat's a good gift, Martha. We can make clothes, but nothing makes a person look more like a hobo than a homemade hat."

I was about to tell her then about the gray man at the store with the short-brimmed hat when we heard a musical "Good morning." A saleslady had approached us. "Last-minute Christmas shopping for the man in your life?"

"Husband," Mother said.

"Oh, husbands are impossible," she said. "I never know what to get mine." This lady wasn't dressed so differently than how I remembered the ladies were dressed for church. She wasn't as striking as the ladies from the first store. Those ladies were triangles, but this woman was more rounded—circles and ovals. They were hard, straight lines, corners, and sharp points everywhere. But this lady was soft, with curves—a woman who could hold a child close without putting an eye out. "Well hello, little darling. What's your age?"

I told her, and it turned out she had a son the same age. She told us he went to school in a town I'd never heard of. Mother spoke differently to this lady, as if she knew her. She let the lady propose several gift ideas—not limited to the clothing in the store—which she followed by telling us what she'd bought her own husband for the last few years on birthdays and Christmases. Mother listened patiently, but the casual way she entertained the salesladies and the way she passively looked at the items in both stores—I began to suspect she'd known what she wanted to give Daddy all along and most of this was only passing time for her. And who could blame her? A trip to town was like stepping into another person's body for a day, like when you wake up from a dream—those first few seconds when you don't know where you are or what life you're living. A little Christmas gift for herself.

"Martha, why don't you look around for a gift for Daddy?"

I almost protested, thinking again of the gray man, but the look she gave me said I had no choice.

"Can I go upstairs?"

"Sure, but come out so I can see you when I call," Mother said.

"You can't be too careful," the lady said. "I guess you heard one of the kidnappings happened in this store. Well, it's not true. One of the girls was *last seen* at our store. Nothing happened here, but that's not how everyone tells it. Business hasn't been great, especially considering the time of year." There were only a few people scattered on either floor. I waited for her to go on, then the woman looked at me a bit too long, which I took as a sign to go upstairs.

Before I could finish weaving through the claustrophobic sales floor, I noticed the metal stairways moving on their own. The steps fit into one another like the zipper on my coat. They kept moving downward, flattening out, and disappearing below the floor. I took a step, and it jammed my shoe back on the landing. I could see a faint light in the cracks between the steps. From across the store, I heard the lady interrupt herself to call to me: "It's an escalator, honey. Use the next set of stairs."

You'll have to forgive me if I'm beginning to sound like an old person, trying to outdo another old person with stories of how backwoods or sheltered I was then—still am, I suppose: I know there are worlds out there much grander than my little corner, and I don't mean to make more of these moments than they were, but frankly, every few minutes of this day was another first for me. Most of the wonders of my childhood were the kind we all have and forget once they become a normal part of our everyday lives—throwaway miracles like a watermelon seedling popping from a little soil in a jar, placed on the windowsill; or a wren's nest appearing almost overnight, assembled in the eaves of our front porch; a quartz crystal you find after skinning your knee along a woodland path—but something about this marvelous invention imprinted itself on my memory, so much that even today I won't deny myself at least one unnecessary ride given the chance. Pretend I forgot something.

I took the escalator up, and it really was a strange thrill. In truth I had rarely been in houses with staircases. An electric staircase. So smooth too. The first ride up and down, I could only watch the stairs and the handrails. But the next ride I enjoyed watching everything below slowly descend as I climbed. I remember thinking, I hope it's like this when we leave this world. Nice and slow and one last chance to see everything again, shrinking into toys, then dots, then disappearing. The ride down was only an excuse to rise again, and after three or four times, I heard Mother say my name, so I leaned against the glass wall of the balcony, watching the women talk.

It's possible they were both talking about the cold, their husbands, or Christmas gifts, but the concerned looks on their faces had me thinking otherwise. Something in me knew they were speaking about the missing girls.

Mother glanced at me on the balcony. Our eyes met, and she must've read these pictures in my face, so she interrupted the lady, and they both walked toward the escalator. I thought if I beat them to the lower floor, we might just leave the store, but before I could reach the down escalator, Mother shouted: "Hold your horses, Martha. Miss Maddie here wants to show me a few things upstairs." I darted to their stairs, waiting to take Mother's hand the second she ascended. I was timid at that age, and Mother had a tendency to be short, but when I took her hand, she had a tender look and said, "We'll only be a few minutes more, Martha, and I want you to help me choose something for your father." And she squeezed my hand, not in any way Miss Maddie would notice. I wasn't alone with my thoughts anymore. We were finding a Christmas gift for Daddy.

Though it was mostly a clothing store on the ground floor, upstairs looked more like a rummage sale. Unlike the gloss and sheen of the new in the previous store, everything in this one looked "lived" to me. Nothing would look out of place if it were to be found in our home or one of the neighbor's. One aisle had books and magazines, and another had old toys, trinkets, and doodads. While I found these alluring, I stayed true to my pledge not to leave my mother's side again. The aisle we were on had serving utensils, flatware, placemats, and other kitchen and dining items. Of the assorted collection there, one item—or I should say two items—caught my eye: a set of silver candlesticks. They were quite ornate, much fancier than anything in our home. The embossed base looked like the petals of a flower. The heftier middle was covered in vines and blossoms, maybe morning glory, and small hummingbirds and butterflies. I thought how fine they'd look on our kitchen table, and I wondered if one day I'd have the money to come back here and buy Mother something so lovely.

"These are sure pretty, ma'am," I said.

"Oh, these? These are just some old consignment pieces we've had here for ages."

She could tell I didn't understand.

"But they are nice. Look here." She turned one around to show a small bird I'd not seen, maybe a bluebird or a sparrow. "We mostly use these to sell our silver polish. See how dark this one is," she pointed to the candlestick on the shelf, "and how bright this one is?"

I don't know why it hadn't occurred to me sooner. One was truly a shadow of the other. I kept studying the two.

"Look here." Maddie brought the polished one close. "A fingerprint. Someone's handled it already."

"Silver's like a magnolia tree," Mother said.

The lady made no expression—almost as if she'd not heard her.

"Why's that?" I asked with the smallest laugh.

"You end up tending to it all year long," she said.

It's true, I suppose. We had one tall magnolia tree in our yard she'd asked Daddy to plant long ago because she liked the blossoms, but it ended up the tree hardly blossomed at all. I'd often seen her piling up leaves and cones to burn in our yard, even in the dead of summer. It never occurred to me that maintaining the tree was a bother, but the way she said it made me think it was a thought she'd had a hundred times before.

But the polished candlestick made me think of a knight's armor, shiny and bright. And the luster of this one only made the other darker one more mysterious. I kept matching the two, searching for the ornate design of the bright one in the dim one. The closer I looked at the faded candlestick, the more interesting it became. You could see all colors in its tarnish. It had a beauty of its own. Mother and Maddie had moved along down the aisle, leaving me considering the pair of knights, two brothers, one light and one dark, both engraved with the utmost care, yet somehow, left to themselves, they would grow to mirror one another in darkness. Staring at them both, I began to be filled with loneliness and, strangely enough, regret.

"Come along, Martha," Mother said, and I joined them on another aisle.

"Ah, here's something for Martha," Miss Maddie said, picking up a doll from the shelf.

"Martha's too old for dolls, isn't she?" Mother said.

"I don't kno-oow," Miss Maddie sang.

I smiled, finally shaken out of my thoughts. I didn't have many dolls growing up, only a baby doll long ago, but this one wasn't a baby. She had slender, porcelain arms; a green-and-navy plaid dress with ruffles on the sleeves and hem; and long, dark hair. Her perfect face was at once childlike and grown. I blushed at secretly wanting the doll very badly. The three of us laughed.

Mother passed on several of Miss Maddie's suggestions for Daddy—cologne, a necktie, an electric razor—and when it seemed she'd run out of suggestions to reject, Mother said it was time to move along to the grocer's. Though I was looking forward to grocery shopping, I felt sad at leaving the escalator; the bright yellow lights; the familiar, homey surroundings; and Miss Maddie's neighborly way.

As we descended the moving stairs for the last time, the lonesome feeling began to swell again. Even the escalator seemed to darken my mood. We still hadn't found a present for Daddy. I watched as the metal stairs fit into one another one last time and thought of a dress catching in its teeth, pulling a body in, stripes on skin. . .

As we walked, we fastened our coats and began preparing for the cold again. I glanced in the men's side of the store and thought I saw a gray hat floating above the racks. It turned one way and the other, but then its tall front pointed toward us and followed as we said our goodbyes to Miss Maddie by the door and walked out into the street, still empty-handed.

"Mama." I pulled on her long coat.

She took my hand and pulled me out the door. "Let's not dilly-dally. I want to have the groceries together before your granddaddy comes."

It was so cold I could only look at my feet and the sidewalk. I struggled to keep step with my mother. We seemed to have plenty of time before, but now she was almost dragging me along to the grocer's.

"Beth!"

We stopped so abruptly I knocked against Mother's backside.

"Beth, it's been so long!" the lady said.

I rarely heard my mother's given name, much less its diminutive. She went by her middle name, Irene. Daddy mostly called her "Mother" around me.

"Victoria," Mother said, flatly.

"Look at you!" the lady said, taking a long look at Mother before landing on me.

"Yes, look at me." Mother let out a long breath that clouded the cold air around us.

The lady had a long, flowing, colorful dress. The fabric had a print with suns, crescent moons, and stars. The hem of her dress had beaded tassels, and her sleeves had a ragged kind of fringe. She had a beige knitted shawl and a bandana across her head. Even under its cover, her untamed red hair lit the entire street. She had fierce blue eyes made even brighter by her dark skin. Mother narrowed her eyes as she looked her over, using her imagination to match her with a memory.

"And this little one!" She reached both arms toward me as if she would smash my cheeks together but thought twice upon seeing the look on my face. Instead, she clasped her hands and pulled them to her chest, her golden bracelets jangling through it all. "What's your name?"

"Martha," my mother answered for me.

"How perfect!" She beamed in the most genuine way. I'd never seen anyone so happy. I began to wonder if she and Mother were once best friends, but when I looked to Mother, let's just say she did not attempt to match this woman's elation. "She looks just like you did, Beth! Those were lovely old times, weren't they?"

"Yes, Victoria. They were."

"Oh, Beth! It's Vicky! You know that," she said, and then to me, "Victoria just sounds so old, doesn't it?"

All the while they spoke, I felt I was slipping into a dream. This unusual lady and her peculiar way with my mother. It sounds silly, but hearing my mother addressed with an unfamiliar name, in Miss Vicky's beguiling way—well, it had the effect of making the woman beside me feel like a stranger. I let my hand fall from hers.

"I heard you were going by a new name, Vicky," Mother said.

"Oh, she doesn't approve," Miss Vicky said to me. "Yes, well, that's who I am now," she said almost in a sigh, "Madame Marie, but that's only to customers." She did a curtsey and a little flourish. "I know it's all over the top, but who will believe a clairvoyant dressed in denim and gingham?"

Mother said nothing.

"A girl's gotta eat. Besides, this may be a show." She brushed her wide sleeves and shook her bracelets. "But what I offer is not," she said.

Mother made a high-pitched shivering sound. "Well, it was swell catching up with you. I've got to get this *little one* out of the cold."

"So precious," Miss Vicky said looking at me, and before we could depart, she got down on her knees and took my hand. I thought I could hear my mother groan above the sounds of the busy street.

The lady brought my palm close to her face. "Much love. As much love as anyone I've seen. A handsome husband one day." She smiled at me and looked again. "And children! Many children!" She watched for my expression. Though bewildered at first, now I was blushing. She looked closer. Her eyes began to flutter. "One child, two . . . thr— . . . oh." Her eyes wide. Her smile disappearing. "Happy lives are often short, but for the rest of us, little Martha, life is long. *You*, my darling, will live forever." Her eyes became misty, and she closed my hand as though she'd placed a coin in my palm.

"Wonderful." Mother took my hand. "Merry *Christ*-mas, *Victoria*," she said and jerked me down the street.

"Merry Christmas!" she shouted to our backs.

"I'm beginning to side with Granddaddy," Mother said as we walked along. "At least the crazies in the country keep to themselves."

I was still lost, pondering Miss Vicky's words.

"Don't you believe none of that nonsense, Martha."

"Is Miss Vicky from the old country?" I asked.

"*Old country*?" she scoffed. "Where'd you pick that up?"

"From the stories you used to tell me before bed."

"Oh. Yes. The 'old country.' Well, she hasn't always been a fortune teller—I can tell you that; she used to be normal folk like us. Her mama and daddy were normal folk anyway."

"Oh."

"Ain't nothing to fortune tellers, Martha. I've never known one that wasn't broke as the rest of us."

But I couldn't so easily dismiss Miss Vicky's reading. She seemed truly affected by what she saw in my palm, and in that instant, I had felt a strange sensation that was impossible to ignore. I contemplated the whole encounter the entire way to the grocer's.

Before entering the store, I scanned both ends of the street and yet again glimpsed the gray man across the way, entering a small jeweler's shop. In the instant I saw him, our eyes met. He paused in the doorway before walking inside. A bell smacked against the grocer's door with a broken, metallic clatter as it swung shut behind us.

My lungs collapsed and my heart shriveled to a raisin in that moment. I couldn't hold it in any longer.

"Mama, there's a man that's been following us around all morning. I saw him in Turner's, I saw him in O'Cleary's, and he just saw me from across the street, and I don't want anyone to take me." I latched my arms around her and wept.

"Martha, Martha. Settle down now." She put her hands in my hair and pulled me close. I heard her speak to someone over my shoulder that it was okay and to "give us a moment."

Mother listened intently as I described the man I saw in Turner's, and when I'd finished, she made me describe him again, but the longer I explained his behavior—how he seemed to follow me to the front of the store; how I could see him in the men's department as we left O'Cleary's; and how he saw me just then and the way he looked at us—the more dispassionate she grew.

Mother said: "I know you might think so, but this town's not really so big, Martha. In fact, there's places and cities much larger than this one. Places with buildings so tall you can't stand far enough away to see where they climb. Places where you can live your whole life and still run across folks you never knew every day—come to think of it, a town doesn't have to be all that large for that—but what I'm trying to say is we're not in the country right now. This is what being in town's like . . ."

I startled as the bell smacked against the door again. Two young men walked in, removed their gloves, and rubbed their hands together.

". . . we're all here for the same reasons. It's only normal we're going to run up against each other. No one's going to whisk either one of us away. You know I wouldn't let that happen." She wiped my face with her knit gloves. "Granddaddy's got you so worked up. I'll be having a word or two with him on the way home. But put it all out of your mind. I was hoping you'd have fun today. It isn't every day we get to do this. Look here."

There were nine bushel baskets arranged in tiers. One had peppermint candy, another gumballs of every color, others with ribbon candy, butterscotch candy, walnuts, pecans. . . . A man with a white apron and mustache took a peppermint stick from the basket, snapped it in half, put one end in his mouth, and gave me the other end. "Here you go, little lady."

"Thanks, Mack." Mother said. "This is Mr. Mason," she said to me. "This is his store."

I took the peppermint stick and thanked him, still sniffling a little.

"It's been an exciting day for her. She's just a little overstimulated," she said.

He and Mother chitchatted before she listed all the groceries she needed—coffee, flour, cornmeal, sugar, and such—only the things we didn't make ourselves, and a few winter treats Mother spoke to him in a whisper. I was far from feeling calm on the inside, but my mother's easy manner with Mr. Mason had a calming effect.

"We're going to look around," she said. "No need to hurry."

It's true I was enamored with both stores we'd visited already, but the grocer's was by far the most magical place we would visit that day. The front of the store had a fresh smell of citrus as we strolled through the produce section. Compared to now, we lived very simply back then. We grew or made nearly everything we lived off of. Most trips to town were reserved for specific grocery runs like these, and more often than not, Daddy or Granddaddy handled these trips since they typically needed something from the hardware store to keep our small farm in order.

Mother walked me down one aisle and the next. This aisle was filled with silver cans of food of all kinds with colorful labels; this aisle held jars of pickled goods, peanut butter, jellies and preserves. She held a jar of peach preserves to the light, but no light shone through its cool, ruby darkness.

I wanted everything.

I wanted big brown boxes to be filled with one of every single item in the store to be loaded into the bed of Granddaddy's truck. I'd ride home in the back on a throne of wood and cardboard if it meant making this dream possible. Mother replaced the jar on the shelf.

"Hold on now. Is that Miss Elizabeth?" a man's voice said as we reached the back of the store. He leaned his heavy, hairy arms on a wooden counter stained with red and brown splotches. His apron was similarly spattered, and he wore a funny white hat. Here the store smelled of pepper and sage. My mouth watered.

Mother introduced me to the butcher, whom she also knew by name. As they spoke, I thought how odd it was Mother knew so many people as seldom as she came to town. This man looked more like Daddy than Mr. Mason and was closer to my father's age. The butcher seemed to enjoy speaking to Mother; in fact, everyone delighted in Mother's company. She seemed different today. She smiled. She spoke more often. I'd heard her laugh more this day than in a month at home. Several aisles down, a voice wished someone Merry Christmas in a "see you later" kind of way, and the bell banged twice against the door.

All the sights and smells made our breakfast seem a lifetime ago. Before I could ask Mother about lunch, behind us I heard, again, the hollow clopping of heels on the wooden floor. I turned to see, and the gray man in his navy coat was walking our way. A scream was gathering in my stomach, but my throat clenched tight. I couldn't breathe. The man's dark eyes were fixed on my mother. I yanked her coat like I was unveiling a marble statue.

"Good God, Martha!" she spun to me, laying eyes on the man. "James!" she shouted.

Everything was flashing green, yellow, and black. The next thing I remember was a sweet smell of tobacco and clean leather and the sound of Mother faintly calling my name. A sharp, cold breeze against my wet forehead brought me out of my stupor, and when I opened my eyes, we were on the sidewalk outside the grocer's, and I was cradled in the arms of the gray man. Had I any strength, I would've bucked like a barn cat, but I thought better when I saw the look on my mother's face changing from concern to something far less patient.

"There she is! She's all right. Just had a little fright," the gray man said and righted me on the ground.

"Thank you, Dr. Winthrop," Mother said.

"*James*, Elizabeth," he said. "She still looks a bit peaked though. Perhaps we should get some food in her stomach? There's a little diner down the way."

"I don't know. My father could be here any moment. He's our ride."

"That's quite all right. Listen, wait here." He darted back into the grocer's. I thought Mother might be angry with me and fully expected a few stern words, but when I looked to her, she seemed unconcerned. She was looking in the store window, touching her hair. The gray man reappeared and said: "That's that. Mr. Mason's holding your groceries for you, and I told him if a man should arrive asking for you, to help load them in his truck. We won't be long. Just a sandwich or a cup of soup."

Mother looked at me, then gently guided me in the direction of the diner. "Let's be fast then."

At the diner Dr. Winthrop pushed the door open and held it for us. Once again, I could smell the tobacco on his clothes as I brushed past his open arms. Inside, the place was alive with voices, sizzling food on a flat iron grill, and clinking silverware and china. We took a small booth at the front. Dr. Winthrop raised a finger to get a waitress's attention, but the cook behind the counter saw him first. "Linda! It's Doc Winthrop," he said.

"Tuna on whole wheat toast, coffee black, right up," she announced, absorbed in furiously wiping down one of her tables.

"Just cool it, Linda," the cook said. "How about you look at what you're doing for a second?"

She was close to shouting back at the cook but stopped short after realizing the doctor had guests. "Oh, my." She stopped everything and approached our table. "What can I get you two?" she asked.

Before Mother could speak, the doctor told her we were in a hurry and suggested the soup of the day would be fine for Mother and a cheese biscuit for me. Mother nodded. "Great," he said. "Coffee for Ms. Elizabeth and a cold glass of milk for the girl."

After the waitress had gone, the doctor said to me, "You had us frightened for a moment there."

I nodded and looked away. I still couldn't speak to the doctor, nor could I displace the image of the gray man from the other stores and the street that day.

"Your knees buckled, and you nearly hit the floor," he continued.

"Dr. Winthrop caught you just in time," Mother said.

"Wouldn't want you to bust your noggin or smash that pretty little nose."

"Can't you say anything to him?" Mother asked.

I could only continue to stare.

"You know, you had the oddest look on your face—like you'd seen a specter of some sort," he said.

"Specter?" I mumbled.

"Specter . . . uh, spirit. A ghost," he said.

Mother sighed. "Well, don't take offense, Dr. Winthrop—"

"Please, Elizabeth, *James*. Don't make me ask again."

"*James*," she smiled, "don't take it personally, but I think my daughter thought you were this evil kidnapper she's heard so much about today. Her granddaddy got her all keyed up this morning, and I think her overactive imagination has bested her."

I blushed.

"Kidnapper? Yes, I heard about that business myself. It's quite alarming to say the least." He spoke to me, "You're right to be on guard . . . . What's this fine young lady's name?"

"Martha," she answered for me.

"*Martha*. You can't be too careful, and if I have the look of a villain, I suppose I better smile a bit more or perhaps wear my hat like this." He flipped up his hat brim and bounced his eyebrows three times. It put me in mind of a straight man's slapdash sidekick.

"That'll never suit you, James. You're much too serious to play the fool."

"I guess you're right." He sighed and turned to me. "You know, in my school days, back with your mother, I only ever wanted to be the clown. Even acted a little in the school plays." He took off his hat and placed it on the seat beside him. "That's a silly dream, isn't it?" he asked me. "But what could be better than making people laugh away their cares for an hour or so? Instead, people mostly only ever see me on the worst few days of their year—for checkups, shots, and illnesses—and then if I chance to see them on the street, one look of their faces tells me they're thinking of how awful their last visit was or how much they dread seeing me again."

"Gee," I had to admit.

All the while he spoke, Mother watched him carefully, resting her chin in her palm, smiling. She sipped her coffee. "But you've done so well for yourself. I'm very proud of you. Who would've thought a dirty little barefooted farm boy would turn out so well? Living your life in town, on your own . . . you must have everything you need, here."

"Yes. Everything." He seemed distracted by the glare of light upon the coffee in his cup.

After the waitress brought our lunch, their talk concerned me less and less, and being a child, my mind drifted in and out of their conversation. He spoke fondly of an older doctor who had mentored him and left him the office and his patients, to the dismay of many. "It seemed," he said, "that the home folks I knew from way back when—they didn't trust me because they knew deep inside I was the same backwoods boy they remembered, and everyone here in town wanted Dr. Amberson's reincarnation."

I couldn't imagine a statelier man than the one before me. Not fancy but dignified: the three-piece suit, the faded pocket watch and chain, the pipe stem rising from his jacket pocket, the hat and long coat, the well-trimmed mustache. I'm not sure that I'd ever seen my father in a suit or anything dressier than his flannels and dungarees in the winter. The slightest of dark stubble could be seen along the doctor's firm jawline. My father kept a long beard. Had I ever seen his actual chin? The doctor's pointed nose; my father's long, arched nose. The doctor's dark hair and eyes; my father's sandy hair and blue-gray eyes.

"Your daughter really is a beauty, Elizabeth," the doctor said.

"What do you say, Martha?" Mother asked.

I lifted my eyes from the knot in his striped necktie to his Adam's apple. "Thanks."

"Brown hair, hazel eyes, the slender face. You know, your mother was a classic beauty in our day, but you bear little resemblance to the way I remember her. You must take after your father," he said.

I looked to him, but he seemed to be looking at my ear or just over my shoulder.

"Oh, she looks nothing like him either. She's only ever looked like herself. I'm not sure who she takes after," Mother said.

Only I seemed interested in our food. I'd been tearing the biscuit apart bit by bit, letting the sharp cheddar string out into ribbons, which I wrapped around the small bits in my fingertips while Mother and the doctor chatted away. As I ate, I thought how silly I was to fear the doctor was a villainous kidnapper, but then I began replaying those short glimpses from earlier and the strange distance he kept. I wanted badly to interrupt their reminiscing with a question or two. I practiced asking them in my mind until finally, in a proper lull, I said: "If you knew it was us all along, Dr. Winthrop, why didn't you say hello early this morning at Turner's or O'Cleary's or, not so long ago, before we were entering the grocer's?"

Mother looked like she'd ingested arsenic—if arsenic made you angry as well as sick.

Before she could speak, the doctor said: "I glanced at you and your mother as you left O'Cleary's, but though I knew Elizabeth had a daughter your age, I couldn't quite glimpse her face enough to know it was her. It's been a few years now, hasn't it, Elizabeth?"

Mother didn't even nod. She only tightened her mouth into a hard-fixed smirk.

". . . And I was only partly convinced when the two of you entered the grocery store; that's what I came over to see—if it *was* you. Did you say you saw me at Turner's? It's true I was there . . . ." He trailed off, looking a little hopeless at my mother, like he'd run out of words.

"It's fine, James," Mother said in a knowing way. "You don't have to confess your daring plot to follow us around all day without being seen. Though you'd think a doctor would have better things to do with his time than follow a couple of backwoods ninnies around."

Mother's tone was hard to distinguish. She was often playful speaking to Daddy and me or Granddaddy, but I never thought her relaxed manner would extend to anyone outside our little world back home. At any rate, the feeling I'd had on the street with Miss Vicky returned, and once again I found myself wondering, Who is this woman?

"I have a solid alibi. I told the nurse I was making a house call," he said with a dapper smile and a shade of embarrassment.

"Do doctors still make those?" Mother asked.

The two laughed and went on talking.

We finished our food, and the doctor paid the bill. Mother said she still wasn't sure what to get Daddy for a Christmas present, and the doctor suggested pipe tobacco, and he referred us to the store down the way.

"*Oh!*" She approved only for a second, then said, "But I don't think so. I'd feel a little out of place in a store like that—being a lady—and with a child in tow."

"I'll walk you there and take care of the whole business myself."

Outside the store, Mother gave the doctor some money. "Which brand does he like?" he asked.

"I'm not sure," Mother said.

"Then I'll get him what I smoke," he said and left us there.

Mother didn't say a word to me. Occasionally, she would glance down the street to see if Granddaddy's blue truck was coming, and when she didn't see him, she looked around the green and gold–painted letters on the window to watch the doctor buying the tobacco.

"But Daddy doesn't smoke," I said.

"Maybe he doesn't smoke because he doesn't have any tobacco."

I thought it highly unlikely he even owned a pipe, but something told me to let it go.

The doctor returned with the tobacco in a brown paper bag. "The difference is in the bag." She attempted to take the bag from him, but he didn't let go. "Don't forget to remove your change and the receipt before you wrap it," he said and released the bag. He tipped his hat to Mother and gave me an oddly poignant smile. As he walked away, it began to snow. In his long coat and hat, he appeared as a tall shadow, shrinking in the distance, turning from a deep navy into lightening shades of gray. Mother and I watched him until he disappeared.

I hadn't noticed how noisy things were in town until this moment, with the snow beginning and the streets having grown remarkably silent and still. I looked up and down the road, and the few people we saw were hurrying for shelter. "Should we go back to the grocer's, Mama? Maybe watch for Granddaddy's truck from the window?"

She didn't respond. She seemed mesmerized by the falling snow.

She was still looking in the gray man's direction when Granddaddy arrived to carry us home.

Daddy got home late in the evening. He'd stopped for a drink with the other men from the sawmill. Most men around home found work there, especially in the winter, when there were no crops to tend to. Sitting at the kitchen table, he still had sawdust everywhere, embedded in his overalls and flannel sleeves and hiding behind his collar and in his frazzled beard. Mother was frying a pork chop on the stove, warming back up the potatoes and green beans we'd had earlier.

"Foreman said after tomorrow we could stay home until after Christmas," he said.

Mother turned from the stove. "Well, what will you do with all your time?"

"I'm going to find a deer stand deep in the woods, tie myself to the trunk of the tree, and sleep the best sleep I've had in years," he said.

"Just don't tie it around your neck." Mother laughed.

"Well, tell me about Martha's big journey today." He looked at me and smiled. We both waited for Mother to begin, but she seemed not to hear. "You know I was pretty worried about the two of you in town today. I've heard stories of some bad things happening out there."

"We had a full day," she said. Again, we waited for more, but Mother stood silent by the stove and turned the pork chop again.

"Saw in the newspaper they found the second girl. But she wasn't . . . right. Wouldn't speak. Didn't act like she knew anybody." Mother brought his dinner to the table without a word. "Hell of a thing . . . ," he said, "and so close to Christmas."

Mother dropped the silverware next to his plate, and it rang out like a telephone. "Sorry," she said after placing her hands down on the knife and fork.

While Daddy ate his dinner, Mother sat down with us at the table. She went over the day's events like a stone skipping on the water. She told Daddy about the stores we shopped in, about seeing Victoria, about running into Dr. Winthrop at the grocer's, and then she stopped. She didn't mention my little episode, thankfully, but neither did she tell Daddy about lunch with the doctor in the diner or the tobacco shop afterward. It seemed strange to leave so much out, and in the lingering quiet, when her words fell short, I couldn't help but wonder at her reasons. Maybe she didn't want to tell the story of me fainting at the grocer's to keep me from looking foolish or to keep Granddaddy from trouble for having put the fear in me to begin with, or maybe Daddy didn't care for Dr. Winthrop, or . . .

"Look at her. She's almost sleeping in her chair," Mother said and stood. She walked behind my chair and put her hands on my shoulders. "Bedtime, Martha. Let's get you dressed."

All day Mother had been pushing or pulling me in one direction, then another, and here she was again, ushering me off to bed, which was odd, really—I could very well dress myself and had been for years—yet this night she took special care to help me change into my sleeping gown. She reached under the lampshade by my bed and put out the light. As I slipped between the covers, I heard her take a deep breath. "They smell like the streets," she said and placed my clothes by the door. She walked over to a chair by the window, but instead of sitting, she stared out the window.

"Clear, bright night," she said. "Stars seem to multiply up through the winter. Look how the light hits that magnolia. Like it's wrapped in tin foil."

She pulled up a chair from the wall to face me and took a seat.

"Why didn't you say more to Daddy about our day—about meeting Dr. Winthrop?" I asked.

Mother pondered this a moment. Moonlight from the window lit her body from the shoulders down. I strained my eyes to see her face but couldn't. "You were looking very tired—like you might slide out of your chair and sleep on the floor. I didn't want to see you pass out twice in one day." She laughed. "Once was enough."

"Oh," I said, as so many children do when they sense adults wish to end what might become a tiresome conversation for them. But instead of turning away this time, I set my eyes upon where I thought her eyes should be and waited.

"It crossed my mind to tell him about James, but then we'd have to talk about *everything*, wouldn't we? Your passing out, lunch at the diner, and then the tobacco shop . . ."

I searched her silhouette for some deeper meaning.

". . . and all this would ruin the surprise of his Christmas present. Wouldn't it?"

I agreed.

"Well, don't sound so disappointed, Martha. It's fun to have a secret once in a while. And anyway, your father doesn't need to know everything."

Having a secret from Daddy didn't feel right. Even as a child, I didn't believe in secrets. School friends would beg me not to tell something that they'd end up shouting to everyone a few days later. I've kept other people's secrets longer than they ever could—long enough to realize that maybe secrets are only ever meant to be shared with a careful messenger, one wise enough to find the right listener, one who will speak at the right time.

I thought she might want to say more about the day we'd had, but leaning forward in her chair to where I could at last see her face, she asked in the most innocent way, "Would you like to hear a story?"

I had long outgrown stories, but I was too tired to protest. She leaned back in her chair, crossed her legs, and rested her hands on her knees. I could barely make out the outline of her hair in the darkness. In her story she said long ago, in a less civilized time, people could turn into beasts of the forest at will but only while they were young. Even then, people never knew what kind of animal they'd turn into until the time arrived for their first change. Which animal they'd become had much to do with their heart or spirit, she said. Once there were two peasant children only a few years older than me who'd fallen in love with each other. They felt the first change coming upon them like a glowing ember inside their bones, but they feared their transfiguration would betray some awful nature they'd not yet encountered. What if one should become a predator and the other prey? So they agreed to meet deep in the forest accompanied by a village woman who was thought to be a witch. They asked her to cast a spell to save one from the other if one should be a rabbit and the other a wolf, for example. When the half-moon reached its zenith, the young boy and girl shrank to the ground. The witch watched, laughing as they struggled out of their clothes, only to find they'd both transformed into foxes. The young girl was a handsome red fox; the young boy, however, had turned into a striking blonde fox. The two foxes, red and blonde, circled and nuzzled one another, purring like kittens. But the witch knew hunters couldn't resist tracking and killing the rare blonde fox for sport, so she made herself appear as a wolf to him, frightening him from the forest. When the young woman resumed her human form, she hated the witch for what she deemed treachery, and . . .

I fell asleep, of course, before the story ever ended.

Mother still tells her stories to my Cindy. Even though she's probably too old for them herself, she's never complained. It's been more than a year now that Mother's been staying with us. A godsend. It was lonesome with only Cindy and me here, even more so after what happened with her brother at the school we sent him to, in the city. It has been good for Cindy having Mother around, and I can tell the stories mean more to Cindy than Mother knows. I suppose they're much the same as the ones she told me long ago, but when Cindy recalls them to me now, somehow, they never sound familiar.

"Children always fall asleep before the endings," Mother said to me at the kitchen table after having left Cindy's room. "But what is life but a thousand unfinished stories?"

I couldn't say, and as usual, I could tell her words were more for herself than for me.

"Maybe it's for the best, though," she said with a sigh into her coffee. "We give the stories to them and let them dream their own endings."

SANCTUARY

My brother had already finished a plate of eggs when I walked into the kitchen, still groggy and a little annoyed to be starting my day so soon. Mother was at the stove cracking more eggs and dropping them into the pan.

"Eggs?" she asked.

I sat without answering.

Mother walked the pan over to the table and doled out two scrambled eggs onto my brother's plate. "You're hungry today. Got big plans?" a kind of false brightness in her voice.

"Yep," he said.

We waited, but no further details were to follow.

"I'd hoped we could do something together, the three of us. We don't often get the chance. Teachers' workday, no shift at the drugstore. Do you guys want to ride to town for lunch? Or we could go on further to the city—make a day of it."

Nothing.

"Or we could finally get cracking at this garden. We should've already had the corn and potatoes in the ground. Had a time getting someone to come till the garden and leave us some rows."

"I really had plans already," he said and rose from the table. He dropped his fork, and his empty plate rang like a bell.

"Plans? What plans?" Mother said.

"Same old stuff, clearing paths. Mostly I wanted to camp a little, on my own, you know?" He glanced at me, but my mind was waking, still catching up.

He went into the living room, unzipped his book bag, and turned it upside down in the corner behind the couch. Its contents tumbled onto the floor, and he raked them with his foot into a tidy pile. He came back to the kitchen and started ransacking the pantry. I saw his hand make several trips where the apples were, a couple sleeves of saltines, a jar of peanut butter, a few tins of sausages . . .

"Wait. Wait. How long are you going to be gone?" I asked.

"How long? Oh. I wanted to do a few nights. That okay?" He looked at Mother.

"You promise not to stay gone too long?"

"Yeah."

"To be safe, to not do anything stupid?"

"Sure. Sure."

"And you're caught up with your lessons?"

"Mostly."

She seemed to be thinking but not all that hard.

"Fine, but don't come home all worn-out and wrecked. You can't be sleeping all day like you have some of these other nights after camping. I want you to finish this school year strong."

He darted out the storm door, his eyes fixed on the shed across the yard, and I believe I caught a rare smile.

"Wait," I said to Mother. "You're just going to let him go out into the woods and be a wild man for as long as he wants?"

"He won't go all that far, and besides, if he gets bored with it, it's only a short walk home."

"So we can just do that? 'See you later, be back when I feel like it'?"

"Cindy, you know your brother's always been a solitary type. Bit of a mope. Did you see how happy that made him?" She read the look on my face and continued. "He's getting older. Teenagers need their space. Especially boys. Boys ramble. Also, it's different for them. It's safer than for girls."

I let out a rage groan and walked out into the yard in my bare feet and gown. I heard a strange sound coming from the shed, lighting up my spine a little. I peeked in the doorway to find my brother taking a file to the bush axe. He was leaning into it as he sharpened the blade. The tool was clamped in our father's old vise grip.

"You ever seen this?" he said, and he produced a cigarette lighter from his pocket. He pinched off the little metal dust from his filings, flicked the flame on, and sprinkled the dust into the flame. The little filings sparkled and faded like a tiny cloud of lightning bugs. "Dad showed me that once."

"Where are you going?"

"You know what? I don't know. Maybe as far as I can. Think about that. I could walk out for the rest of the day, another half-day, then turn around and walk home. Wonder how many miles that would be or what I haven't seen yet out here."

"Is that what you're doing? Then why are you taking the bush axe?"

He turned the vise grip open and squinted as he inspected the blade. "You know me. Always a project," he said. He had on one of Grandfather's old hats, the kind men used to wear back then. It was felt and hunter green with a black band around it.

"I'm going with you," I said.

He looked me up and down. "In your nightgown? Barefooted?"

"Well."

"You want to use the bathroom in the woods for a few days?" He threw the handle over one shoulder and slung his bag over the other.

"Wait for me," I said and dashed back into the house. In the time it took me to change, find my hiking shoes and straw hat, and return to the yard, he had already disappeared into the woods. I called for him and heard nothing, so I began to follow his trail. My brother had carved a wide pathway through the woods that surrounded our home, and it was a sort of lifetime commitment for him, keeping the pathway clean, adding trails to other landmarks he'd discovered, like the boulder field, the pits, the waterfall, the spring, the sideways-growing pine, and so forth, but I figured he'd be on the main path from the way he was walking—like he couldn't waste a second—so I took the main route.

After hurrying through the first stretch of the trail—I don't know why—but it occurred to me to slow down. I'd learned as a child how startling him could work out, but that's not exactly why I did so. I thought it best to watch over him to get a better sense of his plans. Perhaps that's characterizing it too positively. Spying. More or less, I was a little sister spying on her big brother.

I knew going undetected would be nearly impossible. It's awfully hard to walk soundlessly, even on the path, but I knew the trail, its dips and bends, and I knew which lengths would afford me cover. When I didn't see him, I moved briskly to my next checkpoint, where I would stop and listen. Somewhere after the creek, I heard him before I could see him. My brother's voice is rather unmistakable. A kind of thin tenor, mild but clear and sudden. You always had to ask him to repeat himself if you weren't prepared to actually listen. If you were the type to speak over him, you'd find him pretty impossible. Terse to a fault, unless he was really taken with the subject matter.

And though he was alone, this seemed to be his manner at the moment. Downright loquacious for him. I couldn't make out the words, but the inflection definitely sounded as though he was speaking to someone. Particularly after the pauses. Those sentences clearly rang out as replies. I had heard it said my brother spoke to himself often as a child—surely a firstborn thing—but this is something I'd never witnessed before. I carefully quickened my pace to get close enough to hear.

The first words I made out: "You're not going with me."

He stopped and turned.

"I know, but I can go partway," I said.

He leaned against an oak tree while I made my way to him. I needed to catch my breath; I suppose I'd been holding it trying to listen.

"There's something you're not telling us. What's going on?" I said.

He kicked the heel of his boot against the trunk. "It's real stupid," he said.

"Oh, no. What happened?"

He groaned. "Look, I'll make it quick because this is slowing me down: I almost fell off the top of the schoolhouse, and everybody freaked out—"

It went like this: Every year Mr. Steppe would take his physics class to the rooftop of the school. It's a two-story brick building, very old, there's no railing or anything like that, but it's a kind of year-end event for his class, maybe the only reason anyone took physics. It'd been going on forever without incident, but nothing like my brother to find a way. They had this assignment, using only crude elements, to build these little contraptions that are supposed to keep an egg from breaking, surviving the two-story drop. It was a silly thing to look forward to, but everyone did anyway.

My brother's invention was pretty unique. He had woven a kind of nest ball for the egg using grapevines. The egg was suspended in the middle, somewhat loosely, to cushion that final jolt. The whole thing was spherical, with woven layers surrounding the egg so tightly you could barely tell it was in there. He'd built the thing around it. You'd have to cut the thing apart to remove it. I had no idea if it would work, but there was something kind of perfect about the way the egg fit in there so snug, a nucleus in its little wicker atom. I remember him saying, "If you bother to make anything at all, you might as well make it beautiful."

"On the roof," he said, "I suppose I forgot myself for a moment. I was looking out over the treetops, and I think I was daydreaming about flying." He got a faraway look in his eyes, and I could tell he was right back there, soaring over the woods. "I was wondering how far we can see with the naked eye. I was squinting at something moving across the sky, in the distance, trying to determine if it was real. Did you know people report seeing pterodactyls every year? Can you imagine? And where would they live? They're so huge that if they perched in a tree, they'd break the top right off."

"Please get to it."

"Right." He'd started pacing, reliving everything as he walked in a tight little area. "Maybe without knowing, I'd been inching up to the ledge of the building all along. Suddenly, I felt a hot puff of air on my neck—I knew it was Doug even without turning—and, with my trance broken, I was shocked to see how close I was to the edge, how far down it was, and to feel I couldn't step backward, well, I snapped, and in one motion I reached behind me, grabbing the back of his head, and leapt or fell backward. I'm thinking it looked like a professional wrestling move. Anyway, we tumbled over. I fell on him. He had a bloody nose and everything."

"So, you're suspended again?"

"I think so."

"Is that it?"

"No, I think they're coming to see Mom today."

"What?"

"Yeah. I think it's serious this time."

I sat down on an oak root. Here we go again, is all I could think.

"I'm surprised they even let me up there to begin with." He laughed. "I think the only reason they did was Mr. Steppe wanted to see if my egg capsule worked. You know, Doug just put a bunch of cotton balls in a cardboard box." After some silence he said: "He wouldn't have pushed me, do you think? You don't think they hate me, do you?"

I thought this over for a moment. "All it would've taken is for someone to look the other way."

He nodded, sighed. "All right, Cindy. This is where we part ways."

"No, I'm going with you." I stood and faced him.

"You can't."

"Why not?"

Considering his words carefully, he dipped the brim of his hat, and, looking below, said, "Who will look after Mother?" and headed down the trail.

After he'd trekked nearly out of sight, I called after him: "What will you do? Follow the train tracks into town? Are you working on a new path?" No reply. "When are you coming home?"

When I returned to the house, there was a boxy black car in our driveway. It was shiny with tan leather interior. In the back seat there were manila folders filled with paper. I thought I saw my brother's name on the top folder.

I came inside as quietly as I could—I'd even taken my shoes off. Mother was on the couch being addressed by one man in a dark suit who would walk from one end of the room to the next as he spoke. From a chair opposite the couch, the other man spoke very little, only occasionally to agree with the walking man, who was at once pleading and demanding in his tone. I stood listening in the kitchen.

He said: "I don't see that we have any other option. And besides, he's a perfect candidate. You know his IQ is remarkable." When my mother said nothing, the man said, "If it's a matter of funding, you needn't worry about that. There are grants, and the state and the county give us discretion over situations like these. Every year or so we do this. We send gifted, special children to Vanguard Academy, where they can flourish in a way they may not be able to in our school. They have dormitories on the campus. He'll be living just outside the city. There are so many advantages . . ."

It was clear to me now the walking man was Principal Franklin; furthermore, I knew what they were doing.

"Don't listen to them, Mom." I blasted into the room. "They're secretly sending him away because he got in trouble again."

"Trouble? What's this?" Mother said.

The principal sighed. "Your son got into another fight," he said. "One boy said he tackled him and almost threw him two stories off the roof of the school. Maybe broke his nose."

"What in God's name were they doing on the rooftop? Didn't anyone stop to think whether that was wise—to take a bunch of impulsive teenagers on top of a building?" she said.

The man in the chair finally stood. He was largely bald but with a ring of salt-and-pepper hair below the top of his skull. He had hard, severe eyebrows that pulled together in an acute triangle. His baritone voice commanded all of our attention: "She's right, ma'am. We don't know what to do with your son. Frankly, we're tired of making excuses for him when another student goes home with blood on their shirt or with some troubling story of what he did over the summer or over the weekend, and we've absolutely had it. What we're offering you here is a solution for the benefit of all parties involved: Your son, his classmates, and the school."

"Aren't you forgetting someone?" I asked.

They seemed shocked to be hearing me. Mother waited to see what I would say.

"*Us*," I said. "What about his family?"

The phone rang. Mother went to the kitchen. The two men stood silent. I wanted an answer to my question, but as soon as she spoke, we began eavesdropping. It went something like this: "I'm sorry to hear that . . . unfortunate, but I put in for this day off two weeks ago. I'm sorry—I know it's not your fault . . . sure, sure, I'll come in." She slammed the phone down in its cradle, and the bell inside rang a tiny bit.

She entered the room and took a deep breath. "Gentlemen, I hate to cut this short, but they need me at the drugstore. You've given me a lot to think about. I'll talk to him about the roof and see if we can get to the bottom of this—"

"—but the academy, Martha. That's the real matter," Principal Franklin said.

"Of course," she said. "Grab your things, Cindy. We're headed to town."

"What things?"

"Whatever you need to pass the time. Bring a book or two, paper and pen, something. Excuse us, gentlemen," she said.

The men left and drove off, and I thought Mother and I would discuss their proposition, but she said nothing, only a self-pitying bit about having her day ruined by being called in to work—apparently Nancy had come down with something. Before we drove off, I said, "So, we're just going to leave him here?"

"Who?" she said.

I gave her the look I would perfect during the next few years—wide eyes, the half-cocked head.

"Oh. He's likely to be out the rest of the day whether we're home or not. And anyway, he knows where the key is if he does come back."

She backed down the drive.

"I don't like the idea of leaving him here." I said. "What if he needs us? What if something happens?"

As we drove away, she said, "Something *always* happens," but I wasn't sure if she was speaking about my brother or herself.

It takes a while to get anywhere in the mountains. By the time we got to the drugstore, it was lunch. Mother bought me a pimento cheese sandwich from one of the coolers, a bag of chips, and a Coke. I ate slowly, hoping it could occupy at least thirty minutes of the next six hours, until close. The store was relatively busy, it being Friday, so I watched the customers to pass the time. Once, when I was checking my blood pressure for the third or fourth time in the arm clamp torture device, I noticed two women my mother's age in the corner of the store. As they spoke to one another, they never took their eyes off Mother. One had a look of concern on her face, the other a look of glee. She placed manicured fingertips in front of her lips from time to time, like a little finger picket fence. While I could not hear their words, I noticed my blood pressure had changed from earlier. I fought the urge to squirm and break free, but just like the rest of my day, I had no recourse, and so I waited.

We stopped in a diner after Mother closed the store. We spoke very little through dinner and during the long ride home, and after. I'd hoped my brother would be waiting for us when we returned, but I knew he wouldn't be. Mother was right. It didn't matter whether we were home or not.

That silence carried over into breakfast the next day until Mother said: "I was thinking of working in the garden this morning. How does that sound?"

"I wonder how he slept last night," I said. "It didn't look like he had a sleeping bag."

"No? Did he take the tent?"

"Probably." He had a small A-frame tent. A standard-issue army surplus kind of thing. We used to play with it in his room. "What's he doing? Where's he going?" I said, not really expecting an answer.

"Don't you reckon to the train tracks? It would be just like him to camp out near the tracks to watch the trains go by."

That made sense. But then I remembered what he said about walking a full day and a half. It sounded like he had distance on his mind. I pushed a triangle of pancake around on my plate.

"You could go look for him if you're worried," she said.

"Why aren't *you* worried, Mother?"

"Cindy, have you ever asked yourself why we never take vacations, why we never leave the mountains, why we never get farther than Saluda County?"

"Not really."

"We can't afford it—plain and simple. All I can do is make do with the corner we're allotted. There's not much of this world I can offer you, but you know what I *can* offer?"

I shook my head.

"Freedom. Independence. That's it. Sometimes that means nothing; other times it means everything."

I thought on this. "Like Carson," I said.

"What?" she said.

We had a cat for a short time several years ago. A yellow tabby. One of these incidental kittens that appears in your car's motor one morning, crying for food. We fed him for years, even let him sleep in the house when he wanted to, but he was an outdoor cat at heart. He scratched the paint off the kitchen door when we tried to train him to stay in. He couldn't tolerate it. Had to roam at night, hunt. Wonder what finally got him?

"Pack a light lunch and some water. Take yourself a little hike," she said. "But don't go as far as the tracks. If you do, promise me you won't spend much time there. Certainly, don't go walking down the tracks alone."

I gave the impression of a promise, dressed, packed, and left. With the cuffs of my jeans tucked into my socks, bug sprayed, straw hatted, and a bag with a mason jar for water, a few packs of peanut butter crackers, and an apple, striding forth with the walking stick my brother had made me—smoothed, stained, and varnished, CINDY burned into the top—I made my way. In the last twenty-four hours, I'd largely been irritated, wavering between dread and anger whenever I thought about my brother and the men who pretended to have his best interests in mind, so one thing I did not expect was the relief that washed over me when I first entered the woods.

The first stretch, up to the creek, was so familiar to me that it was practically an extension of the yard. The creek was our most frequent destination when it was just the two of us. It was our river, our channel, our moat, our canal—our Styx, Euphrates, and Mississippi all in one, and with crawdads. Depending on rainfall, it could be above my waist or around my knees; this day it was somewhere between. However, wearing pants, it posed a problem. I wasn't interested in walking soggy the rest of the day. I studied both sides of the creek looking for a narrow place or a downed tree. There were a few potentials, but nothing felt sure, so I backtracked toward the spring where the creek narrowed and eventually found high enough ground that I could pole-vault myself across using my walking stick as an aid.

Of course, I didn't account for the depth my walking stick would sink into the bottom, and I promptly found myself soaked and muddy, trudging up the bank on the other side. Lesson learned. Wear shorts if you need to cross, wade through, and find some other way to keep the red bugs, ticks, and poison ivy at bay. So, I followed the creek back to the trail, peeved about my soggy jeans and socks but somewhat proud at not being deterred by the first challenge.

The pathway was littered with the stumps of small trees my brother had felled in service of the trail. They could be treacherous at times— little ankle shoots—easy to trip over and worse, God forbid, to fall upon. But most he'd divided up with his bush axe, and many were already rotting, receding into the forest floor. In fact, I couldn't help but marvel at how clean the path was and surprisingly wide in parts. I remember times when he'd tied neon-orange flagging tape around the trunks of trees to mark the trail, but the way through was clear enough now that anyone could see it.

It wasn't long before I'd reached the train tracks. Occasionally, my brother would take me there. The point where the path met the tracks you couldn't see all that far either way even though the curve was slight. We'd walk several hundred yards in either direction but never much farther. Mother warned against it, and truth be told, it always made me uncomfortable. One of my starkest church memories was a train conductor's horror stories of rolling over hoboes on winter nights. He said they would wait for a train to pass and fall asleep with their necks on the rails for warmth and then fail to wake before the next train came through. This conductor had a long red beard, gaunt eyes, and his voice would shake to speak of it.

I walked up and down the tracks, looking for signs where my brother might've crossed over, but my thoughts drifted back to the headless men who never wake or, worse yet, wake with a few fleeting seconds of light, horn, and terror barreling before them. The sun was hot on the rails, and I was sweating and feeling faint. I couldn't shake the thought that I could stumble, fall, split my head on a rail, and wake just in time to see what those men had seen. Across the tracks I saw what could be the start of a new path, but the way seemed less obvious. Possibly just a deer trail. But crossing over and the thought of continuing my journey without a clear path had me spooked. Getting lost. I hadn't thought of that. What's more, the longer I strode across the weathered crossties, I began to fear that I wasn't alone—that I was being watched. I hadn't thought of that either.

We'd never come up on anyone before, but Mother, more so Grandmother, had often warned us of this possibility. Always listen, Grandmother said. I stopped. Nothing. A hawk, a woodpecker, a few chattering swallows maybe. I began to return to the trail I knew, and then the notion struck me, what if I couldn't find the path home? Suddenly, everything began to seem foreign to me. The woods I'd just come from looked like one uninterrupted band of shady foliage. I couldn't see a clear opening. I heard my footsteps pattering against the crossties and crunching in the rock crush. I was breathing hard, too quickly, and the sun seemed brighter than before. Sweat rolled down my face and into my mouth. I had to stop, had to calm myself. I waited. I looked down each end of the tracks. Everything empty, so I held my breath and listened.

What I heard sloughing through the woods across the tracks sent me scrambling, slipping down the embankment, ducking for cover behind a dogwood's low-hanging branches. The elevated tracks obscured my view of whatever was coming, but in the stillness it grew louder, until I was certain something had emerged from the woods. There were slight sounds, a kind of closed-mouth groaning and awkward, hesitating scrapes in the rocks as it scaled the other side. From my vantage point, it seemed to slowly emerge from the earth, from the tracks of the train, an indecipherable mess of hair, flesh, sinew, and bones. I fought to manage my wheezing breaths until, through the branches' leaves, I could make out its form: upright-walking, hulking shoulders hunched forward, long arms nearly reaching the ground, moving mammalian but unnaturally so, almost as if it was wounded or could only move with considerable pain; three times my size, this flesh-covered brown and gray thing, loping forward, head hung low and dipping with every step, its long, shaggy hair covering its face. In the moment it stopped and turned in my direction, my heart stopped with it, when, appearing like an evening star from what must've been its face, one luminescent, citrine-sparkling eye met mine.

In rare moments of our lives, we are truly surrendered to an experience; the mind becomes an empty, open vessel. In these moments there is no being—only happening—and we, the vessels, are filled, often cracked, sometimes shattered, for in the absolute silence, we have heard sounds and voices; in the empty rooms and roads, we have seen figures and shadows; and in the vast darkness of space, we have found new lights, dancing and erratic or menacing and slow. We are bewildered or amused, ruined or sustained, or, as with my experience, awakened.

It all sent me gulping for air, zigzag dashing, tearing through the forest, until I glimpsed a neon orange ribbon on a tree and, finding our trail, raced along until I reached the other side of the creek, where I collapsed, catching my breath, calming myself, soaked in sweat and creek water, contemplating what I had witnessed, and weighing it against every unbelievable thing I'd ever heard on the playground or eavesdropped from adults who didn't know how closely I could listen, and suddenly, a world of enchantment opened before me, and I knew at the age of eleven, I would very likely never understand much of anything in this life.

I waited there on the home side of the creek for a long time. The creek felt like a protective boundary between me and whatever I'd seen, a blanket guarding against a bedroom shadow. I don't know how long I'd been gone, but it must've been late afternoon, long enough to make Mother nervous, for I heard her voice call my name through the woods.

I stood and ran along the path to meet her, but I found every stretch of the way back home empty.

As I reached the yard, I could see her sitting on the stoop at the back. I paused there and leaned against the railing. I asked why she didn't wait for me, walk with me to the house. She seemed confused.

"I never called for you," she said. "I've been here all afternoon."

She asked me if I happened to find my brother, and it occurred to me how in all the tumult, I hadn't thought of him for maybe a few hours—alone out there, in the woods, in all its strangeness and limitless possibilities.

"What in the world must he be doing?" I wondered aloud.

"Working on a bridge, wasn't he?" she said, almost as an afterthought.

"Bridge? Was that his plan?"

"He didn't say as much, but I didn't see him take his walking stick. Didn't he take a few tools with him?"

"Why didn't you say so this morning? I could've walked the creek both ways and found him."

I was angry with Mother for the span of a shower, but the more I thought it through, this idea didn't make sense to me. If he was building a bridge, wouldn't he start closer to home, and why would he be secretive about it? He'd never built one for our creek, and he probably crossed over ours every day. In fact, why *hadn't* he ever done just that? Also, I had followed the creek a good distance in both directions and didn't see anything. Perhaps there was another stream across the railroad tracks. Or maybe he wasn't building a bridge at all. What would he need the bush axe for? More paths? To where? And didn't he sound like he intended to walk a very long way? Didn't he mention a project? The image of the beast flashed before my eyes. Protection? My brother's out there in the woods with this thing. Questions filled my every waking thought through dinner and after, and when the darkness of my brother's second night alone in the woods settled, I was already fast asleep, dreaming of other answers.

The next morning I made it clear that I intended to return to the woods and find him, but Mother said after breakfast we would be going to church. This wasn't something we did consistently in those days, and, again, I protested on the grounds that he was out there alone and had been now for two whole days, but Mother offered the same flimsy rationale, so I grudge-ate breakfast, and I grudge-dressed in an ill-fitting pink-and-white dress I'd worn last Easter, and I grudge-rode to that little white church halfway between home and town.

I didn't always mind going to church. The routine of it all felt comforting back then—sit, stand, sing, sit, listen, stand, sing, pray, sit, listen—and the people there were nice enough. I liked the beginnings of sermons when the preacher would read Scripture. When the reading stopped, my thoughts began to wander, and that's one of the things I liked most about church, the contrast between feeling trapped and free at the same time, kind of like having your teeth worked on at the dentist. For an hour or so, you surrender yourself to the experience: wearing weird clothes, sitting next to weird people, hearing a man read, speak, and shout weird things. Through it all, I'd find my spirit lifting from my body, sending me anywhere it wanted to go, past, present, or future. With my body physically trapped in the pew, in certain moments, I felt the purest sense of freedom. My mind and my spirit could do as they pleased, and I took comfort in knowing that no one could ever keep that part of me captive.

Placement was important. This day it was perfect: aisle side, end of the pew, so I could lean against the arm armrest, and instead of Mother, Grandmother was beside me; she cared less if I was following along or not. We sat slightly behind my favorite stained glass window.

The multicolored gleam was a gateway for me. The window was rectangle with thin panes around the border, which created a dual-layer frame, but inside there was a more pointed, cathedral-style shape, and at the center of this was a circle with an image. Each window had a different hand-painted scene. My eyes would follow the border, an undulating red line etched into black, like a neon OPEN sign with the letters unraveled; up top a patchwork blue above a cathedral arch; inside the arch were large multicolored rectangles; finally, my eyes would linger upon the image inside. This one wasn't as busy as the others. It was simply Jesus standing at a closed door, his fist raised, ready to knock.

The sermon hadn't started. People were singing "Are You Washed in the Blood?" which always sounded like an advertisement jingle to me. Already I was transfixed by the window. Somewhere in the pastel rectangles, I'd slipped into a memory of when I was six or so. My brother had said he needed to go to the bathroom, and rather than simply stand to let him pass, I seized it as an opportunity to sit in the windowsill until he returned. The windows were recessed, and I was small enough to sit inside with my back against one end and fully extend my legs with my feet flat against the other. The choir was singing. I was trying my best to look through a frosted blue pane when I noticed the smallest crack in a green one. It was missing a triangle not much larger than the size of a pencil point. I pressed my eye up to the hole, only to find my brother, standing there in the churchyard, looking up at me. But he couldn't see me, could he? Maybe just a silhouette of me. He stood gazing up at the window. Was he studying the window or listening to the music and the voices, muffled by brick and stained glass? Or was he getting a sense of church from the outside? Maybe it sounded better out there. When the music ended and the people took their seats, I glanced at Mother, whose eyes told me to return to the pew. I stole one last glance through the hole in the green pane, but when I did, my brother was gone.

I snapped out of my trance as the song ended. The canvas hymnals zipped into their places, the congregation sat, and the pews cracked and groaned. The preacher said a few words, there was prayer, and we were up again. This time it was "Power in the Blood." The old piano had a kind of saloon timbre to it—all those rusty wires and worn-out mallets inside—and above it all, elderly voices all around me singing "power, power, wonder working power," but the whole time it sounded more like *pyre*. I looked around at their ancient faces. My eyes landed on an old-timer, wispy sideburns, gray sandpaper stubble, lips pulled into his mouth, "pyre, pyre, wonder working pyre," faint spittle with every *pyre*. So strange to hear my grandmother singing. It occurs to me now, there was never a lot of singing in my house.

The preacher began reading from Genesis. Joseph. The dreamer. The boy with the rainbow coat. He tells his family a dream. His brothers hate him for it, but the father holds the dream in his heart. I hear the preacher reading, invoking the voices of the brothers: "Here comes the dreamer. Come now, let us kill him . . . ." I see my own brother. ". . . and throw him into one of the pits." I am sweating cold through my dress. ". . . a fierce animal has devoured him." I see the form that followed me by the tracks; I see it shifting, changing. ". . . we will see what will become of his dream." And for the rest of the sermon, I am caught somewhere inside the stained glass window, searching the woods for my brother.

At home Grandmother joined us for Sunday dinner. I'd intended to head into the woods as soon as possible, but when I came back into the kitchen in a different set of clothes, Grandmother said: "Get yourself over here. Someone needs to show you how to cut up a chicken to fry."

Mother was managing the rest, a couple pots on the stove, one with a lump of frozen corn, then a lump of field peas thudded in the next, both from last year's garden. She was slicing squares of butter into them, adding salt and pepper, filling the cast iron with oil.

Grandmother was wrist deep in raw chicken. "You can buy them cut already, but they won't be as good. Don't ask me why. And anyhow, they won't cut the pieces right." She handed me the knife. "I'll tell you what to do."

And we started in this way, me shy about the cold chicken numbing one hand and awkward with the kitchen knife in the other. "*Mother,*" my mother said, watching the tutorial, and she gave her a look.

"Here." Grandmother took the knife and the basin with the chicken. "Young girls don't know how to hold a knife, much less use one without cutting themselves. God knows I was cooking for and feeding my entire family at your age." I was beginning to slink away, but then she said: "You can still help. Come over here. Get over on this side of me." Instead of next to the sink, I moved between her and the stove. "It'd be easier to show if we had a chicken each. We'll do it that way next time. I'll put the knife in your hand, and you'll do it yourself." She raised and flopped over the chicken like she had a hundred more to do—maybe showing off. "Butcher won't cut this part the way we like—we want it to lay flat so it'll fry up better. Here's the part you're most likely to cut yourself if your knife isn't sharp enough. See if that oil's hot," she said. "Good God, don't touch anything!"

"I wasn't going to *touch* anything."

"Maybe you've at least taught her that much," she said to Mother. "Here." She flicked a drop of water into the oil, and it popped. "See? Flop these over in the breader there. Good. Let me show you how to lay them so they'll all fit."

Later we moved all the food to the kitchen table. Mother had set it for three. "Don't you think he might show up?" I asked.

"He can get his own plate if he does, but no, for some reason I don't think he will," she said. "He'll be back tonight."

"Where did you say he was? What's he doing?" Grandmother asked.

"Camping," Mother said.

We sat.

"You said that much back in church. That's not what I'm asking," she said.

"Will you say grace?" Mother looked at me.

"God, thank you for this meal and the hands that prepared it, and we pray now that my brother comes home safely, amen."

"*Safely?*" Grandmother said. "Has he gone to war?"

With everything on the table, we served ourselves. Mother had made biscuits while we fried the chicken. My piece was the pulley, the part with the wishbone. Grandmother took a breast, Mother a leg and a thigh. I ate quickly and was rising to leave when Grandmother said: "Dear, bring the fig preserves. You can eat one more biscuit." The inflection of *biscuit* was somewhat complicated. It simultaneously communicated (a) is that all the time you can afford your Grandmother? (b) where are you rushing off to? and (c) that she thought I was too skinny. I brought her the preserves, sat down, and chose a biscuit.

"What'd you think of the sermon, Cindy?" she said as she slathered a well-browned biscuit with preserves.

"Joseph's brothers were real jerks," I said and tried to eat half the biscuit in one bite.

"To say the least," she said and passed the preserves to me, though I didn't want any. "What about what the preacher said about God's plan?"

"I must've missed that part," I said.

"Mm-hmm. About using 'non-traditional means,' I believe he said, to accomplish His will."

"I couldn't stop thinking of Joseph beaten and muddy in the pit, left for dead."

"They didn't beat him, Cindy. One of the brothers said not to," Mother said.

Grandmother said, "Joseph had a long journey, but it didn't start until his brothers threw him in the pit."

I stuffed the rest of the biscuit in my mouth and muffled through it. "Can I go now?"

"*Cindy*," Mother said, a certain way.

"If you find our conversation lacking, let us detain you no further," Grandmother said, and I rose from the table, grabbed my things, and headed for the woods.

My plan was simple enough: walk until I see him. Keep on the path. I thought, tomorrow's a school day—he's bound to come home sooner than later. And then, as I stepped into the woods, I remembered the men in suits who'd visited Mother and the trouble on the rooftop. I thought how maybe I really didn't know the whole picture about either. Maybe the men did have his best interests in mind. What if things had happened differently on the rooftop? While I'd never known my brother to be the aggressor, that doesn't mean he couldn't have made the first move somehow just by being himself. You could hardly call standing too close to the ledge of a rooftop baiting someone. Would the bad boys have killed him? As I moved along the path, my own words returned to me: *All it would've taken is for someone to look the other way.* A shove at the right second, and with my brother's history, no one would've been surprised. Accident? Incident? Tragedy? They wouldn't even know what to call it. A troubled young man who chose the coward's path. Even if another child or a teacher had witnessed the act, would they be human enough to tell the truth? And me, not being there, I'd have to live with the hurt the rest of my days, that my brother chose to abandon us all. But I would never believe he'd do such a thing, would I? I approached the matter from every angle and was surprised to find I'd already made it to the creek.

Here I hesitated. I thought to take off my socks and shoes, hike up my shorts, and move on, but the moment I imagined doing so, I was waylaid by the full force of yesterday's encounter. In my mind I relived every second and every breath, there at the edge of the woods, where the vision of this strange creature had captured me wholly. Standing there, I carefully pored over the details of what I'd witnessed. Had it been an eternity or half a minute? I didn't have long to absorb much, and I was in such a state, but as my eyes tried to make sense of what I beheld, I felt my mind constructing the thing from the vague suggestions I could make out, to render before me something identifiable, something that didn't defy description.

I sat down by the creek and concentrated until I realized one cause for this impossible task. The creature looked different the longer I watched it. In the span of thirty seconds, its skin turned a paler gray, its spine straightened, its limbs shortened, as did its hair, so that by the time it turned to face me, it was closer to human—even its gait seemed more upright—than when I'd first seen it crest the tracks. To illustrate the creature would have taken several separate sketches, and it occurred to me then that perhaps I'd witnessed the thing mid-metamorphosis, wounded in its evolution, struggling to become.

Afterward, I believe, subconsciously, my mind busied itself building a fortress around the whole thing. I'd passed out as soon as I'd gone to bed, only to wake and be swept up in the day, hustled to breakfast, then to church and back, and through it all, my thoughts turned instead to my brother. I know that seems unlikely—that one could simply move on from such a sight—but don't we do it every day? Our bodies, our minds—they just move on. If we're lucky. Still, I hope to God that every person encounters at least one striking, earth-shattering, mind-bending thing; staring out your kitchen window, you'll surprise yourself how quickly you return to your coffee. But now, sitting alone at the bank of the creek, plunging deep into yesterday's memory, I sensed my life reorienting the fabric of reality around what I'd witnessed.

My mind traversed vast territories those afternoon hours, sitting on the root of a tree, listening to the water trickle, swatting mosquitoes, glancing down both ends of the path: I thought of the weird woodland bedtime stories my grandmother had told me, one about a young maiden who met a demon who, punishing her for her un-possessable beauty, turned her into a catalpa tree instead of a dogwood like she requested; another about an ogre who rips cypress knees from the ground and uses them for clubs to keep people from stealing fish from his bog— all stories, no doubt, meant to keep me from doing exactly what I was doing, sitting alone in the woods. I'll admit they were serving her well this day as I was certain I would either be bashed into little bloody bits of nothing or turned into a tree whose leaves would be constantly fed upon by worms for eternity.

But my thoughts always led back to my brother. What if he never intended to return? He clearly only packed enough food for a few days. Had he secretly learned survival skills? Could my brother snare and field dress a squirrel or a rabbit? He had a lighter, didn't he? Does he always carry one? I never knew him to make campfires. What runaways carry a bush axe? No, he had some project in mind. But didn't he tell me to stay home and take care of Mother? Was there extra meaning there? What would he be building? And why build it so far from home?

Dusk was creeping in. The dense foliage above turned everything darker sooner. I'd begun hearing stirring on the forest floor. Squirrels, most likely. Different birds were beginning to sing. I could hear a whippoorwill maybe a quarter-mile away. The sweat on my shirt was starting to feel cold on my back. Suddenly, the space around me felt closer. I thought of the thing I'd seen yesterday. What if my brother runs into it? Would it harm him? What if my brother knew of it? My foolish eleven-year-old thoughts spiraled from there. I actually wondered, What if he was hunting it? What if he was summoning it? What if he had befriended it? What if my brother *was* the thing I saw?

I heard a distant shuffling of leaves. Perhaps a deer. Larger than a bird or rabbit. Steady, even walking. I perked up like any prey would, balanced onto the balls of my feet. I positioned myself behind a massive sweet gum. The footfalls grew closer. Then a voice. A kind of chittering at first, then a startling sound, short but loud whoops, a thin howl, followed by sounds approximating words. I peeked around the trunk of the tree, far down the path—my brother.

As he approached, he seemed to be speaking, though I couldn't make any of it out. In my relief I leaned against the tree and regained myself but wasted little time in stepping back into the path and calling his name to avoid frightening him or to keep from being perceived as the bratty kid sister, spying on her brother.

Once he was close enough that I could make out his features, I could see he wasn't annoyed. He seemed glad to see me. "Well, look at you, big girl," he said, stopping on the other side of the creek.

I sighed. "It's good to see you."

He took off his boots and socks and, stuffing the socks inside, slung the boots over his shoulder and walked across. "I would've walked up a ways and jumped across, but we're running out of daylight."

"What the hell kind of sounds were you making back there?"

"Oh. Owl, mating call. Depends when you were listening though. Some squirrel thrown in there too."

"Were you talking?"

"Yeah."

"To yourself?"

"I guess."

"Is it an imaginary friend?"

He turned to his left, spoke under his breath as though someone was standing beside him. He paused, nodded, and shrugged his shoulders. "He's confused. He says, 'Don't you see me?'" He smiled.

"Funny," I said.

"Haven't you ever had an imaginary friend?"

"I think it turned out all my friends were imaginary."

His smile faded here from impish to sympathetic. "*We're* friends," he said. "Aren't we?"

My words caught in my throat, but I smiled and nodded. He placed his things on the ground, sat, and wiped the dirt off each foot on a pant leg before putting his socks and boots back on.

"Where have you been?" I asked.

"I've been in the woods this whole time."

"Doing what?"

"Camping."

"Mom thinks you've been building something."

"Oh, really? What?"

"A bridge," I said.

"A bridge." He seemed to be thinking about this. "Maybe I'll call it that."

"Can you tell me more? Is it some kind of secret?"

"Can't a guy have a secret? Anyway, it isn't finished."

"Describe it."

He stood and brushed off the seat of his pants. "So, have you ever seen a Native American fish trap?"

I nodded no.

"What about a dream catcher?"

"No."

"Well, they made these incredible fish traps—they look like a wicker basket squeezed down into a funnel, and . . . it'd be easier just to show you. I'll take you there one day. When it's finished."

Beyond and above the forest, the sun was turning everything golden, but inside, beneath the dense foliage, shadows were turning from green to blue, and an evening chill had settled on my shoulders.

He picked up his bush axe and bag. "Hadn't we better be going? I'm pretty hungry," he said.

"There's something I need to tell you," I said.

"Don't like the sound of that."

I told him how soon after he left home, Principal Franklin and another stony man came by, that they discussed moving him to a different kind of school, a school you live in, for smart kids, far away, maybe farther than town, on to the city, and how they made like it would be good for him.

"—but it's mostly to get me out of there. I know. He's talked to me about it before."

"What?"

"I hadn't told you because it seemed unlikely at the time, but I guess this rooftop situation's really messed things up for me."

"Did you know they were coming?"

"Yeah. The principal had a long talk with me—to me—Thursday after the whole episode."

I was angry, furious, with him for all his secrecy. I have never known how to express my anger to him in any way that displayed an ounce of sympathy or a willingness to move beyond and through a trial or challenge, so I simply clenched my fists and shrieked loud and high enough to scare all the wildlife away, high enough he had to grab his ears.

"Calm down, Cindy. Don't be too mad with me. Don't you think I've punished myself enough over the last three days? My stupid daydreaming—if only I hadn't been so taken with the way those treetops looked, I wouldn't have lost myself and ended up on top of that kid. Now I've messed everything up."

I began to slow my breathing. I sat back down on the tree roots where I'd waited for him all afternoon.

"Look, maybe they're right. Maybe it's for the best," he said and joined me on the root.

"What? You're doing it? You're leaving?"

We sat, not talking for a while. I thought over the last three days and imagined them stretched out over half-years. Far away the quails were starting. A chickadee.

"Like Dad," I said.

"What?"

"You're going to leave us, like Dad."

He let out a deep breath. "No. I'm not leaving for good." He put his arm around me.

"Do you think of him very much?" I asked.

"Sort of. We weren't so close."

"I don't know anything about him," I said.

"He was a quiet, serious man. Worked at the sawmill. Came home late a lot. When he didn't come home late, he'd go hunting. Liked to hunt. I went with him once. His voice changed when he was hunting. He sounded younger. Excited."

I could see in my brother this memory led to something unpleasant. He grimaced as he ground the heel of his boot in the dirt.

"I remember playing a lot of cards with him this one time I was real sick and couldn't go to school. We talked then more than we ever did, I guess."

"What about?"

"Stories mostly. He talked about his father, growing up, hunting stories, work. Not long before he left, he almost died in an accident at the sawmill. He said on the very saw he had been running minutes before, one of the saw blades struck something hard in the trunk of a tree. It caused the blade to eject, and it nearly cut a man in two. Dad had stepped away for a short break. It saved his life."

"Wow."

"He said they found a railroad spike inside."

"What? Why?"

"It's something people would do if they didn't want folks cutting the trees down. It really shook him up. That wasn't too long before he left."

"Maybe that's why he left," I said.

"I don't think we understood each other too well. I'm sure I'm the reason he left—no matter what Mom says."

I thought to ask him why, but I could feel him closing up, so I didn't. I said, "I've been having these weird dreams about him, and then I wake up and find myself wondering what he's up to, where he's living, if he's on his own or if he's found another family. It's stupid, but I wake up and write them down. Or I'll daydream about him and then shake it right out of my head because he doesn't deserve it. But the thoughts always come back."

"You think he misses us?" he asked.

"I hope so," I said.

He nodded.

"I'm going to miss you," I told him.

He pulled me into his side.

"These three days with you gone have felt awful. Church was the worst."

"Why?"

"I couldn't stop wondering about you. I couldn't stand not knowing where you were. I thought maybe you were running away, like maybe you'd hopped a train and were gone for good." I remembered looking at the window, my brother standing there, outside, listening. "I wish we had a stained glass window," I said.

He laughed. "Why?"

"Something calming about it."

"Yeah. Where do you think we'd put it?" he asked.

"Maybe the front door or, better yet, the shed," I said.

"Why would you want it in the shed?"

"Not *inside* the shed but a window for whichever wall faces the sun. Just a closet with a window, but we'd have our own sanctuary. We could go there whenever we were feeling worked up or out of sorts. Sit down in the dirt and just stare at it, think about whatever you wanted to."

"Sanctuary," he said to himself. He could have been imagining the setup I'd described, or maybe he was contemplating his own sacred place. He stood and pulled me to my feet. "Let's get going," he said.

We walked slowly, careful not to trip on any of the severed trunks or roots along the path. On the way we must've spooked a deer. We stopped after hearing it rustle the fallen leaves, then listened to the crackling sound echo and fade as it bounded off through the forest.

After my heart had returned to a normal rate, I asked him, "Have you ever seen anything strange—in the woods, I mean?"

"That's why I spend so much time out here." We continued walking.

"What do you mean?"

"The woods always give you something different, something unexpected."

"Yesterday—" I said, but my voice crimped in my throat.

"What did you see?"

I recounted the whole episode to the best of my ability, every hazy detail, but speaking it aloud had a quelling effect. I began to feel foolish, hearing myself stammer, attempting to describe it, how many times I tried to liken it to something known—it was like, like, like . . . I half-expected him to laugh, but he patiently listened and teased out every facet of my experience.

"It's difficult when we see something no one else does," he said.

And I wanted to ask him had he seen something like this before, but I felt him cooling somewhat, and I didn't want to break the spell of our conversation. No doubt he was exhausted, starving. It wasn't much farther to our house, and it seemed like something else was on his mind.

At last he said: "I don't think I'm as smart as they think I am, Cindy, but what if I went there, to this special school, and there were more kids like me, and less kids like . . . . It might give me a chance to start again, clean slate. You know what I mean? Without . . . so much behind me."

I nodded.

"I might even try being somebody new out there. Somebody else."

"I don't want you to be anybody else," I said. "You're better than they are, and they don't like you for it. That's what this is all about. You're different."

"Hmm."

"It's good that you're different."

"Is it?" he said but less like a question.

I thought about what I'd said, if I really meant it. Hadn't I often whispered, in the pit of my heart: If he could only be less *himself*—at school, at least, around other people. Let me keep my brother *here* as he is, but everywhere else, make him someone else.

"How are you going to be somebody else?" I asked.

"I've been thinking about that."

"Oh?"

"Yeah, I've been watching people and listening. I'm going to do the stuff other kids do. Like that kid Thomas. You know him?"

"Yeah."

"Always looks you in the eyes when he's talking. I see him put his hand on other kids' shoulders. Makes a joke. Kind of goofy."

"You've made me laugh before, but I've never seen you goofy."

"People just want to relax a little," he said. "And talk about themselves. He likes to ask people questions."

"Like what?"

"Anything, even if you know the answer already. People like to talk when they know what they're talking about. I think that's why he asks people questions about themselves. People like to feel learned." He tried out a false voice, something about two decades older than his own: *How's your day been, Cindy? Where'd you get that denim shirt? I like it.*

I laughed a little for the first time in three days. Then slowly, the thought crept in, perhaps I'd somehow tricked myself into believing that he didn't want or need any friends. He seemed so content— hadn't he always sought to be on his own? Perhaps it hurt too much to believe he needed someone. Perhaps I feared that the someone he needed could only be me.

"It'll be better for everyone," he said.

"How so?"

"You might make new friends too."

"Who's new?"

"Well, you might pick back up your old friends?"

"Ugh. Like Mira," I said.

"Mousey Mira wouldn't speak unless it was to go 'squeak squeak,'" he said.

Which I enjoyed immensely. "Do Hannah," I said.

"Hannah, Hannah, prissy snob, always good for a quick job," he said.

I laughed harder at this. "What does that even mean?" I said.

"I'm still working on it."

"Now Calvin."

"Sidekick Calvin, friend of Doug, psychos only need a nudge."

As we neared the path's end, we could see a dim yellow rectangle of light through the trees, our kitchen window, but there in the woods the light was very faint, and I realized I'd been holding my brother's hand for some time. At the edge of the yard, we paused. Close to him, I peered through the darkness to see his face just visible beneath the shade of his green hat. Something about the contour of his jawline had changed, a certain angle now, a new hardness. In the shadows it seemed his cheekbones were higher, his face longer, his eyes grayer.

"It's a pity," he said, looking toward the house, "we'll never know if my contraption worked."

"You mean your physics project?" I said.

He just nodded, solemn as ever, and we walked to the house together, where Mother waited at the kitchen table, a glass of milk and a plate of cold chicken set out for him.

THE BRIDGE

I began again, taking walks alone this week. Cindy left for her last year at the women's college about a month ago. The garden's about done. A few hard tomatoes, nubby cucumbers, spotty bell peppers—all that's left—that and drying-out flowers. Sunflowers and zinnias. Those giant sunflowers that won't finally fall down, standing there like scolded dead men with their big heads hung low. I'd kick them over, but I like to see the birds come by. I miss the goldfinches when the sunflowers are gone. Not much to do in the afternoons now but save my zinnia seeds in a paper bag, go back inside. But I'm going stir crazy. I've got to stretch my legs, and I can't just sit around wishing Mother was still living. Taking care of her here was hard, but now I know how much she gave me those months during her decline. I had someone home, someone to care for, to talk with, to worry over, and it was difficult, yes, and I suppose I was somewhat relieved by the end, but God almighty is it quiet now. So that's why I've started walking again.

For weeks now, I've avoided the woods. I walk all along the perimeter of our yard, sometimes down the dirt driveway to the road, and if I've lost enough of my good sense, I go along the road a way, but it's too hilly, and it becomes too much for me quickly. Every step I think, "Imagine what you've walked so far, how tired you are; double it by the time you get home." Ray used to pick at me for being such a homebody. I think of him more than I'd like to admit, especially now, with everyone gone. I think of them all. My son's been gone a little past six years. Most mornings my brain is like the hard-packed earth. Walking loosens something up. All that blood and oxygen shakes out the memories, I guess. Some good things but many things I'd rather not revisit. I tell myself what's done is done, but then I go on digging those old skeletons right out of the ground. I owe them that. At least that. My thoughts.

I write them letters. Not so many now. Cindy hardly ever replies, and when she does, it's next to nothing. She's so private. Always has been. I'm glad this is her last year at school. I hardly ever write my son. They sent a bundle of my letters back to me unopened from where they're keeping him now—it's not a prison, they tell me, but it might as well be. I've started walking into the woods—just the short stretch to the creek. Not every day either. Sometimes I sit down on a tree root there and watch the water. That's when I remember him the most.

The days are getting shorter. By the time I get home from the drugstore in town, there's hardly light enough to do the walking I've grown accustomed to, so I've started waking with the sunrise. The morning dew soaks my shoes. I think I'll get a better pair with some waterproof. Such extravagance. But the world owes me this—that's what I say to myself when I buy something I actually do need. My routine is to circle the yard once, then head through the woods, to the creek and back several times. It's a well-trod path now. I've trampled out what little undergrowth there was. Didn't he build a bridge over the creek somewhere? Wasn't he always building something? I recall him dragging boards and tools out to the woods. He'd stay gone for half a day, it seemed. What would he have been working on otherwise?

I've found I enjoy the woods stretch of my walk the best, but I am bored with the back-and-forth of it. I followed the creek up both ways, but there's no bridge anywhere. I remember once, he'd tacked two long two-by-four planks together, and they'd use that to cross over. It was a bit of a balancing act. The first time I crossed it, he held my hand and walked in the water, guiding me to the other side. My feet were wet by the end. I suppose a good, hard rain washed it away.

As luck would have it, a storm with heavy winds blew through the other night. Something told me to follow the creek again, and sure enough, a nice tulip poplar had fallen across the creek not too far from his trail. This mossy tree is straight with only a few branches to navigate around, but they give me something to hold onto as I go. It is a good, healthy tree, and it is likely to still be here when I am gone. I tried it out a few times. I might bring the hedge shears and clean it up a tad, and, maybe I'm silly in feeling this way, but it feels like a world's been open for me. The creek had been just enough headache to keep me from going farther before, but now I can really experience all the work he put into carving these paths and trails in the woods here. This must be what he felt every time he discovered something new out here.

I like working at the drugstore because it gets me out of my nest here and into town, and I like church, especially at night because it feels good to be with other people under warm lights. But whether I'm at work, in town, or at church, I find my thoughts returning to these morning walks: I'm always thinking about getting up early, lacing up my new walking boots, grabbing my stick, and heading for the trails. My son carved us all walking sticks. Nothing too fancy but different wood for the three of us. He stained and varnished them and burnt our names in capital letters in the tops where your hand goes. Each morning I take my stick firmly in hand, and I think: This is my choice. This is how I've decided to spend what little time I'm accorded. I don't have to sit around and mope because they're gone. I walk the same paths my son walked, the ones he's left me, and think of them all—Ray, my parents, my children—almost like a prayer or a meditation. And I'm in a trance, the time disappears, and the next thing I know, my little wristwatch is beeping, and it's time for me to return to the house, grab a quick breakfast, and head to town.

The path leads to the train tracks. I walk to the edge of the tracks, but I don't linger there. I rarely walk them. Six years later—it's still too soon. Yet something draws me there. I can feel myself building up to it. I will one day. I will walk them as freely as he walked them.

Today my walk shook loose a few childhood memories from my mind. I was recalling one Christmas we, Mother and I, went to town. I was riding down the main street with Mother and my grandfather, remembering how it looked then, the excitement of being surrounded by new clothes and toys and people but also a twinge of sadness that day. And the next thing I know, my foot is slipping on the cool moss of my poplar bridge. I'm a second before toppling when I somehow have the sense to let my other foot go, and I land on my butt, sitting like the way I've seen ladies ride horses on television. I sit there awhile and think about the possibilities. It's barely a six-foot drop into the creek. Falling in would've probably only been unpleasant. I would've had to drag my soggy self back home, maybe only wounded pride, and even then, who's to know but me? But what if I'd broken a leg, an ankle, or hip? Could've broken my neck. Imagine landing there, helpless, broken, in the water. And if I could've crawled out, could I crawl all the way home to call for help? I'm almost fifty. How is it I've never thought of how vulnerable I am here, alone? I've lived my entire life here this way, as I please, giving little thought to such, but now there's no one here but me.

This morning, before my walk, I left a note in the mailbox for the mailman: "If you ever see my mail pile up for three days, send somebody to look for me." I suppose the folks at the drugstore might think something was up if I didn't come in to work, but I wouldn't bet my life on Nancy, who is more likely to be annoyed at having to work my hours. I've started carrying an old messenger bag of my son's with a few supplies, just for peace of mind, maybe for the time being.

It's been some weeks since my near fall. Colder now. My walks have felt different since then. I've tried to be more cautious, but this has made me tentative, skittish. I see a bad-looking root in the path, picture the toe of my boot catching it, falling, bloodying my face, throwing my shoulder out, passing out from pain, and so on. I'll think: You've got to get control of this. Don't be a ninny or, worse, a coward. And then I'll hear something dash through the woods, and it'll nearly scare the life out of me. Probably just a deer, but my mind leaps to black bear, though I've never seen one in all my years living here. I knew men who used to hunt bear. When I was a child, Father did. I heard something the other day that sounded much heavier than a deer, so I started carrying my son's bear stick. Ursa Stick, he called it. It's about twelve inches long with a sharpened point on one end and a smoothed-out ball at the other. I think it was mostly a joke to himself. Things would have to be pretty dire if it came to needing this pointy little club. I never saw him carry one, but there was a while he would carve one out every month or so. I dulled one using it as a plant peg in the garden. I carry a sharp one now, probably as he did, as a charm.

I was nearing the end of the path, at the train tracks, when, at the final turn, a man was standing with his back to me. He had on an army-green pair of work pants, a long field jacket with a high collar, and a floppy, old hat that looked like it'd seen a lot of rain. He carried a sack over one shoulder, and he held a walking stick. I'd been walking quietly, so my instinct was to back away and go home, but as soon as I turned, I heard him calling me, greeting me. I thought, Do not tell this man anything about yourself. We began to speak to each other, awkwardly, rolling out a few pleasantries, but he seemed easygoing and not all that interested, nor did he seem surprised by my being there. He had a long face that bore signs of having spent years in the elements, gray stubble, dark eyes, and a way of squinting them that made him appear as though he was deeply considering something he could not determine. I said goodbye and returned home, I admit, deeply unsettled.

It's a fantasy to believe we can exist unperturbed by others, even in our own private fairyland. Hadn't I always warned my children about the dangers of walking along the tracks? Trains besides, this was the very thing I'd had in mind: vagrants, drifters, whatever you want to call them, these loners are too far along the edge to be trusted. A pilgrim. A stranger. What moves them to wander? And who knows what they leave in their wake? How must it be to have no home? These questions burned inside me, piling up like embers for days, until we met again, not so far from where we'd first met, sooner than before. So I spoke to him. His voice was deep and smooth except for a slight husky tenor when he'd begin. He spoke in a manner I recall from reading old leftover books and newspaper clippings Father had kept in a trunk by his bed. I said, Where are you from? *From the dust, child. From beaten highways and windswept prairies, hollows and mountains. Everywhere I've been is where I'm from.* Are you staying here? *For a spell, for a spell.* And he asked the same of me, but I could not lie, though I thought to. He said, *Yes, your home is written in the cracks along your eyes, your smile, and you carry it upon your shoulders, upon your back.* It's not easy, I said, being the one who stays. *Whether we plant our roots or tear them from the earth, we bear our burden, heavy in our branches.* Are you so burdened? I asked, but he did not answer. I wished him well and left him there.

The third time we met, we were halfway between the creek and the tracks. I was startled to find him so close. He seemed even wearier than before. I asked him if he was feeling okay. I gave him an apple and a pack of peanut butter crackers that I kept in my bag. He took the apple, polished it on the outside of his jacket, and placed it in his coat pocket. The package of crackers he puzzled over, as if he'd never seen them before, and placed it inside his sack. *It's dangerous*, he said. Excuse me? I said. *Being a woman, alone in the wilderness. You must live near here*, he said. I told him I did. He seemed to know as much already anyway.

I walk now half-expecting to see him. Where once the walk alone occupied my thoughts—the beauty of the forest around me—now, I can't stop wondering whether I will encounter the stranger again. I don't always. I bring him a little something, a biscuit, a blueberry muffin, a pack of crackers. He never eats in front of me. Our exchanges are short, but I've found myself sharing far too much, about myself, about the others, thoughts that have occurred along my walks as autumn has worn on. Today we met not far from the creek. I noticed something odd. His cracked hands are strangely neat, the slender fingers of a banker or musician. He has a look of coarseness about him everywhere but his hands. And was that a lady's ring on his small finger? A tiny golden band. I haven't worn mine in years. Ray and I skipped the engagement part. He said let's get married, and we went ahead. I forget where I put it.

Searched all last night for my wedding ring. I thought it would be in the strongbox with all the papers and deeds, but of all places, it was in the bottom of Grandmother's old brass candleholder—there in the bottom where the wax collects. The gold against the brass was almost impossible to see. I don't recall leaving it there, but maybe there was a time I used to drop my keys and pocket change there. But that doesn't make sense. I wasn't in the habit of removing my ring before Ray left. I'm pretty sure I continued to wear it years after. I tried it on. Couldn't get it past the knuckle. It's in the strongbox now. Funny how you sit in your house, night after night, surrounded by these objects with so much history, so much significance to you, that to anyone else would mean nothing. Strange how we go blind to such fixtures. It was silly to think he'd stolen my ring. Why would he do such a thing? And if he did, why would he be so brazen about it? What's more, would he know this is my house? I keep looking over the rest of the house now, studying to see if anything else seems moved or out of place.

I haven't seen him in three days. Why did I used to take these walks? Wasn't it because I was getting so restless at the end of summer? I needed something else to do. I was bored and lonely. But it seemed to turn into something else. Hadn't it become a kind of way to remember them? To feel closer to everyone in my life who has left me? And now I find my thoughts rarely turning to them; instead, I wonder if I will meet the stranger, and where, and what he will say, what more I will learn. Maybe he's moved on.

I knew I'd see him today. I had only walked the short stretch from my bridge back to the path, and when I looked up, there he was, leaning against a tree, waiting for me, there by the water where I rejoin the trail. Finding him there, waiting for me as I made my way back to the path from my poplar bridge—well, I felt violated, like I was being spied upon, like a secret of mine had been spoiled. He said, *It appears you've found your way.* I usually addressed him first. He reached out his hand. I gave him a chicken thigh from last night's dinner, wrapped in aluminum foil, and a handful of red grapes from my bag. He received them with a cupped, hand. No golden ring, I noticed. I almost said, This is the beginning of the trail, which is obviously untrue. He could clearly see how the trail leads beyond the creek. I said, I have much farther to go, instead. *Your son joins you today,* he said. I told him my son didn't live with me anymore, that he lived with strangers, in a cold, unfeeling place. I looked to his face and noticed for the first time, one of his eyes was green and the other a pale blue. *No*, he said. *Your second son. Go, now. Walk with him*. I felt the blood leave my body. My feet and legs began to push me farther, seemingly without my effort. I walked swiftly, putting distance between us. At the tracks I stumbled up the embankment and sat cross-legged between the rails for quite some time, contemplating his words. I had never spoken so frankly with him about my family. How could he know about my lost son? Aaron. I spoke his name aloud. In that instant I felt him with me, felt him inside me, growing, kicking— the way I'd felt him those last few months—and I felt an unutterable joy. I waited there, caught in this feeling, until the train sounded its horn. I rose stiffly, slowly, panicking inside, but I grabbed my things and stepped away and watched the train until it disappeared, until a gusting wind had dried my cheeks.

At the drugstore I relived every bit of yesterday. A customer would ask me where to find something, I'd ring up a sale, and then I would start it all back over, experiencing it bit by bit. I did not walk today, nor will I walk in the morning. I will keep and ponder these things.

I had never walked beyond the stranger before. That day, when I passed the place where I'd found him waiting for me, he wasn't there anymore. I realize now that our walks had always ended with our encounters—I think because I didn't want to find him, upon my return, at any other point of the trail, standing between me and home. The thought filled me with dread. Something isn't right about this. Everything's spoiled now. They're calling for snow tonight. The first one.

I met him today. Snow was falling. He was waiting for me, standing at the middle of my poplar bridge. Today, elevated above the land, over the water, he seemed much taller than I remember. Less stooped. *Beautiful, isn't it?* he said, opening wide his arms, letting the flakes fall into his hands. I noticed he wore a vest under his jacket. Blue pinstripe. I thought of my father. A gold watch chain led to a pocket there. Didn't my son wear them once, to school? One Halloween? A train conductor. I wouldn't let him take Father's watch, just the chain, so he carved one out of wood, and with a hammer, he fashioned two gold jar lids around the wood to make a case that would open. He carried it with him for months after. He was a child. I reached for the Ursa Stick in my bag. Maybe only to make sure that it was still there. Maybe not. He said, *Would you strike a man with a club for a bear?* I said to him: You are no longer welcome here. I wish you to leave. Do not come back. He lowered his hands and stared at me. He removed his hat and held it over his heart. His hairless head, bare in the snow, gave him a vulnerable, pitiful look. He looked tired. Like he hadn't slept in years, like he'd spent those years on his feet. He reached for the watch in his pinstripe pocket. It's time for you to go, I said. Our eyes met. I watched as the blue eye changed to yellow and, for a few seconds, glowed. *We are of the earth. We are many things. We are what remains.* He blinked, the eye was blue again. *You will not see me again.* He replaced the hat on his head, he turned, and he walked away.

It was a long time before I could go into my son's room. Surrounded by all his possessions—things on the windowsill, on the nightstand, on his bookshelf—I felt suffocated. After the disaster, after it was clear to me my son would never come home again, I gathered all the things scattered around his room and put them in an old cardboard box that I placed on an upper shelf in his closet. In the box were mostly the kind of things all boys find in the woods, but there were other items special to him lying around. The pocket watch he created was one I distinctly remember finding on the bookshelf. He had painted the face to look like my father's: pearly white face, ticks for numbers, careful hands that had the spade shape before the points. I hadn't taken the box down, I hadn't held his things, hadn't even sat on the bed in his room for more than a few minutes since he left. The pocket watch is still there. Eleven thirty-seven.

In spite of everything, I still walk these woods—my son's path, the meandering rabbit trails, my cut-through to the fallen poplar, on to the tracks and back again—but I am not scared. Each day, each step, in blood and breath, I feel my fear drifting away through time.

Here, these dark winter evenings, it seems I have nothing more to write about. I think of my visitor often, but I have no one to tell such stories to now. I am told that last night's dreams, left unspoken, fade off into nothing, forgotten. I have forgotten very little in this life. But I will leave these days here, in this book, and I will never speak of them to anyone. I haven't any room in my heart for such darkness. *Cindy will be home in the spring.* I whisper these words like a prayer when my thoughts become wayward. Though gone, I still possess each of them, Cindy, my husband, my sons. And should we never meet again this side of eternity, I will bear them with me always.

THE AMNESIACS

Tonight I have the misfortune of being stuck with the section by the fireplace where the Morrisons, two white-haired members who tend to linger, paw at each other like libidinous teenagers long after their after-dinner drinks and coffees are gone. As the night wears on and the dining room has emptied, the staff not so quietly sets up and dresses the long tables needed for the enormous buffet that is Sunday brunch, a not-so-subtle hint for the Morrisons to stop nuzzling and go home—we do everything but cut on the house lights—but even after all the racket, the couple remains. The servers are in a hurry because tomorrow is Paulina from Prague's last Sunday brunch, and even though everyone still has to work the buffet brunch, the boys—Burt in particular—want to give her a proper American send-off. There will be liquor, loud music, dancing, flirting, coupling, and high spirits all around at staff housing. Come to the girls' trailer, Paulina and Celeste's. Bring a friend, et cetera, et cetera. Not really my thing. Probably won't go.

After setup, all the kitchen staff, management, and servers leave, except for me. I'm drinking coffee in the wait station, checking on the Morrisons every five minutes. I'm not quite alone. A boy named Mark, who is desperately in love with me, is waiting with me, and I can hear Alec the bartender restocking the bar with clean glasses. Mark seems to think he's doing me a favor by hanging around. He still thinks of me as "new," even though I've worked here almost two months now. He buses my tables from time to time and even runs food for me, though I never ask him to. He says he'll stick around and help me break down and clean up, and he'll walk me to my car for safety. He's nice, but it's all a little embarrassing.

We're sitting on the floor in the wait station, talking, when Alec peeks his head around the corner. "Lovebirds have flown," he says.

I get my tray to bus their table—nothing left now but empty coffee cups and a few saucers smeared with chocolate torte and raspberry currant jam. Mark flips a switch, and the enormous brass chandelier and its children light up the empty dining room. He cuts the gas off from the fireplace.

Alec returns to the barroom adjacent to the dining room. It is fully stocked, but this is a scotch and soda crowd. Rarely will anyone order a drink more challenging than a mojito or an old-fashioned.

"You done in there?" Mark yells in his direction.

"Nah. I'm going to mop, marry some bottles, drink what's left in the spill mat—same old junk," he yells back. "Door's locked. Y'all can leave whenever."

I take all the dirties to the dish pit in the kitchen, and when I come out, Mark's taken off his apron, and his shirttail's untucked. "So, you're coming to the party tonight, right?" he asks.

"I'm not much of a drinker. Not like you guys, anyway," I say. "Did you invite Alec?"

"Alec? I don't remember. Probably someone else did."

"Are you going to?" I ask.

"Alec! Are you going to the party at staff housing?" he yells loud enough to be heard over the television in the bar.

We wait, but it sounds like he didn't hear. He almost shouts again, but Alec yells, "When?"

"Now! It's already started without us," Mark yells back.

We hear a muffled reply that sounds noncommittal at best.

Once everything is cleared and clean, we shut it down and leave Alec to lock up. Out in the parking lot, I ask, "Do you think he's coming?"

Mark says: "That's his way. He makes like he has other plans, but then he shows up fashionably late as usual. What else is he going to do?

We'd walk over to his trailer and drag him out if he didn't. I think he likes to wait until everyone's had a few rounds because then when you walk through the door, they cheer a little louder. Of course, there's an art to it—if you wait too late, then everyone's groggy and passed out."

"Sounds fun," I say.

"It's okay if it's not your thing. They know that, and it'll mean even more to them when you show up," he says.

I tell him I'll go this time, but no promises on how long I'll stay. The drive from the club to my apartment in the city is long enough without being sleepy. He asks me for a ride down to "Rancho Desierto," which is what they affectionately call staff housing. He says he may not be fit to drive in the morning and laughs.

Cool, I think.

On the way Mark says he's spending the night at Nik the Bulgarian's trailer, and he'll catch a ride on the company van back for brunch in the morning. "Nik's got an empty room since that line cook was fired. Too bad about him—drank too much to get to work on time. Shook so bad he couldn't assemble side salads," he says. "You know, he was a smart guy too. He had degrees in philosophy and horticulture."

"That's a sad story," I say.

"They're a sad bunch, kitchen staff," he says. "They've all got some kind of hard luck, whether it's a pregnant thirteen-year-old daughter, a drinking or gambling problem or both, cheating on their wives with the servers, or wives that won't stop cheating on them."

"What's Alec's problem?" I ask.

"Alec?"

"Yeah, there's a bit of mystery to him, isn't there?" I say.

"He's a special case."

"How so?"

"He's got amnesia," Mark says. "He doesn't know anything about who he is or where he's from."

"How is that? With all his stories? It seems like he's lived everywhere a little while," I say. "During the staff meal tonight, I heard him talk about working in a bar in Durango, having run-ins with the Latvian mob."

"Oh yeah, that exiled Latvian princess. But that wasn't so long ago. He can remember recent stuff, anything before whatever happened to him. He's been on the road ever since. Burt thinks he got thrown off a motorcycle or a horse or something—he's got that rugged look, you know?—and it broke something loose in his brain. Me, I think it was something else entirely, like he survived a black bear attack back East or he witnessed something horrible like a drug deal gone wrong while camping in the Pacific Northwest and it traumatized him. Nervous breakdown."

We're passing decadent multimillion-dollar homes, each with their accent lighting and Spanish tile and illuminated fountains, nestled among the sparse trees that will grow out here at the foot of the Sandias. It takes a good fifteen minutes to simply get back on the main road.

"All those stories are interesting, charming even, for a while, but whenever we talk, I always get the feeling he's hiding something. Don't you ever wonder where he's from or who he really is?"

"*He* wonders who he really is. He's got amnesia, Sharon," Mark says, sounding increasingly defensive. "You know, I doubt he's from around here. He doesn't look like us or talk like us, does he?" Mark stares at me. "Come to think of it, you don't either. You sound almost like Tennessee or West Virginia mountains or—"

"Maybe he's just private."

"Huh?"

"Nothing." I pull away from the club entrance onto the highway and point the car to the desert.

Rancho Desierto is six single-wide trailers bought on the cheap a few years ago and moved out to the desert. Staff housing used to be a short walk from the dining room and clubhouse, but the members complained about clandestine midnight gatherings at the pool and loud music coming from the commons, so the club bought a barren plot halfway between their gated community and the city.

When we get there, the music's already thumping through the aluminum walls of Paulina and Celeste's trailer. From a distance it sounds like polka.

"I'm surprised Celeste will allow any of this," I say. Celeste is a shift captain. I learned very quickly, if you're not on her good side, she punishes servers with the worst sections or large-family tables with small children or husbands with wives who talk them out of extra gratuity. She's a senior at the nearby university, majoring in education. She wants to teach high school Spanish. Sometimes, on slow nights, she chats up the Honduran dishwasher in Spanish for practice. He does not seem impressed.

"Celeste's staying with her boyfriend back in town. A bit of good luck for once," he says.

We walk up the stairs of the trailer's tiny deck, at which time Burt comes around the corner of the trailer, zipping his pants and fastening his belt. "Oh, hi guys," he says. "Come on in. Party's on me."

The lights are low inside, mostly just the speckled snow from the television and a light down the hall from the open bathroom door. Someone's burning incense on the stove. Our names are celebrated simultaneously—Sharon and Mark—and it comes out like "Shaaark." Before I can see who's here, Burt's behind us, offering us drinks.

"Good stuff tonight, guys. What'll it be?" he says.

The table in the kitchen looks like a cityscape with bottles for buildings, all shapes and heights and colors catching the dim lights over the stove and above the sink.

Mark wants a Cuba libre, and I don't want anything, but Burt mixes me a cosmopolitan because that's what all the ladies drink at the club. He's elated to give it to me and seems proud that he knows how to make the drink, so I feel pressured to show my enjoyment. I take a sip and do so.

"Shar-onnn!" he says, and a few people around the trailer whoop.

Nik is in the corner with a stack of used CDs previous tenants have left behind and a small boom box he purchased early in the season. He has little use for American pop, so he's dialed in on a Mexican radio station that seems to never break for commercials. He's talking with the Honduran dishwasher, broken Spanish with a Russian accent.

Paulina's sitting on the floor sipping from a short glass filled with merlot, leaning into Vince the Virgin's arms. Rather than fully sensing the electricity in the occasion, Vince seems hell-bent on hearing and understanding her because he was raised by conservative Baptists, and he can't appreciate that a beautiful European woman who will be returning to her homeland in a week is touching his leg and whispering warm, wine-soaked words into his ear. Burt catches me noticing this moment and swoops in. He plops down next to Paulina and clinks his liquor bottle against her glass. She wants the moment back. Vince sips his Coke and grenadine.

All in all there are probably fourteen or so people there, most in the living room and kitchen but a few in the bedrooms on the ends of the trailer. A girl from South Carolina has a huge CD wallet filled with concert bootlegs of some awful jam band with a saxophone she's begging Nik to play, but then a boy comes in with an acoustic guitar. The girl from South Carolina flocks to him, and now she's begging him to play the band's songs. A lanky boy who works with the tennis pro is virtually yanking her away from the boy with the guitar. Paulina steps outside for a smoke. I join her.

She lights her cigarette and hops on the railing of the deck. After a few puffs, she lets it burn between her fingers by her side and sighs. She laughs and says, "You don't like parties?"

"It's a lot to take in," I say.

"What is this?" she says when the language won't quite translate.

"I mean—too much going on," I say. "Music, drinking, shouting, people—it's too much."

She understands and agrees.

"Are you sad to be leaving America?" I ask.

"Oh, so-so," she says.

"You'll miss your roommate?" I say, and she laughs heartily, a cloud of smoke filling the air.

"No, no, no, no, no. Miss Celeste? I will miss the silence that follows when she slams the door on her way to see her boyfriend." She laughs again. "Will I miss America?" she says. "*This*?" She gestures at the expanse of desert darkness surrounding us.

"It's not all desert," I say.

"I know this. That's why I will be traveling awhile before I return," she says.

Burt and Mark join us on the deck. Burt's mop of sweaty, curly hair gives him a wild look, but he has kind eyes. I worry he'll be working as a waiter his whole life. Celeste has harped on him all season about managing his hair, not keeping a dish towel halfway shoved in his pocket, "making fine dining look like flag football," and not loading up dirties on a tray jack near members' tables—all to no avail. He's been a waiter in too many dives now to turn into a server of fine dining. It's also clear he's dated many waitresses in the countless restaurants where he's worked. Paulina smokes more than speaks once he arrives.

Mark says: "So, Burt, how'd you manage all this? The booze, I mean. Did the Proctors' table tip you that well?"

"Let's just say 'Project Inventory Shave' played out flawlessly," Burt says and takes another swig from his bottle.

Mark's face looks immediately ashen. He spends the next few minutes prodding Burt for details until he finally admits that he swiped Alec's key to the liquor room and carted off every partial bottle in the room.

"You can't be serious," Mark says. "They inventory that shit. They'll know right away. You think Alec won't see?"

"I cooked the books, man. I'm no idiot. And Alec's no fink. He won't say anything."

"This is bad. This is very bad. Why were there partials in the liquor room?" Mark says.

"Must've been left over from an off-site party. I don't know," Burt says.

About this time, a set of headlights turns onto the path that leads to the trailer.

"Who's that?" Burt says.

"I don't know," Mark says.

"Celeste," Paulina says.

"Shit!" Mark says.

Burt chugs the rest of his bottle and slams it on the ground below the deck. It shatters.

Celeste's car pulls up. She gets out, alone. "What the hell's all this?" she shouts.

Burt can't explain, lie, or plead fast enough. She's storming into the trailer, and each room she enters makes her angrier. She stomps into her bedroom. Two startled people are on her bed, no longer entwined, still half-naked. We're all waiting for her to scream, bark orders, make threats, explode in a fit of rage, but instead, she grows quiet. The two gather their things and leave her room, and she slams the door behind them.

"Should we move the party to another trailer?" Mark asks above the music, because we're all inside now. "Can you cut it down a tad?" he says to Nik, who rolls his eyes and continues talking to the dishwasher.

"Maybe you should go talk to her," Burt says to Paulina. "She hates me. If you talk to her, maybe we won't have to end the party."

Paulina sighs, says, "Here," and thrusts her drink into Burt's hands, sloshing wine on the carpet. She walks down the hall, and we see her disappear into Celeste's room.

We're all wondering how this conversation is going when the rest of the trailer shouts, "Alec!" He raises both hands in the doorway like a guest about to take a seat on one of the late shows. Burt rushes to the booze island to get Alec a drink. I see he's turning a few of the bottles so their labels face the wall. Watching him check over his shoulder makes me feel complicit somehow. He comes back with a tall gin and tonic. "Where's the goodbye girl?" Alec asks.

The boys catch him up.

Before Alec can respond, Paulina returns and says: "She was dumped by her boyfriend tonight. It was—messy. I offered to get her a drink, and she seemed interested."

"What does that bitch drink?" Burt says, moving toward the table. "Warm vermouth? White wine spritzer? Frozen strawberry daiquiri with coconut rum?"

"Just mix her what you made Sharon and try to be kinder to her," she says.

Paulina brings the drink to Celeste's room, and not long after, the two of them come out to the living room. Celeste is quiet at first. The boys talk about work, Paulina chitchats with Alec, but I can barely hear them. I move in closer.

"You shouldn't leave without seeing the Grand Canyon," he's saying.

"Ah! Spend a whole summer in the desert, only to holiday in a giant hole in the ground. I don't see what the fuss is all about. I'll find some pictures," she says.

"Maybe you're right. You might be more of a redwoods kind of person. I am, myself," he says, and he begins laying out her route, telling her about the waterfalls at Big Sur.

I've heard all this talk from Alec before, and it bores me. College boys like Mark who are itching to conquer the world, starting with America; local girls who've never made it to the other side of the mountains, maybe never even Santa Fe, who fantasize about latching onto someone from somewhere else; Eastern European work exchangers who want proof, who want to believe everything they've been told by their parents and friends about this country and all its glory and contradictions—it's for them, and they can have every last bit of it.

As I try not to listen, a wave of weariness crashes over me. I've worked a double. It's been a long night. I have another thirty-minute drive to my place outside the city. This one drink on an empty stomach is making my face feel warm, like I might sleep standing up. I'm trying to think of a graceful way to tell them I'm leaving when I hear Celeste say, "And where the hell did you get all this liquor?"

Burt's head swivels like a ventriloquist is operating him. His brain's doing cartwheels trying to weave an impromptu web of lies.

She walks over to the table. "I've bartended enough private parties for the club to recognize our labels. Whoever stole all this stuff is in deep, deep—"

"Just hold on a minute, Celeste," Mark says. "Let Burt talk."

While Burt fumbles all over his words, I notice Alec walking over to the table. He turns a few of the bottles around, then looks dead ahead like someone's caught him, like he's the guilty one.

"Did you think we wouldn't notice?" Celeste is shouting now.

Alec butts in before Burt can do anymore damage and says we should reconvene outside. On the deck he says: "Look, he did something stupid. I get why he thought this would work." Addressing Celeste, he says: "Think of it this way—you know we charge members for every seal that's broken." Burt nodding all the while. "These bottles were already paid for. It's really a victimless crime. You can see why he would think that?" Alec goes on. "He's wrong, of course." Burt looking puzzled. "He's taken for granted that every further drink goes back into the profit margin, but you can't expect a server to think like a manager or even a shift captain like yourself. Right?"

Celeste, beginning to feel she's losing ground.

"So, the way I see it, if Burt replaces these partial bottles with full ones, he's only increased the profit margin, and it truly is, as they say, 'no harm, no foul,'" Alec says.

Celeste, looking annoyed and defeated.

"But I can't afford this liquor. That's why I stole—"

Mark elbowing Burt in the ribs hard enough to break one loose.

"All we have to do," Alec says, "is take stock of all you see here—all the bottles on the table and in the trash—and we'll replace them before anyone knows they're gone. The club will make some extra money, and our boy here's learned a valuable lesson."

Celeste, quietly assenting.

Alec organizes the whole operation. I get my pen and pad from my apron in the car and take notes while everyone shouts labels at me.

"Who's going to pay for all this?" Celeste asks, her voice cartoonishly high now.

"Don't worry your pretty little head," Alec says. "Have another drink. On the house."

He tells Mark and me to come with him. He lays out a plan for how to best erase all evidence of Burt's antics. Since we are the most sober available options—aside from Vince the Virgin, who Paulina clearly has plans for—we will accompany him to the city to pick up all the replacement liquor. Alec's sports car only seats two, the company van is out of the question since any extra mileage on the ledger would raise suspicion, and in short, we need my car. I'm feeling dull by the alcohol already—again, empty stomach—so I ask one of them to drive.

"Sure thing," Alec says, leaning on the deck railing like a cowboy against a fence. "Hey, what's this?" He is looking down at the hard ground below the deck. "Broken bottle?"

"Oh, yeah. Burt smashed that one after he drained it. That should be the last one," Mark says. He makes a quick jaunt down the stairs and around to the shattered bottle. He picks up the label with its shards and holds it under the porch light. "MacGregor's Reserve," he announces in his best Scottish lilt.

Alec bites his lip and hangs his head. "Oh boy," he says.

"What's wrong?" I say.

"Get in the car," he says. "I'll tell you on the way."

I glance through the storm door back in the trailer's living room. Burt is talking animatedly to a tight-lipped Celeste, who is attempting to cross her arms and hold her second drink at the same time. Paulina is on the floor with Vince again, giving him a sip of her merlot. Nik has finally ceded control of the music to the girl from South Carolina, and guitars and garish horns are now blaring over a roar of drunken concertgoers. We jump into the car and head out into the night.

On the way to the city, Alec says MacGregor's Reserve is a "single-barrel scotch," and even with the financially well-endowed clientele he pours drinks for day after day, night after night, he can only remember having poured from the bottle a handful of times, maybe after a fluke hole-in-one from Mr. Byrd or the rare late-night drop-in from the septuagenarian rock star, a bass player from a band teenagers mostly know from "vintage" T-shirts. In short, the scotch is not likely to be on the shelves at the grocery store where the club regularly fills their liquor orders, where we're headed.

"I don't know what we're going to do about that one," Alec says. "I don't recall that seal being opened. Surely he didn't drink it all tonight?"

I shrug, but I doubt he sees. I'm in the passenger seat; Mark's in the back.

"Damn shame he broke the bottle. We could've filled it with something else to buy us a little time before we figure out a real solution," Alec says.

We drive on. There's not much to see in this stretch of desert before we get there. Occasionally, there's the shine of an animal's eyes sparkling too far in the distance to identify.

After riding in silence awhile, Alec asks, "So, how did Burt pull off this stunt in the first place?"

Mark leans in from the back and says, "He swiped the keys from the bar while you were gone."

"Oh yeah?" He laughs.

"He probably watched you all night instead of his tables," Mark says.

"Now that you mention it, he did seem very chatty tonight, and he didn't place many orders. And what's this all about?" Alec says.

"He wants to get in Paulina's pants," Mark says.

"And a well-stocked party was going to make him a hero? Sounds right," Alec says. "Sometimes I forget you guys are still in your twenties. Sometimes I forget I'm not."

I can't help but scoff a little at this.

"You wouldn't have pulled a stunt like this, would you?" Mark says.

I see Alec check the rearview mirror. "You know, truthfully, that's a part of my life I don't have anymore," he says.

"You mean you don't remember *anything*?" Mark says, a little too purposefully, and I feel his knee pressing deep into the passenger seat, nudging my back like maybe I'm listening to some other conversation in the car and missing this one.

"It's true. I don't remember too much of my past, particularly anything before my thirties," he says.

Mark's knee grinds into my back again. "What happened? I mean, did you have some kind of accident?" he asks. I send an elbow into the cushion.

"I wish I could tell you," Alec says. "Unfortunately, that's one of the many things I've lost."

"So, you don't remember being a kid or your first girlfriend or what kind of life you had in your twenties—what about your family?" Mark says. "Do you remember your mom and dad?"

"No."

"Man," Mark says.

"Wife. Son. Daughter," I say.

Alec startles and looks at me like maybe he's forgotten I'm sitting here, like he's already forgotten it's my car he's driving. It's been a while since I've said anything. Maybe he thought I was asleep.

"All gone," he says. "I really couldn't say. Some of my earliest memories are of finding shelters and empty houses to spend nights in . . . catching rides with strangers . . . looking out over fields of corn and wheat in the Midwest, big open skies in Montana." As he speaks, all emotion leaves his voice. His brain's on autopilot as his gravelly baritone shrinks to a mumble. "For a time there, it seemed like more than half my life has been behind a windshield, so I started looking for work. I kept thinking if I tried different jobs, maybe some task or action might jolt something loose in my mind, maybe I'd remember"—slow now, like a tape recorder with dying batteries, a robot powering down. We pass under a streetlight, and a streak of yellow moves across the hood and then his face. He blinks hard as if to clear away a blurry mirage in the distance.

When we get to the all-night grocery store, it is very late—homeless people, luckless losers, and manic college kids dragging about. The cold, white fluorescents are nauseating, assaulting my brain, demanding that it's time to be unconscious; it's time to be asleep. Mark and I start pulling bottles while Alec talks to the manager.

"Sad story, huh?" Mark says. "Can you believe it?"

"Funny you should ask," I say.

"What do you mean? You don't think he's got amnesia?" Mark asks. "It's true. That shit happens. You ever see that TV show *Amazing Mysteries of the World*? People get amnesia and end up wandering around homeless, and their families never see them again."

"Seems awfully convenient."

"A psychotic break? I don't see how that's convenient for anyone," he says.

"All that stuff in the car—didn't sound a little rehearsed to you?" I say.

"Don't you think he's had to tell it everywhere he goes? Anytime someone gets close?"

We see a stack of cardboard boxes with legs walking toward us. Alec drops them, and the tumbling sound echoes through the store. "Fill 'em up," he says.

We box what we've already picked. I let them pull the rest while I call out our checklist. When we're done, we have three full boxes.

"I can't believe no one stopped this kid carrying boxes of liquor out the back of the clubhouse," Alec says.

"All it takes is a half-hearted lie when the second party barely cares to begin with," I say and wait for his response. He gives me an odd look, like he's nervous about what I might say next, then I say: "Uhh . . . this?

This box of booze? Uhh . . . it's for an off-site party . . . uhh . . . the Alexanders, I think . . . I'm not working it. I'm only loading up," doing my best Burt impression.

"Sounds about right," Alec says, a little relieved, I think.

"It's when you're not talking to fools you have to be careful," I say.

He studies my face for a second too long.

"What's the holdup?" Mark says.

We bring the boxes to the front. "We good?" Alec says to a skinny, goateed man with black studs in his ears.

"Yep," he says back and waves us off.

We walk through the sliding doors, each with our box, and load them in the trunk.

"Who's paying for all this?" Mark says and slams the trunk.

"It'll bill to the club," he says, and we get in the car. "I told him we had a private, off-the-books party we just now realized we weren't stocked for. Party's tomorrow. What you gonna do?"

"Won't they notice there's been an extra shipment, an extra bill?" Mark asks.

"Tomorrow's problems," Alec says and backs out of the parking space.

It is more than a half-hour drive back to the trailers, even longer to get to the club. It crosses my mind to tell them to take me to my apartment and leave me there—take the car, I'll get it some other time, find another way to get to work, or maybe even never go back. I'm so tired. But then I think back to the thing Alec said about forgetting we're all in our twenties and the way he looked at me in the store, and suddenly I'm silently reviewing every interaction we've ever had together.

Away from the lights of town, we're hurtling down the stretch that's nothing but desert interrupted by the occasional security light above a lone mobile home, far off the road or up the side of a hill. On a clear night, driving through the desert can feel like shuttling through space, but tonight feels like racing through a tunnel in a cave. It takes a sudden gust or a tumbleweed across the headlight stream to remind you all directions are open space and the emptiness runs for miles and miles.

Gazing into the darkness outside my passenger window, I see a faint reflection there from the car's dashboard light. If I look long enough,

I can make out the pupils of my eyes like tiny portholes in the side of a ship. "Do you ever think about your former life?" I ask.

No one replies.

Perhaps Mark is asleep, or maybe both know the question isn't for Mark.

"Like I said," Alec says, "I don't recall any of that; it's just a blank void."

"That's not what I mean," I say. "Don't you ever find yourself day-dreaming or wondering about what was?"

Not a sound.

"Do you ever wonder about those you have left behind? If—wherever you're from—there are people back there, your home, wondering about why you left, where you are, who you've become?" I turn to face him. "Starting over seems to be a luxury only a man could afford"—his eyes still fixed on the road, far beyond the reach of the headlight beams. "Or a certain *kind* of man."

With a sudden move of his hand, there's a click and the headlight beams disappear. He presses the automatic window buttons and the windows open so a roar of wind rushes through the car. He floors the gas, and my car's small engine rises like an amplified chainsaw. I glance at the dashboard, and the needles are pushed way beyond anything I've ever seen in my car. We're gaining velocity every second. The sun-baked road is a dim landing strip, a silver river of ancient concrete in the moonlight that is slowly becoming more visible the longer we soar through the darkness.

"What the hell!" I hear Mark shout from the back seat over the rush of wind assaulting our senses, blowing my hair behind the headrest. Alec lets out the howl of a wild man-beast. He leans the top of his head out of the window, and his thick shag of salt-and-pepper hair frizzes backward, and his eyes are bulging, and his grimacing teeth are shining. "Stop it, man! Stop!" Mark shouts, and Alec lets off the gas and flicks on the lights. A jackrabbit is standing tall on its hind legs, its yellow diamond eyes; it doubles back and forth in our lane, and the car plows right over him with a heavy thump, followed by a sound like rocks hitting the undercarriage.

Mark shouts some indiscernible profanity and catches his breath.

Alec turns to me. "What did you see out there?" he says calmly, loudly.

"What?" I say.

"What did you see?" he says again, sounding now like something between an interrogator and a disciple who'd looked away at the wrong moment and missed a miracle. He rolls the windows back up to hear.

"Nothing," I say in the strange, new quiet. "I couldn't see anything. Just the hint of a road."

Alec settles back into the driver's seat, takes a deep breath, and nods in agreement. "Exactly."

I am lost in my thoughts for some time after this because before I know it, we're pulling into the drive of Season's End, a restaurant only a few miles from the club. This restaurant at the base of the Sandias is really the only other option for club members tired of our selection, and at the end of our season, when we run a limited menu again until Easter the next year, they're apparently the only show in town—or at least the nearest one.

"Look, I didn't mean to rattle you guys back there," Alec says. "I was about to fall asleep, and I could tell you guys were too, so I thought I'd give us a shot of adrenalin. I hate a jackrabbit had to die, but those long-legged freaks give me the creeps anyway." He laughs. "I want you both to come in, but let me do the talking."

It's after 3:00 a.m. This seems like a waste of effort, and I'm not sure why we're making this detour. Alec knocks on the door of the restaurant and waits. The door is locked, but there are dim lights on inside.

"They're closed," Mark says. "What are we stopping here for?"

"They stay up very late. They might be closed, but someone's here," Alec says.

Sure enough, a dark form approaches behind the window, the deadbolt turns, and the door opens. A woman with fried red hair and bright blue eyes looks at Alec and says, "I knew you'd come back."

We walk in through a little foyer area into the greater part of the restaurant. The tables all have upside-down chairs on them. There are rows of white bistro lights draped above them. Tacked to the ceiling are the bare branches of some small tree, and braided in and among its twigs are numerous strands of white Christmas lights.

"I always say that's the only reason anyone comes here," Alec says. "Sit under these lights . . . and you, of course, Gina."

"Oh, I see. You're not coming back—you want something. Typical. Fix you all a drink?" Gina says, already behind her bar, upturning a few rocks glasses.

"A little late, isn't it?" Alec says.

"You tell me. Stephens left about twenty minutes ago; Tracey and Kelly had left the salad dressing containers splattered and sloppy; dishwasher hadn't run the last rack, waiting on these few glasses—which I told him not to do—and Carl left the flat iron looking crusty as hell . . ."

Alec says, "Well, look, we don't want to hold you up any later—"

"Right. Right. I get to listen to sad sacks like Stephens night after night, but when I start complaining, suddenly everybody's in a hurry. Sit down," she says. All this time Mark and I have been hovering silently behind Alec like awkward children waiting to be introduced.

We hop onto a bar seat on command like good boys and girls. There's something disarmingly nurturing in her manner, but when she speaks, it's all drill sergeant. She asks us our drinks. Though I don't really have a go-to, I at least have the sense not to order anything too high maintenance. Mark says Cuba libre, and she tells him, "Just ask for a damn rum and Coke if that's what you want." She had started Alec's gin and tonic the second she stepped behind the bar.

I've never really met a woman like Gina before. Listening to her talk, the way she handles a man—so brusque and matter-of-fact—it surprises me. Gina's skin is as fiery and damaged as her hair, and her lavender eyeliner and dark shadow reminds me of a woman Mother told me of many years ago, a fortune teller Grandmother knew. She looks at least ten years older than Alec, though I suspect they are probably the same age. Still, she is an astonishingly attractive woman. Perfect cheeks and icy blue eyes. She's making small talk with Alec about why we're here, but her words wash over me as I sip my drink. It's too late, and I'm fading, and the drink is only worsening things. Then I hear her say: "Excuse us, children. The grown-ups need to talk for a bit." She waves her hands up at us like a genteel southern woman might shoo a fly from a pie cooling on the windowsill. "Scoot, scoot," she says. I can imagine we're still looking dumbfounded. As we slide off our chairs and move back to the entrance, I hear her talking to Alec, her tone no longer playful, more admonishing: "When are you going to quit screwing around up there and come back on full-time with me. I can't work the bar all night and pick up the slack on the floor and expedite plates in the back. We need you here—*I* need you here," she says leaning into him now.

Their conversation grows to intense whispers. Gina can barely restrain her words. I catch one or two from across the room. She sounds like an angry mother scolding a child in a grocery store cereal aisle.

"What are we doing here?" Mark says.

"I'm trying to listen," I say, but Mark can't take the hint.

"And what the hell happened back there? For a second I thought he was going to veer off into the desert and—what were you saying to him? Why were you pushing him?"

"Because that amnesia business is a cover. He remembers more of his former life than he lets on, but he refuses to acknowledge it."

"You sound very sure of yourself. I didn't know you'd ever spent any time around him," he says. "Him or any of us."

"Let's just say I have a knack for spotting liars. What makes you sure he's telling the truth?"

"This one Sunday afternoon, he was drinking with us at Nik's trailer. Nik had him talking about his travels; he was tracing things about as far back as he could remember, but we were all too far gone, exhausted from the weekend. He was sitting on the floor, speaking about a family he'd met in Utah. He seemed close then, like he was on the brink of breaking through, but the moment passed, and he dozed off, sitting against the wall."

"Utah," I say.

"What's it to you? Are you going to beat the truth out of him? He's a nice guy. Who cares what he did or didn't do?"

"His family. The people he left behind. They deserve better."

"Maybe it's too painful for him," he says.

"Please."

"I didn't expect you to be so cynical, Sharon."

"Now you know," I say.

"Hey, it's not easy to truly know someone. What about you? You never talk about *your* life."

"What?"

"I've never heard you talk about where you're from, your family, or anything you've done. You haven't shared a single memory with me or any of us. At least Alec's grabbed a few memories in the last ten years. He's trying to live his life. What have *you* done?"

"My *grandmother* once told me, the population never grows *back home* because every time a baby's born, a man skips town. Look, people leave their families every day, but we don't fawn over them for their wanderlust or term them 'free spirits' or pretend they're victims. I'm saying, this man, Alec, whatever his real name is, may have chosen to forget everyone he's left behind, but memory doesn't work that way. The harder you run from a memory, the stronger its pull. He—"

Mark shushes me with his finger to his face.

I look to the bar, and Alec and Gina are gone. We can hear their low voices in a back room, but it doesn't sound like normal talking. There's an occasional thump and a knock and a sound like boxes sliding on the floor, a few bottles clanking as they fall on their shelves, a few moments more of this racket, and then it grows quiet except for their voices, soft and slow now.

The next thing we know, Alec's hurrying from the back, raising a bottle of brown liquor into the air. His hair is even more disheveled than back in the car, and his cheeks are red. He reaches into his pocket and tosses me the key to my car. "You're up," he says. "Let's git."

"What was all that?" Mark says when we're in the car.

"It's the MacGregor," Alec says. "I paid a hefty price for this one. I've never made so many promises. I think I might be engaged," he says, straightening his hair in the vanity mirror. He slaps it shut. "Go, go, before she changes her mind!"

It's a short drive to the club. No one mans the gate after work hours. The trails leading to the club are dark and tree-lined. All the houses with their illuminated facades are sitting tight, many of them already emptied, their wealthy denizens migrated to the next seasonal home. I think about their soft, immaculate beds in their clean, dark rooms.

"Watch out now." Alec takes the wheel, his firm grip holding my hand in place as he eases the car back on the road.

"Sorry," I say and shake my head.

"We're too close to derail now," he says. "Gotta stay on track." He holds his hand on mine a second longer even though the car's already righted.

I shake my head, but a warm feeling comes over my face.

"You need me to drive?" he says.

"I'll be fine," I say and sit with a new, rigid posture.

As we near the club, Alec says, "Pull over to the side entry there— the service entry. Wake up, Mark. We're almost done here."

I park at the curb and pop the trunk. Alec hands Mark a box and tells him to walk up the ramp to the door. He gives me one, the lightest of the three, and takes one for himself.

"What about the MacGregor?" I say.

"Special trip. Let's get these inside first," he says.

Alec unlocks the door, and we follow him past the assistant general manager and clubhouse manager's office to the liquor room. He lets us in and tells us to place our boxes in there and he'll sort them out in a second. He leaves to retrieve the MacGregor.

"Say what you will about the guy, but I don't know if anyone's ever bent so far backward to help me out of a jam," Mark says.

I pull a bottle of vodka from one of the boxes, study the label. I can't think about it anymore.

"Except this one time," he says. "One time I was in this bar down-town from my college. I'd passed some big exam or something, maybe delivered a successful presentation, and I was king of the world. I'd had too many drinks too soon, and before I knew it, I'd ordered everyone at the bar a round. Everyone cheered, thanked me, patted me on the back, told me what a great guy I was, congratulated me on my exam or whatever, and I liked how it felt, so I ordered another round. It went on like this at least two more times—I lost count. There was this one guy sitting next to me, the nicest of all the strangers. I feel like he'd had as much as all of us, but to look at him, it was like he'd just walked in off the street. He had these dark, patient eyes. I remember that, and he wore a tailored chocolate-brown suit. Well, the bartender hands me the tab, and I almost fall off my stool. I almost black out right there, but this guy in the brown suit grabs the back of my shirt and eases me back onto my seat. He says, 'Let me handle it,' and I'm absolutely floored. I tell him no, I can't let him do that, and he says: 'Why? It's nothing.' He gives the bartender his card, she rings him up, he signs and puts the card away in his jacket. Out of the corner of my eye, I see him down the last bit of whiskey from his glass, but when I turn to thank him, nobody's there. He's disappeared."

I realize Mark's been staring through the liquor room walls this whole time, reliving this moment, but I'm too tired to offer any real commentary.

"An angel," Mark says. "That's what I think. That's how I tell it anyway."

I ponder the idea of a whiskey-drinking angel, but then my mind awakens once more. "Where's Alec?" I say.

We walk down the hall and to the service entrance, but before we get there, we see a blue strobe flashing on the crape myrtles that line the walkway. A security officer is standing next to Alec, but Alec is doing all the talking. Alec has the MacGregor in his hands and sloshes it every now and again for emphasis. He glances up the ramp, sees us there, and calls for me. I join them, and he introduces me and Mark and, placing the bottle in my hands, says softly to me, "Bring back a house scotch," all the while never missing a beat with his story. I dart back into the liquor room, place the MacGregor on the shelf, grab a bottle, and return to the scene. I give the bottle to Alec, which he hands to the security guard and says, "But this one just got lost on the way somehow." The guard takes the scotch, looks at the label, then to Alec, and says, "Y'all be careful," and gets in his car and heads down to the pool house.

"Taxes," Alec says. "Let's go back inside—one last thing."

We go back to the liquor room, and Alec tells us to replace the bottles where they're clearly missing. When the room looks back in order, Alec takes one of the bottles from the shelves and unscrews the cap. "Remember, these were partials," he says.

He closes the door, and there are a few wine bucket stands for white wine and champagne. He slowly pours several ounces of the bottle in the bucket. "Most of it's swill anyway. Give me that one." He points to another bottle. Mark hands it to him, and he pours again into the bucket. He does this with a good six or seven more bottles, then looks at the MacGregor. "You know what?" he says. "We earned it." He uncorks the bottle. It makes a deep, hollow sound, and he lifts it to his nose. "This will be a first for me," he says. "Here." He hands it to me. "On the house," he says.

It smells like vanilla and cinnamon and maple. I lift the bottle to my lips and take a sip; its oaky, caramel sweetness dances across my palate, and on the finish, a subtle char rises up to meet my breath, warming the backs of my eyes. Mark reaches to take the bottle from me, but I steal another sip before handing it over.

"Hey!" Alec cheers. "We did it." He takes a sip after Mark and places the bottle back on the shelf. Mark dares us to drink from the wine bucket super-cocktail, but Alec says we shouldn't profane the MacGregor. "Let me attend to this train wreck," he says picking up the inventory clipboard. "Y'all dispose of the evidence. Rinse it good and wipe it down."

We take care of everything, lock up, and Alec drives us back to Rancho Desierto. When we arrive, there is no music to greet us. I walk into the trailer, and the place is a refugee camp or a bus station. Among the unconscious bodies, I see a sleeping bag on the living room floor with two sets of bare shoulders, one belonging to Paulina, the other to sandy-haired Vince. Celeste is asleep on the couch, and Burt is curled up on the floor below her like a doting golden retriever. Why no one's using the beds is beyond me. Alec tiptoes around the empties strewn all over the floor and finds one last bottle with anything left. He grabs it and motions for us to step outside.

Out on the deck, the night is quickly fading. It must be close to 5:00 a.m. already because the stars are disappearing. I'm trembling, nearly nauseated with weariness.

Alec hands me a powder-blue bottle. "What you gonna do? Go to sleep?"

"If I could just lay down and fall right to sleep, I bet I could still get three and a half hours before getting ready to leave for brunch," I say.

"God, how many times have I done that math tonight?" Mark says.

"You cheated," I say. "I'm almost certain we lost you a few times in the back seat." I take a sip and hand him the bottle. The gin packs a floral punch from inside my face outward.

"We should drink to something," Mark says. He raises the bottle. "To Alec, fast thinker, smooth talker, and soon-to-be-married man of mystery." He drinks and passes to Alec.

Alec laughs and nods his head. He raises the bottle and says, "To Sharon, a mostly conscious driver and accessory to bribing a security officer." He drinks and passes to me.

"To Mark and Alec, two adept box carriers and not bad company for a Saturday night joyride," I say.

And this goes on for at least two or three more rounds until, to my own surprise, I'm laughing, though I can't say at what. Maybe my exhaustion has finally caught up with me. Maybe it's the memory of the worried look on Alec's face, a grown man negotiating his way into or out of trouble—which I couldn't say—and for what? A stupid kid's second chance to keep a run-of-the-mill job?

I have always felt alcohol to be the great cheapener of experiences. Afterward, I find myself asking: "Was any of that real? Would they have said that or acted this way had they been completely sober?" And so, I rarely partake. I have already made enough choices in my life to fill the rest of my evenings with second-guessing. At the point we drink enough to behave differently, aren't we all just pretending? Who could trust any of it?

And yet, in this moment, I can see us for who we are: sweaty, disheveled, and ruined, arms upon each other's shoulders, our matted heads smashed together, shaking with laughter. We are, all three of us, human wreckage, but Mark and I are young. Alec is not. Despite this, Alec has a deep, resonant, booming laugh I don't tend to hear from grown men. Most I've known are too self-aware, too macho or proud, but he has surrendered completely to an unbridled joy. I may never know this man, whoever he was before, whoever we will become tomorrow, but both feel irrelevant to me now. In this one glimmering instant, I see him unguarded, genuinely himself, and this is enough.

I wake up around nine. Celeste is nudging me with her shoe, telling me we need to leave in no more than fifteen minutes. I wipe my eyes and see that she's already in the Sunday brunch get-up: long-sleeved white shirt, black pants, black apron, gold name tag in place, hair in a perfect bun, her face pale and round as the moon.

I do not remember much of the morning except doing my side work—slicing and scoring lemons, placing napkins in the sweet roll baskets and stacking them by the warmer, organizing extra towels around the cold bar so the ice sculpture doesn't leak all over everything—my head swimming in a thoughtless, tingly haze. I hardly remember dressing in some of Paulina's spare work clothes. I do not remember the ride to the club at all.

It's a quarter after ten, and our first tables should be arriving in fifteen minutes when the clubhouse manager rounds us all up and tells us to sit in the dining room. These shift meetings are typically held by the assistant general manager, a short, fierce woman well into her forties, still with the physique of a college cheerleader, so when the clubhouse manager—a fixer of sorts for the club's day-to-day problems—saunters in with his lumbering Texas shuffle this close to serving hours, we know something's up. The manager places two vodka bottles on a table where some of the foreign exchange servers are sitting. Their twin thuds rattle the silverware and the cups in their saucers.

"These two bottles look virtually the same to the untrained eye," he says. "But you're a bright boy, Nik. Can you tell me how one differs from the other?"

"These two pitiful American 'wodkas' are brothers, I think," Nik says. "They have each made their sacrifices, but one you find 'werrry' displeasing," he says. A Ukrainian girl elbows him in the gut.

"One of these bottles was purchased by the club, and the other was not. Bottles the restaurant purchases have a tiny label with our state-assigned number stamped on them. At least two dozen bottles in the liquor room didn't carry these."

He makes a sweeping look at the faces across the room. They must have been as blank as mine.

"Taxes," he says. "It has to do with taxes. Furthermore, to look at the inventory, there's far more mistakes and written, erased, and rewritten counts than I'm comfortable with. This, in my mind, raises many questions. It's my understanding there was a pretty big party down at staff housing last night that lasted well into the morning. We can't police what you do in your spare time, but when it begins to interfere with the work you do while you're here—that's when I have to step in. I'm looking at all of you, now—look around."

The servers look at each other: baggy eyes, shaking hands, wet hair, sweaty cheeks, distant stares.

"Death warmed over. That's what I'd say," the manager says, tucking his thumbs behind his belt. "You're all unfit for work, and you fail to represent our club's commitment to excellence appearing as you do today. I don't want to end the season on a bad note, so let this be a warning to everyone that the margin for error is now razor-thin. The alcohol situation had to be handled more punitively, but it's already been taken care of. I want each of you to go to the bathroom, splash some cold water on your faces, get those smiles ready, and show me you can do your jobs well, or further measures will be taken at day's end." He takes the two bottles from the table and walks out of the dining room's double doors.

I look over to Celeste, who is clearly avoiding eye contact with everyone.

"What did you tell him, Celeste?" Mark says. "What did he mean 'It's been taken care of'?"

I see poor, naive Burt looking simply, innocently, stunned by her duplicity.

"People were in my bed," she says, as if this were reason enough for all club employees, future and present, to lose their jobs.

"Remember last night," Burt says, "you said: 'How do you do it? How is it that everyone likes you when you so obviously seem to care so little?' You say you try to be nice and you want to be liked, but you don't give an inch when it really matters, and everyone knows it. You care about this stupid place and all their stupid money more than you care for any one of us."

Celeste looks blankly at the table where the bottles were.

"You're the least loyal person I've ever known," Burt continues, "and I'll never trust another word from your deceitful little rule-following mouth as long as I live, and no one here should either." He stands and shoves his chair back under the table.

I can't help but smile behind my hand, but when I look to Mark, his face is red with fury. "What's wrong?" I whisper to him.

"Alec," he says. "He's gone. They fired him. Didn't you notice he wasn't here?"

"What?"

"She ratted him out. All of us, probably. But Alec must've taken the fall."

I rise from my seat and walk through the dining room to the bar. It's empty.

After the shift, the clubhouse manager drives us back to staff housing in the company van with the rest. It is a quiet ride.

Mark and I walk over to Alec's trailer. We knock, but no one answers, so we try the door. It's unlocked, so we go in, calling for him. The place looks like no one ever lived there, recently at least. All of these sad aluminum hell boxes must be at least thirty years old, but inside his trailer, the air seems even staler than the others. The living room is strewn with lamps of all varieties. We walk down the hall to one of the bedrooms. It is loaded floor to ceiling with old credenzas the size of coffins. In another bedroom, a pile of full-sized bed frames, box springs and mattresses, and head and footboards. In the master bedroom, six couches with ripped upholstery and matching chairs are all stacked in pairs neatly atop one another.

"Are we in the right trailer?" I say.

"This is the one," Mark says. "I think." He tips one of the upturned couches over so that it flips and crashes to the floor. He plops down on the couch's back, sinking low into the seat cushion.

I collapse next to him, the gravity of the night before settling into my bones, and I think I may sit here for the next several hours.

"I don't understand," Mark says. "Didn't he live here? Just seems like it's used for storage. Where would he have slept?"

I say nothing.

He takes my hand in his, interlacing his fingers with mine. I let him.

"I need you to help me right now," Mark says.

"With what?" I say.

"I need you to talk me out of believing everything that happened last night was in my imagination. I need you to tell me that he was a real person who really exists because the more I think about this summer, every conversation we had, the more I think maybe you're right that we knew nothing about him. Now I'm doubting if there even was a him, and maybe this whole thing has been some vivid, fevered dream," he says.

Still holding his hand, I turn to him and plant a kiss on his lips, then sit close to him once again. "That's what it's like," I say, but he doesn't understand.

I rest my head deep into the seat cushion. After a minute or two of the quiet, his head slumps down to my shoulder. I look at the clutter and dust around the room and wonder how many people have lived in and left this mobile home, and I think about that—a home you can take with you yet a home everyone's dying to leave—until my eyes land upon one of the translucent windows, clouded with years of cigarette smoke and grime. In the beige light, there is a dark rectangle like a single stained glass panel, the color of this desert earth. There against the window rests a squat glass bottle, half-empty, its remnant amber glinting in the afternoon sun, an elixir for forgetting, forgotten.

DEBUTANTE

Cindy tapped her fingers on the kitchen table, waiting for an old friend to arrive, while Martha looked on, wounded at seeing the warmed-over fried chicken and white bread still on her plate. The dark-stained wooden cabinets and wall paneling swallowed the warm light from the ceiling fixture, five faux candles with little flame-shaped bulbs. Cindy stared at the square design on the linoleum, olive-green grapevines mapping out a grid on the pocked, butter-yellow floor. She wondered about the decades of dinge, surely so deep no mop could ever lift it.

Martha took her plate and set it back in the fridge. "If you won't eat anything, maybe you should drink some coffee. I'll brew some."

Cindy continued tapping.

"Don't you think Thomas might want a cup?"

"Maybe I'd like for my breath not to smell like day-old chicken *or* coffee when he gets here," Cindy said.

Neither spoke for a time, then Martha said, "Well, I'm going to brew some anyway even if it's only for me."

"That's fine," Cindy said. "You know, you don't need my input if you're just going to do what you want to anyway, right?"

Martha sighed. "I thought Thomas might want some since it's a little on the late side and—"

"Tom, Mother. Only teachers ever called him Thomas. Sounds like he's in trouble when you call him that," Cindy said.

"Fine, fine." She filled a pitcher with water and poured it into the coffee maker. "You seem keyed up tonight—more than usual even."

Cindy tapped her teeth.

"Maybe now's a good time to get something out of you."

"What do you mean?" Cindy asked.

"I mean, you haven't said too much since you've been home. I was hoping you'd be a nonstop chatterbox, at least a day or two. Aren't you glad to be home?"

"I'm glad. It's just different. Not here, I mean. Home is always home. I'm trying to say it's different from out there."

Martha sat beside her. "Oh, Lord. We've lost her to the city. She's got too proper to sit and talk with her simple, backwoods mama now."

"That's a pretty uncharitable estimation of things," Cindy said. "Maybe I simply need a little time to adjust to only having one human being to interact with every day."

"Maybe," Martha said. "But I've noticed you do sound a little different."

"Like how?"

"Oh, little things. Like how you said *home* just now—with that *o* like in *crow*." She repeated the word again with the long *o* a few times. "Send a girl off to school, and she comes back talking like the weather woman. I guess that's what the money's for though."

"Mother."

"—can't have my daughter talking like one of us uneducated hicks."

"Mother, please," Cindy said and placed her palms down on the kitchen table. "You're not an uneducated hick. I would never think that."

Martha rose from the table, took three cups and saucers from the cabinet, and placed them by the coffee. "You nervous?" she asked.

Cindy let out a long, emphatic puff of air.

"Well, good God, talk to me, girl. Don't make me play guessing games all night!" She leaned against the counter and waited for her to say something.

"What do you want to know?"

"I want to know it all, Cindy. Like what did they teach you out there? Did you meet any young men? How was graduation? What held you up so long that it took you six months to come home? How long are you staying? Are you home for good? Will you be looking for a job in town? I want to know your plans."

"That's a lot."

Martha brought her coffee to the table and sat. "I can't believe you didn't start right in as soon as you pulled into the yard. I wanted to ask you, but you looked so tired I let you go right to sleep. That's about all you've done since you've been home these three days. Where have you been?" she said.

"Graduation was fine. I didn't come straight home because I had a year lease on the apartment to run out and a few things to take care of besides, after which I traveled. I met a few boys, but I left them out there . . ."

"Maybe if you'd called more often . . . maybe if *I'd* called more often . . ."

"It's not your fault, Mother." Cindy placed a hand on hers. "I was very busy. I had more projects and exams than I thought I could handle, but everything turned out fine. I had trouble finding a job in the city—I guess there were too many girls just like me or better, vying for the same jobs—but now I'm *home*, and I'm trying to plan my next move. Things won't be awkward forever, but I'm going to need a little time to sort everything out."

Martha nodded slowly. "Well, I still want to know everything."

"We've got nothing but time," Cindy said.

Martha sipped her coffee. "When will Tom be around?"

"Soon."

"You can have the den if you want. Or here. Whatever you want."

"I think we may go out," Cindy said.

Martha glanced at the clock over the sink.

"It's not so late, Mother."

"Oh, I know," she laughed. "I suppose you both have some catching up to do."

"Yes," Cindy said. "But you know, we spoke from time to time. He'd call me every month or so, and those first two years he paid me an occasional visit."

"Oooh," Martha nearly sang.

"You know he's engaged to Hannah?"

"Oh," abrupt this time. Martha turned her cup a full circle on the table. The porcelain scraping the wood made a high, hushed sound. "So what's he doing visiting you?"

"Can't you still have friends once you're married?" Cindy asked.

"If you can, nobody told me," Martha said. "No, that wasn't my experience. But the world's changed a lot since I was young—more people, different lifestyles. We didn't have so many options. Still, what could he want with you?"

"Who said he wants anything, Mother? Just to catch up." She waited for a reply. "What's *that* look?"

"You know he's the head editor at the newspaper now?"

"Yes, he called to tell me not long after he got the promotion."

"Hmm." Martha took a sip. "I don't trust them, you know? Newspaper people. Not after how they treated your brother."

"I know."

"The way they took what I said and screwed it all up, the way they made us look—made him look."

"I know," Cindy said. "Tom's not like that. We know Tom."

"We did once." Her eyes trailed from her daughter's to an empty seat across the table.

"Don't worry, Mother. You always worry too much."

They could hear a car turning onto the path that led to their house. Over Martha's shoulder, headlights through the window sent white rectangles racing along the wall. "Must be him," Martha said and stood, sloshing coffee onto the table.

"Settle down, Mother. My God," Cindy said.

"Go to the front," Martha said and sat back down.

"No one ever uses the front door."

A hand rapped on the storm door there in the kitchen.

"See," Cindy said, opening the door. Tom stood on the top step with his sleeves rolled up. He wore a gray fedora with a navy band.

"We don't want any," Martha said.

"Mother!" Cindy opened the storm door, and he scooted in, removing his hat as he did. He had a head of thick, wavy hair, dark with hints of gray, and a five o'clock shadow on a kind face. "She's just joking."

"I know that," Tom said. "How are you, Mrs. Martha? Don't get up."

"Oh, fine. I fixed coffee if you want some."

"Maybe later, Mother. I think we're headed out."

"Oh?" Tom said. "Where to?"

"I don't know. A walk. Let's take a walk," Cindy said.

"A walk? Sure you don't want a ride? I've got a nice, reliable automobile out there, ready to roll."

"You sound like a paper man," Cindy said. "Has he always talked like that, Mother? Like he's reading the classifieds?"

"Not to my knowledge. Wouldn't you rather stay in? I'll stay out of y'all's hair."

"He looks the part too, doesn't he? Spiffed up in his chinos, and that hat? Dear God, Tom," Cindy said.

"Looking the part is 95 percent of the job. You don't look like a paper man, nobody tells you anything."

Martha groaned only loud enough for Cindy to hear.

"Oh, it's your trademark now?" Cindy said.

"Don't mess with him too much, Cindy. He's liable to drive off and leave you. Unless you want to spend the rest of the evening playing rummy with me."

"I do not," Cindy said.

"Thomas. What's this Cindy tells me about you marrying Hannah?"

"Have to make an honest woman out of her sometime. Can't be a bachelor forever. What else would I do with all this money I'm making?"

"Quit your mess," Martha said. "Look at you. You're wasting away. He needs someone to cook for him."

"Then I found the wrong one," Tom said and laughed.

"We really should go," Cindy said, grabbing Tom's arm and pulling him toward the door.

"What about that coffee?" Tom said.

"She'll keep it warm for us," Cindy said.

"Don't y'all need a flashlight? Let me get a flashlight," Martha said.

"It's a clear, bright night; we'll be fine," Cindy said.

Martha moved clutter around in a junk cabinet until she produced a flashlight. She clicked the button, and the light flickered and died. "Lord have mercy. Let's see if I can find some batteries in there."

"No need," Cindy said, halfway out the door.

"Where y'all headed?" Martha asked.

"Out," Cindy said having already pushed Tom onto the steps.

"Cindy," her mother called after her. They locked eyes. Martha gave her a serious look. "You be careful."

"We will, Mother."

"I said *you* be careful," she said in a hushed tone, "careful what you say." Then, loud enough for Tom to hear, "You know, I've always found a nice walk goes a long way to clear the mind." Tom smiled and waved over Cindy's shoulder, and they stepped out.

In the darkness of the yard, Tom said, "Mrs. Martha think we've got minds in need of clearing?"

"Takes a clear mind to clear the heart," Cindy said.

"Did you just make that up?" Tom asked.

"Maybe. Could be something my grandmother said."

Tom leaned against his car. "Look, are you sure you don't want to go for a drive? I'll take you wherever you say."

"*Wherever I say*? Tempting. Get behind me, Thomas. What's the matter? Didn't you wear your walking shoes tonight?"

"Actually, I didn't."

Cindy knelt close enough to see Tom was wearing a leather pair of brogues. Their gloss glinted in the moonlight. "My oh my, Tom. Are you a newspaperman or a banker?"

"Well, how long's it been, Cindy? I didn't want to come over here looking like trash."

"I see." Cindy leaned against the car with him. "If you're not up to it, sure, we can drive."

"No, I'm up for whatever you say. These puppies need breaking in anyway. Where'd you want to go?" Tom asked.

"I don't know. What about the train tracks? We used to walk out there a lot when I was little. My brother loved it."

"Lead the way," Tom said. "Are you sure we won't need a light?"

"I think once our eyes adjust, we'll be able to see pretty clearly. In the meantime stick close so you don't get lost. I'd hate for you to end up on tomorrow's front page."

"Hmm, below the fold," Tom replied.

The home was nestled deep in the woods. From the house a small yard sloped down to a spring situated at the edge of the forest, and from there a nearby path could be found.

The two rustled in the leaves around the spring while Cindy got her bearings. "I believe it's here," she said, pushing a dogwood branch aside.

"If you say so."

They stepped further into the woods. "Well, there used to be a kind of path here. You can almost tell," Cindy said. "My brother cleared it. You'll be surprised when you see how far it goes. He probably did this all with a dull bush axe when he was thirteen or so."

"Oh yeah?" Tom said. "You know, I have very few memories of your brother. He was a couple years above me."

"The path's grown up a bit." Cindy bent a small tree out of their way. "But I think we can manage." She pointed along the trail. "I remember it pretty well. Look, see how it opens?"

He leaned into her shoulder and looked down her arm like he was sighting a gun. "I don't, but I trust you."

"And Grandmother told me blue eyes were nighttime eyes."

"Too long straining at newsprint," he said. "Lead on."

It was a mild mid-October night. Most of the leaves still clung to the trees. It was a clear night, and with the moon nearly full, the shadows of the foliage overhead could be seen on the forest floor. They hadn't walked far before they could better see how to navigate the darkness. Farther still, they could see each other's faces. Tom fairly glowed. She could see his baby-blue shirt and khaki pants. Cindy, however, was harder to make out except for the dotted white flowers embroidered on her navy dress. The times when Tom would fall behind a few paces, her form would nearly disappear into the shadows, except for the tiny white flowers like stars fading behind a cloud.

"So, now that you're home, what will you do? Have you got anything lined up?" Tom asked.

"I've made some phone calls, a few arrangements, an interview or two."

"Yeah?"

"Everybody needs a secretary. I know I'm fit for better, but you've got to start somewhere," she said.

"And you mostly studied business at the women's college?"

"Yes, a lot of business, quite a bit of English as well, literature, writing."

"You sound like a perfect candidate then. I'm sure someone will snap you right up."

"Oh!"

"Sorry about that." He failed to see she'd stopped walking and bumped into her.

They waited.

"Quiet, isn't it?" she said.

"Very."

They listened. Only crickets and a whippoorwill.

"Cindy?" he said.

"I was listening for the creek, but I don't think I can hear it," she said. "The creek's one of the first landmarks."

"Cindy."

"Let's keep moving, Tom. Miles to go, et cetera, et cetera." She began walking. "And what's it like being top dog at the newspaper?"

He caught up. "It's only interim for now. Charlie's health isn't too good, so he stepped down. Stomach ulcers, maybe worse. Anyway, he needs a lot of rest. He'd always liked me. Handpicked me to run the joint until he can get straightened out, but his wife's leaning on him to retire, so who knows?"

"And they don't mind, with your age and all?"

"A few of the older guys didn't like it at first, but I think if they got a taste of this job, they'd want their old one back before the weekend. They're sensible enough to see that."

"A new job and a new bride. You're a lucky man, Tom," Cindy said.

"Yeah. That's true."

Cindy parted some grapevines and pressed her foot down on them for him to pass through.

"We've known each other a very long time—Hannah and I," he said.

"And you're likely to *know* her a very long time too," Cindy said.

"What about you? Do you ever see any of the old crowd? I remember you had several close friends."

"Did I?" she laughed. "I was very close with a few girls for a time, but I grew not to trust them."

"Really?"

"Much changed for me when things first began to go poorly with my brother—coincidentally, when I needed a friend the most. I didn't trust anyone outside of my family for years. Maybe I still don't," she said.

"That's a shame. Really," he said. "You know, I believe one of the first times we ever spoke it was about your brother."

"Oh, no."

"Yes, you told me something very shocking about him. I don't recall exactly what you said, but in my mind I committed myself to keeping my interactions with him limited, if not avoiding him altogether. I think I may have been wary of you too by proxy." He made an amused sound. "I wonder if we would've become friends sooner if—"

"Oh, look!" Cindy pointed along the path to a rock the size of a truck. "That's the first landmark. We take a hard left from here. See?"

He glanced along the pathway and moved hesitantly forward.

"What's this? Independence rock?" he said.

"Not quite. But up top there's some hollows my brother said were bowls. He called this the grinding rock. The Indians would bring their grain to rocks like these and grind it down with another stone. There's some smaller cup-sized scoops he said they'd crack nuts on."

"Where'd your brother learn that?"

"Well, it could all be wishful thinking, but I do remember him learning about this area and the people who lived here before us from a history teacher or school librarian. He'd found plenty of other artifacts. He spent most of his time out here. He didn't like being indoors, merely tolerated our home. He'd get restless, sometimes cranky, sometimes worse," she said. "One summer morning, he was probably fifteen, he'd wolfed down a heavy breakfast, packed a sack with some food, and told Mother he'd be back in a day or so. Turned out to be three. He was testing his boundaries. Mother didn't stop him. I did *not* approve."

"Where'd he go?"

"Another mystery, I guess," she said.

"He was an interesting fella," he said, leaning against the rock next to her, close enough their shoulders were touching. "Pretty fearless."

"Let's keep moving."

"Sometimes I wonder if he wasn't born before his time, you know? Maybe another day or another people would've been more forgiving. Maybe if my brother had been born several centuries ago, he might've been revered or at least accepted. God, I sound like my mother. She's spent the last ten years talking like this."

"What do you mean?"

"She's mulled over his entire life—every moment she's ever shared with him—and when she exhausts her memory, she imagines how she could've changed things. She dreams up another future for him, one that can never be now."

"She feels responsible. She tortures herself," he said.

She walked without acknowledging his words.

"I'm sorry others treated him poorly. I'm sorry for the whole mess. It's no wonder things ended up the way they did. I've always tried to talk the editor out of running those follow-up stories."

Cindy stopped suddenly to face him. "Tell me about the bride-to-be, Tom. I always thought Hannah was a bit snobbish." She shrugged, turned back to the trail, and resumed walking.

He gave a sharp, quick laugh, like a sneeze, and spoke to the back of her head, "Her family was slightly well-to-do, especially for this area in those days, so I guess you can hardly blame her."

"For being uppity? Hmm," she said.

"I'd like to think we've all changed plenty since then," he said. "We've been seeing each other a long time now anyway . . ."

She waited for him to continue. He didn't.

"In truth one of my only memories of Hannah is an unpleasant one," Cindy said.

"Really?"

"It was during a time when my brother's troubles were beginning in earnest. The children had this crazy idea that he'd hatched a nefarious plot to poison the school—and if memory serves me, she was one of the older kids I recall who confronted him. I distinctly remember her standing by while my brother was assaulted."

"Hannah?"

"My friends worshipped her, of course. She was older, very cool, nice clothes . . ."

"You know, I wasn't even friends with her back then," Tom said.

"—and look where you are today."

"Yeah."

"Well, it was a long time ago. No doubt she's a much bigger person now," Cindy said.

"Bigger," Tom said.

They walked silently for a few minutes, only exchanging a word or two to better navigate the dark pathway, holes, tree roots, and spiderwebs to avoid.

They paused to listen.

"Quiet, isn't it?" she said.

"It is," he said.

"I'm still getting used to it."

"Yeah. There's always a barking dog or a loud truck or a honking car or a shouting drunk on my street, but here it feels like we're stepping into the past—like before this land was settled. Imagine how peaceful it must've been. No one for miles. We're like two deer moving unseen through the forest. Hell, why stop there? Through the river of time, we're two trilobites tickling the ground, millennia before the first uttered sounds."

"I didn't know you were a poet too."

"Did I just rhyme? I didn't mean to," he said.

"Maybe I should start reading your column."

"It's slightly worse. Fewer trilobites. No rhyming."

Eventually, the path grew clearer. The ground became sandy and shone brighter in the moonlight. "Well, here we are!" she said. They had arrived at a creek about twelve feet wide. The clear water moved quickly enough a fallen leaf would pass out of sight in a matter of seconds. Tom knelt and dipped his hand in.

"Cold," he said. "Is it deep?"

"Not very. You ready?" she asked.

"Ready? For what?"

"Why, skinny-dipping, Tom. What did you think this was all about?" She laughed and began slipping off her shoes.

"What?"

She walked to the water's edge. "What are you waiting for?" She smiled and turned to face him. He was still standing with his mouth open. "God, Tom, you look like a ghost. I'm only kidding. Get over here and carry me."

"We're crossing over?"

"Yes, this isn't just a walk; it's an adventure."

He looked at his pants and at his shoes.

"I'll hold them for you. Get those socks and shoes off and hike up those britches."

"Yes, ma'am. Whatever you say." He removed a shoe and sock.

"You weren't so willing a second ago," she said.

He removed the other sock and shoe and rolled up the cuffs of his slacks. "After debating stripping down completely, going barefoot feels like a pretty easy request."

"Ooh, look at those ankles! I won't tell Hannah."

"Quit," he said and handed her his socks and shoes.

She hooked his shoes in her fingers. "Well?" she said.

He took a step back from her and looked her over. "Is this a piggy-back situation or . . . ?"

"Do I look like a pig? Carry me!"

In one motion he scooped her up and carried her easily in his arms. She threw one arm around his shoulders and smiled. "Forward," she said, pointing the way. He stepped down into the creek and made a high-pitched sound. The cold shock made him grasp her tighter. "Don't you drop me, Tom."

"Then stop kicking your legs," he shouted. He looked at her knees. They were pale and smooth.

She looked into his eyes. "You're pretty strong for a newspaperman."

"We're not on the other side yet," he said.

The water was ankle-deep at the banks and nearly knee-deep in the middle. "I can't believe I let you talk me into this," he said as he ascended the other side. "How far are we going, anyway?"

"As far as you're willing to follow," she said and laughed deeply.

He lowered her where the ground seemed solid enough. "But you do have a destination in mind? We're not just walking to walk? This isn't some kind of test, right?"

"Yes. No. We'll see," she said and began slipping her flats back on her feet.

"Maybe I don't remember you at all, Cindy," he said. He gathered his socks and shoes, tiptoed over to the base of a large tree, and sat on one of its roots. He brushed the dirt from his feet and began slipping his socks on.

"You mean from those few visits you paid me at the college? Maybe I'm just in a good mood, Tom. Maybe you're not used to seeing me when I'm happy."

He worked his feet into his shoes and stood. "Are you happy?"

She moved in close to him, placed her hand on the back of his neck, then patted his cheek. "Is this how all your interviews go?" She returned to the path. "Move it, Tom."

He followed.

"You know, the longer we walk this path, the more impressed I am with your brother. It must've taken a lot of effort and time to cut a path like this one, especially this wide."

"The path was one of his many obsessions. It possessed him for quite a while—I'm not sure he was ever finished with it."

"What other obsessions did he have?"

"Typically, he would find and collect things—rocks, marbles, buttons, arrowheads, railroad spikes, and anything that might wash up in the creek that wasn't trash . . . but sometimes trash too. The path was different, though. You could tell it meant a lot to him. He would disappear for hours at a time. Sometimes I'd go along with him and watch him work, swinging that old bush axe. He really threw himself into it."

"He must've been quite a young man."

"He still is, Tom. He's not dead," Cindy said.

"Of course. I didn't mean to suggest otherwise. I'm only trying to tell you I don't think he's the monster he's often made out to be. And I'm sorry, Cindy. I'm sorry for everything. I wish things were different for your sake and for your mother's," he said.

"For his," she said.

"Certainly. That goes without saying."

"Yes, it goes without saying. In fact, it always goes unsaid. Why would I think you would be the first?"

They walked in silence for a time.

"I didn't mean to sound that way just now," she said. "Thinking about it stirs up some of those old feelings. I can't think of a single soul outside my family who's ever expressed any pity for him. I'm still very angry. But the hopeless kind of angry, not the productive kind that drives you to act, to change lives for the better. The kind that makes you feel like a useless coward for doing nothing, but it's all beyond my control now."

The path narrowed, and the trees were smaller. The forest walls were tighter with overgrowth, weeds, and bushes.

"What is this?" he asked.

"The next stop on our tour. Notice anything different?"

"Yeah. Tougher walking."

"This was cleared in my lifetime, so the trees are younger, and the overgrowth is thicker. Let's make our way out of it first. Shouldn't be much farther."

Once they'd pushed through the worst of it, they stopped below a massive swamp chestnut oak. "There'd been a gruesome accident at the sawmill where my father worked—at his stall, actually. He said it sounded like gunfire, followed by the sound of a tight string being plucked, and then crashing sounds. The workers killed their engines. Smoke was blooming from one of the machines. The operator wasn't there. They called his name. No one answered. They walked to his station, and there he was on the ground. But there his head was not."

"Geez," Tom said.

"A saw blade had ejected from its housing, flown from the saw, and decapitated the man. Once the mess was cleaned, they inspected the machine and the tree he'd been working on. There was a railroad spike that had been driven into it years ago. The blade had run across the spike, causing it to spring from the machine.

"Grandmother said the townsfolk remembered a biology teacher who'd been a vocal opponent of the sawmill at townhall meetings years ago, who still regularly spoke ill of the entire venture to his students. This enraged parents, who stood to gain money either from the jobs or timber. A very clandestine group had watched the teacher's habits, especially at night. Then one night they found him here."

"Why here?"

"Apparently, these are some of the oldest woods remaining in our county. Look at this thing." It would've taken six men holding hands to encircle the trunk of the oak. The tree had branches the size of other trees. "This is the one."

"The one? What one?"

"This is the one they hanged him from."

"All over a bunch of trees?" he said.

"And a man's life," Cindy said. "The worker who'd been killed had a wife and three children. They were destitute. No one agreed with the men's actions—the teacher had a wife and son himself—but neither did the law look too deeply into the case."

Tom shook his head. "That doesn't surprise me too much."

"It's hard to know what's rumor, but my grandmother told me the chief of police's son was among the posse. Or was it that he was friends with the owner of the mill?"

"Hanging tree," Tom whispered.

"A man hung from the tree he so desperately tried to save."

"It's too poetic to be true," Tom said.

"I doubt you'll find it in your archives, but your paper isn't the only repository for truth. But my grandmother loved a good story," she said. "Often she'd tell them better than they were told to her. She didn't mind making a good story better. What else is there to do in lonely places like where we live? Come on." Cindy led him back to the trail. "I can remember when that area was much clearer, like a little playground in the middle of the woods. Sometimes my brother and I would take walks just to come here. Grandmother said they quit cutting after the teacher admitted to spiking trees for years out here. It was too risky for the mill."

"Why cut out in the middle of nowhere like this? Wouldn't they start closer to a road or something?" he asked.

"Who said we're in the middle of nowhere?" Cindy stopped and pointed down the path. Through the darkness, a paler shade of earth could be seen in the moonlight.

"What is it?" he asked.

"Train tracks," she said. "Those are the rocks they lay the track on."

They walked on to the end of the path and scaled the small berm to reach the railroad tracks. "Well, how about that?" Tom said. "Can't say that I've ever walked on tracks like this, not so secluded anyway."

The rails weren't wide enough that they could walk side by side, so Tom followed. The walking was awkward. The wooden ties were spaced closer than a walking stride, but when he tried to walk naturally, he'd stump a toe or step on a rock. He tried to take shorter steps but still found himself tripping every so often.

"Your grandmother sounds like an interesting lady," Tom said.

"That's true. She loved a good story. Most she told me at bedtime. Never the same one twice unless I asked. She said the stories she told were passed to her from her grandmother."

"You ever think of writing them down?" Tom asked.

Cindy made a short sound to let him know she'd heard his question.

"I'm only saying, don't you think you should record all of her old stories? Maybe someone would like to read them, even if it was just your own granddaughter someday."

"How many decades of my life did you race through? I'm glad you're concerned about the daughter of my nonexistent child."

"In truth my suggestion is meant as much for me as anyone. You know, we didn't all have grandmothers like yours. I have to admit I find your family fascinating," he said, "and the more I learn, the more I wish to know."

"Hmm."

"Is that so wrong?"

"You and everyone else," she said. "In fact, Mother worries that's why you're here. She thinks you only want the inside scoop."

"The inside what? We don't really talk like that, Cindy."

She laughed. "So, you find us fascinating, huh?" They stopped on the tracks. "Any one of us in particular?" She stepped close enough to see his face.

He nodded.

"God, don't say my brother," she whispered.

He kissed her.

She placed her hands behind his back and pulled him in tighter. "Is this what you came for?" she said softly, and they kissed again. "Oh, Tom. Don't look so lost."

"I'm not lost," he said.

"Sure. And I know the way. Follow me." She took his hand tightly and led him farther down the tracks. She walked awhile without looking behind. Tom watched the tiny white flowers down the back of her dress as the crushed stone crackled beneath them.

"What is it about a train that makes you feel restless? Makes you want to leave your life, fly out over this country and never look back?" he said.

"Oh no. The poet's back. Don't be so melancholy. You've always been too somber for your own good."

He sighed. "Haven't you ever wanted to leave?" He tightened his grip on her hand to stop her. "What am I saying? Of course you have."

"I've been gone for several years. Now I'm here. Sit."

They sat on one of the rails.

"I'm tired of it, Cindy. Same four office walls, same problems on the job, same tired news of a boring town in a boring county. Saturday date night at Linguini's, same songs on the jukebox. Sundays at the church, then dinner at her parents' . . ."

She laced his fingers in hers.

"You know, there's a sick joke in being made to write about this place day after day, week after week, pretending like any of it's worth calling news. Who cares? God almighty, who cares?" his last words echoed down the tracks.

"Out of your system now?"

"I'll tell you what I'm going to do. I'm going to sit right here and wait for the next train to come . . ."

"Oh, boy . . ."

". . . Woody Guthrie . . ."

"Tom . . ."

". . . or Anna Karenina . . ."

"Tom!"

"I won't know which until I see the light."

"Are things so desperate? I've never seen you this melodramatic," she said.

"I've never thought of it that way. Jump a train, ride it into a new life; jump it poorly, one-way ticket to whatever comes next. Either way, it's a new beginning." He let out a laugh more like a heavy cough. He shook his head at both prospects and growled as he stood. He paced before her and doubled back a few times before kneeling at her feet, close enough to see her eyes. "You could come with me, you know?"

"What?"

"You're the only thing from this whole forsaken mountain I'd take with me. You're all I'd want."

"What are you saying?"

"I'm saying I'm done with this life. I don't want any of it—except you. You're the only one who truly knows me." He grabbed her hand.

She held her breath.

Each waited for the other to speak.

"Oh, I see," she said at last. "Cold feet. You're being very silly, Tom. As for trains, I'm not sure people really do that. I think that's a bunch of old folk songs anyway."

"Isn't that what your father did?"

"My father?" she said, straightening her posture, releasing his hand.

"I'm sorry, Cindy. I didn't mean to—"

"No, no. What about my father?"

"Everybody said he was a drifter, that he jumped a train after your brother—"

"Stop."

"I'm sorry," he said.

He got off his knees to sit beside her. They sat listening to the sounds of the woods. He ground his fingernails into the rail.

"Ray—my father—left long before my brother . . . did what he did. My father had enough of him—and apparently the rest of us—well before then. There were a lot of little things between the two of them along the way, so I'm told, but I have no memory of these, almost no memory of my father."

"I said I was sorry, Cindy. You don't have to say another word about any of it."

"I know I don't, but I want you to see, aligning yourself with my father's kind isn't romantic; it's selfish. It's the most selfish thing a person can do—to look around at everyone, to see how ravenous we were for love, and then to leave."

"You're right. Forgive me. Don't be angry with me," he said.

"You?" She shook her head. "I've been angry a long time at more people and situations than I care to mention. I've only ever spoken about any of it to Grandmother, and she's been gone a few years—I can't help if it boils over at times. I don't have anyone left to talk to. If you want to know the truth of it—it feels good to speak some of the things I've thought. Mother won't talk about my brother or my father in any serious way. She'll share a casual memory, but they're like trinkets from a former life."

"Don't you ever think about them?" he asked.

"Love is in the wondering," she said.

"How's that?"

"'Love is in the wondering.' It's something else my grandmother used to say. She said if you truly love someone, you never really stop, even if you'd like to. I used to wonder about my father. Often. Mother and I—maybe after dinner, in the quiet evening hours, or on long walks like these—we'd trade stories about him. We'd take turns imagining where he was, who he was with, what he was doing. In a strange way it always made me feel better, closer, almost like we'd shared a lengthy, long-distance phone call with him. I know that sounds ridiculous. Then one day, instead of making me feel better, it made me angry, sad, or bitter, so we stopped. Of course, we were both very hurt, but my mother's disappointment in him didn't last very long. I think she understood some deeper part of my father others couldn't."

"I'm not sure I could get over it. Takes a strong, wise person."

"My mother doesn't have a resentful bone in her body. My grandmother, on the other hand . . . ." She laughed and stood. "Well, let's move along. If we're gone too long, Mother will worry." She helped Tom up and brushed off her dress. "And no more hobo drifter talk."

He brushed off his pants. "Maybe," he said.

They continued down the track. Along the way Tom stumbled on a loose train spike. He'd kicked it, and the spike clanged against the rails with a low ringing tone.

"My brother used to pick those up," Cindy said. "He had several buckets full of them."

Tom picked it up and put it in his pocket.

"He loved the woods, being alone, but nothing rivaled his affection for the railroad. I think it's the whole reason he cleared the path. I used to wonder how far he'd walk these rails. I was so young then, I figured he'd seen both ends of the track and everything in between."

"It's the freedom," Tom said.

"What do you mean?"

"It's about the possibilities. Either way. You have a choice. And in the choosing, there's power and a new life waiting. You think you have to live, grow up, and die where you're born, but here they are: two lines of steel to remind you people choose new lives every day. It's infectious. Don't you feel it every time you hear the whistle blow?"

"I do," she said.

They walked on another hundred yards, this time at a slower pace. Cindy would pause often, surveying the edge of the woods, until at last she glimpsed what she was looking for.

"Here," she said. "We called this the gifting point."

"Another one of your grandmother's stories?"

"No, this one's mine."

They walked over to a cedar fifteen feet in front of the tree line. It had a robust trunk with several missing limbs at eye level. The remnants of those limbs protruded like great thorns. Above these, curvy limbs grew upward like defiant, flexing arms, and the dense foliage rose, spreading an inkblot shadow between them and the stars.

"Someone must have knocked all the lower branches off when the track was laid. Not sure why they would've left the tree in the first place," he said.

"One time my brother stumbled upon the skull of a buck deer. It had a great set of antlers like this." She held her hands apart the breadth of her chest, with her fingers spreading outward as though she held a gigantic bowl. "He climbed the tree and nestled the skull between two of the lower branches, maybe seven feet or more off the ground. You had to look carefully to see it, but it became another trail marker for us. I always liked how clean and white it looked. A night like this one, I'll bet it would've glowed. Can you picture it?"

"I'm not sure I want to," he said.

"Anyway, we'd grown accustomed to seeing it there, right? Then, one hot day, we walked past it, but something felt wrong. My brother held me back. Snake was my first thought. He told me to listen. We heard a great crashing through the woods—quick and noisy like a deer except far heavier and with the regular pounding footfalls that a person would make, and with each stride, a low, visceral sound could be heard. Have you ever pushed over an old rotten tree? It groans as all its fibers give way before falling. That's how this sounded, a steady pummeling of the ground, one thud after another until it faded into the distance."

"Cindy . . ."

"*I know*. It's crazy. But let me tell you the rest. My brother turned and looked up in the tree, but the skull was nowhere to be found. He walked around the cedar, pulling at vines, kicking around in the grass and weeds, and then he stopped. I thought he'd found it, but instead of the smooth white antlers, he held something else."

"What?"

"A jar."

"A jar?"

"Yes, one of those huge pickle jars you used to see on the counters of convenience stores," she said.

"Is that so odd?" he said. "There's all kinds of trash in the woods. People treat them like their own personal garbage dumps."

"But it wasn't dirty like it had been sitting there for years. I've found old bottles and jars before. They become little terrariums, dirt and moss and fungi inside. It was nothing like that. It was spotless even without a lid. A huge, clean, open jar, sitting below where the skull had been."

"I don't think I understand," he said.

"Let's go," she said and motioned for him to follow her into the woods.

"Now I'm not so damn sure I want to walk in the woods anymore. What the hell's in here?" Still, he followed.

"Look, Tom. I can't really say why this felt important to us then, why it does now, but at the time it felt like we'd been given a kind of gift. My brother found and collected everything you can think of out here, but this one felt different—like the woods or something belonging to the woods wanted us to have it. We'd given it something; in exchange we'd received this."

"I'm starting to think the whole point of this walk was to spook me," he said.

"We're close now," she said, beckoning him farther.

A few clouds had begun to obscure the moon, making their darkened way even less penetrable. They had to feel their way through, a few steps at a time, pushing small trees and vines from their way.

"It's been many years since I've been this far," Cindy said. "I suppose you remember a boy from school named Calvin?" she asked. "Gawky, gappy bangs. He was my brother's age, so maybe you don't."

"No, it's coming back to me. I remember he seemed to find himself rather charming? A class clown type?"

"You sound unsure because he wasn't truly funny. Boys dearly want to be funny at that age. So sad when they can't be," she said.

"Yikes. You're making me feel embarrassed for him."

"He was the son of a woman my mother knew, the closest thing my brother had to a school friend for a time—a very short time. Did he ever tell you anything about my brother, anything particularly gruesome?" she asked.

"It's difficult to say, Cindy. I'd heard some odd things about him back then. From whom, I couldn't say."

"Care to enlighten me?" she said.

"I'd rather not. Why would you want to revisit—"

"It's important to me. I'd like to know what you know—what you believe."

He hesitated, then said: "I haven't thought of those days in a long time, but this walk, the crisp air, hearing your voice again, speaking the names of those I haven't seen since they were children—aren't they still children in your mind?—it's all bringing parts of the past back to me. About your brother . . . I heard that he skinned the classroom pet—was it a rabbit?—and kept the pelt inside his pillowcase. That he ripped the livers out of the fetal cats the older kids dissected in anatomy, snuck into the cafeteria, and threw them in the ground beef . . ."

"Is that all?"

"That one time he laid down in the middle of the train tracks and let the train roll over him, but he was so skinny, nothing happened, except the sparks of the wheels tickling his face. That one time he set a fire in the woods to hide something terrible he'd done. That one time he found a book on poisonous plants and mushrooms in the library, that poison in general was a favorite subject of his, and—is that enough?"

"Then you *did* know Calvin," she said and laughed bitterly. "Maybe he isn't worth the credit I give him, but I place much of the blame for the whole mess upon his shoulders. If he hadn't overreacted to some harmless nonsense that happened between him and my brother. If only he hadn't gone to school and run his mouth to anyone who would listen. Maybe if my brother could've made one single friend to defend him at that very cruel age." She groaned. "I'm sounding like Mother now."

"Can I be honest, Cindy?"

She waited.

"At least one of those stories about your brother I received personally from his sister."

They stopped and looked at each other.

"A few others were told to me by children who said you'd spoken to them as well," he said.

Cindy did not reply.

"It's very likely that Calvin and other schoolchildren's whispers are to blame for escalating matters, but Cindy, certainly you remember how you played a part in this?" he said.

"We're almost there, Tom. Let's not spoil a nice walk." She turned and began again making her way to their destination.

He fell in close behind her. He attempted to speak to her twice, and twice she ignored or didn't hear him. When she finally stopped, she turned and addressed him: "Anything I might've said was only meant to subvert Calvin's lies. Calvin was making him out to be a psychotic ghoul, a dangerous freak, a monster. Any story I told them was merely meant to keep those who would harm him away. That's all. Yes, I said some things that were untrue, but he had no one to defend him. I was all he had, and he was perfectly helpless."

"Was he?" Tom said.

Cindy took ten paces from him, and when she stopped, the moonlight revealed her smooth cheeks and sharp nose. He moved to join her, but as he did, he tripped on something large that made him stumble into the light by her side. He looked around to find the path had widened into an open area. Surrounding them was a ring of rocks, black skull-sized stones forming a large circle about twelve feet across. "What is this place?"

"You tell me, Tom."

He thought for a moment. He walked up to the ring and nudged one of the stones with his foot. It barely moved. He stepped over, into the ring, then walked to the center. "I do seem to remember a story—that he had a necklace made from the teeth of dead animals he'd scavenged, that his dad saw him snacking on some roadkill carcass, that it made him so sick, he vomited through his tears, that he couldn't get the image or the memory of the smell out of his head, so he left you and the family for good." He turned back to face her, but she was gone.

"Cindy? Cindy!" he called, but nothing.

He listened. He could hear a quiet sob now and then.

He backtracked, but she wasn't there. He felt his way through the dark, walking around the ring until he came upon her, crouched behind a small tree wrapped with grapevine. She was clutching her hair, hiding her face. He touched her shoulder, and she startled. She eased her fists and parted her hair. Her face was pale and lowered so he couldn't make out her dark eyes. "Why bring me here, Cindy? This place holds so much pain, so many bad memories for you. Why bother to relive it? Why come home in the first place?" He helped her to her feet.

"I'm okay now, Tom. It's okay," she said, forcing a smile. "I didn't know I was going to react that way. I don't think I've cried in years." She tried laughing at herself. "I'm not sure why I wanted to come here. Maybe because I miss how things used to be. Maybe I miss him. Maybe

I'm afraid of him like everyone else and I only wanted to see for myself how I'd behave coming back here. Now we know. I'm a whimpering child still. I'm sorry."

Tom said: "Evil creeps in unchecked when you're young and still learning the damage words can do. How could a child or anyone know the lifespan of a lie or even the truth spoken carelessly or to the wrong person?"

Cindy stepped upon one of the rocks. The clouds had peeled away from the moon, and now shafts of light were streaming in. The perfect circle of dark stones was visible now. She began stepping slowly from one stone to the next as if they provided a passage across a shallow stream. Tom followed.

"My brother was odd. Though I learned very much about his behavior, I don't pretend to understand his actions. There's a touch of truth to what you know. He had amassed an inexplicable pile of dead animals back here, roadkill from the tracks maybe. But I don't think his curiosity held any limits, and it could be that death had occupied his thoughts at the time or what happens after," she said.

They continued moving from stone to stone, watching their step but also gazing inside the ring.

"I believe he and my father placed these stones here before burning it all. It's also true that my father left us shortly after. It's an uncomfortable story, one I'm—I don't want to talk about it anymore," she said.

They had walked very far from her home, and though they were both growing tired, they continued pacing the circle of stones over and over again, each absorbed in their own thoughts. In the solace of this moment, the past, their present, slipped into the ether. Had anyone been witness to the scene, they might have mistaken the two for spirits of the woods, passing in and out of the moonlight and shadow.

At last Tom stopped and said, "Why don't we sit a moment, rest, and head home?"

"I think if I sat down, I'd lie down, and then you couldn't move me. Are you prepared to carry me all the way home like you did across the water?" she said.

"Better keep moving then, but let's leave."

Cindy agreed, but before stepping down, she looked deep into the woods. "Is that our path?" she asked.

"No, it's there." He pointed behind them.

She looked and agreed. "But what's this? I never knew there to be a path that extended beyond this point. Let's go a little farther and see."

"Cindy, it really is late."

"Just a little farther. I'm not ready for our adventure to end. Somehow I feel like there's something more to see." She took his hand. "Come on. We'll be quick."

As they walked, the woods grew sparse, and the trail became indefinite. "I'm not sure, but I think we're nearing the edge of the woods," he said.

"Let's see," she said.

They walked on, but as they approached the end of the trail, they stopped. A dark shape seemed to block the way.

"Do you see that?" she said.

"Yes," he said.

Each stood quietly, trying to focus their eyes or gain a perspective that could make sense of the thing before them.

"It's so dark now. I can't make it out," she said and stepped closer.

"What are you doing?" he asked.

"It seems to be a kind of hovel or nest," she said.

"Let's leave," he said.

"Hold on." She reached out and touched it. The frame was comprised of sturdy materials from the forest. It was fortified by ivy and grapevine and covered with fallen leaves and moss. She stepped into the mouth of the structure, an above-ground tunnel of sorts, but she could not tell how deep or how far it led.

As she squinted into the black, a high yowl in the distance broke the silence. In response another howl much closer resounded. Back in the distance, more howls followed.

She ducked out of the nest, and they looked beyond. Through the thinning woods, an open field shone beyond the trees. The clarity of this night illuminated the earth like a lunar landscape.

"Dogs?" Cindy asked.

"Maybe," Tom said and took her hand.

"Wild, you think?"

"Probably."

They each held their breath and listened. In the cacophony could be heard a range of sounds from the yips and barks of smaller animals to the hoarse, ferocious howls of the larger, older ones.

"Could be coyotes," he said. "Sounds like quite a pack."

Then they heard, above the chorus, one distinct guttural roar that lasted several seconds, that, when it ended, brought everything into a complete silence that did not relent.

"I've seen enough," he said.

"Let's go."

Their pace was brisk, but the growth in the pathway, the often uneven terrain, the roots and debris, and the darkness demanded a careful speed. Nevertheless, their racing hearts and the touch of panic, the ancient stir of primal fear, of feeling preyed upon, drove them nearly to running. They gave little heed to the slaps of branches and the pull of vines and briars upon their clothes as they ran, and when they burst forth from the woods, back to the clearing, it was like emerging from the depths of a murky lake. The two were doubled over, panting, catching their breath.

"What was that? What was any of that?" Tom said between breaths.

"I didn't know I could run that fast," she said. "Oh, I'm trembling."

"Me too."

They looked at each other, both had wide eyes and a wild, unkempt look about them. Cindy laughed first at the sight of Tom, attempting to shake away his fear, and he laughed at her in reply.

"You think we're safe? Don't tell me we need to run the rest of the way," she said.

"I think we're fine. They—whatever—it sounded very far away. Boy, I need to get out from behind the desk once in a while," he said.

They made their way to the tracks, this time walking side by side, both of them between the rails. When their breath had returned, Cindy said, "It's exhilarating, isn't it—to do something that truly frightens you? Scary stories are one thing, but stepping out into the darkness and all its possibilities . . . . We live very safe lives, don't we?" she said. "Don't laugh, but when I was a child, I used to do this foolish thing. Lying in bed on a bright night, I would raise my hand in the air like this," she stopped him and raised an outstretched hand high above, "and I would slowly bring it down until it would almost touch my face. I'd do this again and again. You'd be surprised how few times it takes to begin spooking yourself." She laughed. "Scared of my own hand. That's how fragile we are. That's how prone to fear we can be. Try it."

He raised his hand high and stretched it wide like a puppet master or a sorcerer casting a spell. He lowered it closer to his face, menacingly slow. She moved in next to him, ear to ear, watching as his hand crept in close enough to block out the moon. Her hair brushed his cheek. He reached around her and held her side. With his palm inches from her nose, in a swift motion, he embraced and kissed her. They stayed locked together like this for some time until a low whistle broke the silence.

"Train," she said.

He kissed her cheek, then her ear.

"Passing over Sanderson Road. Few miles out. Whistle blows every crossroad—"

He kissed her lips, long and slow.

The whistle blew again.

"Parker's now. Maybe a mile," she said.

"I don't care," he said and pulled her hips closer.

"You're being silly," she said and kissed his neck. "Let's stop."

"What did I tell you earlier, Cindy?" he said. "Two options?"

Another whistle, much louder, and she could see a faraway light below his earlobe.

"Okay, Tom. It's not funny anymore. Let me go." She twisted, still enclosed in his arms.

"None of this has been silly or funny to me, Cindy. I'm as serious as I can be," he said, tightening his hold on her.

The train whistle blew louder still. The wheels on the rails hummed through their bodies.

"You're right. This *is* exhilarating," he said. The light, no longer a distant star, was more like a headlight now. She screamed. He looked to her and could see the darkness fleeing from her face as the engine's yellow beacon barreled toward them. He grappled her in a bone-crushing swoop, but weary and encumbered, his legs were merely plodding, and he failed to lift one foot high enough to clear the rail. He stumbled. He overcorrected. His shoes rolled in the ballast, and as they fell, he turned so she would crash safely upon him. She clasped him as they touched down, his arms a cage as they made a hard slide on his back before rolling to the bottom of the berm.

The train thundered by in a quaking fury. They were only a dozen feet from the rails, where they lay reclaiming their breath, taking stock of the various hurts, all without moving a muscle, still braced for impact. She was first to move again. Still bound in his arms, she worked her hands up to his face and in searching his expression, somewhere between the panic and relief, discovered in him some indecipherable quality, a suffering or perhaps a yearning, and as the passing of the steel juggernaut rumbled through them, as the tension in their embrace began to yield, she buried her hands in his hair, and she received his kisses, much harder now as if to compete with the terrible force shuttling above them, and his muscles succumbed as their bodies met, the rhythm of the wheels controlling their every breath, their every move, until the silence returned.

They stood and righted themselves. She smoothed her dress and retied her hair while he searched for his hat.

"What are you doing?" she asked.

"Looking for my hat," he said. "Oh." He raised an amorphous shape of black and gray felt in the air. "Looks like I may need a new calling card." He dropped the hat's remains on the tracks. "Let's go," he said. He helped her climb back up the tracks where they resumed walking hand in hand.

Before reaching the path, Tom looked up into the night sky, took a deep breath, and said, "I think I'm beginning to understand the allure of your home, this strange world we've been given."

Cindy smiled.

"I can see how a woman like you could evolve from a place like this.

That goes for your entire family," he said. "Won't you think over what I said—about writing down a few of your stories?"

"You mean my grandmother's stories? Don't talk nonsense, Tom. I'm not a writer," she said. "I'd probably do a lousy job of it. I couldn't tell them the way Grandmother did."

"But that's the beauty of it," he said. "You'd tell them your way." He waited for her reply, then said: "And not only her stories. What about yours? The truth. Isn't it important to record the truth as you see it?"

"Truth the way I see it?" she asked.

They stopped.

"There's only one truth, Tom. There's what happened and what didn't. People say they want to know the truth, but they never do. They only want whichever details bolster their already-made-up minds. They take what they want and leave the truth like your hat back there. I'm surprised at you, Tom. You really don't talk like a newspaperman at all; you sound more like a shrink or a salesman or—"

"Poet. You forgot poet," he said.

"Poet."

They stepped down from the tracks and entered the woods. They didn't talk until they'd passed the hanging tree en route to the creek.

"I can't go back, Cindy," he said.

"What?"

"To the job, to Hannah, to any of it. I feel like someone or something's hijacked my life. The most frustrating part is that I feel like I'm here not because of the choices I've made but for all the decisions I've never taken seriously. I never even considered my life could be anything else, and now I've arrived exactly where that type of inaction leads: nowhere."

"You're starting to sound a little crazy, Tom. Let's not pretend like your life's so awful now. Mother and I are very proud of you, and I'm sure—"

"I've never been more clearheaded in my life. I'm awake now."

They paused for they had reached the creek.

"Maybe that's what this walk was for. I'm here to talk you down—be the voice of reason," she said.

"You think that's why I came to see you?" he said.

"I'm beginning to wonder."

Tom grew silent. He gazed down at the flowing water trickling beneath them, a barely visible cool stream of shadow. "You've called me lots of things tonight. Melancholic, silly, overly dramatic, crazy . . . maybe I'm a babbling fool, but for what I'm about to say—I want you to trust me—I am completely in earnest. You also said I looked lost. Maybe you're right with that one. I haven't believed in a single step I've taken since high school, and now I'm about to marry—"

"Tom, you have to stop. Don't say something you'll regret."

"What's to regret? Words? I've got piles of words—I've got mountains. I retch words in a bucket, slosh it around, dump them on a page, and call it news. But that's not what I'm talking about now, and that's not why I came to see you."

"Why did you come to see me, Tom?"

"The wedding is only a few months away. I had to come see you. Something told me if I didn't see you tonight, I'd never see you again."

"Tom," she spoke his name like a dubious aunt.

"Oh, I'd see you again, but things would be different. We'll be on our best behavior."

"We weren't on our best behavior tonight, were we?" she said. "Was that why you came to see me?"

"Certainly not—I had no idea we would—and that's not what I mean. I mean, we'll be measured in everything we say, there'll be caution, a flatness we won't get over, and we'll be lesser versions of ourselves. We won't be real again, you and me, and I don't think I can bear that."

"So what's your solution?"

"You come with me tonight. You pack a suitcase, throw it into my car, and we hit the highway and never look back, Cindy."

She let his words settle somewhere deep inside her. Below, the water trickled along in a whisper, unseen eddies, whirling in cold darkness, passing over smooth black stones beneath, secrets polished and flattened by time that nevertheless remain.

"You want to know what I think?" She took off her shoes and stepped into the creek. "I think I know why you came to see me. I think you got what you were looking for a few moments ago. Your wedding is a stone's throw away, and your nerves got the best of you. You wanted one last fling, one last reckless act to remember in the tepid moments of wedded bliss to come."

"What?" he said.

She hiked up her skirt and stepped backward across the creek, still facing him. "Or maybe Mother was right: you wanted to hear me spill my guts about my brother and the rest of my family so you can write some salacious exposé because you're tired of writing obituaries and council meeting reportage and—what do you call those old announcements where rich girls like Hannah are 'coming out' into society?"

"This—I can't believe you're saying this," he said. "And for the record, you're the one who suggested we take the walk. You're the one who gave me this backwoods nightmare tour of all the macabre shit your brother dallied in. You've led me every step of the way. And now I've got to reconcile with what I've done—what I can do to save the marriage before we're even married."

"There you are," she said.

"What?"

"There's your answer." She continued backing across the creek. "You haven't exchanged the rings, but your mind's already settled upon that future, so why pretend it can go any differently? It's too dreadful—for both of us."

"Can't it?" He inched closer to the water, unsure whether to charge in after her or to remove his shoes or to simply sit down by the bank and sulk.

She stepped upon the opposite bank and found a place to sit and dry her feet before slipping her shoes back on.

"Damn it all. Damn you and your whole screwed-up family." He hastily removed his expensive shoes and socks and stomped into the water without rolling up his cuffs. His steps made deep, hollow splashes like large stones hefted into a pool. Once across, his pants were wet from the knees down.

"It wasn't so long ago you wanted to know more—everything there ever was or is to know about us," she said.

He sat on the ground across the path from her and put his socks and shoes back on. "Damn things are probably ruined," he said and looked at his pants. "My, what a night."

Cindy stifled a small laugh to see him sitting hunched on the ground, his chin propped by the heels of his hands, like a kindergartener awaiting story time.

"Are you laughing?" he asked.

"A little."

"Damn you and your enigmatic ways," he said.

"You used to love my ways," she said, offering a hand.

"You know, enigmatic is one thing, but being intentionally bewildering . . . ," he took her hand and stood, "Well, that's just cruel."

"It's a woman's dilemma: speak and you're 'mouthy'; keep quiet and you're an enigma," she said.

"Your grandmother?"

"Me."

They spoke very little the rest of the walk. When the lights of Cindy's home could be seen through the final stretch of the pathway, Tom stopped her.

"Something in me makes me want to apologize, but I don't regret what happened, so I can't," he said.

"And I wouldn't want you to," she said. "I'm glad—for all of it."

"Cindy, I have to know—why wouldn't you leave with me? Am I so foolish?"

"What makes you think this has only to do with you?" She looked down the path at the dim yellow light of the kitchen, where the silhouette of her mother sat waiting for them.

"But what will you do now that you're home?" he said. "I don't mean work. What kind of life will you have here?"

"I'm still young, Tom, but I've well learned the more I tell people of my thoughts and plans, the more likely I'll be told I cannot do the very thing I'm set upon."

"Then I won't ask you to tell me anything more tonight, but will you allow me to make one last small request?" Tom asked.

She neither nodded nor spoke.

"I want you to consider writing down your family's stories," he said.

"Do it for yourself at first. Jot down your memories and the stories you've been told by your family. And when you're done, I want you—and then everyone—to see that your family is more than your brother and whatever happened with him."

They walked to the house and up the few stairs to the kitchen. Martha startled at hearing the storm door open.

"Oh, my. It's late. Is it too late for coffee, Tom? Don't stand in the doorway."

"Afraid so, ma'am. How about some other time? Gotta get to the house. News starts early," he said.

"Don't be a stranger," Martha said.

He gave Cindy a look. "Good luck with this one, ma'am," he said with a wave and let the door close itself.

Cindy took the two cups of coffee and warmed them on the stove. She gave one to her mother and sat down beside her.

"Were his pant legs wet?" Martha asked.

Cindy did not answer.

They sipped their coffees in silence until Martha could no longer bear the quiet.

"Well?" she said.

"Well, what?"

"You. Were. Gone. All. Night," Martha said, "And I want details. How did it go?"

"What would you like to know, Mother?"

"I want to know why you have that look on your face. I want to know why you seem different. You're not the same Cindy who left I-don't-know-how-many hours ago."

"I look different? Like Moses come down from the mountain?" Cindy said.

"You didn't get into trouble, did you?"

"How would I do that?"

"Did you get *him* into trouble?"

"You worry too much, Mother."

"How far did you take him?" Martha asked.

"As far as he let me," she said.

"I could just scream at you. I have often told you how you and your grandmother are two of a kind, but this, *this* is all Ray. This is all your father," Martha said.

They finished their coffees and sat at the kitchen table, both too tired to leave, neither wanting to carry the dishes to the sink.

"He loves me," Cindy said.

Martha rattled her empty cup against its saucer. "What?"

"I think he does anyway," she said.

"What makes you say that?"

"We walked very far, Mother, and for so long, and we were so tired, almost to the point of delirium. At one point on the walk, near the end, when we were so far out, I felt a strange clarity, like my life was opening before me. I could see my future, and I could see his future, and it became clear to me that we both have very different paths."

"I take it back. You're more your grandmother than your father," Martha said.

Cindy slid her chair away from the table. She straightened her back like she would stand, say good night, and go to bed, but instead, she looked to her mother and said, "Everyone thinks they know us."

Martha nodded. "They'll never know us," she said.

FROST LINE

Mother knew very little about the house we shared for so long, the one I still live in. A house like this one—old clapboard, slate roof, ivy creeping all around the eaves and up the chimney—has so many problems you can hardly keep up with them. Who works on slate roofs anymore? How much of this house is held together by lead? And how strong does a gust of wind have to be to blow bricks off your chimney? And why would I even know where the damn septic tank is or if it's ever been pumped even once in its whole existence? Live in an old house like mine long enough that you're the sole proprietor, and you'll find yourself asking these questions to no one in particular. Nights I sit here alone in the quiet, I find myself staring at a corner, wondering.

I remember once, when I was six or seven, a massive storm from the coast moved far enough inland that it brought down some of the heavy old trees in and around our yard. The roads were blocked for miles and miles, and power was down for weeks. You'd think a thing like that would terrify a little girl so that she'd never step foot outside again, but my memories largely consist of these few things: the next morning, Mother taking the already softening Cookies N' Crème from the freezer, placing it on the counter, handing me a spoon, and saying, "All yours"; my grandmother showing me how to wash clothes in the creek with an old scrubbing board; the county men and neighbors with their chorus of chainsaws, turning the downed oaks and pecan trees around our home into stackable firewood, enough to last for the next three winters; and my brother, nimbly climbing the woodland wreckage, leaping and dangling from the heavy branches, shaking their leaves, disappearing back into the woods like always. I remember sleeping each evening with the windows open to keep the room from feeling so stuffy, listening for the night sounds of our little home, engulfed in its forest teeming with life, but an unusual quiet had settled upon us, almost like when the heavy snows come and all creation hunkers down waiting for the first sign of welcome. Yet there was something different, something lonesome, about this silence. Several nights like these had passed before it finally dawned on me that I hadn't heard one train whistle since before the storm nor its low tremor rumbling down the tracks, muffled by the dense woods surrounding our home.

If another storm were to happen, they'd simply have to cut me out with their chainsaws. Maybe there's enough of my grandmother's ancient blackberry preserves in the cabinets that I could get by until anyone thinks to do so. These are the restless thoughts I have before falling asleep lately; this wayward meandering tells me we're drawing near to my brother's anniversary, if you want to call it that.

But I shake such thoughts from my head, retrace, double back, distract myself with another memory, another time. I was fretting over the house. I must remind myself that we've always managed to tack it back together, and barring another cataclysmic event, there's no real reason why I can't go on doing so, even alone as I am now. Tonight I'm thinking of the first of our troubles with the water. How many years had it been since Grandmother passed or since we'd last seen my brother . . .

We'd been without water for a week or more—which isn't to say there was no water, only there was no water running to the house. There's a spring down in the woods where we pump our water from. The day we lost water, Mother helped me raise the heavy cover off the well tile enough to shine a light in, see if it had gone dry. It hadn't. Full and crystal clear. I knew it had to be the pipe between the well and the house, which was preferable to a dry well but still a challenge neither of us had anticipated.

I'd spent some time at our small library in town searching for books about plumbing. I suppose I could've simply looked up a plumber in the phone book. This is a thought I would have at several stages of the process, but as you very well know, our family and our house have a bit of a reputation, and in the past, we've had trouble getting anyone to visit, even for commercial reasons. I was sitting at a table near the front desk with my small stack of books when I noticed an old timer in overalls rattling a newspaper, sitting in a small lounge area. I watched as he made his way through the local paper, replaced it on its wand, and moved on to the national. Around here, for a man his age to be well enough to leave his chair, he had to either be rich and have never done a real day's work, or he must have had the sense to find the balance between working enough to keep everything moving and working yourself to the grave. My grandfather, one of the latter, died well before I was born. I only know him from pictures and the rare story from my mother and grandmother. And with Father leaving when I was a child—well, I've had very limited interaction with grown men in my life, especially men of his age. But a simple look at this man's face would tell you plainly that he knew things: he had not been a stranger to hard work; his huge hands looked like they'd been pounded into blunt tools; his face was worn, not so much by sun but by time spent setting his jaw, perhaps contemplating schematics or blueprints—this was evident in how he read the paper, squinting and occasionally dismissing whatever he was reading; and his pinstripe overalls—though they seemed more like a holdover from those days than a real necessity now—had been worn and washed and worn until the denim was soft as flannel.

He saw me looking at him and asked if there was something that he could help me with. Said a certain way, this can easily sound like a "Why don't you look somewhere else and leave me alone?" kind of statement, but he seemed fairly genuine, more so than the librarians there, so I told him that, yes, actually I do need some assistance, and he folded his paper, placed it in his seat, and joined me at the table. He began looking through my books as I described to him our problem. The water pressure had been dying for a week or more. One morning I finally noticed a wet spot in the yard—nothing too miry, more like a discolored patch on the hard, barren ground, under the shade where no grass would grow. Most likely a leak, I said, between our spring and the house. I told him how we lived alone and that we were planning to do it ourselves, as was our nature.

He seemed charmed at the idea of two women—one me and the other near elderly—taking on this task. We looked through the books together, and one in particular struck him as most helpful. The man talked me through the job and had me write down the steps; he even drew a few diagrams. He showed which pictures from the books featured tools we'd need, and when he had gone over the process a few times and seemed to feel confident in my capability, I could see an idea working in him. Suddenly, his hard, gray eyes softened, and he surprised me by saying, "Ma'am, I think I could help you with this, and we'd have it knocked out in a morning—no later than afternoon, tops."

I hadn't known until then that I was feeling a great deal of stress about the whole thing because when he said these words, the tension left my neck and shoulders. Simply looking at the man instilled me with confidence. We would do the job right, we would have water again, and this strange wound the house had sustained would be mended, and Mother and I could go back to living as if the previous week's hand-wringing, silent dinners, and implicit curses for our unique situation had never occurred.

"Where is it you live, anyway?" the man asked.

Here my nerve left me like a ghost escaping my body. I began to describe a route that would take us back to our house. I could see he was making the mental journey as I gave directions. The longer I spoke, the more distant he grew, and I realized I should've just been forthcoming and told him we lived out in the foothills, deep in the woods, exactly where no one ever "happens by," not for curiosity's sake nor even for meanness, much less to favor us with a visit—only lost souls and lonesome transients. And the mailman, I suppose.

I could see he immediately regretted having offered his services.

"It's quite all right, sir," I said. "I think Mother and I can handle it between the two of us, especially with your guidance."

He seemed grateful and embarrassed. "You check that book out—not those, just that one—and meet me outside," he said and left.

I handed the books and my card to the librarian at the desk and told her which one I wished to check out. Her permed hair sat like a mushroom above her head. She looked at my card and at my face, then stamped a date inside the back cover and slid it to me in the most begrudging way, like I'd accidentally found a personal copy of her favorite book. Her lifeless eyes looked like all the coffee in the world couldn't revive her.

Outside I saw a truck that had been blue at one time in its life but now was largely the gray of the metal beneath the paint. The truck had three wooden toolboxes, one behind the cab like most pickups, and two lining each side of the bed. The man was lifting the latches on several chambers on the longer toolboxes along the truck bed, rifling around for some piece or part or tool, grunting and replacing what he was not looking for, and slamming these doors shut. Finally, he made a sound like he'd won a little carnival game. He approached me with a small white device in his hand.

"Coupler," he said. "PVC. Great invention." He handed it to me and showed me how it would work. "Used to have to solder a pipe back together. Headache and a half. This'll probably work with the size of your pipe if the house is as old as you say it is."

I thanked him. I wanted him to know there were no hard feelings, that he need not feel derelict for backing down on his offer to help. "Well, you were our angel today, sir," I said.

"You be careful when you start digging," he said. "My daddy once said, 'Don't start digging unless you're prepared to find.'"

Once we discovered the leak, I'd taken every cheap garden hose on the property I could find and fastened them to siphon water from the spring back up to the house. This worked for a time, but the spring would run over a gallon a minute, and I couldn't let it empty here at the house or in the yard all day every day, so every evening I walked it back to the woods and led the water into a nearby creek. This nightly ritual, though an aggravation at first, had begun to feel like a welcomed pardon from the growingly tense mood at home. Mother and I carried on as usual, but it was so much her nature to worry that by the time the worst of it would come and go, she'd be worn down to nothing and needing a good week to collect herself. This kind of worrying, I find, is infectious, but where Mother frets and paces around every room of the house as the problem worsens, I tend to get angry and curse and rail against our lot. I suppose beginning with a visit to the library is a pretty tepid move, but you rage your way, and I'll rage mine.

On the big day to fix this whole mess, I'd broken down the steps of the job, gathered all the notes the man had given me, and written everything down carefully on an index card. The man mostly verified much of the information I'd already found, but he did offer a few suggestions and warnings as well.

"Is that all you're going to eat?" Mother said, even though I'd left no trace of the eggs, two links of sausage, and two biscuits, one with strawberry preserves, the other with honey.

"I could do this all day, but we've got a job to do," I said.

"Well, I want to help," she said.

"You've done plenty," I said. "It's going to be a long day, and I don't think cereal and coffee would've even helped me get past the ground-breaking stage."

"I *can* help, you know?" she said.

Mother was in her sixties, but she was far from frail. Still, the last thing I needed was for her to pull a muscle or hurt her back. I couldn't care for her *and* fix the water problem.

"Here, take this." I handed her the index card. "I basically have this memorized, but I want you to keep it handy so I don't get off track or forget something important."

"I can do more than that," she said.

"And I may ask you to, but to begin with, let's do it this way. I'll work, you supervise." I threw back the last bit of coffee and placed my cup in the sink. Looking out the window, I could see the faintest shadow, a slightly darker smudge in the stone-hard ground where I suspected the leaking pipe to be. I walked over to a closet and found a wide-brimmed straw hat, the kind we'd garden in, and grabbed my sunglasses on the counter by the door. "I have to gather a few tools from the shed. I'm not entirely certain he'll have everything we need."

Mother had cleared the table and had begun to wash our dishes in the sink with water from a pot I'd filled earlier. "The snake shed? Good Lord, Cindy. You better beat around that place with a stick or something to flush those suckers out."

"I know."

"And black widows?" She shivered.

"I'll be quick," I said and slammed the door behind me.

An already long season had given way to a sweltering Indian summer, and after the garden was finished, we mostly withdrew ourselves into the house after work and on the weekends. There's a natural dimness to our house. The rooms we sit in face north and south, and of course the wood paneling—if you stare at long enough, you begin to see a wall filled with dark unblinking eyes—captures all sunlight, so when you go outside it's like you've walked up from the hold of a ship and stepped out onto the deck after a long storm.

Even with my hat and sunglasses, the light simply assaulted my senses. On the way to the shed, I paused at the place I presumed the leaking pipe to be. I smeared the ground with the sole of my shoe, but it barely disturbed the dirt. Hard as concrete. This would not be easy.

Across the yard is a small shed not much larger than Mother's closet. There is a rusty push mower in there and other yard tools, none of which see much use from the two of us other than the yard rakes. Being nestled in forest, we have more leaves to burn than grass to cut. I hung my sunglasses in the collar of my dress and budged open the door. It's a bit of a nightmare in there, spiderwebs and snakeskins hanging from the walls and the ceiling, enough to make your skin crawl, so I didn't waste time. I could make out the lawn and garden tools upended in an old fifty-gallon drum near the door. I grabbed the shovel and rooted around for anything else that might be of use. I found an old pickax kind of tool. I believe Grandmother used to call it a grubbing hoe—she would use it to dig fishing worms. I took it too. Then, one last thing, I remembered that I needed the pipe cutter.

I could only assume this would be in Father's toolbox—a scarred-up, green metal box that must weigh more than sixty pounds. I spotted what I believed to be the box in a too-dark corner and made my way there. For a second I contemplated dragging it out into the light, but then I heard a loud scurrying in what appeared to be a nest nearby. A big black lizard or a rat, I couldn't be sure, but I shrieked and bolted out of the shed, brushing the dust and the cobwebs from my dress and hat.

About that time, Mother had come out to the yard to see me explode from the shed, flapping like a blue heron, a cloud of dust flying off me.

"Find what you need?" she asked, laughing.

"Enough for now," I said, straightening my dress, fixing my hat and glasses. I put them on and tightened the scarf of the sun hat under my chin.

"You look lovely," Mother said. "Too nice for the kind of work we're to do today."

"Thank you."

"It's your business, but don't you think a dress is an odd choice?" she said.

"I'd take it off, but what if someone came by?" I said.

Mother dismissed my remark. Truth be told, I don't know why I was wearing a dress. Hardheadedness maybe. It was an old dress I found in one of the house's closets, a dress I had the distinct feeling Grandmother had made for Mother or maybe wore herself. The cotton fabric had a peach blossom print and cinched at the waist, with a crochet trim at the sleeves, the hem, and the collar. It was stupid to wear it.

"Still, you look nice in it," she said. "Maybe you should wear it to work sometime?"

I groaned at that—her not-so-subtle way of implying I could do more to turn heads in the office. I felt mean words gushing like bile from some black organ inside, ready to turn to a venom strike, but I would not take the bait. It was too early. We hadn't even broke ground yet.

"Look at this shovel," she said with the blade held between us. The point had been worn away so far that the U was cleft and turning into a W. "How does that even happen?" she said.

"Was Father a gold prospector?" I said. "Grave digger?"

"More likely your brother," she said. "Used it more than your father, I mean."

We walked back to the site. Mother chipped at the ground with the shovel. A teaspoon of dirt moved each time. She furrowed her brow.

"Is this dirt or granite?" She tapped the ground, and the blade clanked three times. Again, the earth barely moved. "Goodness," she said.

"If you're through playing, I'd like to get started," I said.

"Just let me try first, Cindy. I have to see." She placed the blade where she wanted and put one foot on the corner. She stamped her foot there several times and tried different angles. Once, she balanced the entire weight of her body, standing on the edge of the blade, but she hardly scratched the surface.

I held out my hand.

"Maybe it gets softer farther down," she said and handed me the shovel. "Then we can take turns."

"It's not like digging in the garden, where the ground's been broken year after year. I think it's going to take more back than you've got." I lifted the blade several feet from the ground and drove it down with what felt like all my might. It was still a sorry display. Even though I knew what was required, my body would need more convincing. I tried again, still all arms, same result. "You'd think all the water would've softened the ground a little more."

"Maybe you should've left the pump on?" she said.

I raised the shovel again, this time two or three feet, high enough to get my whole upper body into it, not just my arms. I tried to crack my back like a whip and thrust the handle of the shovel in hard, making the tool do more of the work if possible. I remember seeing my brother bring a splitting maul down on a section of oak. To look at him, you wouldn't think he could lift a maul over his head, let alone swing one, but as I would heft and drop the shovel down, I remembered how he threw himself into it, like all self-possession had given way to something else, like he'd yielded himself to becoming a machine in the moment, and there was a kind of soulless elegance to it, and after a while, with each swing a hollow pop, a struggling regroup, and a swing and a pop . . . . Before I knew it, the hole was almost as deep as half the shovel blade, twice as wide, and the sweat was already rolling down my face. "Maybe you should take a break," I heard mother say in between shoveling, but I threw my whole body into it at least three or four more times.

I wiped my eyes against the sleeves that barely covered my shoulders and put my sunglasses back on. "I think you're taking me too literally on this supervisor thing," I said, catching my breath. "I hear you tossing a lot of *maybes* my way, but the thimble-full approach to excavation was going to take us all year."

"I'll go get us some water," she said like a pronouncement. In her voice I could hear that she was already having to exercise patience with me. I gave myself a moment before carrying on. Meanwhile, Mother went to the house for a pail, walked past me without a word, down to the spring, and returned with cold water and a tin cup to share. She also had two five-gallon buckets she must've picked up behind the shed. She flipped these over for seats, one on each side of the slowly forming hole. After we sat, she dipped the cup in the pail. I noticed how the cold fogged the cup, the way her fingerprints slowly disappeared as I drank.

She popped open an old black umbrella I didn't even notice she had. "You'll be so wore out, you won't be able to get out of bed tomorrow," she said from underneath its shadow.

"I've taken tomorrow too," I said.

"Sick day or vacation?"

"Vacation."

"It won't be that," she said.

I handed her the cup. She filled it and handed it back.

"Let's do it this way," she said. "Work a little, rest a little. We're getting paid by the hour anyway."

Mother's demeanor was uncommonly lighthearted this day. Maybe it was the morning sunshine or simply not having to drive to town to spend the day behind the drugstore counter. Truth be told, I'd rather dig a dozen holes than spend another day at the firm answering phone calls, making sure the partners kept their appointments.

"You sweat like your father," she said.

A drop of sweat rolled across my lips. "At least I got something from him." I wiped my mouth with the back of a dirty hand.

I finished another cup of water and gave it to Mother, and we sat in silence a moment.

"Kind of rare for it to be this quiet," Mother said. "So many houses and trailers around here now. Seems like any hour of the day you're likely to hear someone shooting a gun or revving an engine or trespassing on their loud four-wheelers up and down the road and any path they find. It used to be this quiet all the time."

"At least there's a dollar store halfway to town. A few other places. Having people around's not the worst thing."

"Feels less like home, though," she said. "Your brother would hate it. It's changed a lot since—since he was last here."

I agreed, took up my shovel, and went back to work. With each attempt I felt I was still refining my form. Occasionally, I'd try taking shorter digs, but the ground was much harder than I was strong, and this manner only served to wear my arms out sooner, so I realized the wood-splitting, ground-stabbing approach would have to be my go-to. Back and shoulders to break ground, arms and torso to lift the earth from the bottom. As I was learning this, I'd almost forgotten I wasn't alone.

"Cindy. Darling," Mother said as gently as she could, like she was rousing me from having fallen asleep while reading on the couch, telling me to go to bed, "this really isn't lady's work."

I hung my hat on the shovel handle, retied my hair, rolled the sleeves of my dress a little higher, and spat. "Do you know any men?"

"Aren't there a few in church who would help?" she said.

"Potbellied granddaddies and gawky orphans with arms no bigger than mine. And when's the last time we've been to church anyway?" I struck the ground again. "God helps those who help themselves." And again.

"That's not in *my* Bible."

"Well, it should've been," I said.

"What about Tom?"

"Tom?" I laughed. "Tom hasn't got a spare moment between Hannah and the children and the newspaper."

"He's still editor?" she said.

"Apparently, he doesn't even have time for lunch. We would occasionally meet in town when I started at the firm. Of course, he wasn't married long after that." I scooped some of the loose dirt out and onto the growing pile.

"Maybe he thought it wouldn't be proper," Mother said.

"I think Hannah doesn't like me."

"Oh? Then it definitely wouldn't be proper."

"You'd think she could spare him. She's got her children. She's got her house just outside town. Got the vacation home on the river . . ."

"On a newspaper man's salary?"

"Pshaw." I took another hard strike at the earth. "Her daddy's dime, more or less."

"Well," she said, "if he can't make a half-hour lunch without breaking up the marriage, I suppose a morning or afternoon away would be out of the question. Tom always seemed like a bright young man. He's done well for himself with the newspaper, but for some reason I worry for him . . . ." Mother continued, but I carried on with my work all the more relentlessly, the sounds of the shovel at times drowning out her voice, until a sharp pain awoke in my arm. I dropped the tool, sat down, and massaged my arm.

"What's wrong?" she said.

"My arm."

"The broke one?"

"Yeah." I worked my dirty fingers deep into the muscle and thought about the night it happened. My brother, after the first of many periods of despondency, had made a flinch reaction upon finding me where he thought I shouldn't be. I'd startled him. I crashed against a dresser, broke my arm, gashed my forehead. This old pain happens sometimes, but usually it's my head, not my arm. A dull pinprick feeling burrows behind the inch-long scar typically hidden in my hairline, and then I think about him and everything that happened or didn't happen in the years after, and it takes me the rest of the day until the pain subsides and I'm allowed to forget. I began to massage the scar halfway between my temple and widow's peak.

"Cindy, it's sweet of you to do this," she said. "I know we've managed—just the two of us now—for a very long time, but maybe this job needs a certain skill set neither of us naturally has."

My instinct was to be annoyed, but I could see how careful she was being. This, in turn, was making me feel like the heel of the world, that my own mother was walking a verbal tightrope to evade my wrath. I decided then and there to measure my words with the utmost care.

"If you call a plumber, I will go inside and piss on your pillow," I said.

"Cindy!" she said.

"We've already talked about this. No one wants to come out here. They make up stories, their children overhear, they pass them to their friends, and *their* parents hear. . . . We're poison to them and everything we touch. Haunted house, backwoods cannibals, wild forest people from underground caves, an Indian curse that predates everything—they think all kinds of stupid things—so it all comes down to me and you. *We* fix it. We always fix it."

She pursed her lips and made the smallest nod. "I suppose you're right," she said like a sigh.

A slight breeze passed, chilling the damp places where the dress clung to my body. A mockingbird tried out a few tunes overhead.

"Don't hear as many songbirds as you used to," Mother said. "Guess they've gone deeper into the woods to get away from the people."

"What a quintessentially 'old person' thing to say," I said. "Grandmother might've been old, but she never rhapsodized about the good old days like you do."

She seemed taken aback, and I was immediately sorry I hadn't filtered myself better. Maybe it was the pain in my arm doing the talking.

"I guess when I'm old I'll talk like that too," I said.

I thought she was going to freeze me out a while, but then she said, "When that day comes, you'll be lucky if you have someone who'll listen."

I looked in her green eyes for the faintest hint of irony, but they were cold.

She was hurt, and in that moment I wondered if she was closing vaults on the inside that wouldn't be opened for the rest of the day, maybe even the rest of the week. This was our way back then. Our cycle. In a small way I hoped for as much. For this I felt worse.

I stood, picked up the shovel, and stabbed another chunk of earth loose from the hole. Mother went back to the house. I didn't know if I should follow her and apologize. I didn't trust myself to say the right words, and if I found them, would I sound convincing? Was I even sorry?

I ran back through what I'd said a time or two. I pondered her words between shovels. Lucky to have someone around who'll listen, or lucky to simply have someone around? The more I tried to parse out her meaning, the angrier I got, the harder I shoveled, and the quicker the job was over. Fine, I'll dig angry for the rest of the day and be done well before dark.

"'Dig parallel to the pipe so that you don't bring the shovel down across it,'" Mother read from the notecard. She stood squinting at my handwriting, holding the umbrella above her for shade.

"Thank you," I said, heaving the shovel back into the hole. "I'm not so deep yet," I said. "The man I spoke with said they bury water lines below two feet here. He said you have to bury them below the frost line or else when the ground freezes, so will the pipes, and then 'you're in a world of mess,' I believe he said."

Mother sat back down on her bucket. "You remember all those old projects he used to have, your brother?" she said.

"I remember plenty." I struck the earth again and began scraping from the bottom.

"He wanted to build a bridge across the creek that one time. Occasionally Ray would bring home a board too crooked or one with too many knot holes from the sawmill. I don't recall Ray ever building anything except for that rickety shed. But I seem to remember your brother carrying quite a few boards down there . . ."

"I've never seen any bridge."

". . . he wanted a sturdy bridge that arched over the creek in a gradual curve. It would've been simple enough to tack a few boards together for a footbridge, but I think he had something quite magical in mind, the kind of bridge a troll might take residence under. He wanted railings on both sides; he spent days sawing up boards and trying to wrap his head around the problem of the arc; he disappeared into the woods each day after school; and then, one day, he just stopped."

"Did you ask him why?" I said.

"I was afraid he'd feel silly if I asked and he hadn't completed the bridge. I didn't want him to be embarrassed if he'd failed."

"But what if he hadn't failed?"

"If he hadn't, why wouldn't he have said anything? Wouldn't he have told me it was done? Wouldn't I have been able to see that excitement on him?" she said.

I kept shoveling. "I don't recall ever seeing him excited."

"That's not true, Cindy. Don't you remember when he'd find a garter snake or a praying mantis? He'd come show them to us with a real light in his eyes. He'd catch and keep those a day or two and then set them free. Or how about when he'd find a piece of crystal quartz or an arrowhead? He'd be a new fella for the rest of the week. What about the way he used to play with those railroad spikes he'd found, laying down those spiraling rows and designs?"

I lifted my hat and massaged the pain in my head. I hadn't thought of any of that for a long, long time.

"Sit down and drink some water," she said. I sat across the hole from her. She dipped the cup in the pail and handed it to me. The water was warm now, warmer than the sweat rolling down my face. "You don't remember seeing him this way?" she said.

"Maybe once. He was different at school, Mama," I said, staring into the hole.

"But you saw him here, Cindy. The two of us and Mother. We're the only ones who knew him."

I took another sip of water, warm as my mouth, warm as my blood. "There were a few nice times for him," I said in a half-daze. "Maybe recess. There was a little thicket he'd play in alone, finding caterpillars, moving them from one tree to the next."

Mother made a small sound, a nod. I could tell she was pleased to hear this.

"But recess was the only time I'd see him since we were four grades apart." I rubbed my head. "But I do remember once, seeing him in his classroom. He was wearing a black gown-looking thing. But that sounds crazy. Am I making that up?"

Mother laughed. "I made that for his report. He had to give a report dressed as an important person from history."

"Leonardo da Vinci."

"Right!" Mother said. "I made him a beard from Mother's leftover quilt batting."

I laughed as the picture grew clearer in my mind, my skinny brother, one of Mother's old housecoats, a white-bearded shadow addressing a roomful of children who never cared to know him. "I remember now," I said. "I remember the book he read. More pictures than words. He had a story for every picture."

"Do you remember him practicing his speech for the three of us?" she said and sighed. "We're the only ones who can speak of him like this. We're the only people in the world who can remember him this way."

I stood a bit too quickly and resumed chipping feebly at the ground. The air had become very still, and the sun felt hotter than moments ago. I took a long, deep breath and let out a sigh.

"Sit down," she said.

I threw down the shovel and sat back down on the bucket. I felt lightheaded. Mother handed me the umbrella, told me to wait, and carried the pail back to the spring in the woods. Things got very quiet once she left. I wondered if I was about to faint. I looked to the woods where Mother had disappeared. Everything was hazy, rippling like someone had dipped their finger into a perfect pool reflection of our backyard. I closed my eyes, but it was still so bright. I could see a retinal web flashing behind my eyelids, pink and red at first, then black and green. In that utter stillness, I began to fall. I was ten. Grandmother was still living. Snow was lightly falling against the windowpane by my bed. She held a candle in her lap. Her voice, low and warbling. The sheets were warm, but my fingers were cold.

Mother spoke my name. She'd returned with a pail of cool water, which she placed by my feet. She poured a cup over a loose kerchief and handed it to me. "Pat that over yourself," she said.

"All of this digging makes me think of a story Grandmother once told me," I said, dabbing my face and neck.

"Oh?"

I inhaled the first cup and began with another but decided it felt better to simply hold the coolness in my hands and against my face. Before it could warm, I poured the water down the back of my neck, then I drank another.

"Well?" she said.

"Well, what?"

"You going to tell it to me or what?"

"Grandmother said boys ought not be allowed in church. They listen just enough to make them dangerous. Three such boys who lived in these woods were talking it over one day. They couldn't agree over hell or whether it was anything to change their behavior here on earth. One said: 'We can get to the bottom of this. Bring your shovels to my place tomorrow, and we'll find the truth.'

"The boys brought their shovels, and the plan was to dig all the way down to hell and ask the devil to sort it all out—God in heaven, Satan in hell, and everything in between.'"

"Where were their parents in all this?" Mother said.

"Work. Anyway, they found a clearing far enough from the boy's house, and at the end of the first day, they'd dug a nice little waist-deep plot, six-by-three. The next day the hole was wide enough that all three of them could lie down, side by side. They carried on like this for a long time until one day the dirt was piled so high around the rim that between the three of them, they could no longer crawl back out of the hole, even with one boy lifting the other, standing on each other's shoulders."

"Couldn't they just dig out?" Mother said.

"Do you want to hear the rest or not?"

"Maybe they weren't smart boys," she said.

"I thought that much was clear."

"Nightfall came, and the boys shouted and cried for help, but all night long no one arrived. With nothing but nightcrawlers, voles, and moles to keep them company, the boys broke down—each one of them—and they prayed: 'God, deliver us from this pit, deliver us from this grave!' Not long after, they looked up into the night sky—a small rectangular field of stars—and they saw a silhouette roughly the form of a man darken their view.

"'Save us! Save us!' they yelled from the bottom, but the shadow only quietly moved along.

"They raved and wept and gnashed their teeth, but the shadow never returned, and no one came to find the boys. Each of the boys' parents believed the kids were at a different family's house. They stayed there for two days. On the third day it began to rain."

"Lord have mercy," Mother said.

"The walls began turning to mud and caving in. The boggy water rose up to their knees. With what energy they had remaining, they pleaded for deliverance—no longer with words but three separate cries wrenched from their hearts. Together their wails made a high, piercing scream, each fighting to match the pitch of the other. The three voices together, a dissonant keening chorus, rising up from the bottom, fell on the ears of a young boy rushing home through the woods. He and his dog followed the sound to the pit. He couldn't see the boys, but the boys could see him. They screamed to be saved, but the boy remembered hearing how a few neighbor boys had planned to tunnel down to hell.

"He and the dog raced home. Though he was soaking wet, he jumped into his bed and shivered beneath his sheets. His mother and father heard him sobbing and mumbling in his room. They asked him what was wrong, and he told them: A few of the neighbor boys were going to dig a big hole, all the way to hell, and they did it—I heard their screams; they were being tortured. They did it, and now hell's busting wide open, coming for us all.

"The parents worked out the truth, found some rope, and resurrected them from their watery grave."

"Had I known the kinds of stories she was telling, I might've put a stop to them. It's a wonder you ever went to sleep," Mother said. "At least there was a happy ending."

"I wasn't done," I said.

"Dear God."

"You let me tell this much. I might as well finish.

"The boys weren't the same after that. Three days in a grave together had changed them. They didn't wonder about hell anymore; they certainly didn't seek it. They didn't play much in the weeks after. They'd sit together in silence. Until one day, one of them asked, 'What about the shadow of the man we saw on the first night?'

"Someone had heard them. Someone had seen them and did nothing. Who or what would walk away from three panic-stricken children after witnessing them in their direst moment? Surely no human, certainly not a neighbor. The rest of their lives, they never forgot this shadow, and they never walked or hunted the woods alone when they didn't feel it looming behind their shoulder; in their dreams each would see a void darker than night, a form peering above them from a window of stars, blackening out the shape of an indifferent man, this silent witness."

I stood and returned to digging, less furiously than before. I'd sat too long, and I felt silly for getting carried away with Grandmother's story.

Mother sat quietly in the shade of her umbrella before saying, "I don't know how you remember all those stories."

"I was an impressionable child." I chunked the blade back into the ground. I was only slicing thin layers, and even though the ground was somewhat softened deeper down, closer to the water, at this point I was too weak. I leaned on the handle. "You know, Tom wants me to write them down. *All* of them, anything I'd like to tell. He wants to put a book together."

"Tom? A book? Of Mother's stories? You know that many?"

"Kind of strange, but when I try to think back—all the way back to my earliest memories—my mind tends to recall Grandmother's stories. They were so vivid and mysterious to me. And school was difficult, you know?"

"I know."

"Maybe they were a way to escape some of that or to forget what happened with—"

"Don't," she said.

I sat down and removed my sunglasses. I looked her in the eyes. "We never talk about my brother," I said. "We never talk about him."

"We talk about your brother," she said.

"But we never talk about what happened."

Mother's eyes trailed from mine into the deepening hole in the ground. "No. We *never* talk about that," she said.

She watched me work for a while.

Neither of us spoke.

At last she said, "I don't think you should do this."

"What?" I said.

"With Tom. Write the book if you want to but leave Tom out of it."

"Why?"

I could see her searching for delicate, vague words until at last she said, "It wouldn't look right."

I scoffed and shoveled more loose dirt from the hole. "A minute ago you wanted him over here to help us fix our plumbing, but now there's something taboo about him."

"You know what I mean. You know why," she said.

"No, please, enlighten me."

"Cindy." She swallowed hard. She seemed already to regret what she would say. "He's a married man. It wouldn't do for you to spend evenings late working on some project together."

I was livid, but I laughed anyway. "Which one of us don't you trust? You seemed to think Tom was all right earlier. Am I the one? You think I'd seduce him?"

"Stop it! I never said anything of the sort. All I said was that it wouldn't look right. Don't you ever worry about what folks might think?" she said.

"That's gone, Mama. You can let go of that. All these years, all these years—*knowing* what they think of us—and you're worried it could get any worse."

"It can always get worse, Cindy. You're grown, but maybe you're not yet old enough to know that," she said.

I was hardly moving any earth now, but I kept trying. "That's the most *Grandmother* thing I believe I've ever heard you say."

Mother said, "Well, she was *my* Mother. I know you two were close, but I knew her longer than you. I may not know her stories, but I knew the woman, and she *was* a wonderful woman, but she had her flaws like anyone; she had her weaknesses, so trust me when I say it wouldn't look right and leave it at that."

I leaned again on the handle. "You're being disingenuous. Quit pretending you don't want to tell me something."

Mother stood slowly and took a few paces around the worksite, still underneath her umbrella. "There's no pleasant way to say this, but Mother had a fling once, with a man in town. A doctor, an old friend. My father was a hard man in his later years. He was good and true, but it hurt him deeply, and he never got over it, and I suppose part of me didn't either. I don't know who was at fault, Mother or the doctor, maybe both; all I'm saying is sometimes a strong wind only needs a little crack to open a door."

I took several jabs at the ground before speaking. "I'm not sure whom to defend right now, Grandmother, Tom, or me."

"Every person who's ever hurt anyone believed one last lie beforehand: This will only hurt me; I will bear this burden alone." She turned to face the house. "Your grandmother found out the hard way, and it changed us all."

After a while of thinking and jabbing and sweating, I said simply, "You've got Tom wrong."

"I know Tom's a good man. I've never doubted that."

I agreed and started back digging, but then she said, "Part of me always wondered if you two wouldn't end up together. I hoped—"

"Martha, you can take that kind of talk right back to the house." I had pointed the shovel handle at her and then at the house.

She sat there.

"What use is it talking like that? You kill me sometimes. You won't let anything go." I threw down the shovel and massaged my arm. Closing my eyes, I tried to gather myself. I straightened my spine and threw back my head. My hat fell off. My hair, matted with sweat, had come undone and stuck to my neck and shoulders. Still, I clenched my eyes against the sun. "Tom had other plans," I said, shuffling a few steps backward. "I wouldn't interfere with his future." Standing there, the blood draining from my face, I began to feel the sensation of floating, like my legs had disappeared. "He begged me, you know? A few months before the wedding. He wanted me to run away with him. Romantic, huh? Just like him. He's got a poet's heart. Maybe that's why he wants me to write the book. Maybe *he* wants to write one? He's wasted on news. Still, he would've been a fool to walk away from the life he's made for himself. Where would that have taken us? Where would that have left *you*?"

I heard a faint scratching, metal on metal. I looked before me, and Mother had emptied the hole and was carefully drawing the shovel's blade across the bottom, exposing a tarnished copper pipe, smooth and perfect as a bone.

I fell to the ground and dove my hand in, brushing the dirt from the pipe.

"Now we cut the water back on. Now we find the leak," I said.

"*Now* you follow me to the house, and I fix us lunch," she said.

The effort it took to stand let me know she was right. For now I had nothing left, so we returned to the house together.

I left my dusty brogans by the door and went to the bathroom to wash up while Mother banged around pots and pans in the kitchen.

"No fried chicken," I yelled through the door, but I doubt she heard me. It would be just like her to force some grease or gravy on my stomach today. I turned the knobs at the sink. Nothing. The water retreating to the spring made a small, strange sound from the spigot—like the last dying gulps of life. Above the sink a wretched woman in my Grandmother's old dress looked back at me, her hair in matted ropes around her face. She looked feral, like she'd been abandoned to the woods as a child.

I tied my hair back, got a towel, and dabbed off everywhere. The dress fought my movement as I walked back to the kitchen and sat at the table. Before long, a pleasant weariness began to overtake me. The sounds of the crackling oil and the fan above the stove had nearly lulled me to sleep. I felt myself succumbing to the feeling, but soon the jarring knock of a plate being set before me brought me back.

Instead of chicken, Mother had fried pork tenderloin, stewed the last of the summer squash with onion, and boiled some string beans and corn. She'd also fried some cornbread. I devoured the food without a word and drank two glasses of water. As she ladled me a third from the water pail at the sink, she said: "Don't drink too fast. It'll make you sick."

The gravity of my body seemed to magnify as I sat there with my hands clasped around the glass. I felt my posture shifting, my shoulders drooping.

"Why don't you go lay down on the couch, Cindy? Rest up so you can manage the rest of the day," she said.

"I'm afraid I'll freeze up. Besides, I'm filthy."

Mother went to a closet and returned with an old bedsheet. From the kitchen I watched her drape it over the couch and tuck it into the cushions. She came back and said, "Go on."

I dragged myself over to the couch and sat. "I probably won't even sleep, but if I do, don't let me go too long. If I can't shower tonight, I'll burn this house to the ground . . . ." I laid down and pulled the sheet over me. "Maybe run inside before it collapses."

My face was greasy against the clean bedsheet. The room was dark and cool, and though I was damp, I began to feel slightly warm under the cover. I closed my eyes. The same gravity I felt in the kitchen chair was taking me, my whole body melting into itself.

The Riesling laughter of a woman whose evening is only beginning. Linen tablecloth brushes her knees. "That'll be perfect." A baritone voice behind a menu across from her. Silverware clinks upon china, and joyful voices surround them. A gloved hand lowers a plate before her. She looks down. The plate is empty, a pristine circle glowing white and brighter until it becomes the moon. The smell of aftershave and autumn. The moonlight filters through a canopy of leaves, their fiery colors merely muted shades of blue in the night. Together two shadows pass through the forest. A shaft of moonlight reveals that I am the woman, and even without seeing his face, I know the man is Tom. I am leading him by the hand down a woodland path that dissolves and widens until the forest and its cover recede behind us, giving way to a sea of stars above us. I stop, wishing to speak, but in the instant that I begin, a whistle blows, and a field of yellow washes over everything. It swallows and crashes around us. I blink. We are riding coach in a passenger train. We are both much older. He is drinking a gin and tonic, and I am holding a book open while gazing out the window at an endless stretch of golden prairie. My eyes focus on the window's glare to find the reflection of his face; he has been watching me. I turn to him. He places his hand on my knee and smiles tenderly. His wavy hair has much gray, as does the beard and mustache he now wears. I think to ask him where we will go, but I do not wish to disturb this moment. Though we have led much of our adult lives independent of one another, now, together, a feeling of overwhelming warmth blossoms inside me, at the promise of more days to come. This warmth is almost unbearable, but I cannot endure the thought of it ever ending.

"Why don't we pick it back up tomorrow?" I heard my mother say. I opened my eyes. Her face, inches from mine, warped as though sinking into another dimension. "No need to work yourself to death, Cindy," she said slipping into her black hole. "We can finish tomorrow."

Something in me spiked, adrenalin I suppose, and I popped off the couch and wrestled out of the sheet like sloughing an old skin, flailing and stomping. "Nope. No, ma'am. This will be done before the sun sets." I looked to the light of the window. It was clear the sun had passed above and behind the house already. "How long did you let me sleep?"

"Just a few hours," she said.

I let out a sound like a frustrated horse and thundered off to the kitchen for my hat, sunglasses, and shoes. "Get the damn card, Mama," I said, lacing up my work shoes.

The shock of the afternoon heat and blinding sunlight sent radiant waves of rage through my body. Despite the barrage, I felt the dream's residual warmth within me. My thoughts returned to the train and to Tom, his nearness, something about the look in his eyes, and the feeling that we knew each other so much better than we do now, even better than when we were younger. I closed my eyes for a second and felt lost again.

"Cindy?"

Mother's voice was ice in my spine. I felt an internal pop like a breaking bone inside my brain. I said, "I can't understand why this isn't as important to you as it is to me. You *do* know we need water to live?"

"We have water, Cindy. It's inconvenient now, but we still have it," she said.

"That's a beautiful perspective. I wonder if you'd still feel that way naked and shin deep in the cold creek this evening?" She said nothing, so I said, "Read me the damn card."

She squinted and moved the card the proper distance from her nose and read, "'Cut the water on to find the leak.' Oh, wait. Wasn't that a few steps back? Yes. It says to do that before you begin digging and after the hole's been dug to spot the problem. But why didn't we cut it on sooner?"

"I don't remember. I think I had digging on my mind. Go to the breaker box and flip the switch for the pump back on."

As she walked back to the house, I remembered the man from the library saying how it wouldn't be a bad idea to let it run beforehand to soften the ground. Maybe I thought I already knew where the break was or that it would make the pipe harder to find if I didn't stop it soon enough and the ground puddled in too wide of an area. I don't know what stupid thing I thought, but I felt angry at myself for needlessly breaking my back all morning, angry at Mother for not bringing this detail to my attention sooner and for letting me sleep too long, angry at the plumbers for using too thin a pipe, angry at my father for never once being around to repair a single thing in our lives—

"Can you see the leak?" Mother called, halfway back already.

I doubled over and gazed in the hole. My shadow covered everything, so I stepped around, but it was still difficult to see. The water moving through the pipe made a hollow whispering sound. I got on my knees for a closer look. I watched and waited.

"Why can't we see anything?" Mother asked.

I felt something like acid move from the top of my stomach and then downward. I felt a strange sensation where I assumed my kidneys to be. Failure. Systems in my body were shutting down at the sight of this tarnished, seamless pipe.

"I missed it," I said and sat on my heels in wonder. It had never even occurred to me that this could happen. I stared aghast at the copper line for quite some time before I noticed Mother had been speaking.

". . . I went to the church often when you were at the ladies' college. It was nice to sit under the bright lights, especially in the long, dark days of winter, and hear about a different world, a different time. On the darkest nights, he would talk about the afterlife."

I thought I could see water beading on the end of the pipe on the spring side. It looked like more than condensation. I could hear the water moving, whispering.

". . . One night he was speaking about a foolish man who buried his talents. I know it wasn't the point, but I couldn't help thinking about the talents we have, the things we bury down deep, and I got to thinking about you and how smart you are and young and gifted. You're not so old yet. You're thirty. You've still got time to try other things, find out what you're meant for. You're not meant for this, Cindy."

Water was gathering now, moving toward the house, the pitch was changing.

"—and I don't mean *this*. You know what I mean. I mean *here*."

I stood, but the muscles in my back and legs fought to keep me grounded. "We're close now," I said, picking up the shovel. The handle felt smooth and slick. Blisters had bubbled up like eyes below my fingers. I spat in my palm and rubbed a handful of earth in them. It wouldn't be long now. I only needed to pry away a little ground at a time. The leak couldn't be far now.

Through the toil Mother's voice was coming and going, half-garbled like a broken radio signal: ". . . the older I get, the more I think such thoughts," she said. "The afterlife, I mean. I try to picture it, but the preacher says it's more like a great hotel you share with a bunch of strangers, only they won't feel like strangers when you're up there, but it seems to me, if we're all-knowing—he says everything will be revealed—if I know each person as much as I know you, how can a person truly love anyone? If we love everyone fully and equally, will I even care to find the ones I loved here?"

I struggled to work the blade deeper and pry away the ground.

"—I'm worried we'll just ramble around on golden streets, take a look at the jeweled gates on occasion, then just return to our rooms. Jesus, how will we even find anybody? The heaven the preacher describes— the one he says he's so excited to go to—sounds so cold to me."

The falling earth began to bury the pipe, but I wouldn't stop to clear the bottom. Keep going . . . now . . . again . . .

"—and if I don't feel the way I do now, later, when I'm up there, will I truly be me? If all my ailments are gone, if all the pain of this life has left me, how could I be *me*? And if I'm not me, how will I know to find *him*?"

"Him?" I said. I looked to her, but her face was a stone. "Surely you're not talking about *him*. I don't think I know how the whole system works, but I doubt they let you in once you've hurt as many people as he did."

She seemed shaken from her trance and looked at me like we were speaking about different people. "He wasn't a bad boy," she muttered, her lips barely moving. "They'll never make me believe that. I knew him like no one did. He was *good*."

"What about all the trouble at school?"

"They'll never make me believe any of it was his fault. They couldn't understand him," she said.

"What about the incident in the woods? You think all those teeth and bones are still there?" I returned to my work, chopping away, pushing. "I found the skull of a squirrel inside his tackle box. It's probably still there. There are plenty of theories about that whole thing. Most see it as a genesis. You know, some think he made sacrifices—to whom I have no clue."

Mother fell silent. I could see hard beads of sweat covering her face.

"I used to hear him talking to himself—not just at night in his sleep, though that was a thing to hear for sure, but out in the woods, alone on the playground or in his room—and not in any normal way. I mean it sounded like a one-way conversation with someone who wasn't there. He'd ask questions, *and* he'd receive answers." The earth was falling away now, much more easily.

"An invisible friend," she said.

"Don't they say he's schizophrenic? Isn't that what they say when you hear voices?" With a careful step on the top of the blade and a push of the handle, I could lever the blade just so, more ground sliding away into the bottom of the hole.

"We never spoke about any voices. He was imaginative. He was creative. No one would talk to him. No one but us. Who can blame him?" her voice barely audible above my digging. "He needed *someone*."

"What about me?" I struck the earth. "I needed an older brother. I needed protection." Again. "What about us? We needed help. We both needed a father." And again. "You and Father—what didn't you do?"

Her head was tilted to one side, her eyes lifted to me. Her parted lips were barely moving. My once-broken arm felt like a roiling mound of fire ants, surging where the fracture had callused over so long ago.

"Did you ever intervene? Why didn't you stop him when you saw him growing strange? You indulged him by doing nothing. He only got worse. If you'd done anything—if you'd done a single thing—then Father wouldn't have left. And when he did, you just let him leave. Again, you did nothing," I said.

Sweat or tears streaked from her unflinching eyes down her ashen face. The drops mixed with the dust of our work and caked and dried in darkened streaks. My mother, looking upon me, petrified by unspoken despair, weeping the stolid tears of a miracle statue, a saint or martyr mounted high in some lofty, distant balcony. In that moment I wondered if she was suffering a heatstroke or something worse, and a wave of panic and wrath passed through me, but I drove the shovel hard into the ground with everything I had, and a good chunk of earth flopped over into the bottom, and when it fell, a spray of water popped out of the ground, tiny pine needle jets in all directions. The water hissed as it drenched the walls of the hole, gathering in a puddle at the bottom. I reached in the hole with cupped hands and splashed the water on my face. I laughed to feel its coolness upon my cheeks. "What does the card say?" I asked her, my fingers thrust under my sunglasses, still wiping my eyes.

"Cut off the water. Dig far enough below the leak that you can use the pipe cutter," she read.

We both sat, watching the hole fill with water. "Somehow I thought we'd never see this. I thought it'd beat us," I said. I looked at Mother, but again she was entranced, motionless. "Sit here. I'll go cut off the pump."

I absented myself to the side of the house with the circuit breaker. I opened the metal box and flipped the switch to the pump. Alone, out of Mother's view, I leaned against the old house and waited. I wanted nothing more than to be alone—alone for a long, long time. Yet again, I'd said too much. The echoes of my accusations reverberated in my ears, and I felt queasy, like I might retch and pass out there in the grass. I began to heave and wheeze. But only a moment. I steadied myself. I took deep breaths. I patted my face with both hands until I felt the blood coming back. Tears and sweat smeared my face with mud, then dried again. This current within me was subsiding. I could return. We would finish.

I took a deep breath and turned the corner to find my mother, lying on the ground, half-submerged into the hole.

I raced to her and shouted. I fell on my knees by her side, threw my arms across her ribs to flip her onto her back. Her body seized at my touch.

"Dear God, Cindy! You scared the bejeezus out of me!"

"Oh," I said, falling backward. Her entire arm was covered in mud. It was clear she had been emptying the bottom, one filthy fistful after another.

"You thought I was dead, didn't you?" she said.

I said nothing.

"Serves you right," she said. She watched as I struggled to catch my breath, then said: "We should break for the afternoon. You look spent. We'll empty out the hole, and you can finish digging below the pipe once the sun's behind the trees."

I sat there, calming myself.

"You don't look well. Let's go sit in the shade. I'll fix you some water. Go on."

I walked to the porch steps and sat down. The shadow of the house had moved halfway across the yard now. Mother had taken the pail back down to the spring and returned to the house. She set the bucket beside me. "Hold on," she said and went inside. When she returned, she had two packs of peanut butter crackers.

She sat next to me, and we ate the crackers and drank the water in silence. All the while I felt compelled to retract what I'd said earlier or to apologize, but I couldn't lie and say I didn't mean those things, nor was I sorry, so I said nothing.

I returned to the hole. Mother had cleared away a good bit of ground, enough for me to see how to proceed. I took the grubbing hoe and awkwardly punched the blade at the ground on both sides of the pipe. I needed a sturdier base. The only way was to straddle the hole. In this fashion I could come down parallel to the pipe, breaking more ground, pulling the earth toward me. It was at this moment I most acutely regretted having worn Grandmother's dress. The only way was to hike it up nearly to my waist and tuck it under me for decency's sake. But the grubbing hoe worked well and allowed more precision than the shovel. The ground, softer now, gave way easily enough, but this new motion made me tired in a way the rest of the work hadn't.

Mother took a seat and watched. The air was still. As the sun dipped slowly toward the tree line, the shadow of the house crept toward us. Each time I'd glance away from my work, I'd see another swath of yard devoured and the slow blanket of darkness inching its way, urging me onward.

At first Mother made a few encouraging sounds, but she soon fell silent. I was concentrating on clearing the earth from around the broken pipe. Occasionally, I'd stop with the grubbing hoe and, lying flat on the ground, reach in and paw the dirt out from under the pipe. From underneath I could hear the voice of my Mother, though her words were indistinct.

I rose from the ground, repositioned myself, and again struck at the earth below, drawing it toward me. I could hear her now, though once the words finally registered in my ears, it was clear her one-way conversation had been playing out for quite a while. This had a strange effect on me. I felt like an interloper though I'd been there all along. This, coupled with the dress—I looked down at its unfamiliar print and hand-crocheted trim, and suddenly I began to wonder if it was me wearing the dress or someone else.

"—he'd been at that school, what? Did he make it a full year? Weren't they supposed to help him? What did they ever do for him? I wrote him letters, you know? All along. Less toward the end—I mean, not the end but up until what happened. They sent them to me in a box with the rest of his things. Half of them hadn't been opened. Had he read any of them? Maybe they kept them from him. How many times did all those people interview me, the weeks and months after—after it was all said and done and they had taken him from me? Newspaper and magazine people. They come on nice like they care, every five years to the day, like it was his birthday or something, all concerned like they want to help, like those church ladies, pecking at bits of information—more sand in the gizzard, Mother would say. Just when everyone around here seems to let up a little, strange cars coming by, fancy-dressed women with their recorders and notepads—enough to turn everyone cold again, like it happened yesterday. Townsfolk come into the drugstore, and I see them across the floor, down an aisle, whispering behind their hands. Mother was right. So were you. I should've never said a word to any of those people. Any little detail they take and stretch and warp until you can't even sort out in your own mind anymore what's truth and what's their sick little fantasies . . ."

We're close now, I kept saying to myself.

"—what's the use? They know what he did. There's plenty on record about that. Why not leave it? They think if they come around, talk to me enough, they'll get some kind of explanation, but if I can't uncover anything on my own, what makes them think they can? They must think they're smarter than me—smarter than all of us—like maybe if they ask just the right question, they'll get to the bottom of every-thing, everything sorted out and revealed, but I've given them enough already, haven't I? Now every detail I recall, every story I remember, is like a ruby I bury deep inside my heart.

"I ought to visit him. I know I should. But I can't. Can you imagine seeing him like that? You remember how he fared in school—might as well have been in a cell. He was so still when we saw him last, hardly blinked, never spoke, and that was years ago. I wonder now if they can even get him to feed himself. I wonder if he'll always be this way. Won't he turn a corner someday and speak, be himself again. Of course, what you said is true. They tell me he speaks when no one's around . . ."

My arms were trembling with an exhausted fever.

We're close now.

". . . his brother. He speaks to his brother," she said.

I pushed my body out from the hole, placed the tool to the side, and looked at her colorless face, now gaunt and lifeless in the failing light. "Mother, I think you've had enough. You've worked too hard. The heat. You need to go inside."

"He had a twin brother, Cindy. You had another brother," she said.

"What?"

"We knew early there would be twins. Your grandmother had a great intuition about such things. Aside from some bad dreams, the pregnancy was fine—two good, strong baby boys—but something happened there at the end. Your brother was born first, awake but silent and still. The other next. I couldn't see, but I could tell from the looks on their faces the worst was true. So much pain had ripped through my body, but nothing was worse than that moment—like all the blood inside me had soured and spoiled my insides. It's worse than the emptiness that comes after birth, ruin, eating you from within, but then a small cough and a whimper—the first sounds of your living brother—and then a wail.

"I believe he was moved by grief. It took hold, possessed him. He must've felt what I felt. Your brother cried for us all that day.

"We could never talk about it—your father and I. Oh, but I thought about it. Every week, every day. Especially those months before you arrived. Whenever I'd see him playing alone, chattering to himself, hear him mumbling, walking through the woods or murmuring in his sleep—it was always to his brother. Aaron. We named him Aaron. And through the years I could see him grow in the form of your brother . . ."

The shadow had overtaken the yard. Mother's eyes were great caverns.

". . . and so could your brother. Every time he looked in the mirror, he could see him. No one ever told him, yet I'm convinced he felt his presence everywhere he'd go and in everything he poured himself into. Every hole he ever dug, every rock, coin, button, or railroad spike he ever discovered and carried home—they were for him. Every tree he climbed, every bridge he built, every path he cut—it was to get to him. It was the only way he knew to find his brother. And he will get to him, in this life or the next. I pray we all will. And when we do, I pray his twin will know me when he sees me—that we won't be strangers when we get to that land more kind than home."

I crawled away from her, from the whole day's work, and stumbled across the yard to the shed where father left his tools. I threw my hat and sunglasses aside, passed through the doorway, and slammed it shut behind me. I fell to my knees and covered my face in the dust and wept.

Dim strips of light filtered through the ramshackle walls of the shed. Try as I might, my eyes could not adjust to the shapes around me. The longer I tried, the darker it seemed. I stood and remembered my mission: pipe cutter. I pictured the tool the man had shown me from the book. Father's toolbox was somewhere. The corner? I needed light. I turned to open the door to gather what little afternoon sun remained, but the door was gone. I thought to call out for my mother but didn't for fear of hearing my own panicked voice reverberating back to me. I groped through the emptiness, leaning and reaching for a shelf or a wall or a doorknob, but found nothing. The darkness was pulsing somehow, blacker with each increasing heartbeat. I thought to run, to crash into anything if only to touch something, until turning, reaching, opening my palms both forward and behind, I felt the gentle friction of something slide down my fingertips to my palm and, quicker than a gasp, latch around me—a hand.

Not cool nor warm but steady and firm—this hand took mine and would not let go. Another hand enclosed over the top of mine, gently tugging at me. My parched throat stifled a scream.

My eyes had been open wide until then, but now, for fear, I'd shut them so hard, the strain of the muscles of my face rumbled inside my ears, a sound like a gently rolling timpani or a summer thunderstorm miles away.

"Look at me," he said, his voice echoing like a drop of water fallen into a deep well.

I opened my eyes, and in the black surrounding us, his dim form appeared, standing before me, my brother.

"Where are you?" I said.

"Here," he said, expressionless, gazing through me. "You seem afraid."

"I am."

"What's to fear?" he said, staring at his hands clasping mine. "Do you fear me?"

I looked upon him. At first his face was unclear. Dark hair, thin cheeks, hollow eyes, the small mouth, the angular, pointed jaw of a man. I looked and watched as the contours of his face softened into those of the boy I tried to save from the schoolyard ruffians, the ponytailed liars. I watched as his eyes glinted with some unseen light.

"I had two brothers," I said. "Now I have none."

He made no reply.

"I need you now. I've always needed you. Soon I'll need you even more. Mother's getting older. I'll need help. When she's gone, who will I have? I'll have no one. When that day comes, I won't be able to make it. I'll wither into myself. I'll crumble. I won't make it. I'll follow her. I'll follow you. I have lived long enough to know what this world has to offer. What little it has given me, I relinquish. I want none of this. Take it. I offer it to anyone who will have it. But don't leave me here."

"You're not afraid to die; you're afraid of the mortality of others," he said. "You're afraid of the life that comes before and the silence that comes after."

"Yes."

"Such fear." The pressure on my hand tightened. His hands had grown cold as the sweat on my cheeks. "Yet still we live. Each of us."

"What will become of me when I am alone? What does one make of life when there's nothing to look forward to, nothing to hope for? And will I turn from the future, only to flail blindly at the past—like Mother? Will I, looking back, fill my heart with resentment for every-one who's left me? I fear it's already started."

"Yes. You resent them," he said.

"Yes."

"You resent me."

"Yes."

"And now you fear me."

"I loved you," I said.

"But you blame me."

I could not answer.

"You blame me for all that's befallen you. Even now, you are blaming me for the loss of a second brother. Our brother."

"Yes."

"He is forever lost but not only to you—to Mother, to Father, to all of us."

"Can you see him where you are?" I asked.

"Do you see me?"

I nodded.

"Then you see him."

A breeze flashed across my skin, cool like the first whisper of autumn, and I felt a quickening in the marrow of my bones. I slowly opened my eyes to find I was standing several paces outside the shed, my back to the door with my hands clasped before me. I turned my hand over, and in my open palm, I held the pipe cutter.

Before I could attempt to reason with myself about what had trans-pired, Mother had seen me approaching and said: "That didn't take long. I thought you said you needed to search for it."

"What do you mean?"

"You hardly had time to walk over there and back."

I waited for my thoughts to untangle, but the toil of the entire day was beginning to muddle everything in my mind.

"Good thing your father left us the tools," she said.

"To hell with him," I said and laid on the ground. I began working the teeth of the little vise over the pipe.

Mother swallowed. "He's your father. I guess you have a right to say that," she said. "I was awfully sad when he left, angry, that's true, but he didn't take everything with him when he took his love from our family. In fact, he left pretty much everything."

I raised myself to look her in the eyes. "How's that, Mother?"

"Look. He left us all this. More importantly, he left *us*. The three of us. We always had each other. And that's why I felt sorry for him—day one—and why I still do. We had one another, but the moment he left, he had no one. You can curse him for abandoning this," she motioned to the house, the garden, and the yard, "but he gave me a son, a daughter, and a place we could call home."

I thrust my arms back in the hole, tightened the teeth on the cutter, and began pushing the mechanism beyond, down, and around the pipe.

"You know, sometimes the curse of a good memory is a propensity for bitterness," she said.

I pulled the cutter to me and pushed it around again.

"For those old remembered wounds, it helps to have a good imagination," she said. "Remember how we used to dream up your father, imagining his travels across the country? Places I guess I'll never see. After a while it seemed like those stories could've just as easily been about anyone else, a stranger, but somehow I always felt close to whoever we were inventing—it felt real and true, like little daydream postcards from a lost friend."

I brought the cutter back around, and a metal snap severed the copper pipe. I couldn't help making a small, delighted sound. Suddenly, this felt possible. We would finish. There would be water in the house tonight. I spat on the line and polished it enough so that I could see the ruined part. I placed the cutter a few inches beyond. "Hand me that connector, just in case," I said. I took the contraption, lined it up along the ruined part, and made sure I wouldn't cut away too much.

"Wonder what your father's doing now?" Mother said after I'd begun to work the cutter back on the pipe. "Who he's with, what he looks like?"

"Old . . . handsome," I said, tightening the teeth on the metal.

"You speak like you know," she said. "You never did tell me what happened, where you were those months after you graduated from the ladies' college. What was it? God, nearly half a year. All that time, your letters were so vague, the few you sent."

I began cutting the copper.

"You want to know the truth of it? After three months I was scared to my soul I'd lost you. I couldn't sleep nights on end for worrying that you were leaving me. Imagine. Ray gone, your brother gone, Mother passed, and now my daughter, my only family left, she's just a few lines on notebook paper I read once or twice a month. I lived and died with the opening of the mailbox back then. I couldn't eat or rest much after breakfast; I'd spend the whole morning irritable; I'd be hateful to the ladies at work and to the customers; I'd doze off on the drive home, nearly running off the highway; and finally, I had to tell myself: 'Get it together. She's got as much of her father in her as she has of you'—which may be only slightly true; you may be half-Ray and half-Mother—'and if it's in her blood that she must go, then go she must. She'd only be miserable to come home otherwise, and that would just make us all that way.'"

Another metal chink, and a two-and-a-half-inch section of pipe was broken from the line. I fetched it from the dirt and handed it to her.

"Is that all it is?" she said.

"A few pinprick holes are all it takes to ruin our lives for a good week and a half," I said.

Mother read some of the last notes from the card and handed me the coupler again. I laid flat on the ground with my arms in the hole, trying to affix each end of the coupler to the sawed-off pipe, while Mother fiddled with the pipe cutter. "Sometimes I wonder if he's found happiness out there—Ray, I mean. I wonder if he ever thinks of coming home," I heard her say. I didn't answer. I tightened the end of the coupler again and again.

I pushed myself out of the ground and sat on my knees. "Mother." I reached for her hand, urging her to sit next to me so we were eye level.

"We've got to move on from all of this. We can't control a single bit of what's been done. It's over. We can have hope. Hope's a fine thing. We can hope Father is loved wherever he is; we can hope my brother is learning how to *be* again where they've taken him; we can hope that all of the people hurt by his actions will mend and heal and forgive; we can hope everyone in town will just simply forget about us, forget we even exist, but beyond all this hope, Mother, when everything is said and done, we can only choose to move on and live our lives, and if that means forgetting much of what's happened ourselves, then that's what we shall do: forget."

She smiled in spite of herself. She'd intently watched my eyes for every word I'd spoken, but I wasn't sure she'd received any of it. Mother wiped away a lone tear from her cheek. "Forget . . . ," she said, "forsake . . . one and the same. To me." She nodded and stood, brushing the dirt from her pants.

"Let's make sure this whole thing hasn't been one big disaster," I said. "Go into the house and cut on the water at the kitchen. Open the window so we can hear one another."

Mother hesitated before leaving. There were words churning inside her stomach. With a grimace, she nearly shuffled in place as she tried to sort them out: "You think you have to watch over me, take care of me. I'm not so old. How do you think I got along when you were at the ladies' college? It was lonesome, I admit—and I'm so thankful you're here—but I can get along. Because I knew—I know I still have you. Ray, your brother, the baby, they're gone. But I'll always have you, Cindy, no matter where you are."

She walked on to the house, and she did not look back.

I switched on the pump at the breaker box and yelled for her to cut on the water. I could hear a loud rumble and spout through the open kitchen window, a few hard grinding sounds, and then the voice of my mother shouting, "Hallelujah." She came out and around the house to me and said, "A little mud at first, but it's clear now."

"We did it," I said.

"No. *You* did," she said.

We returned to the hole. Thankfully, the coupler was still intact, and neither end seemed to be leaking. Mother took the notecard from her pocket and read, "'Be sure to bury the pipe with fine soil. Any rock or pebble resting on or underneath the pipe is likely to be where the next hole will form.'"

"The man told me this is probably what happened here. Water moving through the pipe makes tiny vibrations, and years of the copper vibrating against stone thins the metal until we end up with water in the yard instead of the faucets, bathtubs, and toilets. It's a wonder it hasn't happened already. I pray it never happens again—for whatever a prayer's worth."

I wasn't entirely sure how to get fine dirt from the hard chunks of earth and clay I'd broken away. Maybe this step wasn't an immediate necessity—we had running water in the house; I could do this tomorrow—but I wanted it finished. I scratched around in the piles of earth around the hole for any dirt that seemed looser and free of rocks, but there wasn't much to work with. I struck the shovel on a larger chunk of clay. "Maybe let's break up a few pieces. See what we have. Just to make sure we don't put anything too large down there," I said. "It's all probably pointless. What's three feet to the hundred or so between the spring and the house?"

"Three feet done right," she said.

We started breaking down some larger hunks. The earth felt cool and pleasant to touch. Mother was taking fistfuls and crushing them together, working the lumps into smaller bits. Occasionally, she'd have a jagged rock or a smooth pebble to toss aside. My mind drifted as we worked in the clay. A passerby might've thought we were two children playing in the mud.

After some time Mother said: "Perhaps you're right, Cindy. I've never been so good at letting things go. How anybody can simply choose to forget—that's always been a mystery to me. A mystery at its best, a shame at its worst. But Mother often told me—implored me, I should say—to seal off the part of me that still worries every day over your lost brother."

"Which one?" I said.

Mother only nodded and filled her hands with more earth.

I'd begun raking the finer dirt into the hole, covering the pipe. I'd pat it down to make sure the ground was good and dense, forming a protective seal around the line.

"I suppose I'm afraid when you get right down to it. That's why I can never let go."

"Afraid of what?" I asked.

"Cindy, when I'm gone—when we're gone—there'll be no one left who really knew him. Not a soul left who might speak warmly . . . ." She trailed off, then said, "Without the two of us, who will remember the best of him?"

After she uttered those words, she crushed two handfuls of hard ground against each other and a spray of dirt crumbled from them. Mother slowly opened her hands but kept them cupped together like she would drink from them. I looked inside the vessel her hands made and could see she held some strange object. It did not appear to be a stone. It looked smooth, metallic, man-made. She rolled it in her palms until it was free of the soil it had been embedded in, and the amorphous shape became a small brass bell.

"What's this?" Mother said.

"A bell?" I said.

She wiped it clean. "Wonder how old it is," she said. Much like the copper line in the ground, it had a rich, dark patina. She broke loose the soil from underneath. "Still seems to have its clapper. Imagine that." She shook the bell, and it made a barely audible clicking sound. "This place—people have been here a very long time for a reason. We're lucky to be here," she said. "For now it's ours."

"Do you think he put it here?" I said.

"It's possible," she said. "Finding things was one of the great joys of his life. Such a simple joy really."

"Maybe he hid things so he could simply lose them, find them himself later on," I said. "Makes you wonder what other secrets are hidden all around us."

"Maybe it was for us to find?" Mother said.

"I could imagine that."

"So can I. I'll bet he was downright giddy inside," she said.

"Well, his version of giddy anyway."

Mother placed the bell in my hands and closed them together. "It's yours, you know?" she said. "All that I have is yours. I know the house isn't much, but I'm proud to have made a life here and to have shared it with you. I'm proud that we belonged to this wondrous old place."

Later that night, after we'd filled in the hole, showered, and cobbled together and eaten a little dinner of canned chicken noodle soup and saltines, we sat on my brother's old bed and talked about those days when he was still a child. I reflected upon my earliest memories of him. We passed the bell back and forth. We had cleaned it thoroughly so that it almost rang. We wondered where it came from, who lost it before my brother found it, why he might have buried it, what other relics must be buried around the old home, and then, what to do with the bell. I suggested we bury it back in the yard—leave it where he left it. Maybe he wanted it there. But Mother thought we were surely meant to find it. She wanted to put it in a box with his things.

"What things?" I asked.

She produced a large shoebox from a high shelf in his closet. It was black and had a white silhouette of a fox. "This was from a pair of leather boots your father wore." The lid of the box folded back like a hinged door. Inside were curios of all kinds, shapes, textures, and colors—things he'd no doubt found around the home, buried in the ground, washed out in the gullies of the fields and forests, hidden under leaves, risen from the creek beds, cast out upon the dirt roads, lost along the train tracks: a hazy glass marble with a gleaming yellow ribbon inside; a blue bottleneck with a cork still in the mouth; an Indian arrowhead with serrated edges and corner notches, the stone a deep, burnt red with a waxy crayon sheen; a quartz crystal, clear and perfect like a miniature obelisk; figures, little people carved from a light wood, maybe from a yardstick; copper coins with the dates and faces smoothed to oblivion . . .

We looked for quite a while through these treasures of his, but when we were done, we both felt saddened at the idea of keeping the bell in the box, sealed away and left forgotten on the darkened shelf of a disused closet, especially after having just been recovered.

"What about the windowsill, there in the kitchen?" Mother said.

We walked across the house to the kitchen and placed the bell upon the windowsill.

"It looks a little lonely there," Mother said, "but I think it would suit him."

It's easy to forget a thing like that, a windowsill trinket, even one your eyes pass over every day for years. Oh, I don't know that we ever truly forget anything, but once in a while, let's say, a random summer day, you might pick a few wildflowers from the yard or the edge of the woods and place them in a tiny old vase from the cabinet and let them sit there in the window until the flowers have wilted and dried into paper. You watch the flowers, and their colors fade, day after day, until it seems more like a painting or a sculpture, and then you can't quite bring yourself to wipe away the dust and the few fallen leaves and petals. But one day you come to your senses—it's only junk now, after all— into the trash, wipe it away, remove the vase, and then you see how this antique green and gold bell has been sitting there beside the vase all along. You shake it—a thing you haven't done in who knows how long—and hear its tinny ring, a few stifled, metallic clicks, and then it all comes back to you: the backbreaking toil, the sweat and the dirt, your mother's words that trying day, your brother's hidden treasures, and how long it's been since you've really thought of them, longer still since anyone has even mentioned someone from your family or given you reason to share a memory of them.

Maybe that's why Mother wanted the bell on the windowsill in the first place, so we'd see it and think of him from time to time. Of course, my brother was never far from her mind. Perhaps it was more for me then. I see that now.

Living alone here as I have these few years, you would think every day would bring a flood of memories, but I don't dwell on the past like Mother did. Still, a little thing like this can sweep me away for a spell. Tonight her words fall so plaintively on my ear now: "Who will remember the best of him?"

Turning the bell in my fingers, I recall how once when we were children, I happened upon my brother kneeling at the bank of the small creek through the woods. His back was to the path, but I could tell he was cradling something in his hands, a crawdad, I thought, or perhaps he was fashioning some kind of creature from the clay in the bank there.

I called to him well before I approached, for he startled easily. I thought he might brush me aside, but he looked glad to see me. He seemed to want me to come over, but his voice was barely audible.

When I reached him, I began speaking, but a small, sharp buzz came from his hands. He shushed me without a sound, just his eyebrows. He parted his thumbs slightly, and the small head of a long-beaked bird appeared. It blinked its tiny black eyes.

"I found it in a spiderweb," he said. "A hummingbird. Look, it's all wrapped up." He pinched the bird's wings delicately against its body and showed me its feet. A white spider line weaved around and through its legs and claws. Securing the web even tighter was what appeared to be a single strand of a woman's hair. "Can you help him?" he asked in a voice so pitiful my heart nearly imploded.

I attempted to pull the binds away from the bird's feet, but the bird flapped its wings frantically and nearly flopped out of his hands onto the ground.

"You hold him," he said. "Let me do it." My brother handed me the hummingbird. "Be careful. Not too tight, but hold him still."

It seemed impossible—how to hold this bright blue-and-green creature carefully enough to keep him in place without crushing him. I smoothed down his wings with my free hand and pinned them. My brother studied the long strand of hair and how it wove through its claws. The hair was gray and black and blended into the spiderweb. He slightly pinched the bird's feet, pulling downward. In this way he was able to free the first claw very easily. The second claw was less forgiving. He attempted to strip the binds down, but the webbing tugged at his foot. With each tug its beak opened, and the smallest sound I'd ever heard came from this little body, no bigger than my thumb. My brother's hands became surgeon's hands.

While he disentangled the other claw, I looked at the bird more closely than I'd ever looked at anything before. Its chest was a deep blue, almost indigo. The blue-green feathers on its neck were like intricate chain mail, shiny fish scales layered and cascading downward, fading from green to orange, yet beneath this rainbow, the underside of these feathers were dark as shingles. Its lavender wings were nearly translucent, its beak a stalk of wheat in early spring, tender, silver, green.

A thing so small, yet it had bones and blood like me, and a heart—a heart that thrummed so fast, you could scarcely tell that it beat at all, yet somehow, in the delicate cage my fingers made, I could feel it, the tiniest vibration trembling through its entire being: life.

My brother stood smiling at me. The bird's feet were free.

My finger, still curled around its neck like a collar, began to loosen. With my hand half-open, I asked him, "Do you want to hold him one last time?"

The bird seemed strangely calm—imagine if two thick-fingered brutes three hundred times your size tried to unbind you and they were passing you one to the other—and somehow it stayed motionless in my brother's hands, a finely painted, hand-carved model of this marvelous creature. He brought the bird close to his cheek to look into its eye, and then he did a strange thing: he enclosed the bird between folded hands and, pressing his lips to the backs of his thumbs, breathed a short, quick breath into them. Then he opened his hands, slowly outstretching his palms, and the hummingbird blinked twice and then zipped away into the trees above.

We watched the bird alight upon a stem of hickory leaves. They barely shivered, barely dipped under its weight. Then it disappeared.

Mother spent much of her last years, even until the very end, ruminating over the question she asked me on this difficult day: Who will remember the best of him?

But what about our lives? Those who came before him, those who lived beside him, because of him, and bereft of him?

Grandmother once read to me, there is no greater mystery than the heart residing within each of us. Could it be we each have someone with us always, a stranger, the presence of another we must forever seek and yearn for or perhaps mourn over?

I have no more patience for the past.

Yet I cannot say what awaits me. Each night before I sleep, I light a candle and sit by the front window of the house. In the window's double pane, I watch the mirrored flame flicker before me, a light reverberating like an echo, cascading out into darkness, until it disappears among the trees. If someone on the outside would see me—a moth, an owl, a brother, some drifter strayed too far from the tracks—what would they see? A sallow face flickering against a cloudy pane, dark eyes watching for shapes moving in the moonlight—to see me vanish from the window, to meet me at the door—what words would greet such a wayfarer? Perhaps only "You're here."

CHIMERA

I am standing alone in an open field. Its wide expanse reaches for miles, yet there is a perceptible tree line in all directions. Having lived my life in these foothills, surrounded by tumbling-down mountains, I find this new landscape comforting, serene. It feels safe knowing no matter where I look, I can see what's coming.

But then I notice, all the while, I have been standing near a small building. There are two large glass panes, like a storefront. They are grimy with dust and maybe smoke. There's a tattered awning above the windows that must've once been navy blue, rippling in the breeze. There is a signpost above me. I look up and see it bears a logo, a set of feathery wings with a red letter emblazoned upon them, and it occurs to me that I am standing in an airfield, the kind I remember seeing once as I drove cross-country.

The ground, everything around me, seems dusty. The field is brown and dry. Even the sky has a sepia tint. No one has been here for a very long time, and no one is likely to be. This realization fills me with sadness, with disappointment, and finally, anxiety.

Then a feeling comes over me that I am not alone. I check my surroundings and still see nothing. I approach the building, peer into the windows—just ransacked shadows. I walk around to the back of the small building. Nothing.

But as I reach the far end, something tells me not to peer around the corner, but despite my inner warning, I do, only to find a hazy brown form approaching in the distance. It is small and very far, but as it approaches, I find myself deeply unsettled. I lean with my back against the building, putting its white cinder block walls between us, but I can't stop myself from peering around. The form has advanced remarkably far in the few seconds I have braced myself against the wall, yet in its slowness, it seems to hardly move. It is still too distant to determine what exactly is approaching. I take another look, and now the form is a mere stone's throw from where I stand. I will not look again. I am backing away from the corner, my mind racing to invent some way to evade it, but after a few paces, I sense that I am being watched. I turn to find the thing looming behind me.

My thoughts disperse in the instant I attempt to process what I am now seeing. I cannot think; I can only absorb what stands before me.

The thing appears mammalian to a certain degree, mostly covered with brown hair. Its lower half is broad, somewhat rotund, and much like a kangaroo, supported by two sinewy legs with enormous feet, which cause it to lean perpetually forward. My eyes travel to its chest to find it has no arms but, instead, large wings that it keeps tucked into its sides, but due to the creature's size, I perceive them to be flightless, like ostrich wings. As I make this association, the creature seems to grow taller, its kangaroo legs lengthening to a bird's. Its chest some-how stretches seamlessly into its neck, and atop its neck—the head of a bird, big as a horse's. I can only see its enormous beak at first. This slightly hooked beak is nearly two feet long and floating near my face. It is razor-sharp and seems capable of inflicting serious harm. This entire time the beak and the body it belongs to, though still grounded, have been hovering menacingly before me, as if to impart that at any moment the beast could attack or charge or flee. I try to further scan its chest and wings, but everything is unnaturally hazy; in fact, its movements seem artificial to me. I become aware of its great height. It has been stooping all this time, and now it leans suddenly back, rear-ing to its full height, opening its wings while lowering its face to me, and tilting its beak downward. I find at the center of its head one dark orb of an eye. It is as wide and black as Mother's cast iron. The eye is translucent, and behind its gleam, gradually emerging from the murky cobalt storm inside, a bright-yellow ring, a perfect golden iris; glowing, the eye fixes upon me, its iris dilating and contracting.

I am completely lost in its gaze. I am transfixed by the glowing ring. I feel myself falling into its pupil and its darkness therein, but the luminous ring of the iris hangs above me, bathing me in light until I am so completely bright, I can no longer be seen. No thoughts or words breach my consciousness for what seems like several minutes until finally I hear a voice—the voice of the beast: "You appear to be troubled."

In a flash we have returned to the deserted airfield.

When I do not respond, it repeats, "You are troubled."

Its beak does not move; its eye does not blink. It seems to speak to me from inside my own mind.

"Perhaps this would comfort you," it says, and immediately its beak recedes into its face. Its great eye melts into an amorphous, viscous glob, which clouds over, turning a milky white. From the tremoring shape, the figure of a human head emerges, a man's face, bald, middle-aged, stern, hollow and unblinking eyes, hard jaw, cracked skin all over, furrowed brow, turned-down lips, and again it speaks without moving its mouth, saying: "Perhaps you can listen, now. Can you hear me?"

Seeing this transformation—the slightly glowing stony figure, a human form emerging from a beast's body—only further horrifies me, yet without nodding or speaking, I think to him, "I can."

From there he begins to speak to me, at length, about the nature of his existence. How, where he is from, he is the only one of his kind. How this creates an unsurmountable chasm between him and anyone who would reach for him. His voice is austere, weary, without passion, yet strangely young despite his countenance. He seems stoically resigned to this existence, and now I can hardly listen for the thoughts filling my mind as he speaks; I have so many thoughts as I seek to attend to his words that I can barely breathe. Through this mental maelstrom, I can only feel. I feel pity for the creature, yet I feel helpless.

When I notice he is no longer speaking, I assume he is waiting for me to speak, and I wish to offer him something, any words to evince sympathy, for it's true, I feel unspeakably sorry for him, for this monstrosity. I think to the being: "We are not so different. Each of us feels this way. Locked in our own consciousness. We . . . ." But the marble visage remains aloof, impervious, and no matter which words I convey with my thoughts, the silence between us is unceasing.

VISITATIONS

When Mother was still living, I'd had plenty to do and to think about. Aside from work, cooking, keeping the garden, maintaining the house, we'd found other ways to pass the time. There was church, a few friendships I'd stumbled into, and an occasional excuse not to go straight home from work. This felt like enough.

Of course, Mother worried about me, wanted to see me married off, taken care of, but I always had a ready comeback, some cutting remark about Ray and how a husband was no guarantee. She'd be quick to point out how he'd given us our home. "What's more, he gave me you," she'd say.

"And?"

"And?"

"A son . . ."

"Yes," she'd say. "I haven't forgotten."

But in truth we lived as though we had. It was easier to never think of either of them, Ray, my brother. We filled our weeks as best as we could, and we rarely spoke of them, but in her final years, this changed. Her thoughts often turned to my brother, and we would sit in his room and remember the good times. I could tell my brother's absence was a weight upon her. Near the end I'd wanted to take her to see him, but in her decline, I feared the trip would be too much for her, and should things go as poorly as our previous encounter, I didn't think her heart could handle it.

Mother's passing devastated me for a time, but day after day, I found myself waking up anyway, fixing breakfast, going to work—I wouldn't say healing or even moving on—managing, I suppose. Staying busy was essential, a lesson from Mother, but there were other distractions. Among them I'd learned that leaving home and occasionally forsaking it all was good for me. I'd often spend the weekends and holidays driving aimlessly, often far enough I'd need a hotel. On one of my driving trips, I'd spent the night in a small town less than an hour from my brother. It took much convincing, but the next day I simply drove home like always. It took a chorus of lies to stay away, to return home yet again, to put him out of my mind, but something found me anyway.

That night I had a strange dream, and it lived inside of me for days after. Soon it became clear what was required of me, where I would go.

Chinquapin Ridge. Another state but still in our mountains. Far enough from home that it takes a three-day weekend or a vacation day to properly visit, which has made seeing him regularly regrettably infrequent, but a little planning and I can see him monthly, sometimes twice a month. Mother, Grandmother, and I visited him once, shortly after he was committed. It did not go well. But once Mother found letter correspondence with him impossible, it was almost like we surrendered him to the state or to death, or both. The number of years we had absolutely no contact with him I do not wish to admit.

But my brother didn't respond to letters, and he wouldn't speak on the phone, wouldn't even hold it to his ear, they said—and the attendant made it clear what an imposition this was, that Chinquapin is always understaffed, that she had several other patients, et cetera—so my brother left me no option but to visit him in the flesh. I told him the day I'd arrive. He said nothing. I called his name twice, and the attendant said, "He heard you," and hung up the phone.

I'm not sure what I hoped to achieve with this visit. I didn't even know for certain if he would receive me. I'd developed the haziest of pictures in my mind, what he must look like—a bedraggled waste of a human, a drooling, catatonic shell that moaned like a creaking coffin lid instead of speaking—but I was surprised to find him not so changed from how I remembered him. His age gathered in the parts of the face they always do, but there was still something youthful about him, the smooth cheeks and narrow chin, the dark, unflinching eyes.

We had to speak in a mustard-yellow room with scratched-up plexiglass between us and an attendant presiding, a burly man with thick black hair on his forearms. The whole time my brother sat there letting me do all the talking, but I watched his eyes. I could tell plenty was going on behind them. After forty-five minutes of one-way conversation, I was at the point of shouting, but I had the sense to calm myself and ask him before leaving, "Do you need anything?"

He lifted his head, looked at me squarely for the first time, and simply muttered, "A visitor."

I inquired about regular haircuts and shaving, about his medications, his diet, his habits. On a later visit, he and I spoke about these. Arrangements were made. With each trip, there seemed to be more blood, more vitality in him, and I could see years fading from his face. No one would ever accuse my brother of being chatty, but there were eventually visits when the scale of conversation almost tipped toward his side. Perhaps it was due to this or, for all I know, his advancement in therapy or met benchmarks, but it wasn't long before they allowed us to meet distantly supervised in one of the commons areas like the atrium, the cafeteria, or more often, the courtyard, under some old oaks by the lawn. The air was fresher there, and surrounded with green, and crape myrtles, I think we could both forget for a few hours where we were.

Being able to speak freely with my brother again—well, I felt like a new, different person than who I knew myself to be at home. I suppose it's who I was when we were children so long ago. I laughed quite a lot. More than I had in years. It was a great relief hearing in his voice his subdued version of excitement and joy. These visits had become a way for us to access so many memories, and I could tell he appreciated the journey of it all, but at the ends of our visits, a certain sadness would settle upon us, and I began to feel the ghost of matters we'd not yet discussed looming thick in the air.

One visit—it had been about half a year—we found ourselves unable to proceed in our normal routine. Perhaps it had simultaneously occurred to both of us that our conversation, which had largely concerned our shared past, had circumvented much of the years we'd spent separately. We knew nothing of each other's lives, who we'd become. I didn't want to speak to my daily life at home, the freedoms I had that he didn't, how my life was turning out; and he hadn't wanted to recount for me the details of his, no doubt, dismal existence here at Chinquapin; neither of us wanted to depress the other, so we sat without speaking, two strangers.

"I'm glad I wasn't there," he said after a prolonged silence.

I've never skied, but I imagined this is what it feels like when the weight of your body first begins to tilt toward the mountain's gravity. Reservations be damned, we were headed wherever, somewhere now, and so I asked.

"Mother's funeral," he replied. "I've played it out in my mind so many times, before and after, but I don't think I could've handled it. I was low then. Maybe physically unable. But to be there, escorted—think of the distraction I would've been."

"I know," I said. "It was hard, especially without you, but you made the right choice."

He covered his face with his hands and wiped his eyes. To speak he'd had to force the words from a clenched throat. "Another visit," he said. "Maybe we can talk about it then."

"Of course."

"But please, talk about something else so I can think about anything else."

"Sure. Like what?"

"Mother, Grandmother—you had them so many more years—"

I nodded.

"—or something about yourself. Tell me something I don't know about you."

So, I told him about my years away at college—nothing much there. But then I recalled my travels to him, the several months I spent on the road, all the places I'd been. He listened with envy and delight, particularly at the thought of living near the desert as I had for a few months. He asked what it was like to stand in one place and to see for miles. It hadn't occurred to me how he'd spent his entire life in the mountains and foothills, never even seen the ocean. I told him how I worked for a time at a dining room somewhere near the Sandias, how I'd met an interesting stranger there—oh, I suppose they were *all* strangers, and all interesting for that matter, but he wanted to know about this man, so I told him.

"What were you doing out there? Why didn't you just go home?"

"I wasn't ready. I don't know. There were several reasons. Running away from some things . . ."

"Running," he said. "Or searching?"

"There were people out there—very much like him."

"Who?"

"Our father."

He nodded.

"Men with secrets, whole lives behind them that they never spoke of. Do you think they ever look back? Do you ever wonder who they would've become?"

"Some don't," he said, with a certain cold finality that wasn't lost on me.

"Before they begin to settle, before anyone can reach for them, they're gone again."

"I dreamed of that life once. It's a fool's freedom. No, I feel more pity than bitterness for people who choose to live this way. I pity our father." A slight smile. "Today anyway."

"Right," I said.

"So, you went home. Then what?"

"It wasn't easy, but I couldn't think of Mother living alone. At the same time, returning, slipping back into my old room—what life awaited me there?"

"Tell me."

"That, dear brother, I've yet to determine."

"True," he said and looked out upon the courtyard, eyeing the patients moving around its fringes, yellow snatches of sun settled low in the trees beyond them. "I wonder what it would've been like to know our family the way you must. I was still a child, you know? Sheltered. I have a version of them, the one they presented to a troubled boy who they worried over more than anything. Tell me about them."

"Tell you about our family?"

"Yes."

"What do you want to know?"

"I can't tell you what I don't know about our family; only you can do that."

"Grandmother had an incredible memory. Always good for a story. Some of the bedtime variety, others not. She knew more people than we did—about town, I mean—and she knew our family better than anyone. She was very funny. I didn't know this about her back then, but when I recall the things she'd say, her voice, I can't help but smile. She could always surprise you."

"How so?"

"She had her secrets, like anyone. I have a vivid memory of a dream she once told me."

"A dream. Who remembers other people's dreams?"

"It seemed important to her. So much so that I had to write it down."

"Do you still have it?"

"Yes, it's in a journal. I have this book of her stories I've been adding to as they come back to me."

"Naturally, you're going to lend me this book one day," he said. "But what about you? Ever had a dream cling to you for a few days?"

"Parasite dream. Yes, I have. Several months back. A strange creature of sorts visited me in my sleep." Something inside was telling me to pump the brakes, that I was saying too much.

"You've been holding out on me." He laughed. "Okay, go ahead."

"I'd rather not. It's hardly sensible. I'm not even sure I remember very much about it."

He scoffed. "All of a sudden your memory's failing you. I doubt it." At this his demeanor changed. He'd grown quiet, ruminative. "Let's talk about this creature. It could be your unconscious is trying to tell you something. I wonder what you think it means. What does the creature represent to you?"

"You've been in here too long," I said.

"Yes, and I've learned a few things too. You develop an immense appetite for reading in a place like this. I've read a bit about interpretation, but I'm curious to know your thoughts."

"Truthfully, I've tried not to overanalyze much of this."

"Context is important," he said. "When did you have the dream? What were you doing, what were you going through, at the time?"

I should've known he'd cut right to the bone, so I told him how I'd had the dream shortly before our first visit.

He nodded like he'd expected as much. "Okay, that's established. The dream somehow was the catalyst that led you here, but that's not the precipitating context. What was going on in your life at the time? Can't you remember any details of the dream?"

"I wrote it down." I wouldn't lie. "It's not something I normally do, but the whole thing had been so arresting—I wrote it out to put it behind me. Honestly, I'd rather not revisit it."

"Can I ask a favor?" he said.

"No."

"Will you send it to me? Your notes?"

I drew a deep breath and exhaled slowly.

"And no edits," he said. "I want pure, unfiltered Cindy-unconscious."

"I'm not sure anyone's ready for that." Still, I told him I would. At least it would give us something to talk about upon our next visit.

At that we sat quietly enjoying the subtle breezes that would move the leaves. It was late summer, and you could feel a certain promise in the air, of relenting heat, of change. An attendant, a powerful, heavy-set woman in a long plaid skirt, approached, said something about visitation hours and my brother's medication. A few patients who had been loitering nearby in a shady spot across the courtyard had seen the lady appear and were making their way to the building, among them a slight young woman and a large hulking man probably older than my brother. They both watched us as they walked past. I was certain I'd seen them before, on other visits. My brother nodded at them and smiled. The attendant, I realized, had only walked a few feet, where she was clearly waiting, watching us. We stared at one another without moving until I inferred this was her way of telling me that it was time to leave. I stood, stretched, and made a show of doing so, "Oh my, look at the time . . . ," and she left us alone and followed the others back to the veranda and into the building.

When I returned home, I found my journal and the several pages that recounted the dream. I thought to tear them out, but I didn't trust myself to stop tearing, and because dream tatters were too damn poetic, I let it sit on my nightstand, open-faced under the lamplight.

As I glanced upon the words, the image of the monster materialized in flashes before me—the mammalian, aviary amalgam; the bright golden iris; the marble visage. True to his request, I rewrote the dream without altering a word. I folded the pages, placed them into an envelope, and mailed them the next day.

Less than a week later, I received a postcard from him with a picture of Chinquapin on the front. On the back, so typical, he'd merely written: "Finished. Let's talk." For this I arranged my schedule and took a few days from work with the intent of visiting for two consecutive days, which I'd seldom done. I didn't anticipate our speaking of the dream the full extent of my visit; it felt more so like a good faith gesture, a way of assuring him we wouldn't simply talk about me or my dream the whole time. But perhaps there was another reason, understood between us, that led me to linger the second day.

We met where I left him last, under the old oak in the courtyard. We sat on our usual mossy metal patio chairs, but this time he'd moved his chair to face me, and he had a notepad tucked under his arm.

"No, this is too intense. I won't be able to think with you looking at me like this," I said.

"Okay, okay." He angled our chairs mostly beside each other again but pointed inward. We'd hardly sat when he said, "Talk to me about this dream you had."

"When I think of it now, the first thing that comes back to me is that luminescent yellow ring in the darkness; then I see its enormous bird head, the beak hovering so close to my face; then the rest of its body— the flightless wings, the feathers, the fur, the powerful kangaroo legs, and the almost pregnant abdomen. The human face comes to me last and the curious things it said."

"A chimera," he said. "A creature possessing many disparate parts. What does that represent to you?"

"Let me think." We sat in silence a moment. I asked him for his note-pad. I found a pen from my bag and began to jot a few thoughts. The more I scribbled, the sicker I felt. It seemed clearer with every word.

"Well, what you got?" he asked when I'd stopped.

"I'm embarrassed to say," I said.

"That's the way this works. If it wasn't embarrassing, it wouldn't be true. Go ahead and tell me."

I'm sure I squirmed before saying, "*You*. I think it's you."

"Ah! I'm the monster! I'm the abominable creature! Just wonderful," he said, but he seemed more amused than anything.

"I never called him a monster in my journal nor abominable—that's *your* take on it."

"No, that thing's just something you'd love to meet and chat with over coffee in a shady place like this."

"Kind of hard to sip coffee without hands," I said.

"Couldn't fit that beak into a cup either," he said. "So, the creature represents me—lurking in the back of your mind, calling you from miles away, and now you're here."

"I suppose so."

"Give me the notepad a second." He flipped back into his notes several pages, searching for something. When he found it, he nodded to himself. "This creature, would you say it looks like this?" He turned the pad to face me and propped upon his knees a pencil sketch rendering of the chimera that was more or less identical to the one from my dreams—one sketch of the creature in full and other, smaller sketches showing details of its component parts: the wings, the abdomen and legs, and the face it last revealed to me.

"I've seen it too," he said.

"What?"

"I've had the exact same dream," he said.

I was aghast, stunned. I sat looking at his vacant stare, which seemed settled a hundred yards past my nose, until he finally smirked and said:

"Come on, Cindy. Am I really that weird still?" And he laughed loud enough to scare the birds from the courtyard.

"What are you saying?"

"I've never seen this wacko thing from your dreams. That's all you. Does everything weird in our family's lives have to tie back to me?"

I felt a mix of shame and relief, but I could tell he was still enjoying himself. I couldn't help but laugh with him. It felt like a spell, really, a kind of trance. Happiness. Thinking on it now as I recount it, I can put a name to it. We were happy.

Afterward he said, "Help me see why you think this thing represents me. I promise I won't be too offended or flattered because—heads up—I think you're wrong, *mostly* anyway."

So, I laid it out for him: "A chimera is a complex creature, multifaceted; that's you. While there was the suggestion of danger with its beak, it causes no harm—you. In the beak and the legs, I see self-restraint, which, more than power, shows wisdom, discernment. The legs, however, are somewhat tempered by the wings. Flightless wings, caught in a barren wasteland—you again, stuck in this place. And the cyclops eye—well, you've always been very intense, you know?"

"And what about the rest? The morphing into a middle-aged man?"

"Here you are: middle-aged." Immediately, I felt I'd tossed this out too casually. "But you're much handsomer than the one in the dream and in your drawing."

"But the rest of it, Cindy. You try to connect with the monster but can't. Let's roll back through it." He flipped to a different page in his notepad. "You were horrified to learn it was human or had a capacity for humanity, yet he states that he is 'the only of his kind,' and in the end, just silence between you two."

"And here we sit," I said.

He nodded.

To have spoken my little synopsis aloud, to have him review the ending back to me—it seemed so obvious, how right I was. I must've known secretly, subconsciously, of its connection. Why else would I have been moved to reunite with him? Laying it bare before him now, I felt more exposed than if I'd shared some guarded secret.

"You may be right," he said, "but let's think of it another way."

He flipped forward a few pages in the notepad. "See what you think about this."

Mythologically speaking, the chimera was part lion, serpent, and goat, but your chimera is unique to you, part mammal, bird, cyclops, and human. What in our lives is an assemblage of related yet fundamentally disparate parts? One that alters and evolves with time? My answer is the family. Your chimera represents us, each member playing our separate roles, yet we're inextricably tied.

The kangaroo feet and legs are our father. Powerful and planted, they serve as a foundation for the family, yet they also signify the potential to swiftly move great distances. While our father fled, our foundation became our home in the woods, which, Mother often pointed out, he granted us.

Perhaps the kangaroo's defining feature is its rotund belly and pouch, capable of carrying its young. This feature is tied to Mother, who, like the kangaroo, holds its children close after gestation, nourishing them in darkness until they are ready to greet the world, until the world is ready to receive them. Again, my thoughts turn to our little home and the lives we made there, comfortable yet insular. As the dreamer's attention is drawn upward, these mammalian features fade from the dreamer's view, giving way to avian ones.

We are the birds, the first signal that this creature has partly evolved, and these striking features form the dreamer's initial impression of the beast as monstrous, a chimera. I am a pair of flightless wings—like the ostrich or kiwi or, more likely, the dodo—awkward and obsolete; I am bound to wherever I stand, paralyzed, which is consistent with the chimera's uneasy, hovering motion and the feelings its movement inspires in the dreamer. As flightless wings, I am simultaneously a vestige, a reminder of our family's evolutionary past, or perhaps a signal of where we're headed.

You are represented by the long, hooked beak, which inspires fear in the dreamer. The menacing beak seems dangerous, but it is the locus of power for this creature. Furthermore, the primary purpose of a beak isn't necessarily defense: it's for consumption, for feeding itself and its young; it's for transporting nest materials; it's for communication, for song. In short you are the most powerful and versatile part of the chimera, but you must bear the burden of responsibility. Our survival depends upon you, and this frightens you somewhat, but you alone are required to defend and sustain the family and our home, and if we have any songs, they are for you to sing.

This brings me to my favorite, hideous detail—the single, yellow, glowing eye. Like the eye atop the pyramid, this eye represents consciousness, enlightenment, and knowledge. Its nearness to the beak, and that it is trained upon the dreamer, clearly links the eye with you. The dreamer is transfixed by a hidden knowledge, yet she dares not to look upon it for too long. But what hidden knowledge?

A single eye also calls to mind the cyclops, known for its power yet, conversely, its vulnerability; such is the way of learning uncomfortable truths. What has occupied your thoughts and your life these few years since Mother's passing? What's unspoken between us? I believe it's what guides you; it's why you're here. But is the knowledge for you to receive or for you to impart? What lies behind its gaze? Terror or redemption? Both? In short you seek the truth, but you are too fearful to ask, yet your unconscious is demanding it.

In your dream the glowing yellow iris encircles and swallows the dreamer. Vision can be all-consuming. But knowledge is transforming; interestingly, the beak and the eye evolve into its terminal shape, the statue bust of a man. The dreamer is bewildered with its partly human form, but its response is sympathy. The emotional journey from dread to bewilderment to sympathy— this is your hope—but sympathy for whom?

In the end the dreamer and the creature meet an impasse once the entity takes its final form, an austere, stony face. This might seem bleak at first, but I choose to see it as the matter being settled or complete. There's simply nothing left to say. But though the matter is settled, uncertainty persists; such is the way of life.

The dream ends where it begins, an abandoned airfield, which, I reluctantly infer, ties in with the flightless wings. Your brother keeps this family grounded, locked in limbo. The dreamer, too, finds herself forever caught in her predicament, left immobile and seeking to know or understand this entity that is ultimately unknowable—in short, simultaneously seeking but also possessing some hidden knowledge.

He placed his notepad on the table and awaited my reply.

"What kind of medications are they giving you in this place?"

"It was *your* dream," he said and laughed. "Do you agree to my interpretation?"

"Can we both be right?" I said.

I let my head fall back against my chair and lost myself in the rustling leaves in the branches above us. The afternoon had turned the yard green and gold around us, but in the leaves overhead, the mottled light had begun yielding to the cool dark, blooming in inky blotches, smearing and gathering with the fading sun.

"Hidden knowledge," I said. "Seems like fancy talk for secrets."

"The bedrock beneath our secrets—that's hidden knowledge, but since it's likely to forever remain that way, we might as well call it mystery."

"So, the mystery behind the dream is that there are deeper mysteries."

"Pretty much." He laughed. "Well, now that's settled. What else you got? Something about Mother this time."

"What do you mean?"

"A secret."

Here my heart flipped suddenly. I winced, no doubt, but when I looked to him, he seemed to be watching the patients in the courtyard. Yes, I had something to tell him, but were either of us ready?

For fear of upsetting him, I blurted something else. "Mother kept a journal while I was away."

"A journal? I don't remember her ever keeping a journal."

"One night I was sitting on the bed in your room. I don't even know what I was thinking about. Probably you and Mother. I hadn't done this without her, but I thought to take down a box of your belongings in the closet, the ones we would look through when we missed you most. For the first time, I noticed a second box. This one had several books in it. Mother's journals."

"And you read them?"

"I did."

"And—"

"It seems that she only kept them in the years she was alone. So, from the time Grandmother died until I came home from college, journaling was a kind of companion for her. It felt like a violation at first, but I was terribly lonely, and to see her handwriting, to hear her voice—I couldn't turn away. After reading a few entries, it felt as though she was with me, like we were speaking to each other, not as mother and child but as confidants, each of us having lived alone in the woods in our old house with everyone we love gone and no indication of their return."

He seemed moved by the thought. I could see him picturing Mother in the living room under a lamplight, scribbling into one of those canvas-bound journals. Or perhaps he was moved by empathy. He has since told me that journaling is encouraged at Chinquapin and something he's taken very seriously in his time there.

"What did she write about?"

"Her days, like everyone, but something else, something peculiar. How she began taking daily walks along our trails through the woods, even so far as the railroad tracks."

He made a small sound at hearing this. I think it pleased him to know that the care he'd taken, you might even say his life's work, was still there and had given Mother an outlet.

"But she met someone there. Someone strange."

"What? Who?"

"It isn't clear, but he said very odd things to her. They spoke often, and though she was guarded about telling him too much, he seemed to always know more about her, about us, about our home, than she could account for. Finally, one snowy day she met him by the creek—he was waiting for her—and she told him she didn't want to see him again. I think he'd disturbed her deeply."

My brother seemed stunned by all this. Speechless.

"Well, you wanted something good, right?"

"Yes, well, I didn't expect that," he said and laughed. "What do you think about that whole thing?"

"The woods are strange. I get a weird feeling there now. I want to blame Mother and Grandmother for all their warnings when we were children. Maybe they primed me for this, but truthfully, I've had my share of weird occurrences. Sometimes very subtle, sometimes not."

"Tell me."

"Subtle like this: Maybe something's really burdening me. I take a walk in the woods to mull it over and to release it. Let's say I sit where we used to, on a tree root by the creek. I get lost inside my head. Terrifically and blindingly lost. My thoughts take me to the darkest places. I'm sinking, drowning in them, utter silence, and before I touch bottom, I'll hear a pop, like from deep inside a heavy tree branch overhead, to startle me from my trance, to save me from myself.

"Something tells me, 'Don't be foolish, you're being superstitious,' but it's happened too many times this exact way not to be meaningful to me. Not only in the woods. In the house too. A hollow, muffled, and sudden sound like a ceiling rafter of the old house, its timber shifting somehow with the coolness of the evening. I used to tell myself it's just the house settling."

"And the not-so-subtle?" he said.

"One clear night—I had only been home a few days from the road—I was walking the trails with Thomas. You remember Thomas?"

"What were you doing with Thomas in the woods at night?"

"Don't interrupt," I said.

"You really *have* been holding out."

"As I said, we were walking the trails. We'd crossed the tracks where we used to, and we found an odd woven structure there."

My brother smiled at this. "I may know something about that."

"I figured as much, but the strange part was after—a chorus of howls in the distance. We didn't wait to find out what was going on. The night only got stranger from there, the woods, the train, Tom . . ."

"That's funny."

"What?"

"You. You're shifting in your seat. I feel like you're skimping on the details here."

"You're watching me too intensely. It's distracting."

"So, tell the rest."

"Not today," I said.

"Okay. Anything else not-so-subtle?"

"Yes, you remember a certain *encounter*, don't you?"

"Of course—if you're referring to the thing you saw along the tracks."

"We never talked too much about it."

"That's true."

"Why?

"I have a dumb kind of theory about things like that," he said.

"Which is."

"The more attention you feed it, the more it appears. They like our curiosity as much as they wish to remain unseen."

"They?"

"They."

"As I recall, you were always looking for something—monster or miracle."

"Is there a difference?"

"For most people."

"Right."

"But I remember how you wanted to catch something unaware or perhaps looking for you."

"Yes."

"And did you?"

He took a deep breath and let it out slowly. "I want to tell you, but I can't without telling you everything."

I said nothing. In truth I didn't feel ready.

"But before I can tell you, I need to know that you've told me *everything*."

In the years after my brother's incident, my mother seldom spoke of him, but gradually, with time and the many walks she would take—down his trails, through the woods, across the creek, and along the railroad tracks—she grew to confide in me more of him, more of our family's past. With every walk she sought the faintest hint, a warning sign, a turning point or moment when she could've interceded and altered his path that it would not lead him here where we sat.

No, I hadn't told him everything. I'd made a mission of protecting him, even until that very minute, but the pull of what remained unspoken between us, like a cosmic black hole, had begun fracturing and distorting everything we'd rebuilt in the past months, so I couldn't guard him from it any longer.

"You had a twin brother. They named him Aaron. They delivered him after you. But he didn't survive. The labor had been difficult. Something tells me this is why I'm here. I cannot say how knowing this will change anything, nor can I say what it will mean; I can only say that I am sad for you, and I wish you'd been told before today."

Until then his eyes had been trained upon me, but having heard this, they drifted out beyond me. He squinted as if to see something beyond the trees, and with crinkled brow he nodded as though listening to an absent voice, whispering to him the words of consolation and clarity that I had been unable to give him.

The lady attendant stepped out onto the veranda and in her booming voice shouted: "Medication, cleanup, dinner. Visitation's over. Atrium in five." Before the echo of her words had ended, she said to no one in particular, at her normal speaking volume, "And y'all better not make me ask twice," and mumbled as she pushed her way back into the atrium.

The slender young woman and the towering man from the day before had been at the farthest point of the courtyard prior to the announcement, but by the time we'd stood from our chairs and gathered our things, they were already in our vicinity. As we turned to the lights of the atrium, I noticed the young woman carefully eyeing both of us, and when she saw my brother's face, she hurried to join him. She placed her tiny palm on the broad part of his back as we walked to the veranda, and the man walking with her said to me, "Watch your step, ma'am. The grass gets slick in the evening."

Walking to the veranda, I began to feel some version of guilt or shame, like after a social gathering, thinking how you'd overshared. Half the day had been spent discussing the dream, the other half our family, and now I'd left him with *this*. I stopped him at the door, my hand on his shoulder. "You know, you don't have to tell me anything. You don't have to speak a word about it. It won't change anything."

"The chimera disagrees," he said, and my brother smiled at me, the way he used to passing a caterpillar from his finger to mine or having shown me how the sunset settled neon pink on a dogwood in our backyard or the way he might after having said something strangely poetic on the school bus, headed home.

Naturally, at the hotel in the city nearby, I couldn't suppress the general feeling of anxiety at what we might say the next day. I thought through all the talks we'd had in a half-year of visits to Chinquapin.

Beyond those difficult early visits, we'd found ourselves settling into comfortable reminiscences, testing our memories of home, the woods, school days, our family. Then, it was important for us to learn how to speak to one another again, to remind each other who we were. Then, it was easy to be swept up into the pure joy of speaking with him, my brother, the only person I have left in this world. But what about now? Who were we now?

The next day we began less easily, fraught with the weight of both our expectations, whatever they were. We both sat in our usual places, each waiting for the other to speak. He looked as though he'd slept very little the night before—the tired eyes, his hair a bit wild, shoulders slumping into himself. It was his posture that concerned me. On my early visits, his body would fold upon itself as if he were sharing a bench seat with others he didn't wish to brush against. Conversation had proved challenging in those days.

But I wanted to be direct with him. We didn't have much time, and this would be our last chance to talk for a month.

I was about to say as much when he began: "I don't know what to do with this information you've given me."

"Nor did I when Mother told me."

"Like learning a fundamental part of yourself has been missing or that your life wasn't what it could have been, that you aren't what you could be."

"Yes."

"Another life."

I could see now. He was mourning. Hadn't we all lost something that day? Had we ever stopped losing?

"I'm sorry," I said.

"For what?"

"For all of us. For everything. Sorry I've upset you. I don't know why I told you."

He shook his head. "You're the only one who could ever tell me the truth, the only one who didn't think I would crumble into ashes upon hearing it. No. I'm glad you told me."

He leaned back in his seat and ran his fingers through his hair. "Now I'd like to tell you the truth," he said. "We owe it to each other, don't we?"

I nodded.

"I tried before. It didn't go so well. You remember?"

"Of course."

"I'd only been here a week or so. It was as soon as you, Mother, and Grandmother could come. They wouldn't let the three of you speak to me together. One by one I listened and watched as each of you struggled to speak to me. They couldn't, but you, you came in, and within minutes you were a meteorite. You were blazing through the glass between us, pummeling me with questions, demanding answers I couldn't give, and I tried to tell you everything, but you wouldn't hear it. You said some cruel things to me then, things I can only assume had been building up since those early grade school days. I needed someone to listen then, but you were too angry, perhaps too young, and I don't blame you, Cindy, but if you, the one person who knew me, wouldn't hear me out . . ."

He swallowed his words here. He didn't have to speak them.

I gave us both a moment, then said: "I'm sorry. For the sum of it. I've made bad decisions. More than I can remember."

"You were a child," he said, shaking his head.

"Yes, but every year you've spent here that I wasn't a child—that's what I want to apologize for now, for the thousands of days I refused to listen."

He nodded, wiped away a tear. "Would you listen to me now if I tell you what happened?"

I smiled, though I was a mess, and told him I would.

He reached for his notepad, flipped the pages, and began.

Life at the new school was different in small ways—the uniforms, the rules and routines, the classes—but in other ways not. Most of the kids there came from wealthy families that knew each other from country clubs and summer vacations and dance recitals and their parents' cocktail parties. Then there were the rest of us, county- or state-sponsored kids. A few were worse off than me—at least I wanted to blend in. Some seemed like they took the whole outcast thing as a challenge. How unlike these vacation home–having kids can I become? It didn't take the rich kids long to ferret me out. We knew our stations, our trajectories. I suppose that was my first good, hard lesson: Reinvention works for frogs and butterflies—me not so much. I'm not sure how that notion ever got into my head. I could act like a different person, but inside I never stopped being me.

But I was a novelty for a time—the rich kids kept me around long enough to teach me a few things, which had me believing I was pulling off the great facade. When at last I fell in with my lot, I found a group of people like me, some much smarter but typically less sociable. I didn't hate it, Cindy. It was easier in many important ways. Being a nobody, when I finally had the sense to embrace it, was the blessing Principal Franklin and the superintendent suggested it might be.

Acclimating to the new system wasn't too difficult. Mainly it was schedules. They were very serious about time. If you were tardy, you lost certain privileges, and then there were "lights out" times, curfews, and a lot of checking in and out if you ever left campus. I learned that if you were in good academic standing, things relaxed a little. You could take more than one town day in the afternoon; you got less guff from the man with the clipboard by the door on the weekends. So, I made it my mission to get good marks and stay under the radar. This meant freedom for me. I could roam around town, spend what little state-issued pittance per diem I had, watch the trains, watch the people. The rich kids had taught me that a pretense helped. They told me to come back with a new library book or two under my arm whenever I came back from town. Staff liked to think we were all just looking for a new place to study whenever we left.

Campus was situated in the southeast edge of town, partly tucked away into the woods but with open grounds and courtyards they took great pride in maintaining, all in all probably forty acres, maybe more if they owned the woods there. It being a prestigious old school, there were some magnificent trees on the school grounds I liked to sit under, some with plaques with the founders' names and the dates they were planted. Naturally, I wanted to explore the woods as soon as possible, but I suppressed the urge. There was one teacher who would take students on bird and flora tours. Mr. Bishop. He was at my hearing. I never missed his tours.

I learned the borders of the town very well. There was a nice park on the northeast corner with a pond and a couple playgrounds for children and, right through the middle of town, the train. I spent plenty of free time hanging around at the station. You could wait inside the depot, and nobody would bother you much, but I usually sat outside on the benches with my books and waited for trains. People boarding the trains would often drag big black garbage bags around. Clothes, I guessed. I thought it weird until I remembered how I didn't have any luggage either. That's the funny thing about leaving home—you learn how much some have and how little others have. I never gave it much thought when we were all still together. Our enough was very little.

Rich kids and local kids often went home on the weekends, some to each other's homes with permission, and the rest of us were left to our own devices. The night curfews on Friday and Saturday were adjusted to allow students to catch the last movie showing at the theater. With a brisk walk back, you could make ten thirty easily. Though I couldn't afford more than one or two a month, I liked going to the movies quite a lot. You won't find this hard to believe, but I'm easily absorbed into the world of a film. I'd walk out of the theater in a daze. As I headed back to the school, the lonely sidewalks felt like another planet from what we were used to growing up. That's when I liked living in town best. One of those quiet walks, it dawned on me how much liberty we were given on the weekends. I didn't need an excuse or permission to leave. Just check out and in, meet the curfew. So, once I learned every bit of the town by walking, I began to expand my boundaries. Old habits.

I couldn't walk so far that I'd miss curfew, but I found I liked the nearer, east end of town best anyway. Woods access was important to me, and it wasn't far to the tracks or the park. I found that from either location I could walk all the way back to the school through the woods with ease. Now I was back in my element. Best of both worlds—town when I felt like it, woods when I didn't. Increasingly, my walks were taking me back to the train tracks. Waiting at the station was one thing, but now I could disappear into the woods by the park, find my way to the tracks outside of town, and walk along the rails like I used to. I started carrying my old messenger bag with food from the dining hall, and yeah, I started finding railroad spikes pretty much immediately. It didn't take long for them to become too heavy on my shoulder. I needed to find a place to stash them.

I walked a mile or more out of town along the tracks and rambled through the woods on both sides for several days. Granted, I couldn't take walks like these often, so it was more like over several weeks. Across the tracks I found an old abandoned house largely obscured from anyone walking the tracks, and though there were people from time to time I'd pass along the way— weatherworn men, drifters, hoboes—they mostly kept to themselves. A few might throw a hand up if they saw me. But this house I found, it had a little front porch, one large room, and two smaller ones—kitchen, sitting room, and bedroom, I think. No working indoor plumbing or anything. Crumbled outhouse in the back. The floorboards were dicey, especially on the porch and in the bedroom, but the kitchen and the larger sitting room were solid. The whole thing was a rat's nest. I broke off some dogwood branches for a broom and swept the pine straw and leaves out the door or into holes in the floor. After I'd tidied the place up, I sat on the floor in the sitting room and nearly cried. A place that was mine.

I dumped all my railroad spikes in the sitting room and started arranging them like I used to. I'd found one spike that was clean, unused, almost shiny. I decided to keep this one in my bag, maybe as a talisman, maybe as a tool for self-defense. Luck and protection—two things I never had much of.

Here, alone, I allowed myself to think of you and Mother for the first time in months. In fact, lots of things came back to me. I missed you guys desperately. I missed our house, the woods, our trails. The new school was my second chance at life, but even though everything was going well, I couldn't shake the idea it could fall apart any day. This discovery of the woods, the tracks, and the old house—though it was a perverse version of home, it made me feel like I could make it. I could tough it out, graduate, and maybe whatever was supposed to happen to me, to my life, it would begin the day I returned home, a new man.

In the late fall the house wasn't nearly as secluded as I would've liked it to be, and I ran the risk of disclosing its location every time I left the school, slipped away from the park, and crossed the tracks. There were people to avoid at every juncture. I never thought much about my safety, only about being unobtrusive or ignored. However, coming across the lone straggler on the tracks or too close to my house would startle me. I'd be lost in thought, collecting more railroad spikes, and suddenly one would appear and break the spell. Most seemed harmless. Some didn't. Few wanted to talk. I never spoke first. Always kept it brief.

I'd brought in dozens more railroad spikes to the house—as many as I could find in a mile stretch. Sometimes, if the weather was bad, I'd go straight there—to my room—uncover the stash of spikes, and stack and line them up like I used to. I liked the sound they made dragging on the hardwood floor or when an arrangement would tumble down, the dulled thunder of knocking wood and ringing steel. In fact, that turned into the game—how ornate can you build something before it collapses?

Like all play, it runs its course, you move on to the next game. One day I began thinking of my old project in the woods back home, what you and Thomas found at the end of our trail. I called it the Woods Weir, though it mostly resembled a Native American fish trap I'd seen in a picture once. Aside from small traps placed in streams, the Native people had another method for trapping fish, something called a fishing weir. One of their legends tells how the coyote taught their people to fish in this way. I envied the Native people for their stories. I think I always wanted the woods to speak to me, to teach me, to produce some spirit to guide me. That's clear to me now.

I didn't have the luxury of tools, so I began the slow process of bend breaking small trees and uprooting vines to work with. When I saved enough money, I purchased the largest pocketknife I could afford. I would have to leave it underneath the porch stairs at the house. Though well hidden there, I'd cover it with leaves. I went to work. Just like the one at home but maybe even better. Not having adequate tools had me using smaller pieces, which gave the whole structure a tighter weave.

I don't know what to say about the Woods Weir except it was something to do. I've always felt lost without a project—a project in the woods, with found materials, even better. Part fish trap, part nest, part horn of plenty, part dream catcher, part tornado. Maybe it's silly, but it kept me grounded; it gave me a purpose. I've only ever felt real peace like that, alone in the woods, busy. Time slipped away from me there. Years after, I came to think of it as a portal. Something I could disappear into. I would begin work, next thing I knew, my wristwatch would beep—hours gone, time to go. Those were the best of my days in the new school. I remember there being plenty of pictures taken, after. What a shame, the things they wanted it to be.

One day I was working on the structure, and a downpour began. The structure was big enough then that I could sit inside and wait it out, but *this rain was remarkable. I would have to make repairs afterward. So I ran to the house, leaping onto the porch and finding a sturdy place to stand and watch the rain, but the wind picked up, and I was soaked and cold, so I grabbed my bag by the doorway and went inside. As I stepped into my room, I was contemplating what a treacherous walk home it would be, how I would need to leave sooner to adjust for the storm, when I noticed I wasn't alone.*

The room was darkened by the storm, but in the far corner, I could make out the form of a person sitting. At first I could only see his legs and boots clearly. His olive-green pants, threadbare with holes in the knees; leather boots with smoothed-down soles. Though his silhouette was unclear, I could see that he had a thin frame, a shaggy head of hair, and that his hands lay motionless by his sides. I had seen transients roaming the tracks and in the city streets before, and most were a certain profile, so I was taken aback when he spoke with a very thin, clear, youthful tone. He could've been younger than me. He addressed me friendly enough. I noticed he was completely dry. He must've been there well before the rain started. As my eyes adjusted, I could see he wore a navy canvas jacket with frayed cuffs and collar. He had a long face, dark eyebrows, dark eyes. He said it was a nice place and asked me if it was mine. I told him no. He looked over at the pile of train spikes. Next to the pile was a kind of freestanding stairway I'd assembled. It was knee high and, I thought, impressive. It reminded me of pictures I'd seen of the Aztec pyramids. He never moved, except for his eyes. "Places like this are always somebody's," he told me. "Did you build that? Out there?" I told him I did. "Cool," he said. "Neat shelter." I leaned against the door frame, slipping my hand into my bag, reaching for the clean spike. I clutched it in my hand. He looked at my clothes, my school uniform. The shock at having someone in the house was fading into something uglier. "What in the world you need a shelter for with a place like this a few feet away?" I shrugged. "Seeing this ain't yours and things being what they are outside—I think I'll just sit here awhile," he said, barely audible above the rain on the tin roof. I looked at my watch, told him I had to leave, and headed out.

That night I sloughed off my wet clothes in my room, toweled off, and crawled into bed. I was stunned, shaken, angry. I felt found out, violated, and depressed. The rational side of me said, You don't own the house; you have no right to claim it for yourself. And then a wave of emotions would wash back over me, knocking me senseless. Still, I found myself saying:

He may not be there the next time you go. He may not even be there after tomorrow. These drifter types never settle for very long. I'd seen them along the tracks, at the park, in town, at the station. New faces every week. They rarely hung around more than two weeks.

Homework became difficult. Focusing in class was impossible. I got poor marks in an advanced math class, and it shook me a little. I was slipping, but I couldn't stop thinking about the likelihood of this person in my house, in my room, inspecting everything. I stayed gone a week before I returned, Saturday evening, the sun already below the trees. Even before I skirted the park and slipped into the woods, I knew he'd be there. As I approached the house, I could smell wood smoke. Someone was camped behind the house, sitting at the mouth of the Woods Weir, tending to a campfire and a small animal roasting above it. "There he is!" he shouted, like he'd been waiting all day, like we were old friends and I was the one paying a visit. He was sitting on an upturned metal pail he must've found near the house. He quickly stood, slid the pail next to him, and gave it three hollow raps. He told me to sit down. I did. Now that we were outside with enough daylight, I could see that he was older than I'd estimated, maybe late teens, taller than me, lanky, swift. He spoke as we watched the flames. He'd pause occasionally to feed the fire, turn the animal, or crumble some green shriveled leaves onto his meal. He said, "You got good food in this city." He looked at me, staring at the animal. "Shit, not this. I caught this earlier. No, all week I've been eating stuff I'll bet even a fancy boy like you's never seen. Hell, I probably couldn't pronounce half of the stuff I've eaten. Amazing what people throw away. Imagine being so wealthy you only eat half a meal or, can you believe, send something back to the kitchen because it isn't 'just so.' Their loss, my gain," the last part said like he'd spoken it to himself many times. His voice was deeper than the one I'd previously heard. I wondered if he had been posturing last time, maybe as a defense. He told me I didn't speak much and that was okay. Though he seemed more affable now, I still felt uneasy, that he posed some kind of threat, something in his confidence and easy manner. I was alone in the woods, except for this stranger. What was he capable of? Though I should have been wary enough not to linger, there was something curious about this man, a few years my senior, who lived a completely different life. It occurs to me now I'd never really known men his age. The adults in my life—all much older—never had much use *for me, nor had they anything to offer aside from what their ordinary lives had taught them, and here was this older kid, talkative, who seemed glad to have someone to listen.*

"I'll tell you what's nice about this city. Up a ways, couple miles, you pass through several crossroads. That's what I've been up to. I haven't been here all week. Up there there's houses like you wouldn't believe. Mansions. And most of them empty. I gotta tell you, that suits me fine. Look at this." He combed his no-longer-shaggy hair from his forehead and flipped down the collar of his jacket, pointing to his clean-shaven jaw. "This is as clean as I've been in weeks." I saw that it was true. He looked fresher than me. Something about his jaw made him appear slightly older than I'd determined, maybe early twenties. In the firelight even his clothes looked brighter. "Look at this," he said. He opened his jacket and showed a red-and-black checkered flannel shirt. "Yanked this from some fella's dresser. He'll never miss it. Smells like it hasn't been worn in years. That's the way with these people. It's nothing for them to lose—and so it's nothing for me to take. Funny how that works, huh? I'll bet they never know when it's gone. Crawdad living. Feeding from the bottom of everywhere's creeks and swamps. Of course, there's an art to it. You don't take from the top. Leave stuff clean, and you can come back again and again—well, unless you know you're never coming back. Then it doesn't matter much how you leave things."

He took the animal off the fire and let it rest. "What the hell you want with all those train spikes anyway?" Just something to do, I told him. "You ought to come with me, see what it's like. Something tells me you're wilder than most schoolboys. A kid that could rig up something like what you have out here could be useful. Resourceful too—you found this house. You built whatever this is, so you could handle a snare easy. With a little teaching, you'd be a tough one. You good in a scrap?" he asked, but I didn't answer. He tore a limb from the steaming animal. "I'd offer you a leg, but a fancy young man like yourself has probably never had meat off a campfire." He turned away from me and took a bite. It sounded crispy. He said, chewing: "Living this way, it ain't always pretty. It's hard at times. But this is better than all the fancy stuff I find in dumpsters and in people's empty houses. That all begins to taste like fat, but this, this is lean, makes you stronger, makes your blood redder. Here—" He reached for something behind him. My stomach went rigid. I tensed and leaned forward. He handed me a clear container with what appeared to be some kind of half-eaten cake. It was creamy and dusted with chocolate or cinnamon. "Maybe this is more your speed." I told him I wasn't hungry. I was.

In the days after, I found myself daydreaming about what the young man had said. Living severed from society. I couldn't decide—had he rejected society, or had society rejected him? Or maybe that wasn't the right question. What does someone gain or lose by living this way? I was still very young then. To be shown another path at such a difficult time was confusing on one hand, exhilarating on the other. I did want to know how to live on my own, to never ask anyone for anything again, to reject all the half-hearted hands that had ever reached out for me, to take, to survive, to live on my own terms. I wanted to know how to set a snare, to live like an animal if I had to. I knew this person's presence was only temporary. While I feared he would still be there when I returned, in spite of myself, I hoped to see him again, to learn what I did not yet know of this world and maybe how to pass through it, unseen.

I approached the Woods Weir that day, half-expecting him there. I could've been wrong, but it seemed as though parts of it had been repurposed for campfires. He must still be here, I thought, but it was strangely quiet. I hoisted myself into the back doorway. Before I could think, two sinewy arms were closing around my neck. I could feel his frame knocking against mine as I struggled. I jammed him against the wall. Dust fell into my eyes. His constrictor hold tightened. I felt my head elevating from my neck. Everything went dark. I awoke on the floor of my room, the sensation of needles in my head and face, sparks in my eyes. I crawled, gasping for breath. "There he is!" he shouted, almost as if he was hovering over my ear. "You feel that, boy? That's life, surging back into your soul! That's blood and electricity all in one, filling up your body, lighting up your brain. Remember it! You won't ever feel so alive as now." I coughed and spat in the dust, on my knees still. The euphoria was imploding, shriveling into a headache. "Breathe deep. It's yours now." I asked him what he was talking about. "Life, young man. It's your own. I've given it back to you. Don't you see?" I sat, regrouping, rattled, determining exactly what must happen next, preparing to bolt or to come at him as hard as I could if need be.

Instantly, I was aware that the person standing before me wasn't the young man I'd spoken with previously. He was dressed the same, same flannel, *same boots, same holes at the knees, but he was much older. Late thirties. The features of the young man were somewhere hidden in this man's face, but at a glance, no one would think them the same person. "I could've left you here with nothing, not even the clothes on your back. Fancy duds. I've seen boys younger than you, tough as nails. What did you learn today in that fancy school? Would it keep you alive or going for two weeks in the places I've been?" The man leaned in the doorway as he spoke, barring my way. He was noticeably frazzled, more haggard than before, under-slept, with thick facial hair, a full beard. He wore a dirty cap now, with the brim pulled down, making only the hollowed bottoms of his eyes visible. He spoke with a sneer. "Think you're tough enough to make it out there? Handle yourself in a fight? Surviving's more than just food and shelter. You've got to want to live bad enough to kill. Could you kill to keep living?"*

I didn't know what to say. I thought of all the threats I'd faced up until then. What? A couple of jerks at school? Who needed to kill anyone? Who, whatever, needed to die? I never wanted anything like that. I felt myself reaching for my bag. "Over there," he said and pointed to the opposite corner of the room, where my bag lay. "Think you could even move me from this door?" I wanted to summon up the blood and the rage to rush him, to press my knuckles into his jugular, to put him slobbering on the ground, but I sat there, cool, waiting. "Wednesday's child. Meek and mild," he said. I could hear the friction of his hands as he rubbed them together. "I could teach you plenty. No one would get the best of you ever again. But maybe I'm wasting my time. I ought to leave you here, just like this." He wet his lips, grimaced. "You've got something special in you, I can tell. But you're going to need something big to bring it out of you, some greater force, but when it does, oh boy." He clapped his hands in one loud, hollow pop. "Fine, fine." He moved away from the door. "You're built for better than this, and when you know you could be better, you're weak if you don't get better. It's time for you to take. Reach out and take it." I grabbed my bag and left the room, never turning my back to him. There was a deadness in his eyes as I passed. They stared past me as I slipped by, like I wasn't there, like nothing had just happened, like he couldn't care less if we met again.

It was at least two weeks before I went back, a long time for me. I tried to put our last meeting out of my mind; I tried to suppress the idea of returning. I suppose I was afraid. I hadn't felt true fear in my life very many times. It hadn't occurred to me how much I could lose in this life. Before I lay choking on the floor, my biggest fear was failing school. In my studies I was a few mistakes from being sent home. That didn't sound so bad at all. My family would be disappointed, and so would I, but then—I'd be home again. But the memory of lying there, gulping for air in the dust, faint taste of blood in my mouth, and everything the man said after, the future he laid out before me—a future that burned everything behind as it blazed onward—was repulsive to me, terrifying. His words repeated in my mind as I tried to sleep. How could you live this way? I ask the stranger, and seeing him before me in a vision, he turns, but this time with the face of my father. Still, I say to him, How could you?

And so I knew I had to see him once more, to ask him that very question, to look him in the eyes, to face him. What's more, I would tell him to get out of my house. It was my house, and he was no longer welcome. And if I needed to, I would defend it, I would drive him from it.

It was Friday, midafternoon. I'd checked out earlier than usual because I noticed a maintenance truck parked in a side lot, near the annex, where visibility was minimal. I told the guard I had to return to my room for something, but instead, I doubled back through campus and to the annex parking lot, hesitating until I was certain no one was around. The truck's tailgate was down, and the toolbox was left open. I scrambled into the bed, looked at my options, and found a ball-peen hammer underneath a bundle of rope and a handsaw. I shoved the hammer in my bag, hopped down, and walked back through the school and out.

After the stranger had gotten the best of me, I realized I had little to defend myself with, aside from the knife, which was hopefully still buried beneath the steps. But I didn't trust myself wielding a knife. On the walk through town, I clenched the wooden handle concealed inside my bag, learning its weight, imagining the moves I might need to make. I made my way to the park, through the woods, across the tracks, and finally to my house. I was fairly tactical in my approach. Like a preyed-upon rabbit, I'd dart for short stretches, hide, wait, and repeat. I startled with every bird or squirrel that stirred in the leaves. I crept along the Woods Weir up to the house, keeping low, trying to manage my breathing though my heart was thumping in my ears. I waited there at the mouth, hearing no one. At the house I stole a glance through a side window into my room. There was a bundle of rags in one corner I assumed to be him. I could see it pulsing, rising and falling, perhaps sleeping. I used the front entrance, which I knew to be quieter, but not before retrieving my knife, opening it, and placing it on the floor just outside the doorway.

I removed the spike and hammer from my bag, and with the spike clenched in my left hand and the hammer in my right, I entered. The floorboards groaned as I stepped through. It couldn't be helped. Old wood and rusty nails. I refused to raid the room, no hasty movements. I kept close to the wall. I listened. Nothing. I risked a glance into the room. Still the bundle in the corner. I took a deep breath, gathered myself, but when I stepped through the doorway, there he stood, looming much taller than I remembered, waiting for me. "Are you going to drive that spike through my heart, young man?" His voice sounded different. Much lower, raspy, weary. I told him I didn't want to. "Maybe you're more capable than I gave you credit for. But no one catches me sleeping." Leave, I said. The stranger only laughed. Then he said, "I wonder how long it takes an old place like this to burn to the ground?" At this I felt the weight of the hammer lighten in my hand as if it was an extension of my arm, a part of me. He said, "Are you slow to wrath, young man, or just slow?" In a flash I imagined every physical step it would take to accomplish the wicked desire of my heart. I pictured every act and the aftermath, but when I looked at his newly frail, weakened form, something turned inside me. There was a hard metal thud at my feet, then the wooden handle of the hammer, knocking against the floorboard.

"Every great man to walk this earth was a loner, like us. These men who traverse space, at some point they had to forsake it all to extend the boundaries of what could be. Spacemen miss family reunions, but guess who the family can't stop talking about when they're gone? That's us, man. Look at you now. Here, with no one."

Still, I held the spike. I rolled it in my palm. I listened.

"Leonardo was the illegitimate child of two nobodies. If he'd been some rich landowner or merchant's son, or the son of a tradesman, he would've disappeared into nothing. Being a nobody bastard has its advantages. He can decide what he will be. Nothing, no one to hold him back. Family, home—nails you to the ground. We need freedom, man. If we don't roam, we perish," he said.

I looked at the spike in my hand, then into his eyes, and said, Leonardo was never a loner—maybe in his thinking—but he always embraced society. He could walk and talk with everyone, rich or poor, and everything he created, it gave them an ideal, something to strive for, art, beauty, excellence, understanding, invention. Everything he left behind was for us, to help us in some way, to give us something to aspire to. What have you left behind? Ashes.

At this he spoke to me in a different voice, deep, resonant, and solemn. "Before the seeds are sewn," he said, "a great clearing must occur. Once the fires have smoldered and everything is destroyed, the earth must be harrowed, and afterward, the first crops always thrive, for the earth is richest beneath a layer of destruction. The violence, the chaos, they are necessary if greatness is to follow. Sacrifice your dreary, trivial life; follow me."

It's time for you to leave, I said.

He turned his back to me, facing the corner. The tattered clothes he wore trembled, and I saw his shoulders stoop, sinking into himself. I could see the back of his head. The wild, flaring hair was lengthening, graying, lying flat upon his head, flowing down around his collar and past his shoulders. I shouted for him to turn, Face me! Now! And when he turned, I saw him.

In my vision, for the span of a few seconds, I saw my father's image in the stranger's face. Now, in the growing afternoon shadows, this man looked nothing like my memory of our father nor, for that matter, did he appear to be the man who had previously stood before me. In fact, he looked far older than before. This man had hard lines of age on his face, a heavy brow. His long eyebrows curved into the corners of his aged eyes, which were faded and tired. His hair, fully gray now, flowed in careful waves from his temple, all around his head, down his cheeks, and below his nose and mouth. His features seemed burdened with the weight of his flowing hair and beard, which fixed upon his face a look of mildly distracted disappointment and upon his mouth a slight scowl, which, even in this new form, seemed oddly familiar, like a face I'd seen in a picture, long ago.

Who are you? I asked him. "Is that the question you wanted to ask me?" he said. No, I told him. Why are you here? What do you want with me? I said. "We are always here, whether we are seen or not, and we shall remain after all things have passed. We desire nothing this world offers. We need nothing.

But we are always amused when we are seen," he said. I told him I didn't understand. "You will," he said. By then all the anger I had summoned had left me. Speaking to this man who seemed to grow frailer by the minute, I only felt pity. "You are more like us than them. This life will be hard for you."

I was too astonished to think or to speak clearly. I could barely remember why I'd returned to the house in the first place, but again the vision returned to me with the lingering question that echoed in my sleep: How could you?

How could you lead a life that torches everything it touches? That blazes through, always taking, leaving nothing? How could you leave when we needed you most?

The man said: "We are, at turns, given to our basest whims, but aren't we more than these? We fail each other, we fail ourselves, we fail our gods, and we bed each night with loneliness and despair; nevertheless, we rise each new morning, to meet the same choices as the day before, and we stand and face them, and trembling, we choose, and we become what we choose. But who can know the full sum of our choices or what we shall choose tomorrow?" His shoulders lowered as he sighed what remained of his breath. "Do what you must," he said.

I never want to see you again, here or in my dreams, I said, and left him standing there in the house. When I stepped onto the porch, the woods were completely dark. It was only midafternoon when I left the school, but now it was well into the night somehow. I looked back into the doorway of the house. It was all shadows. Six or seven hours? It didn't make any sense. I scrambled down the broken porch steps and around the back of the house. I glanced at the Woods Weir, and it was darker than the mouth of a cave. It gave me an uneasy feeling, so I ran for the clearing.

I crossed the tracks. Since it was dark, I walked the rails back into town rather than feel my way through the woods and the park. I could see the lights from the buildings and passing cars when a sinking feeling made me stop. I'd left the hammer in the house. Something in me panicked. Maybe the poisons of a lifetime of accusations. I wasn't a thief. I could come back in the light of day tomorrow. What if he'd taken it? What if he was lurking nearby brandishing the tool, hoping to use it? My thoughts scrambled as I raced back to the house to retrieve the hammer.

Along the way I thought of the man who put me on the floor. I couldn't be caught like that again. Certainly not so close to the tracks. An image flashed *before my eyes, me lying unconscious across the rails. I shuddered. I didn't fear the old man or the young one, but this one . . . I had to be ready for this one, to fight if I had to.*

I returned, jaunting swiftly, stopping on a dime, checking my surroundings and, before moving on, listening. I could hear the train engine. Its horn barely audible, almost more of a feeling than a sound, was still miles away, roaring through some distant crossroads, perhaps another town. I would need to hurry, or else I'd have to wait for the train to pass, and I was already pushing curfew. A freight would barrel on, but a passenger would stop at the station. Then I might be seen climbing between cars. I listened to the horn again, the music it made on the rails. It was a passenger.

When I reentered the woods, things felt different, foreign to me. I was nearing the house, but something made me stop. Suddenly, I felt terribly homesick. Even in the dark, I could tell—these were not my woods, I was no longer wanted here, this was not my home. My hidden house, the Woods Weir, all the hours I'd spent there—none of it seemed to matter anymore. We had no more use for each other. It was a strange sensation, sad but also a relief. I knew then I would never come back. Maybe I'd fail at the special school, maybe not. Either way, something in me turned homeward, and it was almost enough to send me back to the school without the hammer.

But as I neared the front of the house, I could see a dim orange coming from the window of my room, a light that faded through the rest of the place. I watched the window from a distance. The light flickered somewhat. Something like a shadow moved, nothing large enough to be human. I heard scratching, a slight thumping inside. I waited, holding my breath, and an animal appeared in the open doorway. It sat upon its hind legs like a dog. In the dim light I could make out its pointed ears in silhouette. It turned its head in profile, maybe a coyote, maybe not. It hesitated there, almost as if it knew I was watching, as if to give me a clearer view of itself. It turned to me, and as though illuminated from a light within, its eyes shined in my direction, two white stars beaming big as quarters. Then it rose to its feet, padded across the porch, leaped off, and ran into the woods behind the house.

In the doorway you could see down the short hall. It gave the place a sallow hue. I recalled his words, how long it would take to burn to the ground. I leapt across the porch and into my room, only to find the place empty except for a small lantern in the middle of the floor. In a panic I turned, thinking the stranger might be there, ready to teach me another lesson, but still nothing. I do recall the man carrying a bag with him, but I'd never seen the lantern before. I asked myself why anyone would leave a lit lantern in a room like this. My answer: Because they mean to return. I felt a sickness come over me, dread. I couldn't leave fast enough. Then I remembered my purpose: the hammer. I looked on the floor where I'd dropped it. Gone. I glanced over every floorboard of the room. Its emptiness struck me. Nothing. Then it dawned on me.

All those railroad spikes. Gone too. How could that be? Hadn't they littered the floor? There were enough to fill a couple of buckets. But there wasn't anything to cart them away, just a small pail. I'd had to bring them to the house ten or twelve at a time in my bag. Could he have been removing them as slowly as I'd gathered them without my noticing? I saw a few had been left behind, a dozen or more, arranged in a stairway-style structure I used to build. The stairway led into the wall. I ran from the house, heading toward the tracks, to cross over, to race back to the school, to receive whatever would befall me there.

Maybe if I was fast enough, no one would notice. I paused at the tracks to listen. The train had passed its last crossroads and would be coming through in seconds. It was a passenger, all right. I could see its headlight behind me. The crossbars in town were lowering, bells were clanging. I still had a good twenty seconds to scale the embankment and cross over, but my blood went cold. Fear was moving from my stomach through my legs, and I didn't trust myself to make it in time, didn't trust myself not to fall or trip on the rails. I couldn't stop running, but I had no choice but to wait for it to stop, to slip between two cars, then more running.

The engine light illuminated the high grasses and weeds before me for a second before leaving me in darkness. Its rushing vibrated in my clothes as I ran beside it. A row of lit squares passed by me, dining car windows. Some passenger cars had interiors on. Shadows of people. I was breathing so hard. Charging through the darkness, I felt like a secret next to the thundering behemoth, invisible. A phantom. It was exhilarating.

But something changed. A strange, musical pinging sound. Small metal against large, like if someone were firing a machine gun into an impervious metal wall. There was more clattering and grinding, then groaning, followed by a roar like a wounded dinosaur, and I could see before me, nine cars down, buckling off the rails, one car, then another, and another, bowing outward in a chain, heaving and collapsing my way, breaking toward the woods, forcing me back into the trees for safety.

There, behind their cover, each tree was a titan, protecting me as the massive cars tumbled through, taking a few down with them before resting, smoking, among the oaks and pines. The sound of the catastrophe, so deafening and terrifying, was only precursor to the horror I heard after. Amid the sounds of slowing wheels and the hissing of seeping steam, moans and cries, muffled by ripped metal and broken glass, voices of all ages, in agony and confusion, such human suffering—I'll never unhear.

I suppose I was in a state of shock from there. I have little memory of the rest. I vaguely recall the wreckage, smoldering cars, fires spreading out into the trees, sirens, lights, shouting, but my first clear memory was back at the school, checking in, a security guard asking me where I'd been, why my face was covered in cinder, had I been at the accident, him taking my bag from me, finding there—one pristine black-and-silver railroad spike, one stolen, now recovered, ball-peen hammer.

"This," he said, "of course, was enough discovery to bring on a slew of other questions, a lifetime of questions, for me, for everyone, and beyond what I've told you now, I have no further answers." He placed his notepad in his lap and leaned back into his chair. He squinted and rubbed his eyes. He seemed to be at the beginning of a headache. "I told them everything, never wavering from what I've told you now, but in the end I began to wonder if I ever really saw anyone at all. What's more, I wondered if what they thought about me was true, if I was who they believed me to be. And not just my accusers—*everyone*, everyone who had come before them. But I hadn't strangled myself. I didn't rob those people's houses. I didn't own a lantern. And I didn't carefully plot and execute a derailment. But the truth felt hollow the more I ran back through it with my counsel. I couldn't even ID a clear suspect. With each repetition it seemed more far-fetched.

"A railroad man said it was a one-in-a-thousand chance that anyone could derail a train with a railroad spike, but there were hundreds out there, strategically arranged and jammed in place, neatly configured in a way that would bring about all this destruction. He'd also found tampered safety mechanisms, damaged switches.

"It didn't take long for authorities to see a light in the dark of the woods nearby. They found the house, the lantern, and what remained of the spikes inside, the knife by the door. The Woods Weir outside became the stuff of legends—lots of pictures and hypotheses about that in the papers."

He grimaced and shook his head. I could feel him fading, shutting down. Retelling it had taken a toll, and I was already regretting allowing him to relive this, what must've been the worst night of his life. I began to rise from my chair when I was startled to find a small blue plastic cup of water hovering near my face.

"Here," the young woman said, handing me the cup. She was a thin, porcelain pale type, with short brown hair. She indicated with a tilt of her head for me to give the cup to my brother. Once I did, she handed another for me to drink.

"Thanks, Amy," my brother said.

She walked away across the courtyard but stayed within view of us. After he gulped his down, I gave him mine, which he sipped from slowly.

We didn't speak for some time. Where to begin? There were too many questions. I sat pouring over the details of his account in my mind, but to ask about them felt fraught with potential disaster. I wanted more, I wanted to understand, no doubt, as he still does, and so I said, dully, "I don't know what to say."

"You don't have to say anything. It was enough for you to listen," he said, but I sensed he was disappointed with my reply, or maybe he was feeling tired or self-conscious in the silence. "I'd be lying if I said I didn't think of it much anymore. Little things bring it all back—the food cart's clacking wheels moving across the tiles in the lobby, last week the smell of the shorted-out cord of a toaster in the cafeteria—and then I'm lost, surrendered up to the whole saga for a half-hour or so."

"I'm glad you told me," I said. "I know it was difficult. Look at me." He looked me in the eyes for the first time since he began recounting the disaster. "Leaving you here alone for so long—unforgivable. Deep inside, I knew for years that this needed to happen, but I'd been lying to myself, that you were too far gone, that you were past the point of needing anyone, past the point of receiving any kind of help that I might offer, but believe me when I tell you I am still your sister—I haven't been for far too long—but know that nothing you can say will ever change that, and I'm here now, and I will never abandon you again."

His whole body seemed to relax. He slunk lower into his chair, and he gazed upon the branches hanging above us. "I might need to hear you say that again once in a while."

Our favorite attendant walked out into the courtyard and announced that visitation hours would be ending shortly. Her voice, commanding as always, carried to the far reaches of the courtyard, mobilizing Amy, her friend, and a few stragglers who took the long way back to the veranda.

He straightened himself in his chair. "You know, I didn't sleep much last night."

"Why's that?"

"Aside from writing and reviewing this," he held up his notepad, "I must've replayed my entire life with the knowledge of my missing twin brother. I've been aiming it like a light up to the shadows of everything that's passed, and it all makes sense: the lost look on Mother's face when I'd catch her watching me play alone in my room; the lament in Grandmother's voice when she'd remark how much I'd grown since she'd last seen me; and Father . . ."

"What about him?"

"I always thought he left because I was too strange, too unlike him, like he was holding the memories of his childhood up to mine and I never measured up. I wasn't the son he wanted. That may be so, and I've made peace with that, but now I can see it wasn't only that. There was heartache in watching me grow older—there was grief—and nothing I could've done would have changed this. Maybe that's been the greatest gift in learning about our brother. It's rearranging everything in my mind, a lifetime of memories. I'm reliving them now, and I'm understanding." He took a sip of water and cleared his throat. "It wasn't all about me, Cindy. It never was. But I'm still struggling with why they wouldn't let me know. Why did everyone treat me the way they did, like an unsolvable problem?"

"They were too wounded to help," I said, which I suspected to be true. They waited for the right words for fear of saying the wrong ones, but those words would never come, so we passed the years in silence, like stones, grown thick with lichen and moss, until our grief became part of the landscape. "Mother never got over it."

"I see that now."

"And then to lose you the way we did. She was a strong, steadfast woman, but everything had left her permanently fractured. She lived happily enough, but those final years—I wouldn't call that living."

"Did you ever get the feeling that *you* weren't living?" he said. "Sometimes I feel I've spent much of my life watching and waiting for something to happen or for someone to arrive."

"Hovering, wandering around like ghosts. I've felt that way," I said.

"I've felt it most of my life," he said. "Less so since your visits." He smiled. "But what are you waiting for, Cindy? What's stopping you from living?"

The lady attendant returned to the veranda to announce that all visitors had only five more minutes. The sleeves of her navy cardigan were bunched up around her elbows, revealing two muscular fore-arms. She directed this announcement out into the yard even though I was the only visitor remaining and only a few feet away. The rest of the patients were already sitting at long cafeteria-style tables in the atrium, just inside the building. As she turned to address us directly, a door opened behind her, and the large man called the attendant's name, "Florence," like a question.

She looked at us, then back to him. "What *is* it, Darren?"

He sauntered up to her and spoke quietly over her shoulder.

"Y'all *always* do this," she said. "Always right about quitting time, this always happens."

He gave a sheepish look and a shoulder shrug.

"I'll handle it. I'll handle it," she said, sighed, and went huffing back into the building.

"Thanks, Darren," my brother said, and the man left us to ourselves.

"We better go—or at least look like we're leaving," I said.

We stood, and my brother said, "I'm still not sure I grasp its full meaning though, Cindy, about my brother. You've given me a key to unlock so many cabinets and doors inside me. My first days here were difficult ones, as you could imagine. As the reality of my situation began to sink in, I took a long, hard look at my future and stopped being. I quit speaking, quit eating, quit moving. I lived more in my head than anywhere. The longer I lived this way, the freer I felt. I was going to strange, fantastic places in my mind. The things I witnessed there— hard to describe. But best of all was who I was there, who I became. Completely lost on me was the fact that I was dying.

"At the end of one of my visions, I heard a familiar voice saying, 'Leave now and you leave them with no one.' To which I replied, Then let them live as I have my entire life: alone. After uttering these words, faces appeared before me—yours, Mother's, Grandmother's, to rebuke the lie of having always been alone—but then many other unknown faces appeared, and at the end I saw myself, healthy, older, and, perhaps, happy.

"Maybe it was Aaron speaking," my brother said to me.

"No," I said. "It was always you. Look at you now; you've become that person. Your life is proof that you are more than a haunted survivor."

Florence walked across the veranda to find us still beneath the oak tree. She crossed her arms, a bead of sweat rolling down her face, and said, "Visitation hours are *over*."

A sudden wave of anxiety coursed through my blood and moved across my skin.

He reached back to his chair and handed me his notepad. "Here, I'm finished with this. If you don't need it, you can use it to start fires in the woodstove at home. Tear a bit out, wrap it around a pinecone, and send it back into the woods a page at a time."

"You know I'm not using the fireplace anymore. You think I'm up there cutting down trees and splitting firewood?"

"I think you could handle it," he said.

"I'm not going to burn your story," I said. "I'm going to tell it."

He nodded. "Do you think it'll help?"

"It could."

We walked together back to the main building and stood on the paved veranda there. Through the windows, in a shock of white, fluorescent lights, I could see Florence waiting inside for us and Amy and Darren sitting together with a small group of patients at a nearby table. I still felt a slight uneasiness in the air, like something important had been left unsaid. We both leaned against the railing and looked out over the courtyard.

"There's a certain strangeness to our home, isn't there?" I said.

"There's a certain strangeness to everywhere."

I had to agree.

"But I know what you mean," he said.

"I don't know what to make of any of it—not just your part, all of it. Everything strange we've lived through, our house, the woods, maybe it's haunted, or maybe we're all cursed, maybe there's an ancient brooding evil that crops up from the earth, corrupting our lives at turns, or like an old wound flaring up again, maybe it simply wants to remind us that they're here and that to the earth, we're nothing but fleas behind a dog's ear," I said.

"I feel it too," he said. "It's humbling. There's something about our sad mortality wrapped up in all this strangeness, but I don't think it's right to call it evil or even to label it the way some do—supernatural, paranormal, other-worldly. We're too quick to pretend we understand or that we can even *begin* to comprehend any of it. Too quick to term it—miracle or curse, angel or demon, good or evil.

"And it isn't limited to us or our home or the woods. It's simply the world we're given. This glorious place with all of its sorrows, from time to time offers us mystery—something hidden and unknowable to occupy our thoughts and maybe to hope for, for a while. Maybe that's what the mysterious is after all: a chance to bring our awareness to another plane, reminding us how little we know. That was the beauty of being alone in the woods. There I was always surrounded by mystery and awe."

"All these years here—exiled from everything, your woods—I don't know how it hasn't crushed you," I said.

"It did. For a time. But then I found awe somewhere else."

"Where?"

"These people." He nodded back to the windows where I'd seen Amy,

Darren, and the others. "Is there any greater mystery than whatever lies in the hearts of these people around me?" He laughed to himself. I thought of the many aimless wanderers I'd seen here the past few months, patients ambling about in the afternoon sun, each broken, bereft face busy in its own silent purgatory. "I know most of them now. They've been keeping their distance at my request. I told them we'd have a lot to talk about. But there are a few I'd like for you to meet someday. They've also got hard stories to tell—a book in every one—so I visit them and listen. But it feels good to have someone listen to me for a change. Anyway, you've heard my side now," he said. "I must admit— the truth can be hard to believe."

"Yes, hard to believe, often harder to speak."

"Amy, Darren—they've heard my story. What's more, I think they believe me. You believe me. Don't you?" In his voice I heard the child brother I knew from a lifetime ago, the voice that echoes still in my mind, back home on a quiet evening, when my thoughts return to those unbothered summers spent outdoors, rambling in the woods, exploring our tiny, temporary fragment of this mysterious land.

I turned and, taking him in my arms, embraced him, my one and only brother. I kissed his cheek, maybe for the first time.

Imagine that. Such a simple thing.

I heard a door open behind us and a stern voice over my shoulder telling us we'd exhausted our time together, and in her tone was the threat of some vague consequence. As the reality dawned on me of our visit's end and the long, lonely drive ahead, a slight feeling of helplessness came over me, and through my tears, I spoke: "But there's so much left I want to talk to you about, so many questions—so much left to say."

"I know," he said. "Isn't it wonderful?"

ACKNOWLEDGMENTS

I thank God for the moments, memories, and dreams that gave me this book; also, I thank Him for the people mentioned here and so many unnamed. Thanks to my wife, Deniz Alemdar Tuck, for her enduring love and support and for our two daughters. Thanks to my parents, sister, and extended family and to those, especially Adam Tyson and Erin Alemdar, who listened patiently while I blabbed my way through the book's structure.

Thanks to my earliest readers, including Alesia McKeown, Joshua Griffin, and Christopher Brean Murray, and special thanks to Lisa Phelps for reading even the chapters left on the cutting-room floor (and *liking* them). I cannot thank enough Rebecca Hardin-Thrift, who's read every version of this book and who reads closer than any reader could—forever thanks for your incisive comments and tenacious "hype-manship." Thanks as well to Mark Richard and Richard Hatem for their kind words.

Thanks to my many teachers and mentors through the years—Phyllis Hardy, Luke Whisnant, Bill Hallberg, Pat Bizzaro, Peter Makuck, McKay Sundwall, Alex Albright, and so many more. I would like to thank Liza Wieland for her unflagging belief and guidance and Thomas Douglass for his friendship.

Special thanks to *EPOCH* editor emeritus Michael Koch, who first published the story that would become the genesis of the novel. Also, thanks to editors Keith Lee Morris, Ronald Spatz, and Chris Fink for publishing excerpts in their literary journals.

Thanks to Jason Mott for selecting my book among those considered for AWP's James Alan McPherson novel prize, and thanks to the readers at AWP who passed the novel his way. Thanks also to J. T. Hill at AWP, Courtney Ochsner and Elizabeth Gratch at University of Nebraska Press, and the rest of the UNP team.

SOURCE ACKNOWLEDGMENTS

"Twinless Twin" in *EPOCH* 63, no. 2 (2014)

"The Amnesiacs" in the *South Carolina Review* 54, no. 2 (spring 2022)

"Before Crossing the Desert" in the *Alaska Quarterly Review* 40, nos. 3–4 (summer–fall 2024)

"Sanctuary" in *Beloit Fiction Journal* 38 (spring 2025)

James Alan McPherson Prize for the Novel

www.ingramcontent.com/pod-product-compliance
Lightning Source LLC
Chambersburg PA
CBHW021747130126
38179CB00025B/514